SUPERHEROES

SUPERHEROES

edited by

JOHN VARLEY

AND

RICIA MAINHARDT

ACE BOOKS, NEW YORK

This book is an Ace original edition,
and has never been previously published.

SUPERHEROES

An Ace Book / published by arrangement with
the editors

PRINTING HISTORY
Ace edition / January 1995

ACE®
Ace Books are published by The Berkley Publishing Group,
200 Madison Avenue, New York, NY 10016.
ACE and the "A" design are trademarks
belonging to Charter Communications, Inc.

PRINTED IN THE UNITED STATES OF AMERICA

10 9 8 7 6 5 4 3 2 1

For Mom, Dad, Gloria and Bob—
my superheroes

Table of Contents

SUPERHEROES

Introduction

John Varley

I didn't give this essay a title, but if I did it would probably be "What Superheroes Mean to Me." And with a title like that there's just no other place to start with than the Littleton Stamp Company of Littleton, Colorado.

Which is exactly where we *will* start, except for a brief digression to mention my aunt, who was a librarian in Portland, Oregon, and who for many years tore the foreign stamps off all the letters that came into the library until one day, possibly alarmed at the way her desk drawers were bulging, she dumped them all into boxes and shipped them off to me, in Texas.

I kind of liked them. And when the rest of my family heard this, a few other relatives promptly sent me the stamps *they* had been hoarding for years because they were too pretty to throw away and besides, maybe they're *worth* something. (I've since learned that *every* family sooner or later selects someone to be known as "the stamp nerd," usually a thin, studious male with thick glasses. Except for the specs, I fit the part. Thus are philatelists born.)

I bought a stamp album, learned to soak the stamps off the paper backing, and started pasting them into their proper places.

Enter the Littleton Stamp Company. This firm advertised on

matchbook covers and in comic books. The gist of the ad was they would send you 500 (or 700, or maybe it was 1,000) stamps, all different, *FREE!!!!*, if you just sent them a self-addressed, stamped envelope. (anslexusastmpsnaprval)

Eh? What was that? The print was so small and it went by so fast . . . it must have been the wind. Did you hear anything? Never mind. wewillalsoincludeaselectionofstampsonapproval

Hah? Speak up, will you? Heck, I'm *sure* I didn't hear anything, and even if I did, I don't know what "on approval" means, and anyway, I'm sure not going to let it stand in the way of my 1,000 (I'm sure it was a thousand) FREE!!! all-different stamps from twenty-five (count 'em) countries.

So I fixed four-cent stamps to two envelopes—thereby cruelly dating myself to my readers in 1994—posted the letter, and sat back to wait.

The results exceeded my wildest dreams. The Littleton Stamp Company paid off like a slot machine from hell. There were at *least* 1,000 stamps on paper stuffed into a big bag (there were a lot of duplicates, but who cared?). Looking through them, I soon concluded there were a *lot* of librarian aunts out there, and not all of them had a designated stamp geek to send their hoarded treasures to. Obviously, they were selling them to the Littleton Stamp Company. Which, in turn, was *giving* them away in the mail . . .

Did I feel the first chill of doubt then? Hard to remember. Even at that tender age I think I'd concluded that people seldom just *gave* things away. On the other hand, I knew a lot of people thought of these little bits of paper as nothing more than trash. So maybe it was true.

For whatever reason, I put my doubts away and returned to the examination of the treasure trove. And here I discovered something entirely unexpected. In addition to the wads and wads of stamps torn from envelopes, there were these cunning little glassine envelopes. Inside the envelopes, which were printed with legends like "10 Madagascar," "15 Switzerland," "4 Kenya," and "24 Germany," were by far the best stamps of all. These had never been used. They were in sets. From Germany there were a dozen portraits of Hitler, each a different color. From Africa there were sets of wild animals. There were sets from places called Norge, Espana, Helvetia, Suomi, and Sverige, places I couldn't find on any of my world maps.

These were wonderful stamps. They put the others to shame. I simply couldn't believe my luck, that the LSC had sent them to me, for FREE!!!!

Of course, there was the matter of the price printed in the corner of each little glassine envelope.

I wish I could remember all the pro and con arguments I used on myself during the next week. I wouldn't put them down here—they would fill a whole book that would keep Talmudic scholars busy for decades. I just wish I could remember. An exercise in sophistry of that magnitude is *worth* remembering.

In the end, it came down to this: I was pretty sure that some money was expected of me for these stamps, "on approval," whatever that meant. And: I was *damn* sure I was never sending them back. Since I didn't have the money to pay for them, some other arrangement would have to be made. That arrangement turned out to be that I would simply hold on to the stamps. For the verb "hold on to," you may substitute "steal." I don't mind.

I'd never stolen anything before, as far as I can remember. I was amazed at how little it seemed to affect my life. Nobody pointed at me and shouted "Thief! Thief!" I didn't sleep badly. No little worm of conscience ever gnawed at me. Hell, I hadn't *asked* for the damn stamps.

So things were going well, and I was even considering sending off to another stamp company, this one in Pennsylvania, for their Giant Grab Bag of *Five* thousand stamps for only 49¢. I hardly ever thought of the Littleton Stamp Company. What were they going to do? Send a bunch of thugs around to my house to break my legs if I didn't pay up? Ha ha.

That's when the siege began. The first shot was a simple brown envelope in the mailbox. I was only a little curious about it, wondering if it might contain more free stamps, ha ha. It didn't. It was crammed with fliers and catalogs telling me how I might purchase even more wonderful stamps than the ones I already had, some of them for prices that made me sweat just to look at them. And, oh, by the way, we still haven't received payment for the stamps on approval we recently sent you. We're happy that you liked them, of course, but you are now thirty days overdue. We're sure this is just an oversight. Ha ha.

(I have tried and tried and tried, and I *cannot* remember the amount the LSC was dunning me for. Considering the fact that it was the central number of my life for almost a year, I find this odd. I must have simply blanked it out, like one forgets the events surrounding a horrific traffic accident. A guess? I'd say it was around twenty dollars. Pocket change today, of course. Then? Do you remember when Coke vending machines went from 5¢ to 6¢? It was right about that time. We went to the movies for a quarter. Don't ask me what a loaf of bread cost because it was another ten years before I'd ever buy a loaf of bread. Cokes and Saturday matinees were about the extent of my economic knowledge. But let's say it was twenty dollars. Do you have any idea of how much twenty dollars was in those pre-inflation days? Well, it was a *fortune*, that's what it was. You could feed a family of five for years on that kind of money. I don't have the exact figures, but think of fifty or sixty thousand in 1993 dollars. You don't believe me? Just try to find a 6¢ Coke today. Go ahead! Try!)

Please remit twenty dollars. The words burned themselves into my brain (though not, apparently, the numbers). What to do? What were my options?

First, I could ask my parents for it.

Oh, sure. That ought to be real easy. You remember that family of five we could have fed for years? That was *my* family of five we were talking about. There was no way I was going to be responsible for having my mother and my sisters eat dog food for three years. The idea didn't exactly appeal to me, either, for that matter. (Though maybe I ought to get used to it, a part of me was saying—a very pessimistic part that, I'm sorry to say, is with me to this day—because it will be good preparation for prison food.)

It was while trying to imagine ways of breaking this to my parents that I came up with my second course of action, because it would be the first question they would ask me after they'd grasped the enormity of the situation: Why don't you just give them back?

Introduction

Because *it's too late*!

By then I'd learned a little about stamp collecting. I'd learned some of the terminology collectors used. I now understood the meaning of words like uncirculated, original gum, mint, light cancellation. For those of you lucky enough never to have been involved with this terrible hobby there is a simple rule you should be aware of: In philately, the closer a stamp is to the state it was in on the day of its creation, the more it is worth. It should show no wear and tear. It should *not* have a postmark. And it *must* have the same awful-tasting, sticky, easily-breakable glue on the back as it had when it rolled off the press.

Like most young collectors, I'd been using a drop of glue on the backs of most of my stamps. Later, I learned of the stamp hinge, but I never liked them much as they never kept the stamps in place in the album. With the stolen approvals, things were dead easy. Just lick them and paste them in, like you would on an envelope.

Thereby rendering them worthless. (Sorry, all you librarian aunts. With very rare exceptions, any canceled stamp torn from an envelope is of no value.)

My third option was really a lot of assorted options. Option 3A: Run away to sunny California and live at Disneyland. Option 3B: Run away to New York City. 3C: Run away and join the circus. You get the picture. While I spent a lot of time considering these options, I knew deep down I was not the running-away type. Not that I wouldn't like to get out and see the world. I just had barely enough sense to realize I had not the foggiest idea what I'd do once I got out there.

Killing oneself was always an option. It certainly eliminated all one's problems. Let's put that one on hold, until we see what prison's like.

This brought me to the fifth option, the one that had served me so badly up to that point. Sit still and do nothing and maybe the dreaded LSC would forget about me and go away.

They didn't, of course. About once a month I'd find a message from them. These messages got nastier and more threatening. They appealed to my sense of fair play. I remember one phrase as if it were yesterday: ". . . so just send us the twenty dollars and we'll call it 'square'!" Call it square? Call it *square*, you miserable bastards? After you've made my life a living hell? After you misled me with offers of thousands of free stamps, after you cleverly tucked your little time bomb in with the stamps, knowing full well, *counting* on the fact, I shouldn't doubt, that a lot of dumb guys like me would get ourselves in hock up to our eyeballs . . . you want to call it *square*?

I had been reduced to a shattered bunch of nerves, a hollow-eyed wraith whose dreams were now always haunted by the Littleton juggernaut, and I didn't think things could get any worse, when things got worse. The next communication from the Littleton Terror Company had this information: Unless payment is received *in forty-eight hours*, your account will be turned over to *a Collection Agency*.

Well, option number four suddenly started to look much better.

My visualization of a collection agency was necessarily a bit vague, but no matter how I imagined it there were always policemen in the picture, or shadowy guys in trenchcoats or other dark clothing pounding on the door and shouting "Come outta there, Varley! We know you got the stamps!" Oddly enough, they didn't carry guns. I was a lot more afraid of knives, so they carried knives. Even the cops. And after breaking down the door they always dragged me from the house—trying to make myself small and harmless, trying to act as if this was no big deal, as if this sort of thing happened every day and it would soon be straightened out, which was tough to pull off, since I was usually naked or in my underwear when I envisioned this scene, and a large crowd had always gathered.

By then I realized that even killing myself would do no good. The Collection Agency would come around anyway, and they probably wouldn't believe it when told I had recently done away with myself, and would then visit all sorts of atrocities upon my innocent family. So out of a sense of duty, to alert them to what was about to happen, I did what I should have done when the first dunning letter appeared. I turned the whole thing over to my mom.

And Mom took care of it.

I don't know what she did. To this day I have never asked her, and she has probably forgotten by now. I doubt it was a very traumatic event for her. I am now older than my mother was then, and confronted by a similar problem I would probably write an angry letter or make an angry phone call (the LSC really *was* misleading children with its ads, though they did nothing illegal), and if that didn't do it, I'd pay the stinking twenty dollars. A double sawbuck certainly would have put a big hole in our monthly grocery budget back then, but that business about feeding a family for years was maybe a bit of an exaggeration. I've tried to remember if we ate a lot of macaroni and cheese after I told my mother. It seems that we did, but we did *before* I told her, too.

The point is, *she took care of it.* Bingo, and the problem that had been tormenting me for the better part of a year just melted away as if it had never existed. You want to talk about superheroes, you need go no farther than that, in my opinion.

But we will, of course, go farther than that. This book is not primarily concerned with the day-to-day acts of heroism performed by ordinary people (though there are some stories here concerned with that very thing), but about the outlandish acts performed by certain obsessive/compulsive borderline personalities who like to dress up in tight, primary-colored spandex suits, most of them endowed with powers far beyond those of mortal men, and physiques far beyond that of Arnold Schwarzenegger, who like to leap from the pages of comic books and into our hearts, righting wrongs along the way, and who have come to be known by the generic term "superhero."

So just what are superheroes? Why are we so fascinated by them? What part of the human psyche do they come from? Should we look for the roots of the superhero in history, in literature? Was Jesus a superhero? What about Paul Bunyan? Crusader Rabbit?

All very good questions. I don't have the answers to any of them. And the reason is an admission I am forced to make here, since my experience with the stamp company made me a firm believer in truth in advertising: I don't know much about superheroes.

I stopped being a comic-book fan about the time of my traumatic mail-order experience. Somehow, picking up and reading a comic just didn't have the pizzazz it used to hold for me. Part of me really didn't enjoy reading them anymore, probably the same part that had recently graduated to reading books *with no pictures at all* in them, something a lot of my friends thought very weird indeed. The other part was much like what a heroin addict thinks. I was much better off if I didn't let myself get tempted again. From time to time I *would* pick one up, and my pulse would immediately begin to race as I read the ads within . . .

(I can't tell you how sorely I was tempted to buy the Pen-Size, Clips-on-your-pocket SECRET SPY SCOPE, or even better, the X-RAY SPECS (only one dollar) which showed a leering guy looking at the bones of his own hand . . . but behind the hand was a pretty girl and we all knew what he was really looking at, and we all wanted a look at it, too . . . or *How To Build A Body Of Steel*, or *The Unbeatable Self-Defense Secrets of KETSUGO!* Or—and here my heart still skips a beat—the seven-foot-long Space Rocket, for only $6.98. This later evolved into the seven-foot-long Polaris Nuclear Sub (they were obviously stamped from the same mold), and I have a copy of that advertisement before me now, the ad for the sub, and I want it now almost as much as I wanted it back then.

(I lusted after that Space Rocket for many years. It was said to be made of 200-lb.-test fibreboard, with easy assembly instructions. The picture showed lots of happy kids playing all over the damn thing. It had an electrically lit instrument panel and a money-back guarantee: "If you don't think it is the greatest ever—the best toy you ever had—just send it back for full purchase price refund." How could I go wrong? But then the cold hand of the Littleton Stamp Company would touch me, and I just *knew* it wasn't what it seemed. I mean, *six dollars and ninety-eight cents?* Come on. It seemed insanely cheap. So just what *was* fibreboard, anyway? Maybe corrugated cardboard? That's what I concluded, but the notion that I may have missed out on the greatest toy deal of the century simply because I was mail-order gun-shy still nags at me. Did anybody out there ever order the Space Ship or the Polaris Sub? What were they like? Did you have lots of fun?)

This is why I missed the great comic revolution of my generation: the quick rise and ascendancy of Marvel Comics, which in a few years had the old juggernaut of DC on the ropes. My friend Calvin, who probably still reads a lot of comics, told me the reason was that Marvel comic heroes were more vulnerable. More human. Subject

Introduction

to unreasonable rages, like the Hulk, or having the same problems I, as a teenager, was then experiencing, such as dating problems and, possibly, super-acne, like Spider-Man. There were antihero superheroes, supermen with feet of clay, protagonists who not only didn't have the Gotham City or Metropolis police forces at their beck and call, but who were being actively pursued for imagined or trumped-up crimes.

Well, the police don't get on well with the Guardian Angels; why should they like a wise-ass like Superman who goes around making them look bad by showing what a poor job they do? It all made sense, the Marvel universe . . . but what was the *point*? Wasn't the whole idea of superheroes that they were *above* all that?

Apparently not. Marvel-type stories are still around and, from what I hear, even DC does stories like that now. Heck, a while back they even killed off Superman—in seven or eight high-priced issues, certain to be followed by ten or twelve more issues concerning his resurrection. It makes one wish for the good old days of green kryptonite. Or at least it made *me* wish it, but I know I have no real right to, because to this day I've never read a Marvel comic. Maybe if I did, I'd see why they're so much better.

See, what you have here in your editor is a comic conservative. While I'm certainly no expert on either Batman or Superman, I know all the history: Ma and Pa Kent, Smallville, Robin, Lois and Lana, Krypto the superdog, the Joker, the Fortress of Solitude, and so on and so on. And I know a little about the classic Marvel characters. Unless you don't have a television set, you pick up some of this through some mental osmosis. I never watched *The Incredible Hulk* on the tube, but I've seen pictures of Bixby and Ferrigno.

But I must admit to you that I know virtually nothing about any comic character of the last fifteen or twenty years. I don't have any figures, but just from casual observation it seems these have been the very years when comics have had their most phenomenal growth, and the time when they have achieved a degree of respectability. Hundreds of people get together on weekends to buy, sell, and trade comics at astronomical prices.

Sorry, folks. I missed all that. I own one comic book, which I paid two dollars for.

So where do I get off editing a book about superheroes? you are probably asking yourself along about now.

It's a fair question, one that deserves an answer. And just to show you what a generous guy I am, I have *two* answers for you.

The first concerns a story idea I got one fine day a few years ago. It was quite a simple idea, and went something like this: What if Kal-El of Krypton, escaping his home planet's destruction, had landed in the late Soviet Union instead of Smallville, U.S.A.? Maybe he brought Truth and Justice along with him, in his little Kryptonian brain, but how about "The American Way"? I thought there might be a funny story in there, so I wrote it.

That story is collected here, which is only logical when you understand that my co-editor, Ricia Mainhardt, upon reading the story, thought it would be a good idea to put together an anthology with a whole bunch of these alternate superhero stories. It sounded like fun to me, too, so we sent out queries and the stories started pouring in. The best of them are in this book.

Well, sure. (A third answer to the question occurs to me now: It's my book. I've got a *right* to do the introduction. However, I won't use that one.) Sure, but you've admitted you're no authority on the subject, I hear you complaining. Why not let an expert take over? This sounds like a job for . . . somebody else.

Nothing could be further from the truth. There *are* no experts on the superheroes to be found in this book. These are the guys who didn't make the cut into the big leagues. None of them has ever had a comic of his own, much less a television show or a feature movie. These are the superheroes that take Marvel Comics one step further. They're not just more human. Most of them are *too human*. Take Captain Swastika, for instance. There's a tragic story. These are guys whose superpowers can be more a nuisance than an asset, guys like Sound Effect Man, a second-banana superhero if ever there was one. You'll meet these people, and more like them, in the pages of this book.

You know what? Maybe there is something to this Marvel business. Because I like these superheroes more than I ever liked that muscle-bound jerk, Superman, or that gloomy, brooding, boring Batman.

Introduction

So here it is, on approval. Constructed of the finest, sturdy paperboard, seats one, good for hours and hours of adventure, some assembly required. Use it for ten full days and if you don't think it's the greatest anti-superhero book ever . . . well, maybe you'll ask your mom before you buy another one like it.

A Clean Sweep

Laurell K. Hamilton

It's been said that familiarity breeds contempt. How long can even the extraordinary retain its novelty in an everyday world?

Captain Housework materialized on the doorstep of #11 Pear Tree Lane. His emergency beeper had awakened him, code red. Was it his nemesis Dr. Grime, or the infamous Dust Bunny Gang, or perhaps Pond Scum, the destroyer of bathrooms?

He had to levitate to reach the doorbell. As crimefighters go, Captain Housework was on the short side. His white coveralls, silver cape, and mask—formed of a billed cap with eye holes—were gleamingly clean. He stood on the top step shining as if carved from ivory and silver.

He looked perfect, crisp, and clean. And he liked it that way.

The door opened, and a woman dressed in a bathrobe stared down at him. "Oh, it's you. Please come in." She held the door for him, waving him in eagerly.

He stared up at her, a grim smile on his face. "And what dastardly villain is plaguing your home, dear lady?"

She blinked at him. "Dastardly villain?" She gave a small laugh. "Oh, no, it's nothing like that. My husband made the call. Did he say we had a supervillain in the house?"

Captain Housework drew himself up to his full three feet and said, "It was a code red, Madam. That means a supervillain has been spotted."

The woman laughed again. "Oh, dear, no. I've got a party of twelve people coming at six o'clock and my maid cancelled."

"You called the superhero hotline because your maid cancelled." His voice had a harsh edge to it that the woman didn't seem to notice.

"Well, my friend Betty had you over when her kids threw that wild party. You did miracles with her house."

"I remember the incident. I made it clear that it was an exception to the rules that I aided her."

"But you've just got to help me, Captain Housework." The woman went to her knees, gripping his arms. "Please, it's too late to turn to anyone else." Tears glittered in her eyes.

Captain Housework crossed his arms across his thin chest, his mouth set in a firm line. "Madam, I am a superhero, not a maid. I do not think you realize how terrible my foes can be. Have you ever had a wave of black mildew engulf your husband and eat him to the bone before your eyes?"

She blinked at him. "Well, no, but surely that doesn't happen all that often. In the meantime, couldn't you help me, just this once?"

It was true that his archenemies had been lying low for a while. Work had been slow. He stared into her tear-stained face and nodded. "All right, but only this once."

She hugged him, crumpling the bill of his mask. He pushed away from her, straightening his costume. "That will not be necessary. I will get to work at once, if that is all right with you?"

"Oh, that's wonderful. I'll just go get dressed." She raced up the stairs, trailing some floral perfume behind her.

Captain Housework sniffed. He preferred the cleaner scents of household air fresheners. Pine was his favorite.

He sighed and walked into the living room. For a moment his heart beat faster; surely such destruction could only be the work of the Dust Bunny Gang. Sofa cushions were scattered across the floor. A vase had fallen on its side, spilling water. Dying flowers made a sodden mess on the grey carpet. The fireplace was choked with ash and the partially burned carcass of a doll. Toys covered nearly every inch of the floor.

Children. The only natural disaster that could rival Dr. Grime.

Perhaps children weren't as deadly, but they were just as messy.

This was the fifth time in a month that he had been called in and found no archvillain but only bad housework. His name was being traded around like that of a good maid. He, Captain Housework, had been reduced to drudgery.

He, who had fought the great dust invasion of '53, would have no problem with this mundane mess. His superhuman speed would make short work of it all. But that wasn't the point. People did not call The Purple Avenger to change a tire. They called him to save their lives.

Once they had called Captain Housework for the same thing. Dr. Grime had nearly engulfed St. Louis in a giant rain of grease. All cars, trains, and planes had come to a slippery halt. Pedestrians caught in the first greasy rain had melted into puddles of sizzling goo. They had called for Captain Housework then, and been glad to have him. But that had been ten years ago.

Dr. Grime had retired. The Dust Bunny Gang had split up over contractual differences. There just weren't that many supervillains who specialized in true dirty work.

It wasn't really the mundane cleaning that bothered him. It was the repeat business. People had been calling him back again and again to clean up after them. He'd get a house spotless, perfect, and they'd mess it up again.

It was a never-ending drudgery. Even with superpowers over dust and dirt, he was tired of it. They were taking advantage of him. But without any supervillains to fight, a superhero had to fill some need. It was in his contract that he had to be useful to mankind, just as a supervillain had to harm mankind. If all the villains needing his special powers to thwart them had retired, he had to answer the call of need.

Captain Housework sighed and waved a white-gloved hand. The sofa cushions danced back in place, fluffing themselves before snuggling down. "I am a glorified maid," he said softly to the empty room.

The kitchen was the worst. Dishes were stacked nearly to the top of the windows, thick with grease and moldy food. He conjured a super-scouring wind and cleaned them with the force of a hurricane without cracking a dish.

When every room was spotless, he appeared before the woman who had summoned him. "The house is clean, Madam."

"Oh, gee, thanks." She held out money.

Captain Housework stared at the offending hand. "I am a super-hero, not a servant. I don't need your money." His voice was very tight, each word bitten off.

"No offense, I'm just grateful."

"Be grateful and don't call me again."

"But I want you to come back after the party and clean up," she said.

"You what?"

"The maid can't come tonight at all. I thought you'd clean up after the party. The superhero hotline said you would."

"They said I would?"

She nodded. "The operator on the hotline said you would be happy to be of service. She said something about superheroes need-ing to be of service to mankind."

Captain Housework stared at the woman for a few heartbeats. He saw it all then, his future stretching out before him. An eternity of cleaning up after parties, repairing the damage of crayon-wielding tots and unhousebroken dogs. He saw it all in the blink of his spar-kling eyes. It was intolerable, a hell on earth, but the woman was right. A superhero had to serve mankind. If all he was good for was maid service, then so be it.

The woman had been putting on red nail polish. She reached back to tighten the lid, but was unwilling to grip it with her wet nails. The bottle went spinning. Bright red liquid poured out onto the white carpet, trickled down the newly polished vanity.

"Oops," the woman said. "You'll get that, won't you? I've got to finish getting ready; the guests will be here any minute." She stood, waving her nails to dry them. She left him staring at the spreading red stain on the carpet he had just shampooed.

His tiny hands balled into fists. He stood trembling with rage, unable to utter a word. An eternity of this—it was intolerable! But what else could he do? Talk Dr. Grime out of retirement? No, the villain had made millions off his memoirs. *Memoirs of the Down and Dirty* had been a best-seller.

A Clean Sweep

Captain Housework stared at the slowly hardening stain, and a great calmness washed over him. He had an idea.

The police found fourteen skeletons at #11 Pear Tree Lane. The bones were neatly arranged, sparkling with polish, lacquered to a perfect finish. The house had never been so clean.

Time for a Hero

Brian M. Thomsen

Is informed consent a prerequisite for an action to be considered heroic?

The man on the table began to stir.

Good. He's coming around. He's our only hope!

The two doctors in attendance immediately positioned themselves on each side of him, as he blinked his eyes, and began to regain consciousness.

"Thank God you're alright," offered the older doctor. "We didn't know what to do. Why, if you hadn't come around, we would have had to . . ."

"Of course he came around," the younger doctor interrupted. "He's never failed us before."

"Where am I?" said the patient, trying to shake off the last strains of grogginess. "What happened?"

"You're in a special mobile military hospital. I'm Dr. Kirschenbaum," said the older doctor. "The marines brought you here right after you passed out. I've been watching you for the past two hours hoping you'd come around. It's not as if we could treat you or anything, given your advanced physiology and all."

". . . But we knew you'd come around," continued the other. "I'm Dr. Parker, and we knew that it would take more than a direct hit on the forehead from a bazooka shell to stop you."

"Huh?" said the patient, not quite sure if he was really coming around or just trapped in some bizarre waking dream.

"The bazooka shell," repeated Parker. "Don't you remember?"

"No. I don't remember anything. This all must be some dream. Getting hit in the head would kill an ordinary man . . . probably blow him to bits. No, I'm just not awake yet. This is all just a dream," he added, the pounding in his head becoming more and more noticeable. "I'm going to just close my eyes, go back to sleep, and wake up later when I'm not so delirious."

"You can't do that," insisted Dr. Kirschenbaum. "We need you. Surely you must remember the crisis . . . your mission . . . what you have to do . . ."

"What do I have to do?" he asked, hoping that this dream would soon be over.

"Save the world, of course," answered Parker.

"Save the world?" he repeated.

"Of course," Kirschenbaum insisted. "You must remember. So many lives are at stake."

"I don't even remember my name," the patient realized, now painfully awake and aware of his own befuddlement.

The two doctors were shocked.

"He doesn't remember his name," Parker said to Kirschenbaum.

"He doesn't remember his mission," Kirschenbaum said to Parker; then, after a brief inspiration added, "You don't suppose he has amnesia, do you?"

"It could be," Parker said. "A hard blow to the head of a normal man could lead to amnesia. A blow such as one from a bazooka shell to a head such as his . . . who could tell?"

"Wait a second," the patient insisted, interrupting their consultation. "Why do you say 'a normal man'?"

"I'm sorry," apologized Parker. "Maybe I should have said a mortal man, or an Earthman, or . . ."

"Well, what am I then?" the patient insisted, anger replacing his confusion.

"He really doesn't know who he is," Kirschenbaum said to no one in particular, perhaps to himself, perhaps to his patient.

"Who am I?" he demanded, the threat of violence barely masked in his voice.

"Why, you're Meteor Man," Kirschenbaum answered, "and time is running out, and you have to save the world."

For the next few minutes, Doctors Parker and Kirschenbaum carefully reassured the patient known as Meteor Man of his real identity.

They told him the now-famous origin story that had been immortalized in comic books, cartoons, and Sunday features, of how a meteor fell from the sky, and after seven days of cooling cracked open, giving birth to a super-infant, hatched like a chick from an egg. Raised in secret by a retired five-star general and his wife, the super-infant matured and eventually became Meteor Man, strength of a thousand, indestructible, and savior of the planet.

"Surely you must remember the time you averted disaster by extending the course of the Missouri River to put out the raging fires in southern Oregon?" insisted Dr. Parker.

"Or the time you outwitted the deadly brain-stealing ETs from Alpha Centauri?" added Kirschenbaum.

"Or when you single-handedly shielded all of Las Vegas from an atomic bomb blast when you smothered the explosion with your own body," continued Parker, adding, "and lived."

"And lived?" repeated the patient known as Meteor Man, in disbelief.

"Of course," added Dr. Kirschenbaum; then, chuckling, he said, "And who'd have thought a little thing like a bazooka shell would cause amnesia?"

"I don't believe any of this!" said the patient.

"But you have to," said Kirschenbaum calmly. "You've never failed us before, and you are our only hope."

A strange sense of well-being seemed to wash over the confused patient. *Our only hope.* It sounded so familiar . . . but who could believe these fantastic tales of his exploits? And no one in the real world would ever be called Meteor Man. Either he was now in the hands of delusionary madmen, the victim of some bizarre practical joke, or he himself had gone crazy . . . or, there was one other alternative, most bizarre of all—maybe they were right. He was *their only hope*. The whole phrase felt right . . . but it couldn't be.

Trying to maintain a certain nonthreatening calm, the patient responded to his doctors.

"Look," he offered, "I'd like to help, and I'd do anything I could to save the world, but I'm just one man."

"More than a man," interrupted Parker.

"Whatever," he responded, quickly tiring of the annoying little doctor's interruptions, and clarifications. "But what is the crisis, and what can I do about it?"

"We've just received an update from our men on the front," answered Kirschenbaum, now all businesslike and efficient. "The terrorist forces guarding the plant have been subdued by a black-beret insurgency team, casualties listed at seventy-five percent."

"An acceptable number, given the situation," said the annoying Dr. Parker, adding, "so you have nothing to worry about from those migraine-inducing bazookas for the time being."

"We've since discovered that they've planted an Alunarium bomb, which when detonated will create an implosion that will generate a black hole instigating China Syndrome at an almost instantaneous rate which will tear the Earth asunder from core to crust."

"And what can I do about it?" asked the patient known as Meteor Man.

"It's really quite simple," replied Kirschenbaum, producing a mechanical box not unlike an old-fashioned Geiger counter. "All you have to do is carry this magnetic wave transmitter into the plant. The waves will erase the programming of the Alunarium bomb, making detonation impossible."

"What's the catch?" asked Meteor Man, knowing that one had to exist.

"There isn't any catch, at least not for you," answered Parker.

Kirschenbaum explained, "The terrorists flooded the plant area with the coolant from the atomic core. The intense levels of radioactivity would kill any of us, but you're immune."

Parker added, "I remember your comment to the press when you smothered the atomic bomb. You said, 'I feel like I've been out in the sun a bit too long.' Isn't that a scream! A lethal dose of radiation to us gives you a mild case of sunstroke. Walking into the contaminated plant should be a piece of cake."

"You expect me to believe I'm impervious to radiation," said the patient.

"Of course," said the annoying Parker. "You're Meteor Man."

Parker gestured towards the patient's chest.

The patient looked down, and for the first time noticed the large M insignia that covered most of his chest. He seemed to be wearing some sort of garish costume made out of a spandex-like material that hugged the contours of his muscularly masculine physique with a sheen of gold and silver.

His first thought was that he looked like something out of a comic book, but then he caught himself before he said anything, realizing that this would have been just the sort of reaction Parker and Kirschenbaum would have wanted.

"I suppose this is my costume?" he commented.

"Known by one and all," replied Parker. "The savior of mankind, and our only hope in our darkest and direst times of need."

"But dressing in a costume," he added, "doesn't necessarily mean I am some sort of superhero who can fly through the air, leap tall bridges, see through walls . . ."

"You can't do any of those things," Kirschenbaum interrupted. "Your body is impervious to damage from bullets, radiation waves, laser beams . . ."

"But not direct hits on the forehead by bazooka shells," he added.

"Apparently," Kirschenbaum conceded, "your recuperative stamina is one hundred times that of a mortal man. Your strength is that of a thousand, your intellect is off the IQ chart . . ."

"I don't feel like a genius."

"It's probably a by-product of the amnesia," offered the annoying Parker. "I wouldn't worry about that."

"I somehow figured you wouldn't," he replied curtly.

Kirschenbaum looked at his watch and became more concerned.

"Meteor Man," he said gravely, "we are running out of time. I know you are confused, and it all sounds far-fetched, but you are our only hope, and time is running out. What do I have to do to convince you that you are who we say you are?"

Meteor Man was touched by his earnestness and concern. If time was running out, and he was their only hope, then he would have to do something . . . but what if they were wrong? He didn't feel like some sort of meteor-spawn from outer space.

"Dr. Kirschenbaum," he offered, "I really would like to help you, but it all sounds so bizarre. No sane person would believe that he was some sort of superhero."

"Of course not," interrupted the annoying Dr. Parker. "You're one of a kind. That is why you are our only hope."

Both the patient and Kirschenbaum ignored Parker's latest cliché outburst.

Kirschenbaum considered the situation for a moment, and proposed a solution, saying, "If I can prove to you that you are indeed Meteor Man, our invincible hero, then would you save the day?"

"Sure," said the patient, really wanting to help, and also to regain his identity.

Kirschenbaum raised his hand to his face and lightly brushed his moustache, seeming to be in some sort of intense thought. The glow of inspiration illuminated his face, as if he had just arrived at a solution. Dropping his hand from his face to his chest, he reached into his lab coat, pulled out a .44 Magnum, and quickly fired off five shots point-blank into the chest of the patient he called Meteor Man.

Meteor Man had almost no time to react, taking a quick deep breath as he felt the dull impact of the shells against his chest, not even noticing that instinctively his hand had tried to move to block the bullets' impact.

He felt no pain, no harm.

He was speechless. The bullets had impacted, but had not penetrated.

Looking down at his hand, he felt a peculiar sensation of warmth.

There in the palm of his hand were the five shells, tips slightly flattened and worse for wear from their impact with his chest.

"You see?" said Kirschenbaum. "Bullets bounce off you, and though you don't consciously remember how to use your powers, your body and your subconscious do, as evidenced by your catching the shells at super-speed."

Meteor Man just stared at the still-warm shells in his hand.

"Come here," said Kirschenbaum, continuing his quest to prove to his patient that he was indeed invulnerable. "Please put your hand down here on the table."

Meteor Man dully complied.

Dr. Kirschenbaum then took out a surgical saw, turned it on, and proceeded to file down the high-speed blade on each of the fingers of the patient's right hand. In no time at all, the steel blade was reduced to a pile of metal shavings, while Meteor Man's fingers and skin remained unharmed.

Meteor Man's eyes moved back and forth from his unscathed right hand to the shell-laden palm of his left hand.

Dr. Kirschenbaum guided him over to a telemonitor and said, "Observe."

The monitor clicked on.

The Update News Channel was tuned in. A stern-faced anchorman was in the middle of a story:

> "... there is still no word on the condition of Meteor Man, who was apparently dazed when he was hit in the head by a bazooka shell. The thought-to-be-invulnerable hero has faced many greater adversaries before (*visual montage of stock news footage of his earlier exploits*), including the now-famous stifling of an atomic bomb that threatened to level Las Vegas. America wishes Meteor Man a speedy recovery ...."

Kirschenbaum hit the control and froze the screen on a head shot of Meteor Man accepting the Medal of Freedom from President Levin.

Meteor Man looked from the monitor's image to the mirror across the room.

The face was the same.

He was Meteor Man.

It was the only possible answer ... and he was their only possible hope.

He slowly turned back to Dr. Kirschenbaum and said softly, "What do I have to do?"

Kirschenbaum put his arm around the costumed hero's shoulder and said, "Your memory should return in a short time. We can go over videotapes of your past exploits later to try to jog it back into place. For now, we must avert our immediate crisis."

"The bomb in the plant," he stated.

"Yes. All you have to do is bring this transmitter into the plant itself. That's all. A helicopter is waiting to escort you to the plant. You will be lowered down to the ground by a towline so as not to risk damaging the transmitter. All you have to do is disengage yourself from the line, walk into the plant, through the contaminated puddles, and set it down here." Kirschenbaum pointed to a room on a blueprint that had conveniently appeared on the teleprompter.

"You see," he added, "it's no more than a hundred paces from your drop-off point."

"And that's it?" asked Meteor Man.

"That's it," said Dr. Kirschenbaum. "Then all you have to do is walk on out, come back here, and we can work on filling in the gaps in your memory."

"Once again, the Earth will be saved, by mankind's only hope," said the annoying Parker.

"Right," said the tolerant Meteor Man.

"This is the transmitter. It is always on, so you don't have to do anything to it," instructed Kirschenbaum, putting the device into his patient's hands and escorting him to the door, saying, "Your helicopter awaits."

As they were leaving the room, Meteor Man noticed a black beret on a chair by the door. He paused for a moment, picked it up, and was about to put it on and see how it looked in the mirror, when Kirschenbaum gently snatched it out of his hands.

"I don't think that would be a good idea. Some of the members of the team that subdued the terrorists may be around, and they might consider it a bit callous considering their lost buddies, who were not, how shall we say, invulnerable."

"I understand," said Meteor Man, who left the room and continued down the corridor to the awaiting helicopter.

Kirschenbaum looked at the beret in his hand.

"That was a close call," said psychopharmacologist Parker. "Seeing himself in the beret might have brought back a few too many conflicting memories. After all, no matter how many doses of pharmacologicals we inject, it's still impossible to effect a complete past erasure, and restructuring."

"Yes," said psychologist Kirschenbaum.

"At least his task is simple enough. He probably won't even notice any adverse effects until he makes it back here. By then the crisis will have been averted, and he'll be in isolation."

"Where we will let him die in peace," muttered Kirschenbaum.

"Yes, far from the questioning eyes of John Q. Public," continued Parker. "I really have to hand it to you setting up this program. If anyone had told me that we would be able to make your average, everyday soldier believe that he was invulnerable, I would never have believed it. The faked computer-enhanced newscast, the Kevlar body suit, breakaway saw blade. One question: how did he manage to catch the bullets?"

"The bullets were electronically programmed to stop on impact, and activate a miniaturized electromagnet that was tuned to the frequency of a metallic salve that I had coated his left palm with."

"Ingenious," exclaimed Parker. "Where did you ever get your idea for PROJECT SUPERHERO?"

"Where else?" said Kirschenbaum. "The comic books."

"Well, it certainly works," said Parker, patting the older doctor on the back. "In less than two hours we can turn an ordinary soldier with human flaws and instincts for self-preservation into a confident and carefree hero with no other concerns except the completion of his mission. One man dies so that many can be saved. No matter how you look at it, that's a more than acceptable casualty rate. Lt. O'Conner, aka Meteor Man I, will get a hero's funeral, and the day will be saved."

"A hero's funeral," mused the increasingly more depressed Dr. Kirschenbaum. "I remember reading about the Soviet firemen who rushed into Chernobyl to contain the fire to keep the plant from exploding, knowing that in doing so they were signing their own death warrants. I also remember stories of soldiers earning medals that were awarded posthumously by jumping on top of hand grenades . . ."

"That's where you got your idea for Meteor Man smothering the atomic bomb that would have leveled Las Vegas," Parker added gleefully.

"I guess," responded Kirschenbaum, "but you've missed the point. In the past there was a time for heroes, when extraordinary men responded to extraordinary circumstances. No one could predict it, yet somehow, because of the appearance of a few good men, we always managed to survive. It was a time of heroes, and one always showed up on time."

"Now all we have to do is invent our own," added Parker, "and we never have to worry about one showing up too late. We turned Lt. O'Conner into Meteor Man in under two hours, and averted the crisis with three hours to spare. What more could we want?"

"What more could Lt. O'Conner want?" Kirschenbaum responded sardonically. "Maybe just a real chance to be a hero, no deceptions, no false bravado. Maybe all he wanted was the chance to give up his life for the common good. Maybe it was his time to be a hero."

"I'd rather not take that risk," said Parker.

"I suppose you wouldn't," replied Kirschenbaum, turning off the monitor till the next crisis, until the time arrived when Meteor Man II would make his entrance.

Peer Review

Michael A. Stackpole

The law can be extremely complicated with twists and turns. How do the laws of man apply to beings who are only marginally human?

Dan Rather smiled for a second before composing his face into the solemn mask he affected when imparting distressful news to the people of America. "The tumultuous kidnap and assault case involving Maria Hopkins, a desperately ill young woman, her little brother Nathan, and the masked vigilante Revenant took a couple of odd twists today. After the American Justice Commission—a group of superheroes united to uphold the laws of the United States—announced they would hold a hearing on Revenant's actions, news organizations filed suit in Federal court to force the AJC to open their hearing to the public. Lawyers for the networks pointed out that the Federal and States' Attorneys in both Vermont and New Hampshire had refrained from filing charges against Revenant pending the outcome of the AJC hearing.

"The Advocate, charter member of the AJC and its legal advisor, noted that as a legally constituted and privately held Delaware corporation it was not required to open its meetings. Federal Appeals Court judge Elizabeth Kerin agreed with her argument and refused to issue an order opening the meeting. All indications from the High Court are that it will refuse to hear arguments in the case."

Dan let a hint of surprise lighten his expression. "In the most bizarre turnaround in the case, Revenant—who was believed to be in hiding outside the United States—has agreed to attend the AJC hearing, despite his not being a member of the organization. His agreement was deemed unlikely in light of the AJC's involvement with the case and its active opposition to his actions. Nemesis, founder of the AJC and its current president, gave Revenant a personal guarantee of safety and said the hearing would be fair. Revenant, a shadowy figure who has the distinction of being the only superhero ever to make it to the FBI's Ten Most Wanted list, cited that guarantee as the primary reason for his decision.

"*Quis custodiet ipsos custodes*, the Romans used to ask: who will guard the guardians? Now we'll have to ask: who will guard the guardians while they are guarding themselves?"

The desiccating desert heat surrendered reluctantly as Revenant descended the ramp leading into the American Justice Commission headquarters. Built beneath the Arizona Center—the hole for it having been carved out of the caliche by Nemesis and Glacier—the marble-lined walls made him more mindful of a mausoleum than a place meant to be the center for the fight by good against evil. Having holographic images of fallen AJC members built into the walls did not help improve the impression.

The floor leveled out into a small lobby, but the information and ticket booth off to the left was dark, and the tour schedule had a big "canceled" sign taped over it. Continuing on ahead, Revenant passed between two twenty-foot-high statues of Justice done in bronze and into a narrow corridor with a ceiling that sloped up toward the surface again. At the end of it he entered a huge chamber with red rock flooring and copper trim everywhere.

Seven members of the AJC waited to render judgement on his actions. Seated behind a high bench, Nemesis occupied the primary position. On his right sat Aranatrix, Hummingbird and Hammersnake, on his left Glacier, Caracal and Thylacine. All of them wore their costumes, and none had deigned to let him see their bare faces.

As he had no intention of doing that either, he did not take their remaining masked as an insult. His midnight-blue hood hid his face completely except for his eyes, and his cape shrouded the rest of him.

As he walked to the defense table to the left of the central aisle, he refrained from throwing his cloak open quickly—he knew Glacier, Hammersnake and Colonel Constitution would love nothing more than an excuse to pound on him. Reaching the table, he gently flipped the cape back behind his shoulders, then carefully drew and laid his dart gun and shock-rod on the table.

He remained standing, taking his cue from The Advocate and Colonel Constitution at the prosecution table. He bowed his head to Nemesis. "I'm sorry to keep you waiting, but parking is at a premium around here." He glanced over at the superhero wearing red, white and blue. "I hope you validate stubs."

Colonel Constitution snarled immediately. "I'll validate your stubby little . . ."

"Enough." Nemesis rose from his chair, muscles bulging. Though born on a planet in a far distant galaxy and sent to Earth as a child, he did not seem alien to Revenant. His uniform had green sleeves and leggings, with white stripes at the shoulders and waist. The blue of the torso matched the hue of Nemesis's domino mask and was not that much lighter than the color of Revenant's uniform. Unlike the Nightmare Detective, Nemesis did not wear gloves or a cape, and his long, blond hair touched his broad shoulders.

"I wish to thank you, Revenant, for taking part in this hearing. It is less to ascertain innocence or guilt than it is for us to decide if we will establish a policy concerning you. Your participation in the Hopkins abduction has been the subject of debate here." From the way Nemesis looked around and various members nodded, Revenant guessed the debate had been acrimonious. "It is my hope that we can resolve this situation. Agreed?"

Revenant nodded. "Agreed, though, for the record, I would like to point out that I do not recognize your authority over me, nor do I consider myself bound by any verdict that might be reached here."

A suppressed growl from Colonel Constitution echoed through the cavernous hall. The Advocate, in her trademark double-breasted black suit, black fedora, black mask and black gloves, held Constitution in check, but did not spare Revenant an evil glare. Nemesis nodded affirmatively, then seated himself again. "That is understood."

The AJC leader looked at The Advocate. "Please proceed."

"If it would please the . . . ah, you, my esteemed colleagues, let me remind you of the situation two weeks ago that led to the catalog of crimes pending indictment on Revenant. Fearing for the safety of her six-year-old son Nathan, Jeanette Hopkins—in defiance of a custodial order to the contrary—sought refuge near Groveton Springs, New Hampshire. She said her husband and her daughter were members of a satanic cult who wanted to sacrifice Nathan in a foul ceremony. Reverend Bert Sunnington took her in and housed her at his Blessed Haven estate near Groveton Springs, then retained legal counsel for her and immediately appealed the Vermont court's divorce and custody decrees. Her ex-husband Martin was enjoined not to do anything to interfere with her temporary custody of Nathan and, in response to a request by the judge who made that ruling, Colonel Constitution led Strike Team Alpha up to New Hampshire to see that the child stayed with his mother.

"That restraining order in place, Revenant entered into a criminal conspiracy with Martin Hopkins to violate that order and commit numerous felonies."

Martin Hopkins never would have described himself as a brave man. A brave man, he told himself, would be able to fight his own battles. He could not, and he acknowledged that fact right along with his failure in any of a number of other areas of his life. Even this appeal might fail, but he was desperate to do anything that might save Maria. Desperate enough to overcome his fear of anything that even remotely looked outside the law and especially anything that had to do with Revenant.

Martin Hopkins in no way looked the part of a hero and certainly didn't feel it, even though a friend he told about the meeting said he had to have balls the size of planets to actually *want* to meet with Revenant. Short and stout, with a pencil-thin moustache and a double chin that rested on the top of his barrel chest, Martin crept into the warehouse Revenant had designated for their meeting as if he were the lead in a very, very bad spy movie. The belt barely kept an old trench coat closed, and the requisite fedora had given way to a Yankees baseball cap.

Revenant cleared his throat and Martin spun, clutching at his chest as he saw the shadowed outline of a man. "You wanted to see *me?*"

"Whoa, jeez, don't do that." Martin caught his breath, then doffed his cap and wiped his forehead with his sleeve. "I'm sorry, sir, I mean . . ." Frustration and fatigue wove their way through the man's voice, bringing it to the edge of cracking. "Look, I don't have any money. It's all tied up in the operation."

Revenant slipped from the shadows that had hidden him. "You are getting ahead of yourself. You are Martin Hopkins, forty-one, divorced, two children. Maria is nineteen and Nathan is six. You are the manager of Northwoods Lumber." Revenant's voice, calm and even, drained away some of the panic causing Martin's heart to jackhammer in his chest. "Your ex-wife has your son in a religious commune in New Hampshire."

Martin's brown eyes grew wide. "Good, that's good, that you know that stuff I mean. That's good."

Revenant inclined his head toward the shorter man. "And why would that be good?"

Martin swallowed with difficulty, his tongue thick in a dry mouth. "Look, my daughter, Maria, she's in the Medical Center Hospital of Vermont over in Burlington. She has leukemia and is going to die. The doctors say she needs marrow for a transplant and I'm not a good donor. Nathan is, but Jeanette . . ."

A lump in his throat choked off the rest of his words. He opened his hands toward Revenant and sniffed.

Revenant's head came up, and Hopkins felt the man's green-eyed gaze pierce his soul. "Your wife is aware of Maria's condition and will not allow the donation?"

Martin nodded. "I know Nathan would be willing. He loves his sister." Martin swiped at his nose with his sleeve. "Reverend Sunnington—I called him to beg, I really did—said Maria's illness is God's retribution for her sins."

Revenant folded his arms and his eyes narrowed perceptibly. Martin felt a chill run down his spine and could see how the man before him had earned the nickname of the Nightmare Detective. Had he been there just for himself, Martin would have run when he first saw

Revenant, and if Revenant were ever after him, he knew he'd just die.

"I don't know that I can help you, Mr. Hopkins. While I sympathize with your plight"—Revenant shrugged uneasily—"I am only a normal man with a few tricks and a cape. This is the type of case better handled by people like the American Justice Commission."

Martin sagged to his knees. "I tried them. Colonel Constitution says the order is legal and it's a second-amendment issue. I can't fight them." He opened his mouth, then closed it again. Swallowing the lump down, he croaked, "Please?"

The Nightmare Detective remained silent and motionless for what felt like hours to Martin. Finally he nodded. "How long does your daughter have?"

"Maybe a month. The sooner the better."

"Very well. I will give you details for your part in this. You will have your son as soon as possible."

A charcoal-grey gloved hand extended itself from beneath the blue cape, and Martin shook Revenant's hand. Revenant did not seek to crush his hand, and Martin drew strength from the firm grip. "One more thing, Mr. Revenant, sir." Martin freed his hand and patted the trench coat's pockets until he found what he wanted. He pulled a rabbit's foot from his pocket and handed it to the tall man.

Revenant took it, examined it, then shook his head. "I appreciate the sentiment, Mr. Hopkins, but I doubt this will help me."

Revenant made to hand it back, but Martin waved him off. "No, look, Nathan is a smart boy and wouldn't go with you unless you can give him a sign that you're bringing him to me. That's his—Jeanette called it satanic and left it behind when she ran. Give it to him. He'll know."

The Nightmare Detective nodded, and the lucky charm disappeared into a pouch on his belt.

Martin smiled and pulled his cap back on. "I can't thank you enough."

"That may be true, Mr. Hopkins, we'll see." Revenant started to withdraw, then stopped. "You can make a start right now, if you will."

Martin stiffened. "Yes?"

"You're not the sort of man to be associating with those who know how to contact me. How did you get the number where you left that message?"

Martin blinked, then thought for a second. "At the hospital, in a get-well card, someone had put in a note—anonymous. I called."

"Anonymous; interesting." Revenant stepped into the shadows and vanished.

The Advocate turned and pointed at Revenant. "Regardless of the seemingly humanitarian motive of obtaining the marrow needed for a transplant, Revenant mocked the American legal system by planning and executing a series of crimes. . . ."

Revenant held a hand up. "Alleged crimes."

Colonel Constitution looked at him, then sank his fingers into the edge of the copper-covered prosecution table. The Advocate bowed her head, her short auburn locks sweeping forward to half hide her face. "Alleged crimes. Revenant did willfully break and enter into the Blessed Haven compound. . . ."

"I'll agree to entering, but I did no breaking."

Hummingbird, barely visible behind the microphone that was as big as he was, darted over to within six inches of Nemesis's face, then across to Revenant and back behind his microphone in two seconds. "Mr. President, I have a question."

"Proceed."

"How can you say you did not break, when there was a ten-foot-tall fence with razor wire on the top all around the place? Glacier and I installed it three days before you . . . allegedly entered the Blessed Haven sanctuary." His wings humming, he rose above the microphone, his arms crossed over his chest. "You can't fly, so how did you get in?"

"Trees."

The Advocate frowned. "Trees?"

Revenant nodded. "I climbed a tree, walked out on a branch and went over the fence. The fence later went down when Mr. Force-of-Nature hit it."

The Advocate did her best to speak over Glacier's grumbling. "Regardless, you stole a terrified little boy away from his mother, coerced him into criminal action, then assaulted duly sworn officers of the law in the course of their duty."

Coming across the Blessed Haven compound, Revenant conceded to himself that organized religion did serve a purpose. He chose Wednesday night for his penetration of the commune because he knew the adults would all be at services. He knew, from the handful of articles concerning Reverend Sunnington and Blessed Haven, that all children would be in their rooms studying or praying before lights out at 8:30 P.M.—the commune had its own school, and classes started promptly at 6:30 in the morning, every morning.

Actually locating Nathan Hopkins within the 100-acre compound had presented a problem, but Revenant managed to narrow down the possibilities. An old map of the compound run in the Manchester *Union Leader* had showed a set of new buildings under construction and a picture accompanying the same article depicted the construction site as having all the plumbing and electrical fixtures one would need for simple apartmentlike housing units. A later map indicated the same buildings were used for "storage," but the article was talking about Sunnington's "Satanic Sacrifice Succor" program. That meant that Jeanette Hopkins and her son would probably be in the new units—labeling them storage seemed to be a clearly transparent effort at misdirection.

It did occur to him that the new map, which had only appeared two weeks ago in the Boston *Herald*, might have been planted as part of an elaborate AJC trap. He dismissed that idea because Colonel Constitution was running the AJC operation, and "elaborate" became a synonym for "confused" when used in reference to anything he did. The new fence was classic Conny, yet Revenant remained vigilant just in case Constitution had come up with an original idea for once.

If Blessed Haven had maintained a computer listing of its tenants and Revenant had known about it, he could have solved the problem of determining which of the two dozen apartments in the new complex housed the Hopkins family. As he approached the building, weaving his way through the cars in the church parking lot, he started by eliminating apartments connected to patios or balconies where he saw toys unsuited to a boy or someone of Nathan's age. Crouching in the shadow of the BMW owned by the judge who had signed the restraining order, he also eliminated the dark apartments that looked vacant because they lacked shades on the windows.

Moving on, lest the hiss of the car's quickly flattening tire attract attention. Revenant slipped his knife back into the top of his right boot and worked around to the far side of the complex. Apartment 14 seemed a likely suspect, as it had a light on, but no toys on the patio in front of it. He took pride in his deductive ability, then he drew close enough to see a small tag on the doorjamb, just above the doorbell, that read "Hopkins, Jeanette," in a small, orderly hand.

He spent his irritation by raking the lock open with his lockpicks in less than five seconds and slipping into the dimly lit apartment. He closed the door behind him, then flipped the flag lock to give himself a second or two of extra time to escape if someone tried to enter the apartment. He set the heavy pack he had been carrying down in the middle of the living room floor, then crouched and just listened.

The living room and kitchenette were separated by a half-wall. Off to the right a narrow corridor led past a closet to the bathroom— the source of the light in the apartment—and on to two bedrooms. Revenant expected he would find Nathan in one of them, but something didn't feel quite right. He couldn't place it; then he saw a brief flash of light coming from beneath the hall closet door and heard a faint snatch of a hummed tune.

Glancing back out the window and seeing no one, Revenant moved to the closet door. He jiggled the knob, then opened the door. The little light inside snapped off, and Revenant recognized the sound of a comic book flapping shut. In the light that slipped from the bathroom into the closet he saw the comic and a flashlight head down into an empty boot; then a little boy looked up at him.

"Who are you?"

Revenant squatted down. "I'm here to take you to help your sister."

The boy's blue eyes grew wide. "Are you an angel?"

In spite of himself, Revenant laughed. He knew that was the first time and likely the last anyone would ever make that particular mistake about him. "What makes you ask that?"

The boy smiled innocently. "I asked Reverend Sunnington to let me go to help Maria. He said that if Jesus wanted me to help my sister, he would send an angel." The boy reached out and traced the R that made up Revenant's logo on his chest. "You must be Raphael, the helper angel."

"Something like that." Revenant produced the rabbit's foot as if by magic from Nathan's left ear. "I have spoken with your father. He asked me to give this to you."

The boy's face lit up at the mention of his father; then he took the charm and rubbed it in his hands. "If an angel gives this to me, I guess it can't be bad like Mommy said."

"Right. Are you ready to go? It will be a little bit of a trip, and we can't make much noise."

Nathan nodded solemnly and hitched the rabbit's foot to one of the belt loops on his short pants. He stood up and left the closet, closing it very quietly. On tiptoes he crept out into the living room and stopped beside the pack Revenant had left behind. "I have a pack like this. Mommy had me pack it in case we have to go away. Should I get it?"

Revenant nodded and Nathan ran back to his room. The Nightmare Detective dropped to one knee by his pack and unzipped one of the pockets. He pulled out two small plastic bottle-shaped items no larger than the rabbit's foot and set them on the ground. Nathan returned, looping a fuzzy bear backpack on, and Revenant pointed to the plastic items.

"Do you know what these are?"

Nathan nodded. "Party favors. Pull the string and they go boom."

"Right. They're for you. Use them only when I tell you to, okay?"

"Okay."

Revenant shouldered his pack, then crossed to the door. He saw no one through the peephole and no one outside the window. "Nathan, when we go out, we're going to keep to the shadows, okay? Follow me and we'll be with your father in no time."

"Okay, Mr. Raphael."

Revenant opened the door and Nathan followed him out into the night. The little boy trotted along as fast as he could, which was not quite fast enough for Revenant's taste, but the boy said nothing, and that earned him points in Revenant's book. They crossed the open area near the apartment complex and got all the way to the church parking lot before stopping. They hunkered down in the shadows of the cars and Nathan began to hum along with the hymn "Nearer, My God, To Thee."

"Nathan, stop for a second. I have to listen."

The boy clapped his hands over his mouth, then smiled. Revenant looked around but saw nothing out of the ordinary. That did nothing to make him feel any more secure, because he knew that his uniform could render him virtually invisible at night and, without the benefit of starlight or infrared vision devices, his chances of spotting someone were very low. He also knew, from experience, that sound would more likely betray a foe at night, but the damned singing would have covered the advance of Hannibal and all his elephants.

Nathan tugged on his cape. "That car over there has a flat tire."

Revenant laughed lightly. "That it does."

A motorcycle's headlight flicked on from the right. "That's not the only thing that's going to be flat around here." Colonel Constitution slammed his right fist into the front of the knight's-shield on his left arm. "I'm going to start with your head and work my way down."

Nemesis nodded as Colonel Constitution finished swearing to tell the truth. "Your witness, Advocate."

The Advocate came around from behind the prosecution table and nodded to Colonel Constitution. "You were present at Blessed Haven with the permission of Reverend Sunnington to enforce the court order protecting Nathan Hopkins, is that correct?"

Constitution nodded, the red threads on his epaulets rocking gently back and forth. "I was in place at Groveton Springs that evening. Nemesis had agreed to my request to let Strike Team Alpha take care of the Hopkins situation. I had Hammersnake, Hummingbird and Glacier patrolling the grounds. I had been watching Jeanette Hopkins in church to prevent any attempt at snatching her. I had a premonition something was wrong, so I left the church and saw the defendant hustling the child away. I hit my Strike Team alert signal to bring the others to me, then I identified myself to the suspect and asked him to comply with the law."

"And his response to that was?"

Colonel Constitution shook his head, his tricorn hat shifting slightly off center. "He responded by violating my civil rights."

Revenant hefted Nathan up and sat him on the roof of the judge's car, then shucked his pack and set it there. "It's party time, Nathan, and you know what that means. Be ready."

The little boy clutched his party favors and smiled. "Ready."

Revenant stepped away from the vehicle and into the center of the crushed gravel parking lot. "You get one shot, Colonel. Make it good."

Constitution grinned coldly. "I'm going to kick your butt from here to Canada and back, Revenant. You don't stand a ghost of a chance."

"Your puns are cornier than you are." The Nightmare Detective slipped a foot-long silvery tube from the sheath on his right forearm, then shifted it to his right hand. "I bet you call yourself Colonel Constitution because your real name is Bill Wright."

"How did you . . . ?" Constitution snarled furiously and kicked the engine on the motorcycle to life. White stones roostertailed out behind the bike as he gunned the motor, and the bike reared up. The Premier Patriot wrestled the bike down to the ground and aimed it straight at Revenant. The engine roared as the big Harley bore down on him. Constitution hunkered down behind his shield and Revenant watched as Constitution set himself for a shield punch that would put Revenant down for the count.

At the last second, his cloak a swirling satin cloud, Revenant pivoted on his left foot like a matador dodging a raging bull's charge. He stabbed his shock-rod through the spokes of the motorcycle's front wheel, then spun away as the shield clipped him on his right shoulder. Moving with the blow, he ended up flat on his back as the shock-rod locked against the front wheel's fork. The bike bucked forward and catapulted Constitution through the air.

The Premier Patriot flew like a missile and slammed head first into the grill of a Ford Taurus. Radiator fluid gushed out into the air as the hood crumpled and in the driver's compartment two airbags exploded from the dashboard and steering wheel. The motorcycle cartwheeled after Constitution, bouncing high on its tires after an initial somersault; then it balanced for a second before falling over to pin Constitution's legs.

Constitution's nostrils flared as he looked over at Revenant. "If it had been an imported car, I would have demolished it and then him. Because it was a domestic, well, I was hors de combat for the moment, so I didn't see what happened next."

Nemesis looked over at Revenant. "Have you any questions of this witness?"

The Nightmare Detective shook his head. "None he could answer without grinding his teeth."

"You are excused, then, Colonel." Nemesis stared the man back to his place at the prosecutor's table, then looked at Hummingbird. "I assume, Advocate, you want Hummingbird next?"

"Yes, Your Honor."

Hummingbird zipped from his place to the witness box, then hovered before the microphone, his wings a blur. "On my honor, as a member of the American Justice Commission, I swear to tell the complete truth and labor tirelessly until justice prevails."

The Advocate checked some notes at her table, then looked up. "You were next on the scene, correct?"

"I was."

"Would you describe what happened?"

The Wee Winged Warrior nodded almost imperceptibly. "Not much to tell. He tricked me."

Humming like a furious cicada, Hummingbird's first pass knocked Revenant back to the ground. He'd taken the blow full on his back, so his Kevlar body armor helped absorb some of the shock, but the kinetic energy Hummingbird had built up still blasted him into the gravel. Grabbing the shock-rod as he rolled into a crouch, Revenant looked up to see Hummingbird hovering between him and Nathan Hopkins.

"If you want the child, foul one, you must go through me first."

"Have it your way." Revenant slowly stood. "Now, Nathan."

The little boy obediently pulled the lanyard that set off the first party favor. Accompanied by a bright flash and sharp crack, a silvery octopus of fine streamers shot out into the sky. The backdraft and suction from Hummingbird's wings pulled them in, entangling the Wee Winged Warrior before he even knew he was under attack. The streamers enfolded him, and the harsh beating of his wings slowed, then stopped. Yet before he could fall to the ground, Revenant lunged forward and swirled his shock-rod through the trailing tinsel.

His thumb caressed the shock-rod's control button for a second and Hummingbird twitched like a spastic marionette, then hung limp from the streamers. Revenant carried him over to the car and set him down, then peeled the tinsel off and flipped the six-inch-tall man over onto his stomach.

"See that, Nathan? He's a small man in a mechanical suit." Revenant pulled the knife from his boot and used the tip of the blade to pry the lid off the little square box between Hummingbird's wings. "These are the batteries he uses to power his wings. If we pop them out, just like that, he won't get into any more trouble."

"If he's trying to stop you, Raphael, he must be a demon."

Revenant shook his head. "Not a demon, just a confused man. It may be a while before you understand it, but there *is* a difference."

Nemesis stared down at Hummingbird. "You say you awoke in the glove box of a Mercedes Benz?"

The tiny superhero shook with indignation. "I'd been stuffed into a tube sock and had a pillow made out of Kleenex."

"That was Nathan's idea," Revenant interjected quickly. "He'd seen cats about in the compound and thought the sock would make a great sleeping bag for you. In the spirit of things, I figured you'd enjoy a suite at the Mercedes hotel."

The Extraterrestrial Titan nodded like Solomon. "I see. Thank you, Hummingbird. Unless Revenant has any questions for you, I think you can be dismissed."

The Nightmare Detective shook his head, then looked up as Hammersnake moved to the witness box. Stretching his right leg up and over the bench, the Elastic Revenger planted it firmly, then let the rest of his body flow down into place like a man-shaped Slinky. His right hand snapped up cobralike, and he swore to tell the truth as his two predecessors had.

The Advocate glanced over at Revenant, then smiled and turned to her new witness. "In your encounter with Revenant that evening, you suffered a fate similar to that of two other Strike Team Alpha members, did you not?"

"Yeah."

"But in that encounter you learned something that pertains to his motives for being there, and his methods, correct?"

"Yeah." Hammersnake raked rubbery fingers back through rubbery black hair, the tangled mess making an audible snap as he pulled his fingers free. "Do you want me to tell it now?"

The Advocate nodded. "If you please."

"Yeah, right. I learned Revenant works with the Injustice Cabal. . . ."

Revenant and Nathan had hurried along through the night. The Nightmare Detective knew two other members of the AJC's Strike Team Alpha lurked out there somewhere and the only real chance of his defeating them lay in dealing with them separately. "If Hammersnake and Glacier converge . . ."

"Don't worry, Raphael, we have the rabbit's foot."

Revenant smiled and lifted Nathan up in his arm. "Then let's be quick like bunnies and get out of here. Get around there and ride piggyback."

"But rabbits don't do that."

"Angel rabbits have special rules." Revenant shrugged his pack off, then let Nathan settle himself in place. "Ease up on the choke hold there, Nathan."

"Yeah, Nathan, leave something for me."

Revenant whirled and saw an impossibly tall and lean figure silhouetted by the light from the commune buildings. The man stood with his fists firmly planted on his hips, his chin elongated as it thrust forward. He swayed slightly, like tall grass in a light breeze.

"He looks like a soggy pretzel," Nathan whispered in Revenant's ear, prompting a laugh.

"Yeah, laugh there, Casper, because there ain't nothing you're going to find funny when I'm through with you." Hammersnake jerked a thumb toward himself—deftly done without moving his fist from his hip. "I'm Hammersnake, and if you know anything about me at all, you know you better give up now. Don't worry, kid, I'll have you away from him in jig time, then we'll get you signed up with my fan club and get you some action figures and stuff."

Revenant dropped his hand to the holster on his right hip and drew the pistol. Glancing at the selector lever, he switched it over to the second position, then pulled back the cocking lever. He raised the gun to shoulder height, the muzzle pointing toward the stars. "Give it a touch with the foot, Nathan."

As the child happily complied and Revenant drew a bead, Hammersnake laughed aloud. "Shoulda read the press kit on me, irrelevant. I'm rubber. Bullets bounce off . . . OUCH!" Hammersnake looked down, then plucked a silvery dart from his chest. "A dart. Ha! My metabolism is so special that nothing you could have in there could hurt me. In fact, only the venom of . . ."

"The venom of the Haitian solenodon can affect you." Revenant pumped two more darts into the Elastic Revenger, and the man collapsed into a tangle of garden-hose limbs.

"How did you know? That's a secret!"

"Ever since you got bitten by one when fighting Crimson Carnage outside Port-au-Prince, the word's been out on you. The solenodons are being harvested to extinction and the Injustice Cabal's computers list dozens of brokers where you can buy the stuff." Nathan slid from Revenant's back as the Nightmare Detective squatted down and tied Hammersnake's arms and legs around a sapling with a couple of bowlines.

Revenant looked up at the boy. "So, Nathan, you think Hammersnake's a cool hero."

"Not!"

If I ever need a sidekick, Nathan, you're the leading candidate. Revenant took Nathan's hand, recovered his pack and ran off into the darkness before Hammersnake's groans could die away.

✳

"I have a point of clarification, Mr. President."

Nemesis nodded at the woman seated at his right. "Yes, Arana-trix?"

The Mistress of Webs smiled, her silvery costume sharply reflecting the room's muted light. "I have, in spreading my web through the nation's computer systems, come across phantom traces of activity I have attributed to Revenant—though he leaves elusively few clues." She inclined her head toward him, and Revenant returned the nod respectfully. "I would note that the information concerning outlets for the purchase of the neurotoxic venom of *Solenodon paradoxus* has been altered and now, as nearly as I can determine, all requests for same are collected and made available to local law enforcement or Federal forces, as appropriate."

Thylacine down at the end of the bench, smiled beneath his wolfish half-mask. "Mr. President, as you know, Caracal and I pay special attention to crimes in violation of the Endangered Species Act. In Haiti, which is the only place *Solenodon paradoxus* is found, hunting has all but stopped in the past two weeks. I hadn't thought about it until now, mainly because of Haiti and voodoo stories, but rumors of 'The Unholy Ghost' prohibiting poaching and dealing with poachers has destroyed the trade."

Colonel Constitution stabbed a finger at Revenant. "Adding computer crimes and terrorist actions against foreign nationals to your list of crimes now?"

"Alleged crimes." Revenant laughed as Constitution's neck bulged. "And I believe those questions are beyond the scope of your current inquiry."

Nemesis agreed with a nod. "Glacier, you're up next, I think. Thank you, Hammersnake."

Revenant felt the room grow colder as Glacier came around from behind the bench and moved to the witness box. Clad from head to toe in white, Glacier moved with a deliberate slowness. His short-sleeved uniform revealed arms as massively muscled as the rest of him, and icy bracers protected his forearms. His flesh had a bluish tint to it, shades lighter than that used to emblazon the letter G on his chest, but not dark enough to mark him as alien.

After being sworn in he stared at Revenant with arctic blue eyes. "Yes, I was the last of our team to face Revenant in the initial encounter. I determined I would not fail to detain him, but I found myself subjected to an unusual form of attack. . . ."

Without further interruption, but with a few laughs and giggles, Revenant and Nathan reached the fence the AJC had erected. Revenant dropped his pack to the ground, then upended it. In a nice little bundle a padded chain ladder fell out. Revenant undid the cords holding it together, then lofted it up toward the fence. The thick, canvas padding covered the razor wire, while the aluminum rungs provided an easy way to go up and over.

"Okay, Nathan, you go first. Take it easy, and if you see any sharp metal at the top, be careful and don't touch it."

The boy nodded, and Revenant tucked the singleton tube sock hanging from the top of the bear pack back inside. "Go for it. I'll be over in a second."

"Halt!" The bellow echoed through the woods like the challenge of a bull moose to a rival. "I arrest you in the name of the American Justice Commission."

"Nuts." Revenant dug into his pack and pulled out a tooled metal device that looked to be the big brother of Nathan's party favors. He looked up at the mountainous man at the crest of the rise they had descended to get to the fence. "That's Glacier."

The boy pulled his remaining favor from his pocket and smiled. "Is it party time again?"

Revenant tousled the boy's light brown hair. "Yeah, but you save that one for later, maybe for when you see your sister, okay? Up and over for you. Wait for me by that big tree over there, okay?"

"Okay."

As Nathan scrambled up the ladder, Revenant stood up and opened his arms wide. "Let me make this easy for you, Sno-cone, I'm resisting arrest."

"This is ill-advised." Glacier flexed his muscles, eclipsing the moon rising behind him. "I am authorized to use whatever means necessary to detain you."

"Yeah, yeah, you'll put me on ice. There'll be a frost in hell before

I walk as a free man. I've heard it all before." Revenant waved Glacier forward. "Do your worst, just don't take all day, okay, Pokey?"

"Tremble where you stand, lawbreaker!" Glacier shook a fist at him as he began to plod forward. "You shall know the inexorable wrath of Glacier!"

Revenant exaggerated a belly laugh. "Oh, that's rich, coming from a guy who went skinny-dipping and sank the Titanic!"

"Aarrgh!" The Chilled Champion lowered his head and started pumping his arms as he charged forward. His legs, which did not look particularly long because of their girth, ate up the hundred yards separating the two men with deceptive quickness. Glacier's body straightened up as he hit his top speed, and his fists flexed open and closed as if practicing what they would do to Revenant.

The Nightmare Detective held his ground, crouching slightly, as the behemoth rushed toward him. He could feel the thudding footfalls shake the ground. Glacier's labored breathing echoed like a blast-furnace bellows in the night, and the pumping arms reminded him of a locomotive's pistons driving the engine. Twin streams of breath vapor trailed back from either side of Glacier's face, and the air took on the bone-numbing cold of an arctic blizzard.

Revenant drew in a breath and held it, waiting until Glacier came within ten feet of him. He raised the metal funnel, then yanked the lanyard. The blank shotgun shell inside the narrow part of the funnel exploded, forcing everything in front of it out the wide end of the device. The waxed cardboard wadding shot out, smacking Glacier squarely in the face, so he never saw the cloud formed by the pound and a half of black pepper that burst out from behind it.

Glacier sucked in pepper like a Dustbuster in overdrive, and immediately choked and coughed back out as much as he could. Then the convulsive sneezing started, with each intake of breath thereafter dragging more and more pepper into his nose and lungs. The tears running from his eyes froze on his face, forming long, Fu-Manchu icicles hanging down from his chin; then a violent sneeze snapped them off as they bashed into his chest.

Revenant, having spun away from the cloud, lowered his cape and saw Glacier stumbling about blindly. He started to reach for his pistol, then decided against it. Walking over to the stricken hero, he spun the man around so his back was to the fence, then planted the heel of his foot on the point of Glacier's chin in a nasty front kick.

Arms and legs flung wide, Glacier flew the remaining half-dozen feet to the fence and sagged into it, like a trapeze artist dropping into a net. A series of high-pitched *twangs* sounded as the cyclone fence abandoned any pretense of holding Glacier up. It tore away from the nearest post first, dragging Glacier off to Revenant's left as the fence contracted.

Nathan peeked out from behind the tree, then whistled as Revenant limped over to him. "He's out cold."

The Nightmare Detective laughed and resisted the temptation to make it tail off into the sinister tones he used when dealing with criminals. "That's good, Nathan. You're a sharp boy. What do you want to be when you grow up?"

Nathan took Revenant's right hand and they started to walk through the woods. "I want to be a hero—not like them, a *real* hero."

"I think you have a chance, Nathan." Revenant gave his hand a squeeze.

"Really?"

"Really. After all, you've already got the dialog down."

The ice on the witness box bannister cracked as Glacier released his grip on it. "That is what I remember."

The Advocate nodded, dismissing Glacier, then turned toward Revenant. "That is the point when you fled to avoid arrest and prosecution. You also conducted the child across state lines, making the kidnapping a Federal offense. Colonel Constitution, if you would be so kind . . ."

Nemesis frowned. "Colonel, if you please, just remain seated at your table. You are still sworn. I know where this is going, so why don't you catch everyone else up?"

Constitution cracked his knuckles. "With pleasure."

Nathan stopped when he saw the sleek Corvette waiting in the woods. Dark blue on the top with grey trim along the side panels, the vehicle sat with its nose pointed to a narrow road heading east through the woods. "Wow, God lets you angels have really cool cars."

Revenant winked at him as he disarmed the anti-intruder system. "I got it in trade for my harp and a millennium of payments. Hop in."

Nathan slid into the passenger seat, and Revenant closed the door before vaulting the hood and getting in the other side. Nathan had already pulled his pack off over his head and started to fasten the seat belts. Revenant helped him, tucking the pack down in the foot-well, and nodded when he was finished. "Next stop, your sister's hospital, okay?"

"Okay."

Revenant pulled his own safety harness on, snapping the belts into a stainless steal clasp over his chest, then fastened the lap belt low and snug. He punched the ignition code in, bringing the engine purring to life. He let Nathan hit the button that turned the lights on, then brought up the onboard navigational computer. "That dot, it's us. We'll use the old Route 110 extension to a covered bridge over the Connecticut River and into Vermont."

"I like covered bridges. Maria does too."

"Good, you can tell her all about this one." The Corvette roared down the woodland track and joined a paved road about a mile further on. Revenant felt apprehensive as he pulled onto the New Hampshire state route, but it was the quickest way he could get to his destination in the car. A more direct route would have continued through the woods, but the Corvette would have bottomed out a number of times and could even have been put out of commission if a tree had fallen in the thirty-six hours since he last scouted that route.

His confidence grew as they blew through Groveton and turned left. The 110 extension had been graded, but maintained only for local residential use. The dark car moved through the rolling New England hills like a panther eluding pursuit, and Revenant began to smile as the dot on the computer screen closed with the bridge icon.

"What's that?"

Revenant looked over at what Nathan had pointed out and snarled. "That's trouble." A flickering, bobbing light moved through the woods at a high rate of speed. Revenant lost sight of it for a moment behind a small hillock, then saw it bumping its way across a meadow as he crested the hill for the run down to the bridge.

He hit his high beams as the light slowed—it and the 'vette stopping at the same time. Colonel Constitution extended the motorcycle's kickstand. The front tire peeled apart like a retread shedding its outer skin, leaving behind a D-shaped wheel rim. Revenant blinked as the tire spat out road pebbles and tried to straighten up, but Hammersnake's legs quivered and he sat down hard.

Colonel Constitution ignored his battered companion. "It's over, Revenant. Time to take your medicine." Constitution hit a button on his bike's control panel, and two Red Rockets shot out from the launch tubes mounted on either side of the high seat. They arced high into the sky, then arrowed down and slammed into the covered bridge.

The ancient wooden structure had withstood storms and floods in its lifetime, but high explosives were more than a match for it. The twin fireballs blasted the center of the bridge into burning splinters. Cedar shingles flew like autumn leaves through the air, and flaming planks sailed out into the river's dark waters. Jagged beam ends burned brightly, marking where the center of the roadbed had once stood—memorial flames mourning the gap that separated them.

Constitution rubbed his gloved hands together, then made a big show of punching a button on his belt buckle. "There, I've even gone and summoned the Big Guy so he can use his X-ray sight to keep track of your bones as I break them. Get out of that car, and I'll give you a nightmare it won't take a detective to figure out."

Revenant glanced over at Nathan. "Seatbelts fastened?"

The boy nodded. "Check."

"Rabbit's foot deployed?"

Nathan rubbed it. "Check."

"Let's go!"

Revenant jammed his foot down on the accelerator and worked his way up through the gears smoothly. He finished shifting by the time a surprised Colonel Constitution dove out of the roadway. Keeping both hands locked on the wheel, Revenant came around the last bend in the road and started up the slight incline to the bridge. He watched the digital display continue to add numbers to his speed, but he didn't relax even as it cracked triple digits.

"Here we go, hang on!"

The Corvette shot through the fire at the bridge end, the engine screaming as the wheels met no more resistance. Revenant watched as the car's nose touched Jupiter, holding his breath and praying it would stay pointed in that direction for another second and another after that. Then slowly it began to dip, and his first glimpse of flames on the other side seemed to place them just a little more distant than he had hoped they would be.

Nathan shrieked with glee. "We're flying!"

"I guess we are. Brace yourself." Revenant grimaced. "We're landing."

The car touched down hard, sparks shooting everywhere as the vehicle bottomed out on the far side's concrete approach. The impact jammed Revenant down in his seat, and he ducked his head so the rebound wouldn't bash him senseless against the roof. He heard metal scream and felt a bump as some of the tailpipe assembly tore away; then a second heavier thump came from the back.

The car immediately started dragging its tail. Revenant saw one of the rear tires whirling off along the road ahead of them. It passed between two cars parked in the darkness on the Vermont side of the 110 extension, but Revenant ignored them as he fought to bring the Corvette to a stop. He spun the wheel to the left to counter the skid, but the car spun and backed into a roadside drainage ditch with a solid bump.

The navigational computer shorted out in a puff of smoke and Nathan's airbag deployed, but it did not muffle his laughter. "That was great. Do it again!"

"Not right now. We have to give your rabbit's foot a rest." Revenant popped his restraining harness open, then freed Nathan. As the two of them left the ruined vehicle, the waiting cars turned on their headlights and a heavyset man came out of the station wagon.

"Dad!" Nathan, his bear pack swinging wildly in his right hand, ran to his father and hugged the man's legs.

Revenant threw Martin a thumbs-up, then looked at the primly dressed woman getting out of the Infiniti Q45. She pulled a leather briefcase with her and started to open it, but froze when Nathan screamed, "Look out!"

A red, white and blue meteor hurled through the flames burning at river's edge. Propelled like a slingshot pellet by Hammersnake on the far side, Colonel Constitution smashed his shield into Revenant's back, then rolled on down the road until he could bleed off his momentum and regain his feet.

Nathan's warning had enabled Revenant to begin to shift away from the blow. Even so, the shield caught him solidly and smacked him into the side of the Infiniti. Rebounding from metal-sandwiched polymer alloy plating, Revenant landed on his back, momentarily stunned. Feeling flooded back into his arms and legs—pain mostly— but conscious control over his limbs still eluded him.

Colonel Constitution swaggered up into sight at his feet. "Get used to being on your back, because you'll be spending a lot of time in traction." He laughed coldly. "It's party time!"

He raised his shield to bash Revenant with it, but an expanding ball of tinsel shot up from Nathan's last party favor and blinded him. Revenant rolled to his right as Constitution punched his shield down into the road, then swept his leaden left leg back, catching Constitution in the ribs. The Premier Patriot spun away, then clawed the silvery tinsel from his face.

"You've corrupted the minor!"

Revenant rose unsteadily to his feet. "Better that than he grow up like you."

Constitution raised his shield again and closed, but another figure descended from the sky and stopped him in mid-rush by planting a hand in the middle of his chest. "Stop, Colonel." Nemesis looked over at Revenant and held his other hand out to keep them apart. "If you please, Revenant, minimizing the violence would be best for the boy, don't you think?"

The Nightmare Detective nodded. "Just tell that to Captain Collateral Damage over there."

"I'm going to nail your butt!" Constitution's wild gesticulations did not cease even when Nemesis lifted him from the ground. "You're mine. You're under arrest!"

The woman turned from inspecting the dent in her car and pulled a piece of paper from her briefcase. "And you will likewise be under arrest if you continue harassing Revenant, Mr. Hopkins or his son." She slapped the paper against Constitution's stomach. "This is a restraining order compelling you and Strike Team Alpha to stay one thousand meters from Revenant and the Hopkins family."

Nemesis released Constitution. The Premier Patriot unfolded the order, scanned it, then crumpled it up in a ball. "What kind of lily-livered judge would sign that sort of order?"

The woman grabbed a handful of Constitution's tricolored tunic. "*I* signed it, buster. It's got as much force as the order you were upholding over there in New Hampshire, so I suggest you think about that. Then I suggest you start marching off one thousand me-ters to the east and remember to breathe when you're swimming."

Colonel Constitution looked stricken. "Nemesis?"

The AJC President shrugged his shoulders. "We uphold the law, Colonel. Comply with the order."

Revenant winked at the retreating hero. "Remember that breathing thing. Pity about the bridge."

Nemesis dropped to his haunches and smiled at Nathan. "So you're the young man who's going to help his sister get better, is that right?"

Revenant looked back at his car and groaned. "Judge, do you mind if I borrow your car for a quick hospital run?"

She shot him a harsh stare. "After I've seen what you did to a 'vette? You sent Mr. Hopkins to me because I'm smart, remember?"

Nemesis straightened up. "I think I can remedy the problem. With your permission, Mr. Hopkins, I'll fly your son to the hospital."

Nathan shook his head. "Let the angel fly me."

Nemesis cocked an eyebrow at Revenant. "Angel?"

"He thinks the R stands for Raphael. Could have been worse; he could have thought I was a turtle." Revenant shook his head at Nathan. "Naw, go with Nemesis. If we angels do everything, guys like Nemesis won't have any reason to be called a hero."

The Advocate opened her hands. "That covers almost everything, I think. Aranatrix has informed me that some tampering was done with Reverend Sunnington's bank account, deducting something in excess of $467,353 from it. This figure is remarkable only in that it is roughly the amount of the bills the Hopkins family ran up in medical and legal fees concerning Maria's illness. This is just one more count of computer crimes—alleged computer crimes—that can be added to the list.

"If it pleases Your Honor, I rest my case."

Nemesis looked down at Revenant. "You've not questioned any of the witnesses against you. Do you have any witnesses for your defense? The Hopkins family, perhaps?"

"No, I have no witnesses." Revenant stood slowly. "The Hopkins family has more important things to do than to talk here today."

"Do you want to make any comments in your defense?"

Revenant shook his head. "My actions need no defense."

"The hell they don't!" Colonel Constitution shot like a rocket from his chair. "There are guys on Death Row who've broken fewer laws than you have. You trampled all over the very Constitution that I've sworn to defend. You're a lawbreaker—you're worse because you don't even think the laws should apply to you. You offer no defense because there *is* no defense for what you have done!"

"Wrong." Revenant came out from behind his table, shaking his head. "You draw the line at the law. You use the Constitution and the legal framework of this nation like a wall that segregates good from evil. You think and act in a realm of absolutes, rigidly defending the product of a process that you choose to ignore.

"Think." The Nightmare Detective tapped his brow. "Think, dammit. This nation, the tradition of laws you cling to, has undergone multiple changes through the centuries. Why? Because what was once considered just and right is determined, by mutual consent, to be unjust. A thousand years ago it was a man's right—his duty—to beat his wife. In the American South it was once a crime to teach blacks to read. Fifty years ago we imprisoned American citizens just because of the color of their skin and their ancestry. That was unjust, but had you been there, you would have been standing at the gates of internment camps keeping the Japanese in."

The Advocate sniffed. "The Supreme Court upheld the internment order. Extraordinary times demand extraordinary methods."

"Exactly!" Revenant's right hand contracted into a fist. "Extraordinary times require extraordinary methods and yet, fifty years later, reparations were paid to the survivors of internment. We recognized an injustice and made an attempt at making it right again. That's what I did here."

"But the courts were the right place to fight out the battle being waged between Mr. and Mrs. Hopkins."

"No! They were not a good battleground, because resolving it there would have taken time—time Maria did not have." Revenant's head came up. "There was an injustice there, and it was my duty— the duty of every human being who could recognize it as such—to effect a remedy."

The Nightmare Detective looked at each of the AJC members in turn as he spoke. "I understand why you draw the line at the law, because to move past it is to move into an arena with no restraints, no boundaries. I have chosen, unlike you, to live in that region outside the law, because that's where you have to go to hunt down the people who would destroy the world encompassed by the law."

"So," Constitution sneered, "you're admitting you're a criminal."

"No, I admit I am an outlaw, and there *is* a difference. I do have a guide out there: *justice*. Siphoning off money from Reverend Sunnington to cover the operation *was* justice. Forcing Charles Keating to operate one of his resorts for and act as butler for the people he bilked, that *would be* justice—perhaps not under the law, but it would be justice none the less." Revenant's hand opened, then disappeared beneath his cape. "I do not hold you in disrespect because of the choice you have made, and I feel no need to defend the choice I made."

Nemesis smiled. "You were eloquent in your non-defense."

The Nightmare Detective nodded. "Colonel Constitution inspires me."

The Extraterrestrial Titan smiled. "I think, then, we can come to a verdict here. You've heard the evidence. Register your votes, please."

Nemesis waited until the last of his compatriots had withdrawn from the chamber before congratulating Revenant on his acquittal. He offered the Nightmare Detective his hand. "I know you don't think it is important, but I appreciated your participation here. There are times when the American Justice Commission needs to remember that while we uphold the law, discretion, latitude and even dissent are part of the system. I have assurances that the Federal attorney and the State's Attorneys in Vermont and New Hampshire will *nol-pros* the charges against you."

Revenant shrugged. "Better the indictments never go into the NCIC computer than I have to go in and get them out again." He shook Nemesis's hand, then looked the taller man in the eye. "Close vote."

Nemesis nodded. "Not unexpected, given that we do law, you do justice. I had expected the three members of Strike Team Alpha to vote against you. Your work with the computers and in Haiti swung the other three to your side."

Revenant nodded. "And you cast the deciding vote—which had to go in my favor, since you dragged me into this whole affair in the first place."

The big man smiled. "When did you know I was involved?"

"I *suspected* when Martin told me he'd gotten the number he called in an anonymous Get Well card. I'd only given that particular number to a dozen people—including you—and most of them would have been angling for a reward for making the contact, not offering the information anonymously." Revenant shrugged. "*Know*, on the other hand . . ."

"At the river, right? When I flew underneath and gave you the boost to make the jump?"

"Nathan announcing that we were flying was a big clue, yeah." Revenant folded his arms across his chest. "You'll have to be careful there, Nemesis; in doing that you aided and abetted a fleeing felon."

"Not at all." He clapped Revenant on the shoulders. "I just stopped you from illegally dumping your car in the river."

Revenant laughed. "Gotta know the rules if you're going to play by them."

"Or if you are going to be the exception to them."

"Story of my life."

Nemesis walked with Revenant toward the exit. "So now that the

Haitian situation has calmed down and this is over, are you going to take a vacation?"

"I'd love to, but there's always more work to do." The Nightmare Detective shook his head. "I just ran across a couple of IRS agents who have a scam to boost their collection rating. They created a computer program that scans returns to select folks who can't or won't fight an audit. They pounce, the victim settles, and the agents are golden boys."

Nemesis nodded thoughtfully. "You could turn the evidence you've collected over to their supervisor and have them dealt with very easily."

"True, but that would be playing the game by *your* rules." Revenant shook his head. "If I did that, the IRS would reprimand them, perhaps put a negative letter in their files and, horror of horrors, ship them to Fairbanks to run the Alaska office. That's not justice for even *one* audit."

"I see." Nemesis frowned. "Then what, by Revenant's rules, *would* constitute justice in this case?"

"Oh, I have something very special planned. It is guaranteed to fulfill the dictates of justice, and to serve as a deterrent against future crime. I got into their computer and made some changes to their program, directing the selection of their next victim."

"That person being you, I take it?"

"Me? No, that would be too easy." Revenant's sinister laughter echoed through the dark marble corridor. "The next audit on their list is of a guy named Bill Wright."

Shadow Storm

Mickey Zucker Reichert

Heroes often come from the most unexpected places under the most extreme circumstances. Most children have their heroes, someone to look up to, someone to turn to for strength.

Matthew Draybin lashed his hand across his six-year-old step-daughter's face, the slap reverberating through the tiny bedroom. "*I'm* your father, do you understand that?"

Pain lanced through Stacy's head, and her vision shattered in a white flash of light. She cringed, and the next blow caught her across one ear. Tears spilled forth, unbidden.

"*I'm* the one who feeds you." Another smack. "*I'm* the one who clothes you." Draybin whipped his open hand across Stacy's head. "*I'm* the one who has to take time off work when you're sick." His fingers entwined in the sandy locks. He jerked them free, tearing several hairs out at the roots. "Don't you *ever* call me *anything* but 'Dad' again."

Stacy sobbed, curled in a fetal position. Her cheek and ear felt on fire, but she dared not move. She could still feel his slender body towering over her, and the image of his drawn, angry features remained engraved on her eyes no matter how hard she tried to lose it.

Draybin prodded his stepdaughter's forehead with his shoe. "And if I ever hear you call Sean 'Dad' in front of me again, I'll kick you to death. *I'm* your father. Do you understand that?"

Stacy said nothing. She remained tightly curled, waiting for the pain and its source to go away. But the man remained, his presence like a lead weight in the air around her.

"I said, do you understand?"

"I—und—er—stand," Stacy managed.

"WHAT?" His shout ached against her eardrums.

"I—under—stand," she said again, louder, careful not to allow the volume to sound disrespectful.

"Good." Draybin turned and stalked from the room, his footsteps loud in the hallway, then thumping down the stairs.

Stacy clutched at herself, wishing she could bundle her body so small it disappeared. She could hear her mother's lighter footfalls on the landing, birdlike in their grace.

Mary Draybin stood in the doorway for several seconds before speaking. "Oh, Stacy. I'm sorry." She crossed the room, and Stacy heard the creak of her box spring as her mother took a seat on the bed. "Come here, darling."

Obediently, Stacy unfolded, rubbed at her eyes with small fists, and walked to her mother. The woman hefted the girl into her lap, cradling and cooing as if to an infant. "You have to understand, darling. Matthew is your father now. Sean is just . . . well . . . a man the law makes you visit until you're old enough to tell them no."

The closeness, the gentle touch of her mother made Stacy eager to share. "But I *want* to see him. I love him. He's my daddy."

Mary Draybin's grip tightened, and her features flushed. Her wide-eyed stare and stiff smile did not match her tone or coloring. "Not anymore. Matthew is your daddy now."

It was a lie, and Stacy knew it. She had heard her mother and father arguing in the courthouse parking lot where they made visitation exchanges. She had sat quietly in the passenger seat of her mother's Subaru, the window left open a crack; and Mary Draybin's shouts had come clearly to her though she made no attempt to listen. "You'll sign those papers. That girl needs a family, and Matthew and I *are* that family. If you loved her at all, you'd let Matthew adopt her."

Sean Sterner's reply had sounded comparatively soft and controlled. "I will not give up my legal rights to my daughter."

Mary Draybin's voice became a shrill whine. "About her birthday visitation—forget it! And you'll never get another Father's Day. Never."

Stacy scarcely heard Sterner's response. "You can't do that."

"I can, and I will. Sue me. I'll turn around and sue you for more support. You won't be able to afford a house to take her to, and you'll never see her again."

"I won't give up my legal rights to my daughter. Do what you feel you must." Sterner had turned and walked to his battered Horizon. He spun around once to give Stacy a cheerful, parting wave. Then the motor started, and the red Horizon roared off into the darkness.

That night, and every one since, Stacy's mother had become a stranger. She ranted to Matthew Draybin, detailing horrible stories about her life with Sean Sterner that kept sleep at bay and inspired night terrors, though none of the tales were true to Stacy's memories. Late at night, Mary Draybin would slip down to the telephone and shout threats at or cajole someone who could only be Sterner.

Now, Stacy lay limp in her mother's arms, hearing but not understanding, seeking a compromise that would stop the battering and also allow her to please all of the people she loved.

Mary Draybin dumped her daughter onto the bed and gave her a playful swat on the behind, too much like punishment to soothe. "Why don't you get cleaned up, Stacy Draybin? Dinner'll be ready in a few." She whisked from the room as if nothing had happened.

Stacy Sterner, Stacy corrected to herself, clinging to the last vestige of her identity. If she let go, she would disappear. To admit the evils that her mother claimed against her father, she would first have to deny everything her mind and memory knew as fact and to believe that "bad blood" ran through her veins. If she lost her name, she would sacrifice all of her existence until that moment; and she would become nobody.

Stacy slid down the side of her bed, groping beneath it for the comic book secreted beneath the frame. She had seen it in her father's house, had stared at the colorful pages mesmerized, though she could not read them. And he had let her bring it back to this house. "Home," her mother called it and yet it seemed less hospitable than the series of dwindling apartments her father had had to take as he struggled to keep up with the debts Mary had dumped on him as well as the child support she demanded in larger amounts, never satisfied. Stacy had hidden the comic book, afraid of the reaction of her stepfather who saw sacrilege in any but Bible stories.

Now, at six, Stacy had studied the words and questioned enough to differentiate the sound effects: zoo-kowt, kapok, slada-slada-slada, ba-took. And she knew the hero well. Shadow Storm was his name, a massive figure in a red bodysuit that hugged his muscles like skin. The double S's of his crest could come loose from his chest and form lightning bolts or shields or assault rifles as he needed. A red mask hid every feature but his huge, brown eyes; and no one, not even the faithful readers, knew his true identity. But Stacy Sterner did. And when she spoke it, as now, he came to her:

> "Sean Sterner, big as can be
> As Shadow Storm, please come to me."

Light flashed, blinding in the small bedroom. Then the figure from the comic book appeared before her, large as life. He stood in the same dignified pose as on the cover, legs slightly apart, cape flapping though there was no wind, arms folded across his muscled chest. "Come here," he said.

Stacy ran to him, tears streaming down her face.

Shadow Storm held her with all the tenderness her mother could not seem to muster, his silence speaking volumes after her mother's attempts to soothe had only made her ache with need. He smelled of the old house, where they had lived together as a family, never quite happy but familiar. She also caught the aroma of baking chocolate chip cookies and the greenery smell of the field where her father had taught her to catch a ball. Among it all, she found the faint fragrance of her father's aftershave, that which had given his identity away months ago. "I love you," she said.

"I love you, too," he replied.

The door rattled open, and her mother's head poked through the crack. Shadow Storm disappeared, replaced by Stacy's blanket, mashed tightly in her embrace. "Dinnertime, Stacy."

"Coming, Mom." Stacy returned the covers, knowing better than to be late.

Two days later, Stacy sat on the terrace, watching passersby from over the waist-high barrier. Though eleven floors up, she could still distinguish enough to tell men from women; and, as always, she recognized the plaid fedora well before its wearer stepped over the blocked border from the street to the sidewalk and headed in her direction. It had become a daily ritual. "Business" brought Sean Sterner past the New York skyscraper that housed his daughter every afternoon once school let out, though twenty-seven miles separated the apartment building from his place of employment. Stacy had discovered him the first time by accident, but she had never failed to wait and wave since that day.

As he came upon the layered balconies, Sean Sterner stopped and looked up.

Though Stacy could not read his expression, she waved vigorously. He returned the salute, followed by a broad circular motion that he had explained during visitation meant "I love you."

"I love you, Daddy," she whispered, returning the gesture fervently. "I love you, too."

Then he was gone, headed for whatever business he needed to attend to. Moments later, the balcony door whisked open amid the jangle of the wind chime swinging from its frame.

Stacy turned, seeing her mother framed in the entry, holding the glass door ajar with her elbow.

"Your father wants to talk to you." Mary Draybin spoke in a somber tone, her expression grave.

Stacy froze, terror sparking through her. Experience told her he would not strike her two days before visitation. Her mother and stepfather had made it abundantly clear that horrible things would happen to her and to Sean Sterner if she ever told about or showed him the results of Draybin's temper. Slowly, head sagging, she trailed her mother through the kitchen and into the living room where her stepfather waited. Her mother sat in a chair and pretended to read the newspaper.

The coiled posture and purpled features of Matthew Draybin told Stacy all she needed to know. She fled for her room in terror.

Draybin chased her. "Run from me, you little bitch, and it'll go much worse for you."

Stacy knew he spoke the truth, but fear would not allow her to return. She raced into her bedroom, slamming the door closed behind her, and huddled on her bed. She buried her face in her pillow, hoping he would choose not to follow her, wishing he would just fade away.

Draybin stomped after, screaming and swearing. Stacy covered her ears, blotting out the sound. A moment later, the door slapped open so hard that it bounced nearly closed. He crossed the room in three strides, and she heard the crackle of paper near her nose. "What's this?" he demanded.

Trembling, Stacy freed one eye to look. He held one of her first-grade papers from school. He pointed to where she had written her name: Stacy S.

"Stacy S? Stacy S!" Draybin slammed his arm into her shoulder, and she tumbled to the floor, crying, fighting not to scream. "You are *not* Stacy S. You are Stacy Draybin now! Stacy Draybin!" He kicked her in the ribs just as she took a shuddering inhale, hammering the breath from her throat. She gasped for air, but her lungs would not function. Panic descended on her, along with an air-starved dizziness that blurred the world to gray. Unable to speak, she sent a mental summons, desperate to halt the barrage of pain and cling to the tatters of her life: *Sean Sterner, big as can be; As Shadow Storm come to me. Quickly, please. I need you.*

He came in an instant, a sudden wall between the battering fists and Stacy. He took the blows without a cry or whimper, using his own face and body to protect her. Draybin took no notice of the superhero who answered her call. His clenched hands crashed against flesh he seemed unable to tell from hers, despite its iron hardness.

Shadow Storm tore an "S" from his chest, shaping it into an invisible barrier that fielded the attack, though Draybin seemed to have no more awareness of this than of the hero's sudden presence. Stacy caught her breath, and the pain of the first two blows ebbed and disappeared.

At length, the assault stopped. "Stacy Draybin," Matthew warned one more time. Then he stormed from the room. As always, Mary Draybin slipped in for her usual ceremony of supporting her husband and comforting her daughter, as oblivious to the superhero as Matthew Draybin had been.

Shadow Storm stepped back into his usual pose, an "S" still missing from his bodysuit, blood trickling from beneath his mask. Standing as sentinel and guardian.

The weekend passed too quickly for Stacy. She did nothing that anyone would consider special with Sean Sterner. He could not afford to take her to amusement parks or on trips, but the time spent cooking hot dogs over a grill, clambering on playground equipment, and putting together puzzles they had done a million times seemed enough. There was a quiet normalcy to her time with her father that she would not have traded for all of Disneyland. With him, she could forget the chaos and terror of her other life.

But, as always, it ended too soon; and Stacy found herself back in her normal routine, counting the days until the next visitation. She wished her father would call sometimes, but she understood why he chose silence instead. More than once, she had heard her mother claim Stacy was away while she sat next to her on the couch. Other times, Matthew Draybin slammed down the receiver without a word of explanation. The few times Sterner got through, her mother and stepfather listened on the extensions; and Stacy feared even to call him Daddy in their presence. Sterner gave up on telephone contact, torn in another way from the daughter who loved him.

That Tuesday, as usual, Stacy headed for the balcony, the concrete wall cold and hard against her abdomen. She watched patterns of people flutter by to the music of the myriad sparrows and pigeons that roosted in the building's cracks. It seemed like an eternity before the familiar plaid hat came into view, and a second lifetime passed until Sean Sterner paused and waved.

Engrossed, Stacy did not hear the tingle of the wind chime nor notice the second presence on the terrace.

Grinning, Stacy returned a vigorous greeting. She made the circular motion, a code they alone shared. "I love you, Daddy," she whispered. For that moment, time seemed suspended.

Then, reality intruded. Fingers seized her arm, bruising, and jerked her away from the ledge. She watched in terror as Matthew Draybin leaned over the side to focus on the figure far below. Then, he stepped back, spinning Stacy to meet his hard, blue gaze. "I am your father."

Stacy struggled to break free, but his grip tightened and he seized her other arm as well. He slammed his knee into her crotch so hard that the pain made her knees buckle, and she slumped. He kicked her in the chin, and her scalp smacked against the concrete. She heard a distant, desperate shout from below. Draybin hefted his stepdaughter, pinning her against the concrete slab. "You ungrateful little bitch, I'll throw you over. I'll just goddamn throw you over!"

Terror exploded through Stacy's mind. She wrestled desperately, kicking, swinging, and writhing without conscious direction or understanding.

Then HE came without her needing to call, bringing a gust of wind so violent that the glass door to the balcony shattered, raining fragments. He clutched an "S" in each fist, muted to the shape of glowing clubs, and he charged Matthew Draybin with a bull bellow of fury.

Stacy and Shadow Storm fought together, a wild blur of fear and fury. Her fists pummeled flesh, though a red fog of need and hysteria blinded her to whose. She could hear the meaty thud of club against body. Then her mother's scream tore her attention to the broken terrace doorway. Mary Draybin stood, freeze-framed in open-mouthed horror.

In the instant that Stacy paused and looked, Matthew Draybin seized both of her flailing arms in a viselike grip. At the same time, Shadow Storm's club caught the stepfather a solid clout across the ear. Impact hurled him sideways, twisting over the concrete barrier. His hold winched tighter instinctively, and Stacy flew over the balcony wall and into oblivion.

Stacy screeched, hands clawing air in helpless desperation. Air whistled and surged around her, spinning her in a crazed circle that severed Draybin's grip. She tumbled past three balconies, the scream an unstoppable constant in her ears. Then, strong arms enwrapped her, crushing her against a massive chest covered with tautly stretched red fabric. The S's now served as hawk wings, gliding superhero and cargo gently toward the concrete sidewalk.

Stacy clung, all fear dissolving in an instant. She clung to the solid reality of her savior, knowing a strength and security she had no wish to question. The faint fragrance of his aftershave cut through the damp, smoggy air. She felt a sudden jolt as he landed, then realized that other arms held her now: still huge, though not quite so mountain-hard and clothed in a cotton button-down shirt she knew well. She huddled into Sean Sterner's grip, flinging her arms around his neck and burying her face into his shirt. He hugged her, at first with shocked hesitation, then with a vigor that all but suffocated her. They both cried.

Stacy heard Shadow Storm's whisper in her ear. "Stacy Sterner, little and free: You have no more need of me." Then, all hint of him was gone except for the tattered comic book still hidden beneath her bed.

Stacy did not look back to see him go.

Red and blue dome lights strobed across the skyscraper's brick and concrete. Stacy clutched Sean Sterner's hand, sweaty from long contact, but she would not release it. A round-faced, paunchy officer had been speaking with them for longer than half an hour. "I still don't understand." The policeman flicked dark bangs from his eyes. "You caught her?"

"Yes."

"After she fell eleven stories?"

67

"Yes."

The officer glanced to the chalk outline that denoted Matthew Draybin's landing and the blood splashed in a wide circle around it. Two of his companions approached from the crowd of spectators huddled at the perimeter. "Excuse me a moment, please." He trotted over to meet them.

Stacy released Sterner's hand to catch him into an embrace. He clutched her in silence, and the hushed union seemed to Stacy to radiate love and safety.

The policemen spoke softly beneath the hubbub of the crowd, but Stacy could hear every word.

"There's a dozen witnesses say the girl and man fell together."

"All of it seemed in slow motion, least the part with the kid. He fell fast enough."

"This other guy seemed to have plenty of time to get beneath and grab her out of the air. Why they didn't both get driven ten feet under the concrete . . . can't explain it."

"Once heard of a baby-sitter moving a minivan to save an infant."

"Guy once flipped a Volkswagen to save his wife."

The paunchy officer finally added his piece. "Girl says some cartoon superhero carried her."

"She's hysterical."

"Ought to see her mom. Had to crate her off to Bellevue in a jacket. Kept babbling about a huge, red devil with fluorescent fists."

Stacy had heard enough. "Daddy, where'd they take Mom?"

Sean Sterner knelt to Stacy's level, concern clear in his dark eyes. "They took Mommy to a hospital. She's upset about what happened, too. We can visit her anytime you want to, okay?"

"Okay," Stacy said.

The policeman returned. "You're free to go now, Mr. Sterner." He smiled crookedly at Stacy, still clearly puzzled. "You might want to get her to a doctor. Looks like she got a bruise or two from the fall."

"Thank you." Sean Sterner took his daughter's hand and headed away from the crowd amidst a chorus of murmurs and whispered comments. "Do you hurt anywhere, Stacy?"

"Uh-uh." Stacy squeezed his three middle fingers in her small grip.

Sterner studied his daughter, worry and caring clear in his gaze. "Do you want to visit Mommy now?"

"No, Daddy." She clutched him tighter. "I want to go home."

They headed toward the red Horizon.

Empowered

Alan Dean Foster

In comic books, superheroes are individuals with extraordinary skills or powers who decide that their special status requires them to take actions outside the law. Because they appear to be on the side of justice, serving the common good, we tend to forget that they are at heart vigilantes.

They'd used too much explosive, but Kreiger didn't care. The stuff didn't do anyone any good sitting in the basement of the safe house, and the one thing he sure didn't want to do was use too little and risk blowing the whole job. So he'd told Covey to use all he wanted, and the demo demon had taken him at his word.

Besides, Kreiger liked big explosions.

Covey had certainly orchestrated one. As he and Kreiger and the rest of the gang hunched down behind the truck, the force of the blast blew out the whole back of the building. Even before the dust had begun to settle they were up and running, masks and filters enabling them to breathe where others could not while simultaneously disguising their identities. Across town Joaquin and Sievers were faking their bank break-in, drawing the majority of the police to their nonexistent robbery. By now those two should be on their way to freedom via the carefully plotted sewer escape route.

Meanwhile, except for its now numbed and bleeding private security force, the special colored gem exhibition at Vaan Pelsen's was open to anyone who chose to saunter in without buying a ticket. Needless to say, Kreiger and his team didn't have any tickets. They never paid for admission.

Some gems lay scattered like electric gumdrops among the rubble, but Covey's careful placement of the explosives the previous night had only destroyed the back third of the store. Save for shattered glass and bodies, the front portion was largely intact. One guard had somehow survived uninjured. He was quickly gunned down by Pohatan, wielding his Uzi.

Not being averse to physical labor, Kreiger carried his own canvas sack. While Pohatan and Covey kept watch over the street, where dazed pedestrians were stumbling about looking for help, Kreiger and the rest of the team efficiently and methodically helped themselves to the necklaces and rings, watches and bracelets, settings and loose gems from the demolished cases. No alarms rang in their ears. The explosion had destroyed them as well.

Anything worth obliterating, Kreiger mused as he worked, was worth obliterating well.

Having rehearsed the heist for months, they worked fast, intending to be long gone before the first of the duped city police could make it back across town from the faked bank robbery. Still Kreiger urged his people to move more quickly, and to leave nothing behind. Ignoring the shocked and moaning injured among the store's staff, they roughly shoved bleeding bodies aside in their quest for the last of the stock and special display. In less than ten minutes they had reassembled and were heading for the remnants of the back door.

Where a lanky green figure waited to confront them.

"Who the hell is that?" Pohatan gaped at the caped, emerald silhouette.

"Doesn't matter," snapped Kreiger. "Shoot him."

Reflexively, Pohatan brought the Uzi up and squeezed the trigger. The compact automatic buzzed.

Before the bullets could strike home, a giant oak sprang full-grown from beneath the crumbled tarmac between the gunman and the green figure. Slugs thudded harmlessly into the thick wood.

Kreiger's jaw dropped. His careful plan contained no contingencies for inexplicable interference.

The green-clad man stepped out from behind the tree. Lean muscle rippled beneath his tight suit (spandex? Kreiger wondered dazedly) and he wore a green band across his eyes.

"Give it up, Kreiger. It's all over."

"Like hell." Kreiger turned to his men. Already the distant complaint of sirens could be heard approaching rapidly from the north. "Get him!"

Pohatan threw his massive bulk at the figure, only to run headlong into a dense grove of new-sprung spruce that hadn't been there when he'd started his charge. Brownlee succeeded in reaching him, whereupon the figure's arms seemed to metamorphose into long vines. They wrapped around the startled assailant, lifted him effortlessly off the pavement, and flung him clear over the ruined store into the street beyond.

While the rest of his team rushed the floral fighter, Kreiger raced for the truck. A glance back showed that they were having no better luck than their colleagues.

Kreiger stabbed the key into the ignition and fired up the big engine, slamming the truck into drive. He accelerated as he bore down on the green shape, who had just disposed of the rest of Kreiger's colleagues. No time for him to get out of the way, though. Kreiger grinned. He liked running over people almost as much as he liked big explosions.

Giant roots erupted from the ground immediately in front of the truck. Wide-eyed, Kreiger tried to swerve. The roots twisted and grabbed at the truck, coiling around both axles and lifting it off the ground. As the solemn-faced green man looked on, they heaved the vehicle sideways. It smashed into a pair of parked cars, rolled over, and came to rest among the tables of an outdoor restaurant whose patrons had fortunately run inside and stayed there when Covey's explosives had initially gone off.

The first patrol car to arrive in the parking lot behind the smoking ruins of the jewelry store disgorged a pair of stunned officers, who gratefully took delivery of the still-alive (but badly damaged) Kreiger and the rest of his gang. As the cops looked on, a brace of flexible willows emerged from the earth to lightly grasp the green figure. Bending their crowns to the ground, they aimed him skyward.

"Wait a minute!" yelled one of the officers. "Who are you? *What* are you?"

"Call me *Earth Spirit*," the green man intoned. "I was once one of

you, one of the teeming masses. Now because of an industrial accident I'm somewhat more, and this is what I intend to do with my
newfound powers. Spread the word among lawbreakers and polluters.
Let them know they're safe no more!"

With that, the willows sprang back with tremendous velocity,
sending the green man soaring out of sight. No doubt another tree
or bush was waiting somewhere to relay him on his way or cushion
his descent. The officers exchanged a glance, then set themselves to
watch over the battered gang until backup and medics could arrive.

"You know, you're a very difficult person to locate."

"How *did* you find me?" Earth Spirit stepped back into the cave.
"And how did you get past all the thornbushes and poison ivy I
brought forth to discourage interlopers?"

The small, heavyset man set himself down in a high-backed chair
which was growing right out of the cave floor. He mopped at his
sweat-streaked brow with a monogrammed handkerchief. "Nice
place you've got up here. Spacious, but a little dark for my taste."
He smiled. "I'm mildly claustrophobic."

"And hugely curious," said Earth Spirit. "You haven't answered
my questions."

"I put out the word quietly. Announced a reward for information.
Local farmer noticed a lot of sudden growth up on this mountaintop
and got in touch with a regional contact of mine. At that point I
decided that a personal visit was in order. May I call you Earth? It's
a lot easier, I prefer to be on a first-name basis with people, and
besides, the other half's copyrighted."

"If it'll make you comfortable." The green one settled himself into
a chair opposite. A compliant vine handed him a drink.

"As for the thorns and the ivy, as you can see, I dressed accordingly. Abercrombie and Fitch. I'm not used to this sort of thing. Silk
three-pieces are more to my taste."

"You're from the government," Earth Spirit surmised.

"Not at all, though I'm sure they'll be here shortly. My name is
Lemuel French. I'm a lawyer."

The green man frowned. "What would I need with a lawyer, Mr.
French?"

The smaller man stared at him in disbelief. "You really don't know? Well, maybe not. Ever since the Vaan Pelsen's debacle you've kept pretty quiet, except for vine-wrapping the occasional mugger."

Earth Spirit smiled. "My actions seem to have had a deterrent effect on local crime."

"That they have. It's one of the problems you're going to have to deal with."

"Problems?" The vine held the drink neatly.

"You're really out of touch up here on this mountaintop, aren't you? No paper, no cable."

"I prefer the company of the natural world," the green man said stiffly.

"You want to live like a Granola that's fine with me, but your activities impinge on the real world. That's why I sought you out. See, I believe in what you're doing and I want to help." He smiled broadly. "For a fee, of course. We really need to discuss your putting my firm on retainer."

"I told you, I have no need of a lawyer."

"So you said." French popped the polished brass clasp on an elegant eelskin briefcase and removed a thick sheaf of papers. "Copies. You'll be served as soon as they can find you. That gives us some time."

Earth Spirit eyed the papers in spite of himself. "What is all that?"

"Let's see. Where to start?" French shuffled the sheaf as cleanly as a Vegas dealer handling cards. "The first suit is from Vaan Pelsen's Inc."

"Vaan Pelsen's? Why would they want to sue me? I saved their merchandise."

"But a lot of it was damaged in the gang's escape attempt. Fancy gold work, that sort of thing."

"They wouldn't have it to fix if I hadn't stepped in."

"I agree completely, and I'm sure the court will take that into account." French had his reading glasses on now. "Here's another: 'Mildred Fox, plaintiff for Sissy and Michael Fox, juvenile principals.'"

The green man looked baffled. "I've never heard of these people."

"They were dining in the restaurant where you threw Mr. Kreiger

75

and his stolen truck. Ms. Mildred Fox is the mother of the two named children. She claims that her kids suffered severe emotional distress from nearly being struck by the escape vehicle, and that among other things they now refuse to ride in the family minivan, thus forcing Ms. Fox, a working mother, to sell it at a loss and buy an ordinary car. Claimant further deposes that her children now experience uncontrollable fits at the sight of any large delivery vehicle."

"This . . . this is ridiculous!" Earth Spirit sputtered.

"I heartily concur, and we'll make Ms. Fox and her well-coached little schemers look that way in court." As if by magic more papers appeared.

"Is there much more of this?" Earth Spirit regarded the phone book–sized pile with growing trepidation.

"Depends on your definition of 'much.' A Mr. Colin Hvarty is suing you for medical expenses pursuant to a broken leg and sprained back, plus possible concussion."

"I never intended to break anybody's leg, not even one of the robbers!" the green-clad man protested.

French looked up and smiled apologetically. "Apparently Mr. Hvarty was standing in the street opposite Vaan Pelsen's when he was struck by a flying crook. Did you happen, in the course of your work, to perhaps fling one or more of the miscreants in that direction?"

"I didn't mean to hit anybody."

"Well, you did." French adjusted his glasses. "We'll have to see about getting you some liability insurance, though after the business at Vaan Pelsen's you'd better be prepared to deal with an outrageous monthly premium."

"Superheroes don't need liability insurance."

French peered over the top of his glasses. "Is that so? You want to perform good deeds in *this* country, you'd better make sure you're fully covered before you start.

"The owner of the parking lot behind Pelsen's has presented a bill for the following: to wit, expenses directly related to removing a large oak tree and a number of smaller growths from his property, and repaving the damaged area. The owner of the restaurant where Ms. Fox and her offspring suffered their trauma is suing for damage to eight tables and chairs, umbrellas, railing, landscaping, and assorted crockery, glassware and utensils.

"A Mr. Loemann and a Mr. Kelly are suing for damage to their respective vehicles. Those are the two cars you unfortunately hit with the getaway truck. Or rather, their insurance companies are suing you. A local nature organization has filed a writ to prevent you from utilizing any vegetation of any species whatsoever in your crimefighting activities until you can present them with an acceptable environmental impact report demonstrating beyond argument that your work does not involve the use of dangerous chemicals, stimulants, or scientifically unapproved bioengineering. The local office of the Food and Drug Administration wants to talk to you about essentially the same thing."

"Go on." Earth Spirit's expression was grim.

"I intend to. The municipal police have a warrant out for your arrest for interfering with police activities. I don't think we have to worry about this one. They don't want to jail you; just co-opt you."

"I don't work for anybody. I'm independent."

"Then you're going to be butting heads with the local law enforcement bureaucracy from now till doomsday. Bureaucrats don't like outsiders poaching their turf. They're afraid you might apply for and get a government grant intended for them."

"But I'm helping them in their work, fighting evildoers."

"You're not going to have enough time to fight the local school bully. See these?" French waved another entire sheaf of papers. "Subpoenas. Calling you as a witness in the Vaan Pelsen's case. Each robber has requested and been granted an independent trial, so you'll have to give testimony in all of them. Also, at least two members of the Vaan Pelsen's gang are suing you, including Kreiger. They claim that since you're not a member of any recognized law-enforcement department, you had no right to interfere, and that they've suffered irreparable mental harm as a result of your activities."

"I was making a citizen's arrest."

"They claim use of excessive force. Among other things."

"That's outrageous! They had explosives and automatic weapons."

"Maybe we can cut a deal. I'll speak to their people."

The green man's chest expanded proudly. "I don't have to belong to an official organization. I represent the *Earth*."

"Not in this county you don't. And don't go on boasting that you're some kind of foreigner. This is a conservative community." He murmured half to himself. "We can use temporary insanity in at least half these cases, if we have to. I mean, just look at you."

Earth Spirit blinked down at himself. "What's wrong with me?"

"Grown man living alone in a cave atop a mountain? Talking to plants? Running around in green spandex?"

"It's not spandex."

"Whatever. So long as there's no brand-name infringement involved." French sighed tiredly. "Then there's the government."

"What about the government?" Earth Spirit said darkly. "I'm trying to *help* them."

"Why do you think the local police bureaucracy is so afraid of you? If some superhero starts dropping out of the sky on local criminals and the crime rate falls to zero, what do you think happens to their budget? Not to mention their jobs. They're terrified you'll stick around.

"As for helping the government, the spin on the street is good, but they're wary. Nobody knows which party you belong to."

"I belong to no party. I belong to . . ."

"The Earth; yeah, yeah, you told me already. Even worse. A third-party iconoclast. They want to know your name."

"I am Earth Spirit!"

"Sure, okay. But they can't find anybody named 'Earth Spirit' anywhere. You're not on the tax rolls, so they want to know if you've filed any returns. You may be 'of the Earth,' but if you want to practice your profession in the U.S. you'd better be able to prove that you're a citizen. Or else have, you should pardon me, a green card. Do you even have a Social Security number?"

Earth Spirit looked away, clearly uneasy. "If I give up that kind of information, I'll have to reveal my true identity. I can't do that. Criminals could threaten me and my work through family and friends."

"There's always the witness protection program, but I don't think it would work for superheroes. Eventually you'd forget yourself, make a redwood sprout in a mall or something."

"This is all that Kreiger's fault," Earth Spirit growled.

"Maybe. You can't do anything about him, though. He's had a restraining order put on you. You can't go near him."

"Why would I want to go near him? He's in jail, where his kind belong."

"Are you kidding? His lawyers had him out of the hospital and back on the street in forty-eight hours. Bail."

Earth Spirit rubbed at his forehead, above the mask. "Is there much more of this?"

"It's not all bad news." French inspected fresh paper. "Mattel wants to start a line of 'Earth Spirit' toys. Two major fashion houses want to license your costume as the basis for new lines of men's clothing. Oprah, Jay, Phil, and Joan all want you for interviews. *Time* and *Newsweek* are preparing features . . . you can't *buy* that kind of publicity. CAA and William Morris are vying to represent you on the coast, and each claims to have multi-picture deals already cut and waiting for your signature. Personally, I'd go with CAA. They already have Hoffman committed to play Kreiger.

"There are book offers all over the place, and I think that with your okay I can get this incipient Kitty Kelly exposé nipped in the bud. We'll also make arrangements to protect you from the people at *Hard Copy*, *Inside Edition*, and *Geraldo*, though even I can't do much about the tabloids. Have you seen the *Enquirer* or the *Star* this week? No, of course you haven't."

Earth Spirit looked up. "That's the *good* news?"

"Impressive, isn't it? You stand to make millions. Of course, there's the matter of my firm's fee, but I'm sure we can come to an equitable arrangement. Oh, one other thing."

"I can't imagine."

"The FAA wants you to cease and desist all this flying about. They're worried about your influence on air-traffic patterns. Better you should take a cab."

"To fight crime?"

"Why not? The cabbies in this town can get around pretty good."

"What about the government? Why should I have to worry about tax returns? I have no income."

"You're going to. You might as well cash the checks as they come

79

in because nobody'll believe you don't have any income anyway. It's un-American. Don't worry. The accountancy firm that's associated with us will make it effortless for you. And you can use the leftover money to fight crime in whatever way you wish. If there is any."

"Crime?" Earth Spirit murmured uncertainly.

"No. Leftover money."

The green one rose dynamically from his chair and began to pace, fingers flexing like questing stems behind his back. "All I wanted was to help people and battle the forces of evil."

"And you can, you can," French insisted soothingly. "It's just a question of going about it in a careful, intelligent way . . . and making sure all the proper forms are filled out and filed beforehand."

Earth Spirit halted abruptly, and French flinched. After all, the fellow *did* have superpowers . . . and was doubtless a little off to boot. That bizarre outfit . . .

"All right," he said finally. "I'll hire your firm. On a case contingency basis. Get me clear of this Vaan Pelsen's business and then we'll see."

"That's fair enough." French rose, and they shook hands.

"Would you like me to have my friends ease you down the mountain?" Earth Spirit said in parting. "It's a difficult hike."

"Tell me about it," French grumbled. "I'll walk, thanks. Even though I think I shook the couple of paparazzi who followed me from the city, you'll be safer if I don't draw attention to myself. You needn't apologize for your naivete. It'll be much easier now that I know you're not some nut and that you understand what it means to have to work within the system."

Earth Spirit waved. "Oh I do, Mr. French, I do. Now."

Six months later the first deposition arrived on Tonga, advance scout of an irresistible paper army, but by that time Earth Spirit had already moved on once again, to a land where lawyers were less numerous still.

Passport problems were already beginning to dog him, though, and in Singapore he barely escaped having his suit and mask garnished for nonpayment of one claim.

Handing On the Goggles

B. W. Clough

Passing on the mantle from father to son is a frequently
repeated theme in traditional storytelling. Contemporary
storytelling requires something a little different.

The problem with my daughter is that she has too much energy.
Way too much energy! Rollerblading, karate, managing the metal
club, marching in pro-choice demonstrations—and today she still
found time to come over and harass me.

"This house is too much for you, Pop," Cath said. As she moved
down the sofa, plumping each pillow in turn, her chains jingled and
swayed. "You ought to move to a condo."

"Your mother loved this house," I protested.

The dangling silver skulls in her ears clanked as she whirled to
glare at me. "Mom passed away in 1989, Pop! And look at this mess."
She pulled three Iron City beer cans, a used plate, and a cloudy glass
from under the end table. "While you're away I'm definitely going
to spring-clean."

"Don't bother, Cath—you're so busy all the time." Actually I
didn't want her messing with my stuff. "I'll have someone come in
and clean, when I get back from the reunion."

"Men are another *species*," Cath grumbled. She whizzed over to
the bookcase and began straightening books. "Visiting battlefields?
Looking up the people you tried to *kill?*"

"We were all fighting the Axis together—the Greeks understood that." It was scary, like watching a tornado. I sat tight, not daring to recline my chair back. There was more crockery, I knew, underneath the Barcalounger.

Suddenly she hauled a book off the bottom shelf. Dust rose in clouds, showing white on her black leather jacket. "Now you could easily toss these—"

"No!" I yelped. "Cath, those are mine!"

"Pop, you don't even read them," she said patiently, the way you'd talk to a baby. "Look at the dust." She let the volume fall open on her miniskirted lap. "This one's nothing but a scrapbook. 'The Gazorcher Saves Tot from Ledge.' It's so juvenile, to adore superheroes these days."

"That does it!" Creaking, I stood up. My own daughter, the punkette, calling me juvenile! I felt in my pants pocket for the ring. "Watch this, Cath."

Too late I remembered why my costume had goggles. The air swooshed past, buffeting my face and bringing the water to my eyes. Stopping was always the devil, too. I missed the TV by a whisker and skidded painfully into the panelling.

"Jesus! Pop, what the hell?"

I took a hanky from my sweater sleeve and blotted my eyes. "I wish you wouldn't swear, Cath. Indulge an old superhero, okay?"

"*You?* Pop, you were the *Gazorcher?*"

"Yep, that's me." I hobbled back to the Barcalounger and sat down to nurse my bruises. "The master of line-of-sight teleportation himself. Pittsburgh's own superhero."

"Ohmigod!" If she laughed, I promised myself I'd rewrite my will. But she just sat on the linoleum by the bookcase, flabbergasted into immobility. "Pop, how is it done?"

I showed her the ring: an old, old bronze signet, the design worn almost away. "I got it in Heraklion."

She leaned to look, her unpleasant jewelry jingling. "A guy in a toga appeared in a puff of smoke, and told you to fight the Nazis with it," she guessed.

"No, I think that was Captain America. I bought this in a junk shop. Some Cretan must've dug it up. The past few years I've read up on it—this is Minoan work."

Cath stared wildly around at the bookcases which lined the rec room. "All your books about ancient Greece," she said.

I nodded. "This is the lost ring of King Minos, Cath. He ruled a naval empire back then. Bet gazorching was really helpful to him."

"And—wait a minute, Pop! And you're taking it back to Greece next week?"

"Well, you know, Cath, it might be a really significant artifact. The archaeologists would like to see it, I bet. I thought, when we do the tour of the air base outside Heraklion, I'd pretend I just found it, in the grass or something. It's not like I had a sidekick, to hand it down to . . ."

I could tell from Cath's sudden blowtorch glare that I'd said something sexist again. "What about me?" she demanded. "Why can't a girl be the Gazorcher?"

"Uh, there are reasons, Cath." I could feel myself going pink with embarrassment. "You know what a gazorcher is?"

"It's a gigantic slingshot arrangement, right?"

"Fraternity men at CMU use them to lob water balloons," I mumbled. "In my day the Pi Lambs made 'em out of bicycle inner tubes. But in the beginning, when the frat first invented them, we used, uh, women's undergarments."

Cath looked at me as if I were stuck to the bottom of her shoe. "You used bras. Great! I always knew frat men were adolescent swine, and this proves it."

"You could use another name," I suggested quickly. "How about the Feminist Avenger? Nail rapists. Embarrass dirty old men. Testify at Supreme Court confirmation hearings."

That made her laugh. "Are you serious, Pop? Would you let me inherit the superhero job?"

When I looked at her, so competent, so full of bouncy energy, I had to say, "You've already inherited everything you need, Cath." Besides, she wouldn't need a cape or anything—the studded leather dog collars and the green streak in her hair were terrifying enough. Batman would have nothing on her. I put the ring in her hand.

She closed her fingers slowly around it. "This is amazing. I can't believe it. My father, the costumed crimefighter. Would you, you know, teach me how to use it?"

"You bet!" The last time Cath wanted me to teach her anything, it was how to ride a two-wheel bike. All of a sudden I felt great. There's life in the old boy yet!

Suddenly she seemed to have second thoughts. "One more question, Pop. Why'd you quit? How come the Gazorcher retired?"

That's Cath all over, examining the drawbacks before committing herself. "Look it up in the scrapbooks," I said. "The Gazorcher's last case was in October 1967. And you were born—"

"November second," she said. "Oh, Pop, you're kidding! It was *my* fault?"

"It wasn't anybody's *fault*," I corrected her. "But your mother was ill, in the hospital for six weeks. What was I going to do, leave you alone, a newborn baby? It was easier to just hang up the goggles."

"Child-care pressures did you in." For the first time today Cath stared at me with not astonishment but respect. "I'm gonna tell my women's action group. They'll award you an Honorary Ovary. It's a pin—you can wear it on your lapel."

I winced. "Uh, thanks . . . Oh, the goggles! Now those are essential; you'll see what I mean. Let me look upstairs, see if I still have mine." Come to think of it, the Gazorcher's goggles were black leather too. Obviously it was meant to be.

She Who Might Be Obeyed

Roland J. Green and Frieda A. Murray

We all influence the people around us in little ways every day; some more than others.

What Cynthia Binder now called the Obedience came on when she was fifteen, long enough after menarche so that Dr. Rupprecht had eliminated any possible connection. (As far as one could eliminate any hypothesis about a unique phenomenon, at least.)

Her father had left when she was three, under circumstances her mother never talked about. She really didn't need to; Gerald Binder never contacted his family again. They weren't even sure that he was alive.

The desertion raised Cheryl Binder's consciousness, to the extent that she switched from playing doormat for her husband to playing doormat for her "sisters." Her daughter was fairly sure that didn't extend to sex with the odd gay or bisexual member of her half-dozen women's organizations, but it covered everything short of that.

Of course, everybody has to have a vacation from being unselfish. Cheryl Binder's vacation was her daughter. All the orders and refusals she wouldn't give her colleagues at work or her sisters at the meetings, she gave to her daughter. The sense of being a Marine boot came to Cynthia fairly soon after she heard of the Marines.

Shortly after that, she took a firm resolution. She was going to be *absolutely* unselfish. She was never going to take out frustrations on

85

her family. She would have a corner to hide in, or a punching bag to use, or some way of handling the bad times besides beating up on the people close to her.

Maybe it was that resolution that triggered the Obedience. Within a year after she made it, Cynthia discovered that if she stood close to someone and asked them in a certain tone of voice to do something, they would do it. She had to speak aloud, she had to watch her volume as well as her tone, and she had to make the request something that helped others rather than herself.

Not that she felt she had to play martyr, either. She was able to use what she then called the Voice (a term picked up from Frank Herbert's *Dune*) on unwanted boys, to keep them out of her pants, tops, or anyplace else she didn't want them, which was mostly anywhere within ten yards of her.

Fortunately she had quite a few classmates who were better-looking and more interested; she was able to direct the boys elsewhere. She never used the Voice on another girl to make her say "Yes," or on a boy to make him ask the girl. She did arrange for a few boys to notice girls they might otherwise have overlooked, then let hormones settle the issue.

That kept the boy problem down to manageable proportions, and let her get on with more important jobs.

There was the time one of the teachers seemed to be having a problem with what they then called Black students. He thought any of them who got an A on the math test were cheating. When the school's best halfback, Rackham Peavey, got two A's in succession, the teacher hit the roof. For a while, it looked as if Peavey was going to be off the team.

Cynthia Binder's commitment to civil rights was offended. Peavey had studied like he'd never studied before, and earned those A's fairly. She was even more offended, because she'd used the Voice on him, suggesting that he might study harder instead of hanging out three nights a week with a bunch of friends who were the next thing to a gang.

(She wondered if he'd thought she would go out with him if he got an A. He'd never seemed the kind of Black guy who thought a date with a white girl was some sort of trophy, but you never knew with men, Black, white, or polka-dotted! Experience might cure the ignorance, but getting the experience could be a pain in the *tuchus, zudik*—enough already. . . .)

When she heard the rumors of the cheating scandal, she managed to get close to the teacher, then say, as if she was talking to herself or maybe another student, "He really doesn't want to get Rack Peavey kicked off the team. Rack didn't cheat, and everybody will be pointing fingers if the team loses without him." She didn't add, "That will dump any chances of being vice-principal next year," because she wasn't supposed to know that, even though it was all over the school.

The teacher dropped the charges, Peavey played, and the team went to the regional semifinals. In fact, Peavey got such a habit of studying that the last Binder heard of him, he was a resident in internal medicine in D.C.

Then there was the time she and a bunch of friends had gone out to a party where liquor was served. The guy who owned the old Chevy Impala wagon took on a lot more than he could handle, let alone drive with. He was the biggest of the bunch, though, so even the guys didn't want to argue with him.

Neither did Cynthia Binder. But she didn't want her friends involved in a drunk-driving arrest either, still less an accident. She had to whisper this time, but she'd got the bugs out of the Voice enough to make a whisper count if she kept the command simple.

"Lou can drive us home. You're a better driver than he is when you haven't had six beers, but Lou's had only two." (Actually Lou had stuck to Diet Pepsi, but she didn't want to make him sound like a complete dork.)

So Lou drove them home, and dropped off each girl at her home, while the original driver—Carl, that was his name!—escorted them to the door. Behaved like a gentleman, too, or so the girls all said the next day. (Cynthia took it for granted that boys would behave like gentlemen around her, Voice or no Voice. Among the boys who classified girls as Do's or Don'ts, she was definitely a Don't.)

It was that way through high school. In college, she set her sights higher, both personally and academically. The academic sight-setting came naturally. She knew she had the smarts and therefore the duty to get high marks and "realize her potential." (Although that potential didn't include medicine; one biology class taught her she'd never have the stomach for that much blood.)

The personal sight-setting was a little more complicated in practice, although her original motive was simple enough. Her sophomore-year roommate was a near-victim of date rape (liberally assisted on both sides by too much beer), and the thought came to Cynthia as she held the roommate's head over the toilet:

Suppose I can teach the Voice to others? Suppose Jean could have told that jerk to go pee up a rope and made it stick?

There were a lot of questions she knew she had to answer before she started setting up as a Voice guru. Did liquor or drugs (on either side) make the Voice less useful? Suppose you wanted a guy, and wanted him to touch you *here* but not *there?* Could you use the Voice, and would that be selfish? And so on.

By the end of college, she had learned quite a bit about the Voice, including that it absolutely would not work on her mother. (She'd suspected that while she was in high school; more systematic tests made it certain.) She'd learned about problems she'd never read about even in the women's studies and psychology courses, and she'd learned that she could do very nicely without sex for a few years, thank you.

In the year she graduated from Northwestern University, everything happened at once. Her cousin, a Marine, was killed in the Beruit barracks bombing. This left her Aunt Louise, her mother's older sister, a childless, well-off widow.

Cheryl Binder was all over her sister—"like an oil slick on a reef," as Cynthia put it—laying up treasures in sisterhood heaven by "taking care" of her sister. This turned the long-standing tension between the sisters into a full-scale estrangement, which in turn led to Aunt Louise having a full-scale bout of clinical depression.

Enter Cynthia Binder, using the Voice to get her aunt to a doctor recommended by a friend whose father was a colleague of Dr. Eva Rupprecht. Exit depression. Exit also the secret of the Voice—Dr. Rupprecht put the various twos together and came up with a sum so close to the right one that Cynthia didn't feel called on to argue about the rest.

She might have been able to argue more effectively if Dr. Rupprecht hadn't been as immune to the Voice as Cheryl Binder. Rupprecht could neither hear nor learn the Voice. She did, however, suggest a few things that might help Cynthia with her career as a superhero.

"What did you call me?" Cynthia remembered asking.

"A superhero. You know, like Spider-Man and the Black Canary."

Cynthia concluded that Dr. Rupprecht read more comic books than she did. She tried to make a joke of it.

"I don't have the figure to go running around in a cape and tights."

"That could change. But you're right about not being conspicuous." Dr. Rupprecht twirled a lock of her gray hair around one tanned finger. "Keep a low profile for a while. Be sure you can save yourself before you try saving the world."

"I'll need help to save even one street. Or haven't you been reading the papers?"

"You don't need to be sarcastic. You don't need to rush things, either. May I suggest a bargain? I'll help you work out a series of tests to give the people you're trying to teach. That may eliminate a few bad apples. It will certainly save you time."

"What's the catch?"

"You promise to get yourself professionally established over the next five or six years. Then we can go into business."

It sounded like a prison sentence, and Cynthia knew her face must have showed it.

Rupprecht's eyebrows rose. "That's a problem I have with comic books. The world is so grateful to superheroes that they never have to worry about paying the rent, finding a parking place, or changing the diapers. Gratitude doesn't cover those things, as you will learn."

"I don't see myself with a child."

"Like your figure, that may change. What do you think?"

Cynthia's first thought was that tens of thousands of women were going to be murdered, raped, or otherwise mistreated in those five or six years. Her second thought was that even if she spent all her time finding the mistreaters and using the Voice on them, she'd only be able to save a fraction of the women. And Rupprecht's offer of help made a lot of sense, if training other women was going to be systematic and effective.

"It makes more sense than just winging it."

"Most things do," Rupprecht said austerely.

In the long run, it did not hurt that Aunt Louise died a year later. Cynthia managed not to blame herself for the long-neglected heart condition that finally caught up with her aunt.

She couldn't help a tormented month of sleepless nights when she learned that Aunt Louise had left half her estate to her niece. Had she somehow conveyed a suggestion of this to her aunt, back when they were meeting almost every day and sometimes talking for hours? Had she used the Power of Obedience (a term Rupprecht preferred to the Voice) to make herself rich?

Time and sleeping pills quieted the agonized self-questioning. (Sleeping pills also knocked out the Power of Obedience, so Cynthia went off them as quickly as possible.) She set up a trust fund with most of the money, swore not to touch her capital, then took enough to pay her way through Northwestern's Kellogg School of Business. She came out with one of the best MBA's in the country and was fast-tracked in a major Loop marketing firm for the next four years.

By then she knew that the best place to find women to train in the Power of Obedience was an executive-search firm. As soon as she thought she had the experience and contacts, she downsized her employers by one junior executive, pulled out enough money to rent an office and hire an assistant, and treated Dr. Rupprecht to lunch at Ricky's.

The campaign to give "empowerment" a whole new dimension had begun.

June 17:

After six years Cynthia began to feel it was like one of those World War I battles. The kind where lots of men marched into machine-gun and artillery fire, and when the smoke had cleared most of them were lying dead on barbed wire or in shell holes and the survivors held a few more miles of mud and enemy trenches.

In fact, there'd been only one dead, but Cynthia suspected that was more good luck than good management. The spring had run her list of failures up from ten to twelve, which was fast going but partly due to luck. Again, good or bad? She wished she knew even that much.

One of the potential candidates, a medical technician, thought Cynthia was trying to seduce her and took off running. She got out of range so fast that Cynthia didn't have a chance to do anything about her prejudices, let alone give her a thorough testing.

The other was a bookstore manager with her own set of hangups. She was a devout New Ager, and insisted everything Cynthia wanted to teach her be translated into a New Age vocabulary.

What Cynthia knew about crystals and channeling could be written in the corner of a postage stamp. This was inevitable, since none of the literature on the subject seemed to be written in English and Cynthia was relentlessly monolingual. However, it probably cost her at least a chance to evaluate the bookseller.

Or did it? Someone who thought that in a previous life she had been a Tibetan guru and Cynthia one of her students might not be the best candidate for learning the Power of Obedience. Cynthia managed to find the woman a position with a new superstore opening in the North Loop, and hoped that she wouldn't start channeling while meeting sales reps.

This left Cynthia facing the second half of June exactly where she'd been in March. Maybe a little poorer, too. She'd managed her April tax payment without dipping into her capital, but it left her short of liquid cash.

This didn't bother her. What did get through to her was an argument with Pat over a modest, quite reasonable request for a raise.

"The cash flow can't stand it," Cynthia said.

"So improve the cash flow," Pat said.

"How?"

"For one thing, you might spend less time finding accountants for women entrepreneurs just starting up. I know all about the sisterhood side of it. Do you know about the money side of it? Around here, that seems to be the downside."

Cynthia couldn't reply. That, she realized later, was the first piece of good luck she'd had in quite a while. If she'd spoken, she'd have said something ugly enough to make it impossible for Pat to go on working for her. Then the rent-plumbing-diapers side of her super-heroing would be up the creek.

See if Rupprecht can find a tranquilizer compatible with the Obedience was her mental memo, before she started flipping through the resumes—

June 20:

Francine Latrilla looked like Barbra Streisand's baby sister, complete with the nose. Cynthia wasn't surprised; Mediterranean, Ashkenazic Jewish, and African-American faces overlapped a good deal.

Latrilla's resume made her face a secondary consideration. She had a B.S. in computer science and seven years' work experience. The last two were with a games firm in the northwest suburbs. They were downsizing after having to cancel two games because of a religious righteous wing boycott. Francine hadn't been pink-slipped yet, but she knew her next promotion would be after her supervisor died, and the super was two years younger than she was.

"Male, of course?" Cynthia asked.

"As far as you can tell with his clothes on," Francine said. "I never tried to get them off, either. Talk about the classic nerd!"

The interview went on from there. In spite of herself, Cynthia liked Francine's forthright, even salty tongue. It might make her hard to place, and would certainly limit her to firms where she wouldn't have easily threatened males over her, which eliminated a lot of possibilities.

"—move over into educational software," Francine was saying. "There's a lot of that action in Chicago."

Cynthia tried the Obedience, at the lowest level. "You don't need to tell me so much that I already know."

Francine blinked. "In a hurry?" She sounded almost petulant.

Better than being dazed. And I've given up hoping for someone to recognize what I'm trying to do—

"I will be. It's after one."

"Tell you what," Francine said. "If you let me go on, I'll take you out to lunch. Yeah, I know about business etiquette. But my dad always said I could talk a dry sewer into backing up. I figure that if you have to put up with that, I ought to do something for you. What about it?"

It seemed like a remarkably good idea, and she was even willing to trust Francine's judgement about where. The woman's clothing suggested that the budget would be halfway between fast food and power lunch, but Cynthia realized that she was almost too hungry to care. Brown-bagging it was fine in principle, but the refrigerator in her studio was not only too small to let her entertain, it was too small to let her keep a week's supply of lunch fixings. . . .

"Let me check the calendar—nope, nothing until three-thirty. Let me warn Pat and get my raincoat—"

"You'll melt. The sun's come out again, and I don't think the clouds are coming back."

"Umbrella, then." And why had she felt as if sweat was oozing on her neck and arms when Francine said, "You'll melt"?

From Cynthia Binder's Journal:
June 24—Dr. Rupprecht says Francine Latrilla is qualified in all re-spects to learn the Obedience. (I have decided I am not going to use the word "Power" anymore. I am not living in a horror novel.)

She also says that I may have more trouble than usual, teaching Francine my principles of unselfishness. Maybe she was trying to tell me something, but she's found at least one dark side to everybody who's got as far as the examination. Not that she's always been wrong, either, or Lainie wouldn't be dead—and I will *not* think of that. Pat's face these days is giving me all the guilt I can handle.

August 2—First practice session with Francine today. The usual rou-tine, and she's quite promising. I usually don't get so much cooper-ation and matching voice tones until I've told the trainee what we're up to, and not always then.

Or am I using the Obedience on her, at an unconscious level? (Was that what scared off the girl—she acted seventeen even if she was twenty-four—who thought I was a gay seducer?) Check with Rupprecht if that is possible.

Also check if Francine has ever had voice lessons. She certainly has a good ear.

August 11—Francine is definitely moving along faster than usual. Against my better judgement, I am going to try her out in a public setting next week.

August 15—Francine and I attended the Feast of the Assumption Mass at Holy Name Cathedral. Not something I would have done by myself, but somehow it doesn't surprise or bother me to learn that she's a reasonably observant Catholic. ("By my own standards, at any rate," she says. "Maybe not the Pope's, but the Pope's a man, so what does he know?")

Got back to find an answer to my query among Francine's co-workers. Nothing that I can really use for her job search, and no record of voice lessons, but one thing interesting if a little kinky.

It seems one reason her supervisor was down on her was that he dared her to play strip role-playing. (I've heard of strip poker and even strip chess, but strip *Dungeons & Dragons*?). Anyway, she won by a mile. It was embarrassing to the guy, or maybe em-bare-assing would be a better way to put it—

Come on, Cyn. You have enough vices. You don't need to develop a taste for locker-room puns.

August 19—Francine's briefing before our first public test. I thought it went well. She did say right off that it sounded like something I'd given before. I did my usual "neither confirm nor deny" routine, and she said that she appreciated confidentiality but that I wasn't a Pentagon press officer. Polite impasse. I suspect Rupprecht is partly right—I can teach Francine my principles, but I can never teach her to carry them out in a way that people will recognize as being unselfish.

Never mind that. The state of mind is what counts, as far as Rupprecht and I have been able to figure it out. What the other party *thinks* the state of mind is doesn't seem to affect results.

August 20:
The trouble started the moment they walked into Martina's. There was a line, every table was filled, and the hostess had no record of their reservation.

"Let's make her remember," whispered Francine.

"It may not have been recorded. We can't force her unless we know it's her fault."

"I know whose fault it will be if we have to stand in line for half an hour, and in these shoes." Francine was wearing a new pair, which supported Cynthia's theory that after foot-binding was outlawed in China, all the Chinese makers of women's shoes had emigrated and infiltrated the West's shoe industry.

"Francine, you are a pretty poor hand at laying guilt trips," Cynthia said, trying to put warning into a whisper. Francine shrugged, but didn't say anything else.

At least not until they were seated, twenty minutes later and in the smoking section.

"Either he puts that out," Francine said, pointing to their neighbor, who seemed to be a chain-smoker, "or I have a fatal sinus attack right now."

"We're in the smoking section," Cynthia replied, with the patience of one speaking to a small child.

"I can read," Francine said, with an adult frown. "Have you heard of secondary smoke?"

"It was as much your idea as mine not to wait for a seat in the nonsmoking section."

Another silence, which lasted through ordering from a waiter who even Cynthia wasn't too cranky to notice was remarkably easy on the eyes. Francine looked as if she was memorizing his features for her private fantasies tonight, at least.

Then the steaks came, and they were both badly overdone. Cynthia took up knife and fork with the determination of a Crusader riding out with sword and shield, but Francine signaled the waiter.

"I ordered this steak medium, not charred. Could you take it back and get it right this time?"

The waiter was a professional; he didn't look embarrassed or argumentative. He swept the steak off with the grace of a dancer, then returned just as Cynthia found the right words for broiling Francine.

"The cook says those were the last steaks. May I recommend the fettucine Alfredo with chicken? A complimentary round of drinks will come with it."

Francine nodded, then added hastily, as Cynthia glared, "I'll pass on the drinks."

"Good idea," Cynthia said, when the waiter left.

"I did remember what you and Rupprecht said about liquor. How about you remember that people sometimes do civilized things without being asked? That guy's a pro. I didn't need to use any whammies on him."

Considering that the waiter had been studying Francine almost as intently as she him, that was at best a half-truth. But there was nothing good that could come of calling Francine a liar now.

They munched their way through a really excellent fettucine Alfredo without any further conversation. Cynthia's mind was too busy, turning over the thought that this public test was way premature, to make polite chitchat.

"More coffee, people?" the waiter asked. Even standing still beside their table, he had the elegance of a big cat. Cynthia was trying to keep her eyes off him. Francine wasn't even trying.

"Thank you," Francine said, but Cynthia put a hand over her cup. The waiter filled Francine's cup, then signaled to the busboy to clear the table.

"I'll bring the dessert menu in a moment, but I warn you we're out of eclairs."

"Temptation, get thee behind me," Francine murmured.

Cynthia's temptation was to use the Obedience on Francine, to keep her from making a pig of herself if not from admiring the waiter. She thrust that temptation behind her much harder than Francine looked to be thrusting the desserts.

Francine ordered Black Forest cake; Cynthia ordered a brandied pear. As the waiter left after delivering them, Francine's eyes followed him.

"I'm trying to raise barriers to sexual harassment, not increase it!" Cynthia whispered fiercely.

"Admiring him isn't harassing him, or is it?" Francine said. "Have I said a word?"

"No, but you've been thinking very loudly. What if he hears?"

"If he hears, then I'll wait and see what he says."

"What if he's gay?"

"Wouldn't it be nice to make him straight for a day? Or a night?"

Cynthia glared. "If that's your idea of a joke—"

"Ease up, Cyn."

My god, what have I done, loosing Francine on the world? Her face twisted, and she barely recognized her own words, there was so much rage in them. "Are you going to treat the whole Obedience as a joke? Are you going to go around playing with people's minds for fun? You selfish, bitchy pseudo-male—"

For a moment she thought Francine was going to slap her. The waiter, just coming out of the kitchen, seemed to think the same.

"Oh, for God's sake, Cyn. Lighten up and get off my case. Or drop dead!"

Sweat not just oozed but poured out of what seemed every square inch of Cynthia's skin. Lights flashed behind her eyes, blurring her vision of the dining room. Her right ear felt as if she'd ruptured an eardrum, and other pains throbbed in her jaw and rumbled in her stomach.

She tried to stand, held out a hand toward Francine, and felt her grab it. Then Cynthia's legs were giving way under her. She had enough control to guide her fall—or was that Francine and maybe even the waiter guiding her?—to miss the table. Her chair crashed over, though, and her dessert slid off the table and landed on her J. C. Penney's executive ensemble.

Snatches of dialogue, heard through a green fog (why green?) shot with orange flame—

"—call the manager—"

"—paramedics on the way—"

"—diabetic or epileptic? I had a girlfriend who had petit mal epilepsy."

That was the waiter. So much for his being completely gay. Good luck, Francine. Whether from Obedience or not, her hostility to the other woman had faded.

Cynthia's last conscious thought was that whatever her "mal" was, there was nothing "petit" about it.

August 21:

Cynthia Binder's first conscious thought was recognizing that she

97

was in her own bed at home. Her second thought was that it was a good sign she could recognize that much. Whatever had hit her at the restaurant hadn't given her amnesia.

Francine Latrilla's face loomed above. Cynthia focused enough to see that the other woman looked exhausted. She might even have been crying, which would be a first for their association.

"How are you feeling?"

"Tired. Confused. Not disoriented—confused. Just—wondering what happened. The last thing I remember was you telling me to get off your case or drop dead." She forced a smile. "The next time, give me a chance to take the first choice before you hit me with the second."

Francine winced. "That—look, I have a confession to make."

"You spent the night with the waiter."

"I spent the night right here, on your floor, rolled up in a sleeping bag the waiter loaned me. Not with him in it, either. That's for another day."

"Did the paramedics come?"

"Yes, but all your signs were normal by the time they got you to the ER. You were even awake and talking normally. Do you remember that?"

Now that she concentrated, Cynthia did remember bright lights and people in scrub outfits asking remarkably rude questions. She'd thought it was a flashback to her aunt's death, but the calendar on the wall wasn't right.

"I do now. So confess. I won't use Obedience to make you, but—"

"If you did, you might put the same sort of whammy on me that I did on you. If we each knocked the other ass over elbow in two days, somebody might get suspicious."

"Somebody is suspicious. Me, and right now." Cynthia sat up. She still had yesterday's underwear on under her nightgown.

"All right. I've been in your files."

Cynthia didn't throw anything. She simply sat staring at Francine until her eyes blurred again, this time with tears.

Francine patted her shoulder. "Remember, I know computers, and

I have a few contacts in the hacker community. I called in markers, and they helped out without knowing what they were helping me with." She went off into a long monologue on the security problems of Cynthia's software.

Cynthia blinked and cleared her throat. "Francine, if you don't finish your confession before I stop crying, I am going to get out of bed and strangle you with my bare hands."

A moment later, she realized that she'd slipped into Obedience voice. Francine's eyes widened, and she put a hand to her throat, as if she already felt angry fingers tightening on her windpipe.

"All right. I peeked. I think I've figured out what's wrong. You need to be selfish."

Cynthia heard the words but no sense in them. "Run that past me again. Slowly."

"Look. Take the time you saved that football player. You wanted the team to win, didn't you? That meant more parties, maybe enough for somebody to invite you to one?"

If it's Confession Time—

"Yes, I guess I did."

"Right. So I suspect that your Obedience worked a lot better, because you would get some good out of that halfback's staying out of trouble."

Cynthia tried to clear her head by going back over the details of the Rackham Peavey affair. She finally had to get up, take a shower, and call up the Obedience files on her computer.

She was red-eyed from fatigue, not weeping, before she finished, but by then Francine's off-the-wall hypothesis began to make sense. Enough sense that she felt a wave of guilt sweeping through her, from not considering it before. A good many other incidents took on whole new dimensions, when looked at in this new light.

Take the case of Lou the designated driver. Cynthia hadn't wanted her friends to be hurt. But she was going to be in the car too. And she hadn't wanted the two-block walk home from the usual drop-off point, so that probably accounted for the door-to-door service.

Probably. She wouldn't go farther than that. She knew that some of the reluctance was not wanting to admit how wrong she'd been, or what her being wrong might have cost others.

But—

"What about the failures?" she asked, between bites of an anchovy pizza that Francine had somehow caused to materialize on the coffee table. "What about the ones who couldn't even use Obedience against a polite pass? It worked well enough when I was a teenager, even in college."

"Maybe you need to be in some sort of danger, or the pass needs to be less than polite?"

"Maybe, but how many polite passes have you had in your life? Enough for one hand and maybe a couple of fingers on the other?"

"About that. You're right. If a little selfishness helps, then Obedience ought to knock out *any* kind of pass. As long as the woman using it has her mind made up, anyway."

Cynthia said nothing. It was nice to think that women always had their minds firmly made up about sex or no sex, unambiguously and finally, before the date reached the propositional phase. It was also unrealistic.

"What about laying the whole thing before Dr. Rupprecht?" Cynthia said. She really wanted for the first time to dump responsibility for the Obedience in somebody else's lap.

Then she realized that Francine was sitting down by the telephone and punching in Dr. Rupprecht's number. She had slipped into Obedience—and there was just enough selfishness in her wish to get in touch with Rupprecht that Francine was snapping to it like a Marine boot or a trained dog.

"Hey, wait," Cynthia said. "What about an experiment or two first?"

Francine stopped dialing. Her eyes were blank for a moment, with the familiar stare of someone coming up from under Obedience without realizing they'd been there in the first place.

Then she smiled. "I think we just had one. I *had* to call Rupprecht. I would have tried to call her if the building had been on fire and the roof ready to fall on me."

Cynthia curled up in her sling chair and contemplated the rug. She wanted to believe Francine. But short of hooking her up to a lie detector, there was no way to be absolutely sure. (And Obedience might scramble a lie detector. A lot of things did.)

100

"Maybe. We need another. What about the waiter?"

"Now who's treating people as pawns? I was thinking about your assistant Pat."

"Pat? I've never tried Obedience on her. It would have been—selfish."

"You told yourself it would have been selfish to exploit a black woman trying to make good. But have you really helped her that much, running your business so that she's making twenty percent less than she could make elsewhere?"

"Maybe not."

"No maybe about it. Cyn, you zigged when you should have zagged. You were so damned determined not to go your mother's way that you set yourself an even higher standard. One that screwed up your talent, if I might be crude about it."

"Don't be that crude around Pat. Her dad's a Baptist minister."

"I won't. How about calling her?"

This time Cynthia knew that somebody was using Obedience on her, and that it was working. Not enough to wipe out her own firmly held convictions, though—which might have something to do with the sex problem.

"Look, let's agree on what experiments we're going to do with Pat," Francine suggested. "Then maybe we should run the list past Dr. Rupprecht first. She knows Pat. She can tell us what would be safe."

"That still leaves the problem of working with Pat afterward. I don't want her to quit—"

"Cyn, let me make you an offer. If Pat quits over this, I'll go to work as your assistant. I've sneaked a look at most of your files anyway, and I certainly know office equipment. I even have a little money to throw into the pot."

"Not on pot, I hope?" Francine's cheerfulness was infectious. Did Obedience need a little fun along with a little selfishness, for full effect? *That* might be the key to the sex problem.

One thing at a time, though.

"You're on. Now, which of us orders the other to call Pat over here? And this is not an order, but I wouldn't mind a beer. There's some Michelob in the fridge."

From Cynthia Binder's Journal:
September 13—Dr. Rupprecht has finished analyzing the results of our experiments with Pat and the waiter. (At least Francine says that she experimented with the waiter. Either she is telling the truth or has a very good imagination. I could hardly ask the two of them to let me videotape the proceedings.)

She agrees with Francine. A little selfishness, like a little garlic, does a lot for Obedience. She is not sure why it worked for me in sexual situations when I was younger but hasn't worked for the adults I've taught since.

She does have several theories, connected with age, hormones, sex drive, self-esteem—any or all, take your pick. She also suggests that while she's working on the Big Problem, all is not lost. Spreading Obedience around could reduce teenage pregnancies, waitresses getting their bottoms pinched by the cook or the customer, female executives having to attend skinny-dipping parties, pornographic pictures hung up in offices—a whole bunch of things.

Rupprecht says that the largest building is built one brick at a time. I told her that metaphor is out of date. She said all right, call it one girder, but the principle is the same. I have to agree.

September 22—Gave Pat a twenty-five percent raise. We can afford it. I have placed four women in the high five-figure brackets, and I have one nibble from a woman whose asking price is in the low sixes.

October 19—The first six-figure placement! Francine and I went back to the restaurant where it all started. Her friend Mel is now the headwaiter. Has she been teaching him Obedience without a license, or just self-assertiveness?

November 23—Our business needs a lawyer on retainer. I tried Obedience on one, to make her speak English instead of legalese. It worked! This might be a bigger breakthrough than a cure for sexual harrassment!

December 11:

"Hello, Cyn. I have the position."

Francine sounded so delighted that Cynthia had to laugh. "Good. Anybody there looking for a position?"

"You kidding? They were hanging on for dear life with three people. They may need a fifth before long. And do you know who our newest client is?"

"Mel?"

"I didn't know you were telepathic as well. Yes, Mel. He's opening his own restaurant and wants to subcontract the payroll. It was his own idea, too."

"Good. Let's get together next week."

"Fine. Call you Saturday?"

"Perfect."

The line went dead. Cynthia swiveled her leather chair, resisted the temptation to put her feet on the new rosewood desk, and frowned.

Mel might have decided on his own to open his own restaurant, and as long as he was using his own money (or money the bank intended for him), well and good. But—had she accidentally set somebody up in business as an embezzler as well as a restaurateur?

Well, she could at least get to the truth, since it involved money, not sex. Surprising how many problems had money at their roots, not sex.

Memo to Pat: Buy four dozen "Girls Just Wanna Have Funds" T-shirts, in assorted sizes.

She'd wanted to have something to hand out to clients for fun. The "She Who Must Be Obeyed" one didn't quite make it (besides maybe giving too much away).

She started sorting her mail. The newspaper was near the top. On the front page was a grim-looking couple and a headline that Cynthia realized she'd been dreading to see for months.

Cynthia Binder, closet monarchist. Cynthia remembered when the couple had been a good deal younger and not nearly as grim. She remembered when the wife was a classic English-rose beauty instead of looking as if she'd been to the wars.

That woman needs Obedience, even if it violates all kinds of protocol. Now, how to get access to her?

Memo: check out health clubs. Cynthia now had a one-bedroom apartment, but there still wasn't much room for fitness equipment since they delivered the new computer. A little trimming down wouldn't hurt, just in case she wound up having to look good in a cape and tights.

And the Sea Shall Cast Him Out

William Marden

One of the tenets of superhero lore is that truly powerful beings must always be in control of their emotions because stray anger might kill innocent people or even level a city. This leaves us with the question: how do they deal with . . . passion?

She rose out of the sea like a dream long forgotten.

Sunstar watched her walk naked out of the surf onto the fine white sand of the Caribbean island called Haven, the sight causing his body to flare with the brilliance of a small star.

Cecil, an island fisherman, mended a net with his twelve-year-old son while talking with one of the island's superhuman tourists. He grinned at Sunstar.

"Do you always ogle naked women when they walk ashore?" Her voice carried hints of cold undersea currents.

"I think, Sea Witch, that you have never gone anywhere that you haven't been ogled."

She did not give him so much as the hint of a smile, but her lazy, impersonal gaze made shivers run up and down his spine.

"Men. You always think with your glands."

She walked past.

"Fortunately."

Cecil shook his head.

"Be careful, man, that one will eat you up and spit you out."

The fisherman's words flashed through Sunstar's mind that evening as he sat at one of six round tables on an open deck facing the ocean, a strong rain-laden wind blowing off the water through the tropical darkness.

Sunstar leaned forward and with the tip of his finger lit a large black cigar that Professor Power held. Adjusting his old-fashioned spectacles, Power said, "Thank you. As I was saying, my young friend, I was truly impressed with the job you people at the Bureau did in stopping that Genotype Corp. hijacking last week."

The tall, hawk-nosed individual washing down coconut-wrapped shrimp with a coffee liqueur—dubbed the Mind Master by the public relations experts at the Bureau of Extraordinary Talents—said, "That's big of you, Prof, considering you masterminded it."

The Professor shook his head, saying, "You flatter me, but I'm afraid that is an unvarnished falsehood. Anyway, it doesn't really matter on this lovely island, does it?"

"It will when you leave here, Professor. Three security guards were killed, and two civilians. What does that bring your tally to, anyway? Word is, you're directly or indirectly responsible for at least twenty thousand—including that fission fiasco in Mexico City."

Power waved a finger at an ashtray on a neighboring table and after it floated to him tapped his cigar gently against it, saying, "Nothing like that. You and your fellow BET agents have the same vested interest in painting me as a mad killer that your predecessors in the FBI had in building up the Dillinger mystique."

"Hey, no shop talk," Harley Speed said, uttering his first words of the evening, staring at both men with cold, flat menace. "This is the only goddamned place on Earth I can go and get treated like a halfway normal human being, instead of walking death. Anybody tries to screw things up, I'm going to be very unhappy."

"You're right, Harley," Power said. "We need the neutral ground of Haven too greatly to bring in our outside quarrels."

Power rose from his seat and paced back and forth, unconsciously levitating so his feet hovered six inches above the ground, staring out into the darkness from which the wind and the sound of surf came racing to shore.

"You Bureau agents need Haven for the same reason my freelance colleagues like Harley and the lovely Witch do. We—products of the nanotech, biotech and cybertech revolutions, and a little alien meddling—need contact with our own kind. The people you serve are not your equals."

"A guy named Hitler felt the same way once," said the sixth member of the table, the spectacularly blond Lady Mischief.

"Ask yourself, my dear, why you do not seek rest and relaxation skiing in Colorado, sunbathing on the Mediterranean or sipping hot chocolate in a Swiss chalet," Power said. "Instead you come to this tiny flyspeck—although an enchanted one—to mingle with your worst enemies. Doesn't that seem somewhat strange?"

"It does." Sunstar stared into the upturned face of the Witch. "But sometimes you get lucky. Sometimes."

She followed him to the beach minutes later.

"They say that you could fry a woman, immolate her, incinerate her from the inside out while making love," she said.

He turned to say something, but found her in his arms. The world disappeared under the thundering rush of black water as the sea swept over them and pulled them out away from the land.

They hung suspended as if in the depths of space, currents of freezing cold and lukewarm water sending them bobbing up and down like corks, their clothes fluttering away from them like tropical fish.

There was no oxygen, but he did not drown and did not breathe. Big-eyed fish and fluorescent creatures from a madman's dreams crowded about them as they swirled nakedly about, two beings made one, joined at the thighs and the mouths.

She clawed and scratched and tried to suck his entire body into hers. He screamed in molten ecstacy as he exploded, the water around them vaporizing, energies from the stars turning a good chunk of ocean into superheated steam, instantly cooking fish to the point that their flesh fell off their bones. The force of the blast hurled them into trees and onto the homes of Haven, making this a miracle day residents would talk of for generations to come, the day the sea rained fire.

He had no conscious memory of how he made his way back to the beach afterwards. He found himself rocking on his knees back and forth in the surf. Which were tears and which were the ocean's salt he could not tell. He had always known inside that he was no longer human, that he could never lose control with a woman that way. Despite her crimes, he didn't think the Witch deserved to die that way.

A soft touch on his shoulder brought his dripping face up to stare blindly at the figure standing beside him.

She sank to her knees next to him, kissed him with lips that tasted of salt and blood and iodine, saying, "Do you understand now, my beautiful Sunstar? I can't kill you, even if I wanted to. And you can't kill me. How do you kill the sea? I am immortal in my element, a molecular pattern that cannot be destroyed."

Her kisses drove the fear away.

"That's why we wanted each other. You could never love a human woman without killing her. And no human man could ever love me and survive. We were made for each other, fire and water, sea and sun."

The next four days dissolved into a blur, mornings waking on the beach with the sea lapping around them, walks where they sometimes saw and waved to Cecil and his son.

Professor Power smiled knowingly at them, and Lady Mischief only shook her head. Sunstar knew he faced lectures when he returned to the Bureau, but it didn't matter on those nights when the two of them would meld into an impossible creature of passion, one that fire could not destroy nor water quench.

He woke up alone on the beach on the fifth day. He found the Witch at the tourist office, making arrangements to leave.

"I don't know what to say."

"Don't say anything."

"I've got to. It's just that—I can't let you go like this."

She stopped, looked at him with the cold look of a stranger.

"That's your hormones talking, Sunstar. You're a government agent. The next time we meet you'll try to kill me, or vice versa."

"No, I couldn't do that. Not now. Everything's changed."

She turned her back and walked to the beach.

"The only thing we had was great sex," she said. "If we don't kill each other, maybe we can get together again. But no promises."

As she stepped into the surf, he grabbed her by the shoulder. Flame leaped up around his hand, and he smelled burning flesh. She gasped, but twisted away from him and fell into the water. A moment later she arose, her bare skin free of blemish.

"I'm sorry," he said, "sorry. But, your going doesn't change anything. We're different people than we were five days ago, and it's much more than just sex."

She shook her head.

"I shouldn't do this. It would be better for me if you stayed a lovesick fool. But you deserve better than that. So this is my last gift to you, my beautiful human star. I give you your freedom."

Like a fish leaping into the waves, she was up and then gone under the water before he could move.

That evening the trawler brought in the bodies of Cecil and his son. They had drowned hours before.

The message appeared clearly when the boy's small body was placed beside his father.

"NOW YOU ARE FREE."

The Defender of Central Park

Josepha Sherman

A tree grows in Brooklyn. Lots of trees grow in Central Park.

Deep within the heart of the great tree, something stirred, yawned, opened its eyes—then froze in confusion. This was not the forest, not the springtime, not even the good, proper feel of Mother Rus. And this tree, this huge, once-wonderful tree, wasn't even alive any longer!

The being uncurled, peering through solid wood as easily as though it was glass . . .

Ach! What was this place? Bright as day though every sense screamed it was late night: human bright, with strange, strongly gleaming globes on poles placed everywhere, with yet more light blazing from the windows of the buildings that—how could this be?—were tall enough to nearly touch the sky!

What have I come to? Where is my forest? What oh what am I to do?

Wait, the being decided. Wait. This was plainly some vast city. And sooner or later someone human must pass, someone of the old blood and knowledge . . .

Tanya Hanson switched off the computer and got to her feet, stretching stiff muscles. Being an associate producer at a New York news station might sound like a glamorous job, but it meant long

111

hours of overtime and not all that much in the way of salary.

It's a start. Besides, it's not as though I've got somewhere better to go.

Grimly, she fought to block thoughts of Dave from her mind. Tall, handsome, with such a charming smile—as long as she was properly deferential. It was over, had been over the first time he'd slapped her. An accident, he'd claimed, something that would never happen again.

You bet it won't! Tanya thought, snatching up her coat and heading for the elevator. *I may be overworked and underpaid, but at least I have my freedom.* And then: *God, how melodramatic.*

At this hour, the elevator was nearly empty; she and the two other late-night workers studiously ignored each other as only a true New Yorker can manage. Tanya waved good night to Hal, the building's night watchman, and hurried out into Rockefeller Center, wincing as the cold, clear air hit her. For an instant she paused, glancing warily left, right, looking for that one tall figure . . .

No one. Maybe Dave really had taken seriously her threat to call the cops. At any rate, he seemed to finally have given up watching her. Tanya started forward again, giving a mental nod of greeting to the huge, brightly ornamented tree towering over her. A sure sign the world was changing: this year the tree was a present from New York's so-called Sister City, Moscow.

Sorry, Yeltzin. Looks just like any other fir to me, and—

A cold, rough hand touched hers. "*Spohkoyni nochi, gospadeen,*" said a sudden voice, and Tanya gasped and whirled, thinking wildly, *Dave—no, no, Dave doesn't speak Russian and I don't think muggers do, either!* "Get your hands the hell off me or I'll—Oh, come on, E.T. was just a movie!"

"*Ya ny snayo*—" The . . . whatever it was (odd, she couldn't see it clearly even though the street was brightly lit) held up a hand (Green fur? Tanya's mind gabbled, it has to be a glove, surely), then started again in careful, heavily accented English. "Your pardon. I thought you speak mother tongue, too."

"M-mother—Uh, no. Why would I speak—I'm American, not—Look, I don't know who, what, you are, but if you're lost, the Russian Embassy's over on the east side, somewhere in the Sixties I think—"

"I am lost," the creature agreed. "Very. You must help."

This was ridiculous. She couldn't be standing here talking to a . . . thing in the middle of the night. Even at this hour there should be lots of people around—this was New York, after all—so why wasn't anyone stopping or staring?

No one stared in New York. "I—I've got to go," Tanya said in panic. Blessedly, a taxi stand was nearby. Practically running, she threw herself into the first cab and stammered out directions to her apartment.

Overwork, she told herself. That had to be it. She couldn't have just been talking to a green-furred Whatever. *Overwork.*

She could have sworn there was someone lingering in the street below her apartment, a tall figure . . . Daringly, Tanya pulled up the window and leaned out to look; Dave wasn't the sort to take a potshot at her.

But then he hadn't seemed the sort to hit a woman, either. Tanya hastily pulled her head back inside, telling herself sternly that, no, no one had been out there, she was starting to get paranoid—

"*Gospadeen.*"

Tanya whirled, just barely stifling a scream, and snatched up a paperweight, hefting it, ready to throw. "How did you get in here?"

The weird Whatever looked even more weird standing in the mundane reality of her living room. Tanya reached out a wary hand for the lamp nearest to her, fumbling with the switch. Ha, there! But even in the sudden blaze of light, she couldn't quite see the creature clearly: a vague blur of greenness perched tentatively on the side of her couch. "I clung to strange vehicle," it said. "That one in which you rode."

"Th-the cab? But *why*? Why are you following me?"

The thing sagged. "No choice. You are of right blood."

For one ridiculous moment, she could only think of green-furred vampires. "But I'm not Russian!" she protested. "My last name's Hanson; that's hardly a Russian name—"

"Your mother's mother was of Rus. The blood is in you. Besides," the creature added wearily, "I could find no one else."

Tanya warily lowered her throwing arm, but she didn't let go of the paperweight. "Let's start at the beginning. Who *are* you? And . . . what?"

"Why, have you never heard of *leshy*? No? I am Forest Lord in my realm, *of* forest, part of it, lord of birds and squirrels— Or I was." The being, the *leshy*, sighed. "Winter came. I slept in tree as always." It shrugged helplessly. "I woke here. And where *is* here?"

"Uh . . . New York City. America. The New World. You . . . don't understand, do you?"

"Far from Rus?"

"Very far."

"Ach." The *leshy* seemed to shrink into itself. "What am I to do?" it murmured. "Where am I to go?"

Unexpected pity roused. "I don't suppose the Russian Embassy . . ."

Suddenly fierce green eyes glared at her. "I am not some little lost human! I am *leshy*, of Old Magic! But," the being added plaintively, "what good is that in this stone-and-metal place? I need forest."

"I'm afraid Central Park's about it."

"Ha! You shall take me to this place, yes?"

"No! I mean, not now!"

The *leshy* blinked. "Why not?"

"Because—because it's the middle of the night! You don't go wandering in the park at night unless you *want* to get your head bashed in!"

"It is the home of monsters?"

"Human monsters. Predators."

The being's chuckle was soft and totally alien. "Think you any human frightens *me*?"

"Well, they frighten me. Look, I have to be at work tomorrow morning. I can drop you off at the park on the way. But tonight you'll have to find your own— Hey, what—"

The *leshy* was rushing to the open window in a blur of motion. There was a wild, savage whirl of wind, a frightened yelp, the fading sound of running footsteps— Then the *leshy*, grinning broadly, was settling back onto the arm of the couch.

"He was out there. Watching. Maybe planning to climb."

"He? Who? *Dave*? Dave was here?"

"Not," the *leshy* said with great satisfaction, "anymore. Who is he, this 'Dave'?"

"My ex. Boyfriend, that is. He doesn't want to believe it's over." Oh, wonderful, here she was discussing her private life with a—a thing out of folklore! "Look, uh, *leshy*, thank you for scaring him off."

"Vodka."

"Ah, what?"

The *leshy* grinned anew. "Thanks are best given and friendships sealed with vodka."

"Uh . . . sure." A drink wouldn't be a bad idea right now, not at all!

She wasn't quite sure what happened after that. There was a time when the two of them, human and not, were sharing their woes, Tanya about Dave, the handsome, selfish, deceptive Dave, the *leshy* about its lost forest.

"What am I to *do* now?" it asked softly. "What purpose have I?"

"Don't worry," Tanya murmured sleepily. "We'll think of something. Tomorrow."

And tomorrow it was, all too suddenly. Tanya groaned, flinging a hand over her eyes, then flinched as her outstretched fingers touched fur.

"*Dobrahyee utro*, good morning," the *leshy* crowed.

Tanya sat bolt upright, clutching the blankets about her, staring at the being perched lightly on the windowsill. She rubbed her eyes. "You're worse than a cat."

"Never mind, never mind, it is morning and you shall show me this Central Park where I may live."

"Morning," Tanya grumbled. "It's barely light."

Why had she drunk so much? And gotten so little sleep? If there were any justice, the *leshy* would be showing some signs of the weird night, too. But the creature seemed disgustingly awake and full of energy, urging her on from behind the closed bedroom door as she dressed and did the best she could to look human.

Which, Tanya realized with a renewed shock, the being on the other side of the door was most certainly not.

115

It's all right, she told herself sternly. *I'll take him, it, whatever to Central Park, and that'll be the end of that.*

It really was ridiculously early; the streetlights were still giving more light than the sky. Tanya shivered in the chill air, clutching her coat to her, glancing about. The streets of New York are never quiet, but no one was on the sidewalks save a few fanatical joggers. Not one of them seemed to notice the small green shadow lurking at her side.

"All right," Tanya muttered, "let's go. We have a good walk ahead of us."

"This is it?" the *leshy* asked doubtfully. "So much pavement."

"It gets better further in. There's even a bird sanctuary in there."

"Let us see."

"Hey, wait, I can't— Let go!"

But the *leshy* was pulling her into the park with all the enthusiasm of a child. A child with a grip like iron.

"Look, I have to get to work!"

"It is early yet, you said so yourself. Come, explore with me."

"Do I have a choice?" Tanya muttered. Like many another New Yorker, she'd never gone beyond the edges of the park; she'd never realized there were so many dark, secret corners. "Look, I really do have to be getting on."

The *leshy* released her without warning. "This is almost forest enough," it muttered. "But it is *made,* not grown from Nature. There is no—no *heart* to it, no real purpose for my staying here."

"I'm sorry," Tanya said, and meant it. "But—"

"Not your fault. You did your best. Go on, now, go."

Tanya hesitated uncertainly, then walked resolutely away.

She hadn't gotten too far before a too-familiar voice murmured, "Good morning."

Tanya stopped short. "Dave."

He looked so amazingly normal, so totally sane and . . . safe that his sudden humorless little chuckle was all the more chilling. "Bet you thought you could get away from me. Bet you thought I would just let you go."

116

"It's over." *I will* not *let him know I'm afraid.* "We both know it. Now—"

"It's not over, Tanya. Not till I say it is."

God, why had she let herself come to this place? The narrow path wound too much; she'd never be able to get away. And a scream wasn't going to be heard by anyone but squirrels. "Don't be stupid," she said as calmly as she could. "We had some fun together, but—"

"Don't mock me, Tanya. You know better than that."

Tanya stared into his cool blue eyes—too cool, too controlled for the anger in his voice—and felt a new shiver prickle through her. *How could I ever think I loved him?* Oh, ridiculous question! He was handsome and charming, and she'd never once guessed, not till the end, that it was all a sham. She'd never once guessed just how shallow his veneer of sanity might be. "I—I have to get to work. Let me pass."

"Oh no, Tanya. No more games."

Panic exploded into anger. "Dammit, it's not a game! Get out of my way!"

She tried to push past him, but Dave's hand pulled her to him; his arms crushed her against him. Tanya tried to bite, tried to kick, all the warnings she'd ever heard about women needing to learn self-defense echoing in her mind; too late now, too late, he had one hand over her mouth and his weight was forcing her to the ground—

A roar like the anger of all the world split the air around them. Stunned, Tanya felt Dave torn from her, leaving her huddled, staring at—at *what?* At a whirlwind, at bird, beast, thing, at all the raw Power that was a forest, that was a *leshy*, that was enfolding Dave in primal savagery.

Dear God, and that's what I shared a drink with!

She had no idea what Dave saw, but whatever it was, it clearly held a world of horror for him. Tanya heard him cry out, a child's cry of sheer terror. With that terrified cry, Tanya realized, the last of his sanity had snapped. And when the incredible whirlwind of Power cast him away, he staggered blindly off, eyes wild and hopeless, no longer a menace to anything but himself.

"Dear . . . God."

"Are you hurt? Are you?"

It was the *leshy*, a small, green-furred creature once more. "I'm all right," Tanya said warily, "I—I think. Was all that . . . you?"

"Yes, yes!" the being crowed. "Tell me, quickly, was that a common thing for this park, that attack? Was he the sort of predator you mentioned?"

"Uh . . . yes. M-more or less. There are worse."

"Ha, good! A true challenge!"

"What are you—"

The *leshy* laughed. "This is a poor forest, but forest it is. It needs a Forest Lord, a protector."

"Not against everyone!"

"No, no, I never did ban my forest to humans who came in peace. But you saw what I did, what I can do against those who mean harm." The *leshy* laughed again, high and wild as the wind. "Thank you, human friend, thank you for bringing me here and giving me a home."

"You mean," Tanya said slowly, "you're going to stay here. You're going to hunt the predators."

"Of course! You saw what I can do." The *leshy*'s small, strong hand caught hers and pulled her to her feet. "I have a purpose now, human friend. I am, and shall remain: Defender of Central Park! Now go, off with you. You have your work to do. And I—oh, I have mine!"

Reflected Glory

Paul Kupperberg

We've seen many examples of people who've said "enough" and proceeded to take matters into their own hands. Sometimes they're hailed as heroes, sometimes they're damned as villains. Usually the only difference is . . . spin.

Weiser is the name, public relations is the game.

I wouldn't be surprised if you'd heard of me, seeing as how, for a humble press flack, I'm pretty well known. I was lucky enough to be the first victim he ever rescued, just about three months ago, when he revealed his existence to the world. But a guy in my line of work takes it where he can get it. Usually, the p. r. guy humps along quietly in the background, aggressively selling his clients to the people who can get their names before the public while keeping the lowest personal profile possible for himself. But since this all fell into my lap, I'd have been a schmuck not to take advantage of it. See, the way I figured it, the better my face is known, the easier it is for me to get my foot in the door and, by extension, my client's names into the newspapers and their smiling faces on the TV talk shows. Talk about understatements. Being a public figure in my own right gave me instant credibility with the publicity suckers who control the media. Celebs trust fellow celebs. They believe everybody else wants something from them, which is usually the case, but closer to insight than I generally like giving these people credit for. Doors open for a guy whose name is followed by the label "Ultima's best friend."

Of course, we're not really best friends. Or any kind of friends for that matter, sure as hell not the "pals" the tabloids have us pegged as. At best, we can be called acquaintances. *Business* acquaintances, at that. Sure, I owed him for what he'd done for me, saving my ass the way he did, but I like to think I've more than returned the favor for that over the last couple of months. Now, I do a job for him, and we both got what we needed out of the relationship without the bother of a friendship mucking up the arrangement. Me, a guaranteed table at Elaine's, more high-profile clients, and a big, juicy bank account, and Ultima, publicity that kept John Q. Public from finding out what kind of a monster he really was.

Since when does reality have anything to do with public relations?

"Where do I come from? You know I can't tell you who I really am, right? Nobody knows that. Nobody can ever know, otherwise I'd never have a moment's peace for the world camping out on my doorstep, wanting me to do for them. Or wanting to do me harm for what I've done when I'm off my guard, being who I really am when I'm not being Ultima. So for our purposes, I'm just Ultima, that's it, okay?

"Sounds pretty silly, I know. I guess the strangest thing to realize is that the role models for what I am come from comic books. Except the world's not like comic books. The real world doesn't need me, not the way they'd need me if I were a comic-book hero in a comic-book world, fighting the hordes of bizarre and powerful comic-book villains populating those pulp realities. There, when I punched someone, I wouldn't take their head off. My blow would send them smashing through a wall, but they'd always get right back up and come at me again. In the funny books, people like me aren't murderers.

"Uhm . . .

"Maybe you don't want to use that part in the book, Jack."

Three months ago . . .

I'd spent most of my life avoiding working for a living. I started by spending six years in college, drifting between a variety of majors and interests until the scholarships ran out and my parents were fed up supporting me. The last major I'd absolutely, positively committed my academic energies to the semester I left school was journalism, so, on my own and without the comfortable cushion of parental financial support, I worked up a fake resume that would have been impressive for someone twice my age and applied to every newspaper in the New York metropolitan area. I was just young and cocky enough to expect a personnel manager to fall for it. I was lucky enough to find one gullible enough to do just that and landed a gig on *The New York Daily Press*, a tabloid with a marginal regard for integrity and enough advertising revenue not to have to worry about it.

I'd stepped into something too good to be true for a know-nothing, inexperienced kid of twenty-four. All I had to do to sustain the gig was be reasonably competent at my job. Only problem was, I sucked big time at straight, honest reporting. So big that I couldn't hack it at a newspaper where hacking was the minimum daily requirement for collecting a paycheck. When it came to the concept of writing the facts and just the facts, I missed the point. I had a tendency to dress up a story, add a little pizzazz when I felt the facts were dragging down the truth. Even at the less than journalistically pure *Press*, making up the news, even selected bits and pieces of the news, was frowned upon. The city editor tried to get me to see the light, but I was young and a major butthead to boot and wouldn't see the error of my ways.

In short, I was fired.

But my nine months on the paper taught me two things. Number one, I really hated punching a time clock and working for a boss.

And number two, a few strategically placed contacts could alleviate the necessity of number one.

For reasons having more to do with a drunken office Christmas party encounter in a dark stairwell than any indication of real ability on my part, the *Press*'s gossip columnist, excuse me, *social* reporter Dayle Schuyler, took a liking to me. "Public relations, doll." She winked at me when I stopped by her office with my belongings in a box under my arm to inform her of my termination on my way out of the building. "I bet you'd simply shine at p. r. And besides," she said, leaning forward with elbows on her desk and breasts pressed between upper arms to show an abundance of middle-aged cleavage, "with a little help from your friends, you shouldn't have trouble placing items and impressing prospective clients."

Dayle winked again.

I took the hint. Dayle set me up with a couple of contacts and placed a batch of items in her column and the columns of her fellow gossipmongers. A rising lounge singer here. A struggling stand-up comedian there. An up-and-coming starlet. A corporate executive considering public office. A local TV talk show host looking to syndicate his program nationally. One by one, little by little, the client list grew. Not that I was getting rich, but I was making a living and, for a guy three years into a career in a risky profession, I figured I was doing reasonably okay. By working twenty, twenty-five hours a week tops, I was bringing home bacon enough to keep a roof over my head, pay my bills, and indulge in sufficient wine, women, and song to keep any young man happy.

That's about where I was at three months ago, on the night of my twenty-eighth birthday to be exact. I'd spent the evening with a group of friends in a Greenwich Village club, drinking a succession of toasts to my birthday, our health, one another, the bartender, our waitress . . . just about anybody or anything that moved. By 2 A.M. closing time when the party broke up, I was sauced beyond all reasonable expectations of remaining conscious. But you know how it is, the drunker you are, the deeper into denial you get, so I staggered off on my own to find a cab to take my snockered butt back home to Brooklyn thinking I was fine. Just fine.

I wasn't. I took a wrong turn somewhere and wound up in the warehouse district over by the West Side Highway. There's not a lot going on over there at that hour. Even the hookers and junkies who took over the area after dark had pretty much called it quits by then.

But not the muggers. At least not the three sleaze-buckets who came at me from an alleyway, oozing out from behind a parked truck cab, probably just lying in wait for a drunk like me to roll. I tripped to a halt as they blocked the sidewalk, too drunk to figure out what was happening right off.

"Give it up," one of them said to me, holding out his hand.

I smiled like the zonked-out goon I was and waited, swaying in the wind. "He's wasted," the second one said.

"Cool," said number three. "Makes it easy."

That's when I saw the baseball bat in the first guy's hand. The tire iron gripped by the second. Number three had a gun, and when he lifted his arm with the barrel sticking out of his fist and at my face, reality cut through my alcoholic haze: I was being held up.

Number one smiled a greasy, nasty smile and took a step towards me, hefting the bat like he was stepping up to the plate to bash out a homer. Only it was my head that was about to go flying over the center-field fence. I knew I was supposed to duck, but I couldn't move near fast enough as the bat whizzed past my head, cracking alongside my left temple and sending me to the pavement like a discarded paper cup. Number one laughed. He was enjoying himself something fierce, no doubt about that, but his buddy with the tire iron wanted to play too, and that cost me a busted rib and a bruise that took two weeks to heal.

In those couple of seconds between the first blow with the bat and number three aiming the gun at me again, I found instant sobriety and the realization I was about to die.

And that's when he came.

From the sky, like he'd jumped from the roof above to land be-tween me and the three thugs, only he came down as soft and as easy as a feather. He hadn't jumped. He *flew* down.

Flew freakin' down!

Okay, I figured I was seeing things, a whack to the head on top of about a dozen straight Stolis will do that. A guy, looking to be about nine feet tall from my vantage point close to the ground, wearing midnight blue spandex tights and a black leather tunic jacket with the collar turned up, boots and gloves, a black cowllike mask covering his face from the nose up, swooping down from the sky like a saving grace from heaven above.

The muggers took a step back from him, no more sure of what to make of this guy than was I. But he knew what he was doing; at least he gave the impression, and I was in no position to question anything he did in the next eight seconds.

The first second his hand shot out and closed around the gun.

Second two: the startled mugger pulled the trigger as the man in spandex squeezed. Even over the sharp retort of the firing gun, I heard the screech of bending, twisting metal, the crackle of breaking bone and the mugger's pained gasp as the costumed man crushed gun and flesh together.

Three: my savior pulled back his hand, fingers clenched into a fist, then snapped it around, backhanding the gun-wielding thug across the face. His head snapped around with the crack of more breaking bones.

Four: as the first man crumbled to the ground, the one with the bat started swinging on the masked man. His forearm swept up to block the Louisville slugger, which snapped like a twig against his arm.

Five: the man's fist shot out, straight as an arrow, into the bat guy's face, striking hard enough to send a spray of blood splattering from the point of impact. I later learned that the single blow shattered the mugger's skull like an eggshell. Meanwhile, the last mugger was in mid-swing with his tire iron for the back of the masked man's head.

Six: the tire iron *wrapped* around the man's head . . . *literally* wrapped around it, bending around his skull like a piece of flexible wire instead of a length of iron. The man grinned at that, amused by the mugger's sudden realization of fear. He reached up and snatched the bent iron from the other man's grasp.

In the final two seconds, he grabbed the last man before he could run away and, with one hand, wrapped the bent tire iron around the mugger's neck. And then twisted it, tight, like a twist tie around a Baggie. The mugger gasped and, eyes bulging, went down to his knees, fingers clawing desperately, futilely at the twisted loop of iron choking the life out of him.

But the costumed man was no longer interested in him. He turned to me and knelt down, smiling, dark eyes blazing through the eye-holes of his mask. "Are you all right, sir?" he asked, speaking for the first time since alighting to save me.

"Uhhh . . ." was the best I could manage for the moment.

Behind him, the last mugger gave out a final, horrible gurgle and toppled to the sidewalk.

My eyes went wide at that, and he looked back over his shoulder at the dead man. "He won't be bothering you anymore. None of them will ever victimize anyone again."

He really talked that way, like some pompous heroic figure out of a bad movie. Some counterpoint to his having just casually murdered three people in cold blood while I watched, huh? It was too much irony for me to deal with right then and there.

"I . . . uh . . . thanks . . . I guess," I stammered. I wasn't sure he was finished killing. Fact was, he was just getting started, but people like me were safe with him. He always chose his victims from a very select group of individuals: criminals.

"Just doing my job," he said modestly. "You appear to be in need of medical attention. I'll have the police send an ambulance."

I nodded, feeling a sharp twist of pain from where the bat had met my head, and realized I was bleeding. But even with the hurt in my head and ribs, I knew I had something here so, as he straightened up to leave, to fly away, I shouted, "Wait!"

He looked at me. "Yes?"

"Who are you? I . . . I mean, what should I call you?"

He smiled at that. "I don't know yet. I've been debating that question myself." He shrugged. "I mean, do you think I really *need* a name? Like Zorro, or the Scarlet Pimpernel?"

"Oh, yeah," I said. Was I really having this conversation? "People're gonna have to call you something."

He looked at me, thoughtful, for long seconds. "What's *your* name?"

"Weiser," I said. "Jack Weiser." I managed to pull myself into a sitting position, ignoring the pain in my side for the time being. I reached into my pocket and pulled out a business card.

He looked at it and smiled. "A publicist?"

I nodded.

"Then maybe you have a suggestion."

And then he lifted up into the sky, looking every bit like a movie special effect. Only there was no crane and wires to haul him skyward for the camera. He did it under his own steam.

He was really flying.

This guy was the ultimate human being. Ultimate man . . . *Ultima.* Had a nice ring to it. At least it sounded good to me at the time, when I told the cops what had happened. Of course, by then the

125

paramedics had given me something for the pain and I was well on my way to lightheaded.

But the name stuck. Ultima didn't seem to mind.

"I've always been different, as far back as I can recall. And before. There are family members who would tell how my mother bragged that I never cried, that I never needed to cry because she would always know what I needed, when I needed it, almost as soon as I myself knew it. The other mothers, she said, were always jealous of the close bond between us, almost as though we could read one another's minds.

"That wasn't quite true, although they were on the right track. While I can't provide you with a scientific explanation . . . there's so little anyone knows about these matters . . . suffice it to say I was born with certain psychic abilities. Powers of the mind. As an infant and child, these abilities manifested themselves in a very basic manner, creating a silent link between myself and my mother. She could, on some level, hear my needs as I had them, reading the thoughts that I was able to broadcast as some sort of primal reflex. No one else heard these thoughts.

"I can only assume that her ability to know what I was thinking came about through the natural bond between mother and child, that instinct through which a mother recognizes her child's cry and the child its mother's touch. In no other way have I ever exhibited any sort of telepathic ability.

"When I was old enough to move beyond that, when I was finally able to start articulating my needs, my abilities began manifesting themselves in other ways, as in my enhanced strength and speed, et cetera. They're all, so to speak, in my mind. You could run every conceivable physical examination you wished on me and detect nothing whatsoever different or unusual in my physiological makeup. Everything I do, I do with my mind.

"What do I remember about my mother?

"Not much. She died when I was three years old. Of a brain hemorrhage. Why do you ask?"

Ultima's premiere performance left me up to my armpits in trouble, sprawled bloodied and dazed in one of Manhattan's seedier neighborhoods with three brutally murdered corpses for company. Under the best of circumstances, the N.Y.P.D. hates setups like that, but add a story about a costumed flying perpetrator to the mix and they get downright ornery towards the idiot who tells the tale. Especially when his blood alcohol scores higher than his I.Q.

The cops couldn't decide whether to book me for murder, ship me over to Bellevue for observation, or just toss me into the deepest, darkest cell they had in the 10th precinct and leave me there until I was sober and could come up with a better story. I can't say I wasn't sympathetic; if I hadn't seen it happen myself, I would've doubted my own story. As it was, even while I was having my head sewn closed by a doctor in the emergency room of St. Vincent's, I figured I really should have been having it examined from the inside out instead.

A flying man. Killing blows. Solid iron bending around a human skull.

Yeah. Right.

The detective investigating the case was called out of the room to take a phone call in the middle of his interrogation, which was still taking place while the doc taped up my dinged ribs. Just my luck, I remember thinking; a few more bodies had probably been dropped on the pile and, since I already had those first three stiffs, I wouldn't mind a few more. But then Sgt. Jepson came back into the examination room, his previously ruddy complexion now as white as the bandages circling my ribs.

He started to speak, or at least he tried. All that came out at first was a series of unintelligible grunts and squeaks. He finally caught himself, cleared his throat, and said, "You can go when the doc's done with you, Mr. Weiser."

"I can?" That was news. A few minutes earlier, he was about ready to hang me, forget about gracing me with the "mister" in front of my surname. Now I was being told to split with all the respect due a sober, taxpaying citizen.

"Uh-huh. We got your statement." Jepson was distracted by whatever it was he'd been told on the phone. I had a feeling I knew what it was, that my story'd been somehow verified, otherwise no way in hell would he have let me walk out of there. But for my own peace of mind, I needed to hear it from him.

"Then I'm not a suspect?"

Jepson shook his head, chewing on the inside of his cheek and looking at me like I was from another planet. "Not even close."

"Don't think I'm looking a gift horse in the mouth, Sergeant, but why the change of heart?"

He didn't want to answer, probably because once he said it, he'd have to believe it, and that was out of the question. But I was asking, and he was better off practicing saying it to me than trying it out cold on his superiors. "Because, Mr. Weiser," he said, with just this side of a sigh, "of the two calls I just took. The first was the preliminary report from the forensic field investigators confirming a situation having taken place that pretty much matches your story."

"No kidding?"

"Why're *you* so surprised?"

I shrugged. "Relieved is more like it. So what else?"

"Your flying man . . . what'd you call him?"

"Ultima," I said.

"Yeah, him . . . you sure that's what he said his name is?"

"Well, no. He didn't exactly have a name, so when I asked what I should call him, he said I should come up with something."

Jepson stared at me. I shrugged and grinned a lot like the idiot I was feeling. "What can I tell you?"

The sergeant ran his hand through his disheveled black hair and shook his head. "Man, am I supposed to believe any of this? I don't care what that loon calls himself, okay? He's real . . . about half an hour after your run-in with him, he showed up on the FDR Drive and ran interference for some of our cars chasing down two perps in a high-speed pursuit."

"Did he . . . y'know . . . was he driving or did he, uhm . . . ?"

"Fly. The son of a bitch flew. We got half a dozen cops who eyeballed the whole thing. So, you're in the clear, Weiser. Put your shirt on, go home, and we'll be in touch if we need anything else from you."

He stalked out of the examining room without another word. I had to call one of my old pals on the *Press* to get the lowdown on Ultima's encore.

Two punks had jumped a guy as he was coming away from an automated teller machine, took his wallet, watch, and rings, shot him in the stomach, and then took off in his two-year-old Oldsmobile at something like sixty miles per hour. The first patrol car picked them up as they sped up York Avenue and tried to pull them over. That trick didn't work and the punks took their show onto the FDR at 63rd Street, where two more cop cars joined the chase. The Oldsmobile wasn't stopping for anything or anyone, at least not until Ultima flew in and landed smack-dab in front of it.

They were just going to run him down, leave him as a red smear on the pavement, but how were they supposed to know there was a real live superhero in town? The car hit him going better than eighty. It might as well have hit a brick wall.

The front end accordioned against Ultima and went from eighty to zero in that split-second. The punk doing the driving wound up with the steering wheel punching through his chest and died instantly. The other one wasn't so lucky. He went through the windshield and landed behind Ultima. The cops caught up with what was left of the Olds by then and they reported that Ultima was ready to leave at that point, but that the punk had kept hold of his gun even with his trip through the windshield and was still conscious and feeling hostile towards the guy who'd wrecked his brand-new car. He took a few shots at Ultima, hitting him, the two cops on the scene swore, at least twice before the masked man turned on him and kicked the gun from his hand. He was reaching for him by the time the cops had drawn their guns and used the punk for target practice. Scored a couple of bull's eyes, too. The punk died on the spot from the gunshot wounds.

The cops had absolutely no idea what to make of Ultima, so they kept their guns trained on him while they called for him to drop to the pavement. Ultima smiled at them, tossed off a salute in their direction, and then lifted up into the sky and flew away. The cops were way too stunned by that bit of business to do anything but watch him disappear into the dark of night.

There were three other fatal incidents involving Ultima that night with five more thieves and two rapists buying the big one at the hands of the world's first real superhero. There was also a major five-alarm fire in a Bronx tenement that he put in an appearance at, rescuing seven residents trapped by the flames. The firefighters and onlookers on the scene cheered him like he'd single-handedly won the World Series for the Mets. The next morning, pictures on the news programs and in the papers of Ultima rescuing a frightened three-year-old girl and her kitten from the burning tenement overshadowed the news of the eleven dead at his hands. He'd caught one hell of a break with that fire, that's for sure, but it must have made obvious to Ultima what I'd figured out within minutes of our first meeting:

He needed someone to handle p. r. for him something fierce!

"You know about the flying, of course. To tell the truth, I don't know exactly how I do that. It's not like I flap my arms or anything. I just think about flying and it happens, I take off. I don't know how fast I go, I've never actually clocked myself, although I once kept pace with a commercial airliner for several miles.

"I'm very strong. I can smash solid steel the way an ordinary man might crush a soda pop can. And you know about the time I battered my way through a concrete bunker wall to get to that kidnapped child. That took a bit of effort, though. The concrete was about a foot thick and I had to beat on it for a good minute or so.

"Which would have been quite painful, if I felt pain when I'm active. Well, no, actually, that's not quite right. I can feel pain, it just takes more than the usual things to get to me. Invulnerable? Not exactly, although when I'm being Ultima and sensitized to danger, I'm fairly close to it. Otherwise, I can stub my toe just like anybody else. Otherwise, bullets can't penetrate my skin, but they will leave bruises. Fortunately, I heal rather quickly, although I wouldn't like to have to go head-to-head with, say, a mortar shell.

"What else can I do? You've seen it, Jack. Sometimes, I don't know my own strength. What more do you need to know?"

After that first night, Ultima was all anyone talked about. The things he'd done had, prior to his appearance, been the stuff of big-budget movies, cheap TV shows, the comic books. Now it was real, page one, top of the program, Jay's/Dave's lead joke news. The talk shows quickly booked scientists denying the possibility of Ultima's existence or trying to explain how his powers worked. The Court TV cable channel hosted a roundtable of experts discussing the legality of his actions. The State's Attorney got busy looking into whether Ultima could be indicted even as the mayor's office tried to track him down to give him the key to the city. The Police Commissioner issued a loud "no comment" but quietly instructed his officers to bring Ultima in, not for questioning, of course, but for a discussion on his tactics and intentions. Mister Rogers went on PBS stations to tell kids not to be afraid of superheroes, they were your best pals in the neighborhood, and the Fox Network announced its desire to enter into negotiations with Ultima or his representatives for a brand-new series of cartoon adventures based on his life.

Ultima was hot.

He was hero, he was villain. He was an enigma, he was the answer to New York's prayers. He was a saint, he was a devil in leather and spandex.

He was a publicist's dream.

He was a million bucks waiting to be pocketed.

I made sure I got my name in the papers posthaste, again courtesy of my friend at the *Press*. The other New York papers and wire services picked up quick on the story of Ultima's first rescue and pretty soon I was looking frequently at my own face on the local and network news, talking the man up big time. Sliced bread? Penicillin? Open-heart surgery? Give me a break, all second-rate next to Ultima. I'd be humbled just to have the opportunity to thank him, in person, naturally. Just us, me and him, face to face.

So I could pitch a deal for my services, services he was going to need bad if his first night on the town was any indication of how things were going to be.

The next night, and the night following it, Ultima was just as busy as he'd been on the first one, appearing all over the city to rescue people from crime, disasters, and their own stupidity. Even people inclined to attribute the stories to a hoax or some bizarre mass hysterical reaction were starting to buy into Ultima's existence. People who felt they'd long ago had to abandon the streets of the city to the criminal element applauded his actions. Civil libertarians were aghast at the body count Ultima was toting up.

All I kept seeing was a business opportunity passing me by.

Then, on Ultima's fourth night, I got my wish when he showed up at my window.

At the time, I was living and working out of a third-floor apartment in a Park Slope, Brooklyn brownstone. It was close to midnight and I'd just turned off the television after taping my appearance on *Nightline* where Koppel and I had been discussing the rise of urban vigilantism. There was a tapping at my living-room window, which I assumed, since the fire escape was outside the bedroom window on the other side of the building, to be from a tree branch or a loose cable wire blown by the wind. But when I glanced towards the window, I saw a face.

Wearing a mask.

As much as I wanted to talk to Ultima, I assumed he'd pick up the phone and call me. Or show up at my front door. Sure as hell not at my freaking window at midnight, giving me what, at twenty-eight, I just knew was what a heart attack was going to feel like. With my heart still thumping like bongos in my chest, I unlatched and opened the window.

"I understand you wanted to speak to me, Mr. Weiser," he said. Oh, yeah. I should mention he was hovering outside the window, hanging suspended in mid-air. As often as I'd see him over the next few months, the flying was the hardest thing to get used to.

"Yeah," I stammered. "I did . . . I mean, I do. Uh . . . how'd you know where to find me?"

He held up the business card I'd given him three nights ago. "You gave me your address."

"Right." I nodded. I'd rehearsed what I wanted to say to him a hundred times over the last few days, but now, face to face, with him standing on nothing outside my window, I lost it. "Look, mister . . . eh, Ultima. Do you mind? I mean, the name? It was the best I could do on the spur of the moment."

"Actually, it's a bit much." He shrugged. "But it seems to have stuck. I can live with it."

"Great. Great," I said. Lame.

"Well, Mr. Weiser, if there's nothing else . . . ?"

"No!" I took a step forward, reaching towards him. "Don't go yet. I've got to talk to you, okay?"

"If you want to thank me, there's really no need. I don't do this for gratitude."

"Why *do* you do it?"

"Because," he said and smiled, "I can."

"Yeah, okay, that's all well and good, but I've got to tell you, man, you're . . . look, Ultima, you want to come inside? Take a load off your . . . your whatever you use to fly?"

He was still smiling as he floated in through my window and settled on the floor. I think my reaction, which was probably a whole lot like your average six-year-old seeing *Peter Pan* fly for the first time, amused the hell out of him.

"Now then, Mr. Weiser, what can I do for you?"

"Actually, it's what I can do for you, uh . . . Ultima." It sounded goony to call a grown man that, but I had nobody except myself to blame for it.

Ultima looked at me, waiting.

"Okay, look, you know I'm a publicist, right? The way I figure it, I'm just the kind of guy you need."

"That seems awfully, I don't know . . . commercial. I'm not an actor or politician."

"Right. You're a vigilante. A superhero, something no one's ever seen before," I said, talking fast. "Well, let me tell you, Ultima, you plan on being different, you need someone to put the right spin on that difference for you. You're different *and* people, even the bad guys, wind up, you know . . . well, dying because of what you do; you need to have the rest of the world told what you want it to be told before it draws its own conclusions."

He nodded and stroked his chin in thought.

I hurried on. "You see it happening already, right? Some of the press is starting to make noise about the cops getting you off the street."

"They can't," he said simply, stating a fact of life.

"You don't have to tell me, man. I've seen you in action, but whether or not they can isn't the issue. If the cops give in to the pressure and start getting in your face, it's going to make doing your job a hell of a lot tougher than it already is.

"But get public opinion cooking on *your* side, pal, and there's nothing the cops'll be able to do to you. If this whole killing-the-bad-guy thing grabs hold with the public and they become afraid of you, you're lost. But set yourself up as a hero, *their* hero, and you're golden."

"I only kill the ones who resist," he said. "If they cease their aggressive behavior and surrender, I have no reason to hurt them."

I nodded vigorously. "Exactly! And that's what we've got to play up for the public. Right now you're a mystery man, a spooky guy in a mask." I paused, uncomfortable about bringing up the subject but deciding, what the hell, it was going pretty good, let me go for broke. "Speaking of the mask, Ultima, the whole costume, in fact . . . it looks kind of thrown together. Makeshift, if you catch my drift."

Ultima caught it, looking down at the leather-and-spandex concoction he had on. "It is."

"We can do better. You know, brighter, friendlier. Then I'll need some good pictures of you wearing it. And video. Is it okay if I arrange an interview for you? Something high profile, Mike Wallace, Ted Koppel, like that? That way you only have to do one, two tops, to get the maximum exposure."

Ultima was starting to smile now, watching me as I paced the room, working up ideas, spitting them out as fast as they came to mind.

"Is that all?" he asked finally, when I had gotten around to the subject of him and the covers of the news weeklies.

I stopped cold. "You just humoring me?"

He shook his head. "No, actually, much of what you say makes sense, Mr. Weiser."

I smiled. "Call me Jack. What should I call you?"

"Ultima will do just fine, Jack."

"Right. Look, I don't care who you really are. I mean, that's your business. So, okay, I make sense. But . . . ?"

"But I think we should take it one step at a time. The costume, the pictures, those are fine. But I need to think about anything beyond that."

"Gotcha." I nodded. "This is new territory for both of us. Okay, let me get started with the costume. I know a designer who can help. I'll get some sketches done up and get back to you with them.

"Uhhh . . . *how* do I get back to you?"

"I'll be in touch with you," he said. "The same time and place tomorrow night all right with you?"

"That's another thing you might want to think about, Ultima. This whole night thing of yours? Makes you look like a stalker. Says vampire to me. Any chance of showing yourself during the day?"

"Well, perhaps on the weekend," he said, thoughtful.

I must have looked confused because he smiled again.

"I *work* during the day, Jack. I have to pay rent and eat, you know."

"I spent most of life hiding my abilities. I was, I think, afraid of what I could do because I didn't understand it. How could I? I was different, strange, some sort of bizarre mutation beyond understanding. I realized, of course, that I needn't have been afraid of anybody who might have had problems with the fact of my abilities. I was stronger, smarter, faster than anyone I knew, but that wasn't what I was afraid of. It was the mere fact of my difference. Children and teenagers want to fit in with their peers, not be singled out for being different. Certainly not for being some sort of freak.

"I was in college the first time I allowed myself to use any of my abilities in public. A girl and I were walking across campus late one night when two thugs jumped out at us from the bushes. I don't know what they wanted, whether it was my wallet or her . . . well, her. Either way, they meant one or both of us harm, so I didn't have any choice, really. I stopped them from hurting us, which meant hurting them instead, rather badly, I'm afraid. We left them there after I was done and never once did the girl imagine that I was anything other than a normal boy who reacted out of fear in a normal way. She went on about the effects of adrenaline on a person under stress, you see?

"She never once stopped to think that there was anything even remotely abnormal about me because she had no other expectations. There was no such thing as a 'superhuman' in her, or anyone else's, realm of expectation, so it never occurred to her to believe I was out of the ordinary.

"I was the only one who knew I was different, so I was the only one who would have known what to look for.

"After that, I realized that I could relax some. If no one was looking

135

for a superman, no one would know what one looked like or how one acted.

"It's only lately that I've ruined that for myself. Now I've got to be careful in my . . . well, in my secret identity. Lord, does that sound as ridiculously pretentious as I think it does?"

That's how Ultima, the super human, became my client.

I had my costume designer friend whip up some sketches, but nothing really clicked. Everything he did came out looking like a Broadway version of a superhero by way of Liberace. In desperation, I hoofed it over to the local comic-book store on Seventh Avenue and asked around for an aspiring comic-book artist looking to make a quick few bucks. There was an eighteen-year-old with a sketchpad browsing through the latest releases who was happy to oblige and, ten minutes later, in exchange for fifty bucks and a hastily scrawled signed release relinquishing any future claims to the costume, I left the store with what I needed.

In between doing what he did—I hadn't yet started to force myself to use superhero jargon, like "crimefighting duties" and "nightly patrol" that I would adopt for public statements—Ultima stopped by my window that night and approved the design and left me with his measurements. Bright and early the next morning I was at a tailor shop picking out fabrics and promising the world to the old man if he would deliver the finished product in forty-eight hours.

Meanwhile, Ultima continued to dominate the news and public mind of the city and the country. He was out there every night, stopping crimes, rescuing damsels and dudes in distress, and mounting an awesome death toll. For the most part, he remained true to his word, didn't often inflict more damage than was necessary to subdue a felon. If they resisted, even in the slightest, they were dead men, but if they stopped, dropped their weapons, and hit the ground in surrender, they'd live to be led away in handcuffs instead of riding an ambulance in a body bag. That's not to say he didn't occasionally get carried away or fail to pull a punch in time, but in the heat of those tense moments, most happening faster than victim or surviving perpetrator could follow, it was hard to really pin anything on him.

I called a press conference for the Saturday morning after Ultima's costume was ready. I got a lot of skepticism from the assignment editors I contacted, and the turnout was piss-poor considering what I was promising, but that would be the last time one of my announcements was ignored—because from that day on, I was the man who could not only promise but actually *deliver* Ultima.

Pretty cool, huh?

The conference was for noon, on the open Long Meadow in Brooklyn's Prospect Park, leaving Ultima plenty of room for a dramatic entrance.

A dozen print journalists, two camera crews from local stations, and one radio reporter were all we drew to the lush, green lawn. I welcomed them, thanked them for coming, spoke a few words about how the world of fantasy had finally met up with real life with an honest-to-god superhuman who'd come to take on the bad guys for those of us who couldn't fight back on our own. Ladies and gentlemen . . .

Ultima!

He came floating down from the sky, resplendent in his new duds. Camcorders whirred, still cameras clicked like locusts on autowinders, and everybody gasped at the sight of Ultima, clad head to toe in a yellow, formfitting bodysuit, his mask leaving his eyes and the lower half of his face exposed. Black leather gloves and boots covered his hands and feet, a waist-length black leather jacket was buttoned at the waist, and on his chest the *pièce de rèsistance*, a stylized black "U" set against a diamond-shaped field of crimson.

They gasped. They gaped. I think the radio reporter wet himself. I was loving every second of it.

Ultima landed beside me, gentle as a leaf, smiling at the reporters like everybody's best friend. They didn't wait for his feet to touch the ground before they started shouting questions at him.

I managed to get their attention long enough to say that Ultima wouldn't be taking any questions himself but that I, as his representative, would be happy to help them. Who was Ultima? Where did he come from? Why was he doing this? Was he working with the police? On and on and on, talking to me but keeping their cameras on Ultima, who stood with arms folded heroically across his chest, smiling but staying mute like I'd instructed.

We gave the press fifteen minutes and then Ultima waved farewell, thanked them for coming, and lifted off into the sky, more shouted questions trailing after him. It took me another half-hour to finish the reporters off and send them on their way to file stories to their hearts' content. It couldn't have gone any better and I couldn't have been more up, and seeing police detective Sgt. Jepson lounging at the entrance to the park I was leaving through, smoking a cigarette, didn't darken my mood.

"Yo, Sergeant." I smiled. "Should've come to the press conference. I could've introduced you to Ultima."

"That's okay, Mr. Weiser," he said, grinding the half-smoked cigarette under the toe of his scuffed shoe. "I don't have to meet him. Something tells me we don't have a whole hell of a lot in common anyway."

"You sure? He's a nice guy."

Jepson looked at me through narrowed eyes. He wasn't a happy camper. "He's a murderer, Mr. Weiser."

I shook my head and wagged a finger in his direction. "Correction. He's a hero."

"Working ahead of a string of corpses isn't my idea of a hero."

"To each his own, Sergeant. Was there something you wanted from me?"

"Nothing official," Jepson said, then turned his eyes to scan the sky above. "Look, Weiser, you see this Ultima goon as a meal ticket, but I don't think you know exactly what it is you've latched onto. In six nights, he's killed forty-seven people . . ."

"Any innocent bystanders in there?"

"No," he said. "All of them were in the process of committing one felony or another. But that's not the point, at least not the way I see it. This guy's set himself up as judge, jury, and executioner for the criminal element, all on his own volition. Hell, I'm an employee of the city and I don't have that sort of authority, so who appointed him?"

"If he's done something wrong, why didn't you bust him when you had the chance?"

Jepson gave a sour little laugh. "Right, like he's gonna come along peacefully just because we ask nice."

"Not to mention that you guys"—I smirked—"wouldn't want to look bad by getting your asses kicked by Ultima in front of the press."

"What would be the point? The D.A.'s looking into pressing charges, but there's no paper out on him yet and until there is, we don't have anything *official* to bring him in for, forcibly or otherwise."

"Then why the visit, Sergeant?"

"Doesn't mean we wouldn't like to talk to him, unofficially, if he'd come in on his own."

"Just to talk?"

Jepson shrugged. "The department wouldn't mind knowing what his intentions are."

"Not that we've discussed this or anything, but Ultima doesn't seem to have any interest in talking with you guys."

"He's gonna have to, sooner or later."

I laughed. "I've got to tell you, Sergeant, from what I've seen, that man doesn't have to do anything he doesn't want to do."

Jepson pulled a pack of cigarettes from his shirt pocket and started to shake one loose. "Sooner or later," he said, "we all wind up doing things we don't want."

For a cop, he knew a good exit line when he spoke it. He walked towards his car, parked at the curb. I guess I was supposed to stop and think about what he'd said, feel remorse for consorting with a monster like Ultima.

Guess again.

"Why now? I've spent my entire life up until now just like everybody else. I often thought that I should somehow capitalize on my powers. I mean, why work so hard when I had these abilities that could earn me a small fortune with minimal effort?

"But it shouldn't work that way. At least, I don't believe it should. Obviously, if I was given these powers, it was for a reason. God doesn't hand out such gifts for no reason.

"That sounds pompous, I suppose. I know I'm not the most easygoing man in the world, but I can't help being who I am, the way I am. I never asked to be some sort of superman, but I've tried to live with it the best I

can. Just knowing what I was capable of shaped me into the man I am today.

"Do you believe in destiny? I know I do. I suppose I have to, all things considered.

"I'm sorry, Jack. What was the question?"

The next month was a nonstop blur. Ultima was everywhere, including the cover of *Newsweek*, which, I think, impressed him, but he played things too close to the vest for me to be sure. But it didn't matter, not with the way things were going. Ultima kept fragging bad guys, the cops kept trying to find a reason to go after him, but a public opinion poll in that same issue of *Newsweek* indicated that some sixty-seven percent of those polled agreed with Ultima's methods. People were fed up with surrendering their streets to crime, sick of the legalities that kept the cops from landing on criminals with both feet, tired of a judiciary with its system of revolving-door justice that put murderers and rapists back on the streets as fast as the cops could pick them up.

People were afraid, and Ultima offered relief from the fear.

Any authority looking to prevent Ultima from doing that risked, at best, having public opinion turn against them or a reelection yanked out from under them and, at worst, a lynching.

Besides, Ultima was having an effect on New York. The crime rate, in general, was plummeting as the bad guys decided to back off rather than chance an encounter with him. Those who didn't stop were taking a twofold risk, of having their heads handed them by Ultima, or of being attacked by a mob of citizens inspired by the hero's example. All of a sudden New York, that cesspool with stoplights, had declared war against criminals, and nobody was taking prisoners.

The city was becoming an inspiration to the country, and Ultima was poster child for the revolution.

Ultima never personally paid me a cent for the work I did for him, but our relationship was profitable nonetheless. New clients came knocking at my door, leaving me with hefty retainers and their reputations to mold. Licensing concerns arrived with hats in hands, seeking to buy the rights to slap Ultima's face on everything from lunchboxes to video games, to create action figures in his likeness, to sell replicas of his costume, to share fictionalized versions of his adventures with the public via cartoons, comics, movies, and books. Ultima himself had a short attention span when it came to dealing with the business end of his life. In fact, he wanted nothing what-soever to do with it. Seeing as how I was the one selling his repu-tation to the public, making them forget the methods he used to achieve what he did for them, he left these matters in my hands. I told him the exposure was good for him, that while his actions spoke for themselves, the creation of an Ultima mythos by way of licensing bits and pieces of himself made him appear friendlier and infinitely less threatening. Familiarity would breed comfort.

Except for agreeing to talk to me for the book about him, Ultima didn't care, just as long as he was allowed to get on with his work. He trusted me to handle these things—and the money they brought flooding in—for him.

Naturally, I did that on the up and up. The last thing I wanted or needed was to have Ultima pissed at me, not because I was afraid he'd hurt me but because I didn't want him taking his business else-where. I set up a concern, the Ultima Fund, to handle things. Of course, as chief operating officer of the fund, I drew a nice salary for my efforts, but the bulk of the money went, at Ultima's insistence, into a charitable trust to help the homeless and disadvantaged. For both moral and tax reasons, Ultima refused to take a cent from any deal. He didn't want to even *appear* to be profiting from his powers and the suffering of others. Besides, if he took the money—even though it would have allowed him to quit whatever day job he held and spend more time being a superhero—he'd have to file a tax return, which he couldn't do without revealing his real name. The way the bucks were coming in, we could have supported him in a lifestyle of his choosing by hiding the money going to him in petty cash, but he'd have none of those financial shenanigans.

So, okay, he was too goody-goody to be believed, but it worked for him and didn't hurt me any either. I was getting mine and getting it without compromising my heartfelt lifelong quest to maintain a minimum workload for maximum profit.

Could it have been any better?

Okay, possibly. Most everybody I knew from the days prior to my becoming rich and famous had suddenly decided that I had, in one way or another, become a moral and philosophical monster. Go figure, right?

Dayle Schuyler was the first to articulate this when I ran into her late one evening at Elaine's. I was with a prospective client and her entourage, so when I saw Dayle sitting with her escort—some young, up-and-coming singing Broadway stud—when we came in, all I could do was wave and keep moving. It was almost an hour before I could get away from my client to drift past Dayle's table and say hello.

Dayle was clearly not overjoyed to see me, her greeting colder than I might have expected even taking into consideration her being with a new beau.

"Smile, Dayle." I grinned. "I'm one of the people you like, remember?"

"Mmm, yeah," she said, patting the stud-boy's hand. *Him* she gave the smile while she asked him to be a dear and make himself scarce for a few minutes. He gave me a dirty look as well as he headed off to the bathroom to check his coiffure or oil his vocal cords.

"What's with him?" I asked, leaning over to kiss her cheek. "Don't tell me he's jealous."

"Remo doesn't know who you are, Jack," she said.

"You're acting like you don't either, Dayle. I do something wrong?"

"Just about everything."

I leaned back. I stared at her. I held up my hands in a gesture of helplessness. "Do tell."

"Think Ultima," she said. She hadn't called me "Doll" once yet, which meant I was in deep shit with her.

"What? You want an interview, some insider stuff for your column, you know all you've gotta do is ask, Dayle. There's no reason to cop an attitude with me."

She sighed and rolled her eyes. Along with the missing "Doll," she'd also failed to flash her décolletage for my erotic edification, and any time Dayle didn't show cleavage to an admirer such as myself was a bad time indeed. "Buy a clue, Jack," she said, throwing an angry hiss into even those nonsibilant words. "How in the world can you act as the public mouthpiece for that . . . that monster?!"

I was stunned. I showed her my stunned face. "Hey, p. r.'s what I do, Dayle. What *you* told me I should be doing."

"I never said anything about representing murderers. Actors, politicians . . . even talk-show hosts, but not mass murderers. There's got to be a limit."

"You're kidding, right? Ultima's one of the good guys. The only people who get hurt are the bad guys."

"If I don't believe in state-sanctioned capital punishment, I'm certainly not about to condone some lunatic in a costume taking it on his own shoulders without benefit of a trial and a jury verdict."

"Oh, come on, isn't that just a touch bleeding heart?"

"What if it 'is? That doesn't change what's happening. That doesn't make the, what . . . over one hundred by now? . . . people he's killed any less dead."

"That's up to the cops to decide, isn't it? I mean, if Ultima's wrong, they'd've come down on him by now."

"Get out, Jack," she warned. "Get away from that homicidal maniac while you still can. The cops are just waiting for their opportunity. He's just a sleazy murderer with good p. r. thanks to you. Bet once you finally come to your senses and wise up, that will make you feel just so pumped up with pride."

I tried to laugh it off, but Dayle wasn't joking, Remo had returned from the john, and I had a client waiting for me. I told Dayle I'd see her later and was heading away when she called after me. I stopped, looked back, and waited around long enough to hear her say, "Be careful, will you, Doll?"

"Still . . . it's difficult sometimes. I never asked for any of this, no matter why it came my way. I have all this power, so I'm forced to use it in the pursuit of good. Yet, what is good? Should I be using it to find ways to shelter the homeless? To feed the hungry? To save the environment? Or to do as I've decided to do and reclaim the cities for its people?

"I do what I must. Who would do any less in my place?

"Well, yes, certainly there are those who would take advantage

143

for personal gain. But I won't take any manner of remuneration for my efforts. I think it would be wrong. Wrong. Even if I have given my life over to this.

"Would I have done anything different, knowing what I know now after doing it all this time?

"The killing . . . perhaps I would have learned to better control my strength. I can do just about anything I can conceive except . . . except pull my punches enough to keep from killing anyone I strike in anger. And it's so very hard not to be angered when I come upon someone abusing someone else. Human beings live inside such thin shells.

"They're so damned frail . . ."

"This," Steve Gilman said, "is totally bogus." He flipped the prototype of an Ultima action figure back onto my desk with a gesture of disgust.

"What's the matter with it?" Bernie French asked, reaching for it from among the litter of similar items there. We were in my apartment, my *new* apartment on Fifth Avenue, in the den where I had been going through some proposed licensed material when they'd been the first to arrive for the apartment's inaugural poker game. I'd given them the grand tour, finishing off with the grand floor-to-ceiling window view of Central Park spread out below, beyond the apartment's wraparound terrace. They did the appropriate oohing and aahing over the view, but what caught their attention were the toys.

Steve made a face and shrugged. "I don't know, man. All the stuff Ultima's done for New York, for our boy here," he said, pointing at me, "I think it kinda sucks ripping him off with shit like that."

Bernie laughed and flew the Ultima figure past Steve's face with a loud whooshing sound.

"It's cool with Ultima," I said. "He's authorized me to cut these deals for him."

"That's what I mean. It's like, he's a hero . . . even if he's okay with this, I don't know if he *gets* it, you know? I mean, he's busy being a hero, he hasn't got time to really think this stuff through. But it, I don't know . . . it cheapens him. Ultima dolls. Ultima un-

144

derwear." Steve looked at me, deadly serious. "It's disrespectful, Jack."

Bernie punched him on the shoulder and laughed. "It's *what?*"

"You heard me," Steve said. I think he was embarrassed to cop to this kind of hero-worship. It was one thing admitting you thought some hyperthyroid basketball player was cool, but you'd never think twice about buying a T-shirt with his face slapped on its front.

"You're nuts, pal," Bernie said.

"Yeah. Besides, man," I said to Steve, holding up an Ultima beach towel, "there's something deeper than respect at work here."

"Paying the rent on this joint," Bernie jumped in with and started howling with laughter.

I smiled, tapped the tip of my nose, and then pointed at Bernie. "Bingo!"

Peer pressure caught Steve square in the chest and he backed down, but he still wasn't happy with what was happening to Ultima. He just wasn't unhappy enough to risk further ridicule over it. It was his problem anyway. Ultima and I were okay with it, so the last thing I needed to hear was whining about a perfectly acceptable business practice.

Especially one I was cleaning up with.

". . . I don't know where I expected this to lead, Jack. I thought, when I started, that it was the right thing to do. I'm still not sure that it can't be right. But for someone else. I don't think I can go on the way I've been going.

"Why?

"I'm seeing them all the time now. In the street, at work, on television. And, worst of all, in my dreams. Maybe it's because I'm not sleeping as well as I should these days. At first, I thought it was because of all I had to do. Working during the day, prowling the city as Ultima most of the night. But that isn't it. It's not that I haven't time to sleep, it's that I can't. I think I'm afraid to, because of what I might see.

"I can't forget them no matter how hard I try. I know that they're bad, that they're harmful parasites. When it's a matter of their lives versus the lives of their victims, there shouldn't be a question. There

isn't . . . *but I have to ask whether I'm the one to continue making the choice, night after night, time and again.*

"Who's 'them'? The victims. My victims. All two hundred and six of them. I know every one of their faces, every one of their names. I can tell you where each and every one of them died and how I killed them. You're surprised I would keep count?

"I'm surprised you don't . . ."

Today . . .

Ultima was waiting for me when I got home, standing in the cold dark of night on my terrace. I walked into my den and switched on the light, jumping in surprise when I glanced out the window and saw the figure silhouetted against the glow of the city's lights. He would have waited out there all night rather than bust the flimsy lock on the terrace door to come inside. Hell, even if it was unlocked, he wouldn't come inside without an invitation.

A Boy Scout. Skeptics and Ultima's detractors thought it had to be an act, but it was the real him, through and through.

I flipped the latch and slid open the door, speaking his name.

"Hello, Jack," he said without turning around. "I hope this isn't inconvenient for you."

"No, no problem," I said. "I told you, Ultima, you're always welcome here."

"That's good," he said softly. "It's nice to know there's someplace I'm welcome."

"Are you nuts?" I laughed. "You can go anywhere in this city you want."

"Yes, but will I be welcome," he asked, starting to turn from the terrace railing, "or will people just be too afraid of me to turn me away?"

He didn't sound right. I suppose I'd been catching hints of this tone in his voice over the last few interview sessions for the book, but I'd chalked it up to his being tired. The man worked hard at what he did; it's no surprise there would be times he'd be at an ebb. It had to come with the territory. But this was a whole other sound, beyond tired, well on the way to bone tired.

"Is something wrong, Ultima?"

He shoved his hands in his jacket pockets as he walked towards me, his eyes holding mine, then past me, into the apartment.

"I guess you could say that." He was behind me now. "Don't you think there's anything wrong, Jack?"

I turned and saw him, standing beside my desk, eyeing more merchandise bearing his likeness or distinctive "U" logo. "Nothing I know of. The city's safe and sound, business is booming, everything's right with the world."

Ultima didn't respond, still looking at the toys, but with nothing on his face to tell me what he was thinking.

Finally, he said, "I stopped an armored car robbery out at Kennedy Airport this evening."

That wasn't like him, bragging on his exploits. Usually it was like pulling teeth to get him talking. "Yeah?"

"Eight men," he said, his voice getting lower, low enough that I had to strain to hear him over the sounds of traffic filtering up from the streets thirty stories below. "Two of them ambushed the guard on duty at the armored car company's hangar, bypassed the security system, and let the rest of the hijackers inside.

"It took them only a few minutes to fan out through the building and overpower the company's personnel, armed and otherwise. Three guards were shot dead resisting them. Then they consolidated the contents of several armored cars into one and took off in it. One of the men they shot was able to trigger an alarm before he died. I happened to be passing the airport when I saw the police converging on the hangar, mere moments after the stolen car had fled. I remembered having seen one of the company's cars speeding onto the highway from the airport as I was flying by overhead. On a hunch, I turned around and went after the car.

"I caught up with it on the Van Wyck. The driver was keeping to the speed limit in order to avoid suspicion, but as soon as I flew across their bow in an attempt to get them to stop, he hit the gas. I stayed right with them, trying to get them to stop. To do it the easy way. But they opened fire on me through the car's gun ports. I had no choice. They *left* me no choice.

"They cut across three lanes of traffic in an attempt to get off the highway at the next exit. I thought that was for the best. It was late, but there's usually a lot of traffic because of the airport. I certainly didn't want to risk innocent bystanders being caught in the crossfire or hurt in a traffic accident.

"Once off the highway, I was free to deal with them. There was roadwork being done on the highway, and the construction crew had left equipment on the shoulder. I used a temporary concrete road divider to block their way. They tried to go around it, but when they saw there wasn't enough room to make it, the driver hit the brakes, but not soon enough. The armored car hit the edge of the divider and flipped over onto its side."

Ultima paused, taking a deep breath, almost as though he were trying to maintain his composure. "They kept shooting at me through the gun ports, and I suppose that must have angered me, because the next thing I knew, I was standing on the side of the car, ripping the side door of the rear compartment from its hinges with my bare hands. Then I was reaching inside, where six of the hijackers were huddled. I . . ."

He paused for another deep breath and continued. "I don't re-member exactly what happened, who I got to first, but . . ."

Ultima's hands came out of his pockets and he held them up for me to see. His gloves were off, his hands covered with dried, dark splotches of blood. He just stared at those bloodied hands for the longest time, almost as though he'd never seen them before, like somebody else's hands had somehow found their way to the ends of his arms.

"I killed them," he whispered. "All eight of them, numbers two-twelve through two-nineteen."

Just listening to his voice chilled me, made my mouth go dry.

"The first two went easy, and then the rest tried to surrender. They knew who I was, what I did. They knew better than to resist me, but I couldn't stop. I didn't *want* to stop. Other men live ordinary lives, don't spend their nights riding the skies, seeking to commit murder. I could have elected to do the same, I suppose. No law demanded I don this costume and do what I do, but I believed in a higher calling. What's the saying? With great power comes great responsibility? I believed that."

I knew what was coming, what he was going to say, but I was afraid to speak.

"But that's not entirely true," he said, looking up from his bloodied hands with eyes sadder than any I'd ever seen. "Power itself isn't enough. It takes a wiser man than I to command it, to control it as it must be if it's to be a benefit rather than a curse. I guess I believed the ends justified the means, and for a while I suppose I had fooled myself that was enough. But with all the deaths . . . how can I continue with the charade?

"Especially after tonight. I was so angry with the hijackers . . . no, it wasn't just them. It would have been whoever I happened to come across tonight, because any criminal would have been all criminals at that moment, one of the breed which *forced* me to become Ultima . . .

". . . A killer."

"Ultima," I said, slowly, carefully. "I think you're overreacting. I mean, you've been under a lot of pressure, you're not getting enough sleep, you said so yourself. Maybe all you need is some rest or . . ."

"I don't think you understand, Jack," he said, smiling sadly. "It's finished."

I pretended I didn't get it, but Ultima wasn't in a pretend mood. His reality was too painful for him to ignore, and when I tried telling him otherwise, using the word "hero" in the process, he shook his head violently. "I'm not a hero," he insisted. "I'm just a man with far too much blood on his hands to consider himself anything but a murderer."

We argued the matter for the next hour. I insisted what he'd done for the city far outweighed the lives he'd taken, that the people who died chose the life that led to their deaths at his hands. But that no longer mattered to Ultima, not with the ghosts of all those dead haunting him.

He picked up a bright yellow Ultima Halloween costume from my desk and closed his fist around it. "You've never killed anyone, Jack," he said, as though my clean hands explained everything.

"No, I haven't," I said, feeling my anger grow. "But I learned this much from you, Ultima . . . threaten my life, and I'd kill without hesitation."

149

"Easier said than done," he said and let the cheap imitation of his costume, now stained with the blood from his hand, drop to the desktop. "I flew around for a week before I showed myself that first time, the night I rescued you, afraid to jump in because I wasn't sure I could do what was needed. Afterwards, I became afraid when I saw how easily I did it."

"So what're you saying, Ultima?"

"I said it. I'm finished. I'm going to tell the world that what I've done was wrong, just as wrong and as corrupt as the deeds of those I killed. I can't stand the thought of anyone continuing to believe me some sort of heroic ideal. I have to impress on them that I know I was wrong. Then"—he shrugged—"Ultima will simply cease to operate and disappear forever and I'll try to put it all behind me."

Ultima smiled at me. "I know how disappointing this must be for you, Jack. In your own way, I know you believed in what I was doing. And I want to thank you for that."

"A lot of people believe in you," I said, moving around behind my desk, grabbing at the merchandise piled there to show him. "Look at all this! It's not just toys and gimmicks . . . people want to own things with your name on it because you *mean* something to them."

"Then they had better pick a more meaningful icon. I'm sorry, Jack, but I've made my decision." He was at the door now, stepping out onto the terrace. Ultima smiled back at me, the tension out of his face for the first time since he'd gotten here. "Thank you, Jack. It's been a pleasure knowing you, my friend."

And then he lifted off into the night.

Son of a bitch! My meal ticket was literally flying out the window, and there was nothing I could do to stop him. He'd tell the world that he was a murderer, not worthy of their adoration.

Or their merchandising dollars.

And in that split-second, three things popped into my mind. The first was something Ultima had said during one of our interviews for the book. I'd asked if he was invulnerable and he had said that when he was expecting danger, he was "fairly close to it. Otherwise, I can stub my toe just like anybody else."

The second was what I had said just minutes ago, that I would kill in an instant if my life was threatened.

And the third, that I had a gun in my desk drawer, one I'd picked up not long after I had been mugged. Sure, Ultima had saved my life that time, but I couldn't count on his always being there in case of trouble. There'd been a half-dozen street corners within spitting distance of my old place in Brooklyn where handguns could be had for the right amount of cash, so I invested in the concept of better safe than sorry.

I pulled open the drawer, my hand closed around the handle of the gun, and as fast as it takes to tell, I was on the terrace, looking at Ultima's back as he lifted off into the night. I steadied myself and took aim.

"Ultima," I called out at the top of my lungs.

He hesitated in mid-air and, hovering not a half-dozen yards before and above me, he turned.

I fired twice.

I was counting on Ultima not expecting an attack from a friend, not being on his guard, with his powers at rest. If he could stub his toe just like anybody else, he could also die like anyone else.

He jerked, his eyes going wide with pain and surprise. I couldn't say where I hit him, but I'd aimed for the crimson emblem on his chest, and he clutched himself there in the instant he remained suspended overhead. Then, as though the string that had been holding him aloft had been suddenly severed, he tumbled head over heels from the sky.

Ultima's eyes held mine for that instant before he fell, but I turned my head away, not wanting to see what was in them. Pain? Betrayal? Forgiveness?

It didn't matter. The deed was done, and I could live with it. I'd acted in self-defense, to preserve my life.

I had to call the cops, of course. Tell them about the two men who had ambushed me on my way into the apartment, robbed me of cash and jewelry at gunpoint, then shot Ultima when he was coming in for a landing on my terrace, expecting to find only me, his friend, before they escaped with my property. I had Ultima's own words on tape to explain how their guns, catching him unawares, could kill him. Their masked faces made it impossible for me to ever identify them.

151

I practiced going over my story a few times while I hastily gathered and dumped my wallet and as much jewelry as I could find down the incinerator, along with the gun, which I made sure was clean of fingerprints. Just in case.

Of course, even if the police ever do find the gun, I don't expect them to suspect me, but to believe it the work of killers getting rid of a murder weapon. I had the perfect alibi, didn't I? Ultima, the living superhero, was making me a rich man.

But I knew the public mind better than they did.

I knew a dead martyr was worth as much, probably more than, a living superhero.

Super Acorns

Mike Resnick and
Lawrence Schimel

Even super acorns don't fall far from the tree.

"As the oak grows, so shall the acorn."

Dear Ma:

Yes, I know I haven't written in a couple of weeks, and that I promised to write you every day, and yes, I'm getting my greens. And it's my cholesterol count you're worried about, not my chlorophyl count. Trust me on that; I'm a doctor, remember?

Anyway, I haven't written because I'm tired. (No, don't send any chicken soup; the last time you did, it leaked through the package and stained my copy of *Playboy* in a very delicate place.) And I'm tired because I went into pediatrics instead of something restful like geriatrics. I mean, I could really get into sitting around watching a bunch of old codgers give up the ghost.

Uh . . . I didn't mean that quite the way it sounded, Ma. Besides, you'll be shopping up a storm long after I'm in the grave, which could be the middle of next week the way things are going.

Pediatrics isn't exactly what I expected it to be. At least, not *my* practice. For example . . .

153

Whoops—another Code Four Emergency. Gotta run. I'll write again later. If I can keep awake.

Love,
Harvey

Dear Ma:

Yes, I'm remembering to floss after each meal. Honest.

Anyway, the crisis is over. For the time being. I put Valium in all their formulas, so I ought to be able to finish this letter before the next emergency.

In answer to the question in your last letter, I can't call from work because we've only got two phones here, and I'm not allowed to use them even for a medical consultation. The green phone is for when a superhero needs an ambulance, and the red phone is a direct line to the White House.

You know, when I got the highest grades in med school, I figured I was going to get a plum job, and truth to tell, when I first was approached for this one, I jumped at it. I should have stopped to figure out why the guy who was leaving for duty in Mozambique looked so damned happy. You remember how you used to spank me and then make me stand in a corner when you caught me playing doctor with little Doris Mishkin who lived upstairs? I felt very lonely and isolated, like everyone in the world was against me (except maybe Doris). I hadn't felt that way again, until I took this fershlugginer job.

You figure at least the superheroes would appreciate us, maybe even feel a little gratitude to us for saving their lives, but the truth of the matter is they hate us for seeing how vulnerable they can be, for seeing the man or woman beneath those crazy colored pajamas. Is it *our* fault that they come in here with only half a blood-soaked costume left?

Of course, I don't have to deal with that very often. What I *do* get to deal with are all the parents who hate me because I know they're more afraid of their children than of going up against supervillains. (You wouldn't believe how hard it is to make them come and pick up their children sometimes. They think that because they

154

pay for this place with their private funding they can use it as a day-care center.)

Damn! Gotta run again. I forgot that Valium doesn't work on the plastic kid.

Love,
Harvey

Dear Ma:

Yes, I thanked Aunt Sophie for the sweater.

Today I had to help out in obstetrics. All the nurses quit in the middle of a delivery, and there was another woman in labor waiting her turn. They needed someone to assist, so who do they call on? Me.

The delivery room is split down the middle by a curtain, and as I get there, some guys from Maintenance are leaving the far half of the room, and they're furious. Seems the doctor broke two of their diamond-tooth saws and their best laser drill. The Platinum Woman is giving birth, and as best I can determine, they couldn't get her to dilate enough, no matter how much oil they tried to use as lube, and had to do a C-section.

When the other doctor sees me, he nods and says, "Take care of the woman in the next room, will you?"

So I go next door and introduce myself to the woman, and all that. We go through the whole procedure, and everything is going wonderfully except that there's no baby. Like it was a placebo birth or something. She's pushing and grunting and everything, just no baby.

When it seems like half past forever, I tell her to try to put a little more effort in it. She tells me to go to hell and that the baby is already out.

Well, damn it all, nobody told me it was going to be an invisible baby!

So I pick the thing up, and carry it to the other room as best I can under the circumstances, and hold it up in front of the other doctor. He's got a huge mask on, with a visor, and sparks are flying everywhere. There's a large arc welder set up next to the bed, and he's welding the Platinum Woman's abdomen shut. It doesn't look

155

very sanitary, but I decide that now is perhaps not a good time to mention it.

"What do you want?" he yells at me over the noise from the machine. "Can't you see that I'm busy?"

"The baby's out," I shout back.

"So what do you want?" he shouts back. "A medal? Go cut the umbilical cord and tie a knot."

While I'm wondering how to explain to him that the baby's invisible and I can't *see* the goddamned cord, he yells at me, "Here, take this!" and tosses me a pair of shears that are really mangled and notched. "Give them back to Maintenance when you're done," he adds, and turns back to his welding.

Great, I think as I go back to my delivery room, now I have to take the blame with Maintenance, too. They're all against me here, Ma; it must be latent anti-Semitism.

Anyway, I've still got this invisible baby to take care of. I take a good look at it, or where I think it is, and try to figure out how I'm going to do this. By feeling along its body with one hand, and holding the scissors in the other, I find the umbilical cord. For a minute I worry about the malpractice suit they can launch against me, but then I realize there's no way they can produce the evidence, unless the kid learns how to turn *un*-invisible when he grows older. If it *is* a he, in the first place, which I really hope it isn't. It's one thing to have to deal with cutting an invisible umbilical cord, but if it's a boy, he'll never survive the *bris*.

Then, just as I'm about to actually go through with cutting the cord, the alarm goes off in Room 14.

Have I told you about my ward, Ma? I get all the problem kids, and Room 14's got Pyroman's bouncing baby boy. The kid's got a problem that's not totally unlike, say, bed-wetting, except that since he's a pyrokinetic, he sets his bed on fire in his sleep instead of just soaking it like any normal kid.

I have to drop everything and race back to my ward whenever the alarm goes off, since I'm the only pediatrician on duty and I don't want to wind up with a suit for negligence or anything. (Besides, I get enormous satisfaction out of blasting the little bastard with the fire extinguisher, for all the trouble he causes. It doesn't do him any harm, but it feels good.)

So I put the scissors and the baby down and go put the fire out, and when I'm done I go back to obstetrics, to see how things turned out. The moment I set foot in the delivery room, the doctor starts screaming at me, accusing me of stealing the baby and calling me all sorts of names.

I tell him the baby was invisible, and he tells me not to be absurd and that it'll never fly in court, and I keep explaining that I already got three babies in the ward that can fly and what we're talking about is one that can disappear.

Well, we still haven't found the baby. Right now I'm hiding in the prep room in Nephrology, waiting for the hubbub to die down, which is why I've had so much time to write this long letter. But I'm out of paper now, so I guess I'd better close.

Exasperatedly,
Harvey

Dear Ma:

Yes, I'm remembering to wear my overcoat when I go out.

Well, we finally found the baby. Dr. Yingleman almost crushed it to death when he was *schtupping* a nurse two rooms away. It gave out a scream that cracked his contact lenses, and after a little feeling around, we located it—it's a *him*, poor devil—and moved it to my ward.

Then, while I'm standing there in the nursery, warming a bottle of motor oil for the platinum baby, in comes this couple carrying a bucket of water.

"There's been a horrible mistake here," the man says to me. "I can fly, and my wife can see through walls, and you've given us a baby that turns into water." He holds up the bucket. "What are we supposed to do with him? The first time we try to toilet train him, he's going to get flushed down the drain."

I say maybe he can fight crime by turning into water and invading the bad guys' hideouts via the sewer system, and they just glare at me.

"This is totally unacceptable," says the woman. "We expected something that could fly and see through buildings."

157

"Can *you* fly?" I asked her.

"No," she says.

"Can your husband see through walls?"

"No," she says.

"Except for the greenhouse," he adds thoughtfully.

"Well, then, be grateful your kid can do something. You could have had one who couldn't fly *or* see through walls."

"But a child who turns into water . . ." says the man dubiously. "The dog might drink him by accident."

We talk about it a little more, and finally I suggest that if they can just make it through his adolescence, they can put him in a squirt gun and have him transform once they spray the bad guys, which sounds silly as hell to me in retrospect, but he kind of likes the idea, and she decides they can tint him with decorator colors so they don't accidentally mix him into a cocktail, and they finally leave.

Then Mrs. Blumberg—you know her as Mighty Wench—brings Philbert in to get his shots, and the second she leaves to go visit the Golden Swan, who got nailed by Falconman the other night and is recuperating down the hall, the kid turns difficult and says, "If you try to give me a shot, I'll hold my breath until I turn blue!"

"So hold your breath," I say, pulling out a syringe.

He takes a big gulp of air, and tenses, and squeezes his eyes shut. I lean forward with the needle, when I notice he's really starting to turn blue.

At first I am amused by it, but then I began to worry: What will Mighty Wench think if she comes back and finds that her precious little Philbert suddenly looks like a Smurf? And just as I'm worrying about it, in she comes, and takes one look at the kid and walks across the room and takes the syringe away from me and throws it through the window and the last I see of it it is going into orbit and will probably prove a traffic hazard to Skylab or whatever we've got up there these days. As she's walking out with Philbert, he turns and sticks his tongue out at me.

You ever see a 48-inch-long blue tongue? Me, I'm going to be seeing it in my nightmares for the next half century.

Worriedly,
Harvey

Super Acorns

Dear Ma:

Yes, I'll get a haircut as soon as I have time. I promise.

Things are really getting hectic around here. Broke nine needles trying to give Steelman's kid a shot. The plastic kid keeps disguising himself as a raincoat and going home wrapped around Nurse Murchison. Whiz Kid's daughter found out that I like to root for the Pirates, so she races to Three Rivers Stadium and back—a little journey of 5300 miles round trip—between every pitch to tell me what's going on. (Yeah, I know she's only 14 weeks old, but she not only talks and runs, she's committed the entire works of Danielle Steele to memory.)

Still, I have my few moments of triumph. Finally figured out that if I put one crib upside down atop another, it would prevent the Levitator's baby from floating away. And since I couldn't stop Foghorn's daughter from sneezing, I rented her out to the construction crew that's tearing down 4th Street between Main and Elm; she leveled the whole block with two sneezes and a sniffle.

Biggest problem now is little Malcolm, the Vanisher's son. *He* can't vanish, but he can make other things vanish. Last night it was Nurse Murchison's uniform. Maybe I shouldn't have looked so approving, because this morning he repeated his trick, and she blamed me. And now I hear that six CATscan machines have disappeared into thin air.

Oh, and there's little Penny, the Changer's kid. About an hour ago I found a 30-foot python on the floor. Just as I was about to evacuate the room and call for help, it changed back into Penny. So now every time I see a spider or a crumpled piece of paper or a half-eaten sandwich, I have to check and see where Penny is before I stomp on it or throw it out or, God forbid, eat it.

And to think—I turned down the Mayo Clinic for *this*.

Unhappily,
Harvey

Dear Ma:

I've *had* it with this place. Today was the last straw. I get to work, and what do I find waiting for me in the nursery?

Copycat's kid.

You remember Copycat? She's the one who can change her appearance in half a second, so that she can look like a gang member and infiltrate the enemy.

159

Well, I have a feeling her kid is going to grow up to be Xeroxman. He can reproduce himself endlessly, and even as I write this I am surrounded by 78 identical babies—all with dirty diapers.

I'm getting out of this madhouse and into some sane practice, like maybe pathology or forensics.

Exhaustedly,
Harvey

P.S. Yes, of course I'm changing my underwear every day.

Dear Ma:

It's blood pressure, not blood *pleasure,* and yes, I'm watching it.

Concerning pediatrics: Maybe I was a little bit hasty.

This morning they bring in a corpse, and I am in the middle of the autopsy when what's left of the body suddenly sits up and asks me what it died of this time.

It's Spiritman, of course . . . and when I'm done with him, I have to work on the Spook and then Zombie Girl and then the Vampire Bat, and I find that I am not cut out for discussing the whys and wherefores of their latest fatalities with a bunch of super-corpses.

I've got to get out of this place.

Distractedly,
Harvey

Dear Ma:

You really didn't have to send the soup. In fact, I rather wish you hadn't. It leaked through while it was sitting in the mailbox and totally ruined my severance check.

Things are going along fine here at the HMO. I set a broken arm this morning, treated my very first case of gout, and gave a businessman with high blood pressure a low-sodium diet, all before lunch. I feel like a totally fulfilled person.

There's only one problem.

I'm bored.

Love,
Harvey

Vets

Richard Lee Byers

Those individuals who experience life-and-death situations every day frequently feel disassociated with the rest of us mortals. They live in a world of special rules that only other veterans can truly understand.

Something inhuman shrieked. Jarred awake, I thrashed, and demolished the bed. As I hit the floor, I realized the phone was ringing.

Prior to that night, I'd gone without sleep for three days. Three days of stumbling over decapitated children, rousting lowlifes, and, at the end, nearly taking a plasma bolt through the chest before I KO'd Dr. Mayhem. I wanted to yank the phone out of the wall and close my eyes again. Instead I fumbled clear of my tangled blankets, shredding them in the process, sat up, and groped for the howling instrument on the nightstand.

"Hello," I croaked.

"Frank?" It was Malcolm, one of the two vigilantes I'd sponsored in the program. "I'm sorry to call so late, but Sandy left me."

I'd been expecting it. He'd been talking about his marital problems for the better part of a year. I rubbed grit out of my dry, aching eyes. "Oh, damn. I'm really sorry. What—"

"She said she never saw me. But I was protecting people. I was protecting *her*. If Crimson Lion had nuked Florida, she would have died with everyone else!"

"I know," I said. "She does too, and maybe after she's had a chance to think—"

"No," he said. "She's already screwing somebody else. George, from her office. Apparently it's been going on a while. I bet she even told him my secret ID."

I tried to think of some comforting twelve-step platitude. Perhaps because I was still groggy, nothing came to mind. "I know it must hurt like hell. It sure did when Barbara left me. But try to remember that there are still good things in your life. You do the most important job in the world. People look up to you—"

He laughed. "Bullshit. Most of them take us for granted until a threat gets past us. Then they bitch. The rest hate us, 'cause they're jealous of our powers, or worry that we'll get sick of baby-sitting them and throw in with the bad guys."

"I don't think most of them feel that way," I replied, though actually, there were plenty of days when I did. "But even if they do, it doesn't matter. *You* know what kind of man you are, what you've accomplished."

"Yeah, and what have I got to show for it? A plate in my skull. Headaches. Scars. Nightmares. Superpowered psychos out for my blood. Do you realize we've been doing this silly job since we were teenagers? And the pressure never lets up. I am so fucking tired!"

"Then take a vacation. I'll cover for you, patrol Miami a couple nights a week." I cringed at what I was saying. I had my own problems; that's why I was in the support group. I was afraid that if I had to be responsible for Tampa and another city too, I'd start drinking again. But Mal sounded so near the edge that I had to offer.

"No." I felt a guilty pang of relief. "I can't. Warhead escaped from Raiford, and I'm the only person his illusions don't affect. But I am going to let off a little steam. Pay Sandy and George a visit."

My hand tightened on the phone. The plastic creaked. "You don't want to do that. You joined the group to keep from abusing your powers."

"It won't be abuse. The two of them deserve punishment as much as Oleander, Isotope, or any of those freaks."

"Hold off just one day," I said. "I promise, you won't feel this way tomorrow."

"I don't care. I feel it now."

"Think of the consequences."

"Good point. But there won't be any consequences if I go in invisible, *kill* the fuckers, then burn the house. That way, there're no witnesses and no evidence."

I could tell he meant it. For a moment, I wondered if I was still asleep, having a nightmare. "That's a hell of a fantasy, but you're one of the good guys. You could never carry it out."

"Tonight I can. I'm going to find out what one of our enemies feels when he blasts a normal into pulp."

"I'll tell you how you'd feel. You'd hate yourself."

"You think? I think it'll be satisfying, like when you squash a roach."

My mouth was dry. My head throbbed. "Please, *think*. If you really wanted to do this, you wouldn't have phoned me."

"Maybe part of me wanted you to talk me out of it. But you didn't, so the other part wins."

"But now that I know, you can't go on."

"Why not?" he asked. "Even you can't get here fast enough to stop me. I'm just a block away from George's place. Look, I'm sorry I called. It wasn't fair to drag you into this." He hung up.

I was still wearing most of my grimy, smelly costume. I'd been too exhausted to peel it off. I snatched my cowl, boots, and gauntlets off the floor and yanked them on. If Mal hesitated before going after Sandy and her lover, maybe I *could* reach Miami in time to stop him.

But he didn't and I didn't.

The burning house was easy to spot from the air. As I approached, Mal, visible now, flew up to meet me, the silvery wings of his Daedalus harness beating. "I told you you'd be too late," he said.

"Yeah," I answered. "Shit."

"We were both wrong," he said. "I don't regret it, but it wasn't fun either. I didn't feel anything. Are you going to try to arrest me?" He faded.

My fists clenched. Then I remembered how he'd gotten gored pulling the pin out of the voodoo doll Hellpriest carved in my image. The night he'd rescued me from Imperator's torture chamber. All the times we'd talked about the stresses no normal, including our wives, could understand. I felt how sore and tired I was. My hands opened. "No. I won't fight you."

His form became opaque. The sparks dancing on his fingertips winked out. "I'm glad. I don't want to fight you either. What will you do, tell somebody?"

I supposed so. Then someone else, someone who wasn't his friend, would hunt him down. Except . . . there were so many menaces, and so few of us vigilantes, and no one else with precisely Mal's abilities. Those talents saved thousands of lives every year, had saved the fucking *planet* more than once. What if they were needed to save it again?

At least that was my rationalization.

"I'm not going to do anything," I said. "I guess you couldn't help what happened. Just . . . don't call me for a while, okay? Not unless there's an emergency."

"All right," he said.

I wheeled and flew away. The lights below me looked as distant as the stars above. I imagined I could fall for a million years and never reach them.

Four Tales of Many Names

Gerald Hausman

The concept of the superheroic figure is neither uniquely American nor exclusive to this century. Most cultures are rife with legends of individuals who have special gifts.

The Story of Hawk Storm

After he was too old to go into battle any longer, a warrior often taught the young men the secrets of the hunt, how to steal horses, the art of touching an enemy on the breastbone, surprising, but not killing him; what is called counting coups. When he grew older still, a warrior did not instruct young men; he told stories around the winter fire to children, and they listened, for they could see that his face was as the face of a rock that has been worn by wind, lashed by rain and bitten by frost. Such was the old storyteller known as Many Names:

When I was young there lived a boy in the skin-tent next to mine whose mother was killed soon after he was born. When I knew him he lived with his grandmother. Now this boy had surprising powers for one so young. He liked to sit in the grass and watch the rock swallows. Once he told me: "You see how they fly, bunched close; that is how we should run." And this boy showed me how to run, elbow to elbow, drawing strength from each other.

165

He became known as Dove Running because, even more than the rock swallows, he watched the doves, imitated their movements. Now one time when he was a little older, but not yet a young man, his grandmother was stolen by the ones they call the Wolf Eyes. The Wolf Eyes took her to the desert where the people live who take silver out of the earth. The Wolf Eyes have a deserved reputation for cruelty; and they beat her when she brought them water from the river; they beat her when she brought them firewood. Sometimes they beat her for no reason, just because she was one of us, their enemy.

Now Dove Running had followed his grandmother into the south country, where he called upon the power of the dove people to come to his aid. There he found that his prayer was answered, and one day he walked into the camp of the Wolf Eyes, unseen. The Wolf Eye women saw something, looked up from their work: they felt something come into their camp, yet they could not see it. What they saw was a small grey dove that ducked into one of the brush shelters. Ignoring the little bird, they went back to their pounding. Now, Dove Running landed on the shoulder of his grandmother, and he saw, looking down on her scarred arms, that she had been freshly burned with fire-sticks. Then he turned back into a boy, and his grandmother caressed and fondled him, but she said: "You must fly home, little one, the Wolf Eye chief lives in this shelter, and soon he will return. Surely, when he sees you, he will kill you!"

"I am not afraid of the Wolf Eye, Grandmother," the boy said. But, just then, as they were talking, the Wolf Eye chief suddenly entered the shelter.

"What do you mean by whispering to that dove?" he demanded of the old woman, and knocking her down, he grabbed up the grey dove and squeezed it until blood squirted out of its eyes and tiny white bones stuck out of the bloody feathers.

"Is that all there is to your sorcery?" The chief laughed fiercely, and he threw the bones and feathers out of the doorway of the brush shelter. Now when this happened, the grandmother let out such a wail that it could be heard from far away; and she began to attack the Wolf Eye with her fists, but he pushed

166

her away, saying: "Pitiful old dog, your teeth have no bite." Then he went outside, but had not taken two steps when those little dove's bones, lying in the dirt, flew up into the air and came together in a dark cloud of dust, out of which flashed the wings of a great hawk that flew into the chief's face and tore out his eyes. But before the cruel chief fell to his knees and covered his face, the hawk whirled about and soared into the brush shelter, picked up the grandmother by the back of her buckskin dress, and flew away with her. That same day he brought her home; and the people said it was a great thing that had happened down there in the desert; and after that they knew Dove Running by the name of Hawk Storm.

The Story of Fire Storm

When next they met around the storyteller's fire, the children asked Many Names to tell of the worst danger that Hawk Storm ever faced; and so he told them of the time he got his second name, which is what this story is about:

This was long ago, when the people called the Burnt Moccasins attacked Hawk Storm's hunting party. But today, as I tell it, it seems like yesterday. You see, my friend had been known by the name of Hawk Storm for some time, but it was a boy's name. He had done more impressive things after receiving the name, earning him even greater favor as a young warrior, but it was not until he met the Burnt Moccasins on the field of battle that he was given his man's name. You see, the Burnt Moccasins had been hunting Hawk Storm, and they finally caught him, tied him to a huge, lightning-struck sycamore. Now, that, as everyone knows, is not a good-luck tree; and they tied him there in the middle of a thunderstorm, hoping the tree would be struck again by lightning—and presently it was, and it started to burn. Now Hawk Storm called for his ally, the hawk, but no hawk came.

"Why, Grandfather," one of the children asked, "did he not turn into a hawk himself?"

At this the old chief scowled. "You mean to say, you do not know the answer to that?"

Confused, the child shook his head.

"When you are a man of power," he said wisely, "you do not waste your power needlessly."

"But, Grandfather, he was going to die—" the child protested.

"He was not given magic power to save his own life," the old chief admonished, "but to save the lives of others."

This seemed to satisfy the children, who once again fell silent, so that Many Names then went on with his story.

Now when Hawk Storm prayed for an ally to come, Raven heard his cry, and came to him. Yet the flames from the burning sycamore blazed so close to his feathers that he, himself, was caught on fire, and burnt black, just the way you see him today.

When Hawk Storm prayed again for an ally to come, Screech Owl heard his cry, and came. Yet the flames heated his eyes so badly they turned red-orange, and they have been that way ever since that time.

Again, Hawk Storm prayed for an ally to come, and Brown Snake appeared, wriggling into a hole in the burning sycamore tree; but he too was burnt black all over, and to this day, when we see him, we call him Black Snake.

Now the fourth time Hawk Storm prayed for an ally to come, Spider Woman spun a fine silk thread, and dropped it from a cloud. Then she came down from the sky, and with her sharp teeth she nibbled the bonds that bound Hawk Storm to the burning sycamore tree. And that, grandchildren, was how Hawk Storm escaped his death and bested the warriors of the Burnt Moccasin people.

"What happened to them, Grandfather?" one of the children asked.

"Well, they burned their moccasin feet black, walking all over looking for Hawk Storm," Many Names said. "And that is how they got the name Blackfeet, which is what we call them today."

"Grandfather, what of Hawk Storm's new name?" asked another child.

"That, grandchildren," the old chief chuckled, "is for another time."

The Story of Water Spider

The next time the children gathered around Many Names, he told them that the new name of Hawk Storm was Water Spider.

"Why did they call him that?" a girl asked.

"Well," the old chief explained, "you remember how he was saved by Spider Woman? That meant that he was favored by the spider people. So his new name came from one of them."

"But why Water Spider?"

"They say that only Water Spider can come out of a fire without getting burned."

"What happened to him after that?"

And Many Names told them:

Water Spider continued to be a great warrior. One time he fought a long and hard battle, and was coming home with three of his friends; he had injured his leg, so his friends had to carry him between them. Their village was still a long way off, they were being followed, and night was coming on fast. At last, they came to a little canyon where a stream ran between the rocks, and one of the men said, "I will go down there and bring up a water-skin full of water." But while he was climbing down into the canyon, he got the idea that they should leave Water Spider there; that way they might still have a chance of eluding their enemies.

And so these two cowardly companions pushed Water Spider over the edge of a cliff. Then they ran back to their village, arriving safely, and telling everyone that Water Spider had fought bravely, but in the end, had been overcome, and had died with an arrow in his heart.

169

Now, in the meantime, Water Spider found himself lying in a forsaken canyon with two broken legs. The only thing he could do was crawl along on his belly, seeking some kind of shelter for the night.

After dragging himself for many hours, he found a small cave, pulled himself into it, and let out a long sigh of relief. At the back of the cave, he saw firelight flickering, and an old naked man with no hair on his head, sitting on a rock. The old man's legs, such as they were, were withered and useless, and his arms did not seem much better, being small as a child's.

"Welcome, grandson," the old man said cheerfully, and he offered Water Spider a fresh killed rabbit. Water Spider noticed that there were two fang-marks at the rabbit's throat, but no other mark on the body.

The old man just smiled, saying: "That is how I always kill them, right there, on the neck. But I am getting too old to hunt; if only someone would drive the game to me, I might yet make a good hunter. But as you can see, I am just too old to move about the way I used to."

Water Spider let out a pained laugh. "You are doing better than I, Old One," he said, then added: "In the morning, I will see what I can do to help you." So they shared that rabbit, and soon after, went to sleep. Water Spider noticed that the old man snored; and when he snored, he made a rattling noise that sounded as if it were coming from his backside.

The next morning the old man showed him how to slide out of the cave, how to move along the ground on his belly. "We are not much good," the old man snickered, "but there are two of us." That morning, they caught a quail by the river; Water Spider drove it in the direction of the old man, who killed it in the manner of the rabbit of the night before. Proudly, he showed off the puncture marks. "I always get them like that," he bragged.

Now in the days that followed, the two hunted together every morning, and always, it was the same: Water Spider drove the game in the direction of the old man, who somehow managed to make the kill with just one shot. "I would like to see the bow you use to do that," Water Spider said, but the old man just replied, "Sometime you will."

One night, as they were preparing to go to sleep, Water Spider watched the old man place his head straight out in front of him, resting it on a rock. Soon he was snoring with his eyes wide open, his tongue poking out and quivering as he slept. The next morning Water Spider thanked the old man for sharing his lodge with him, but he said the time had come for him to go. The old man was sorry to hear this. "We have hunted well together, grandson," he said. "But if you must leave, I want you to take this little bag; put it around your neck for safekeeping."

"What is it, Grandfather?"

"It is the medicine I use to put my enemies to sleep."

So Water Spider thanked him very much, and crawled out of the cave, and slowly climbed up out of the canyon. It took him a long time, but when he got to the top, he knew there was no sense in trying to walk; his legs still would not support him. But after all this time with the old man, Water Spider had gotten used to traveling in this way; in fact, he had gotten good at it. First, he moved his shoulders, then his belly, then his hips, gradually sliding himself along with his knees and toes. It was a slow way to go, but it worked, and he had no choice in the matter.

So he traveled all day and all night, stopping only to drink water from a small spring. And the next day he continued to travel steadily toward his village, stopping but once, to eat serviceberries, then moving on. By nightfall of the fourth day, Water Spider saw the campfires of his village, and tears came to his eyes because he never thought he would see them again. However, as he started down the hill through the grass, he was seen by some scouts—as it happened, the same ones who had tried to kill him.

"Look who comes crawling back after all this time," the first said.

"Yes," replied the second, "it is Water Spider, who was once our friend, but now our enemy; for, given the chance, he will tell how we betrayed him."

"I shall tell no one," Water Spider said grimly. "Just help me get home the way you were supposed to."

But the two men could not take the chance that Water Spider would keep his tongue still on their behalf. Nodding evilly, they notched arrows and drew their bows on the unarmed man at their feet, who, seeing that they were about to kill him then, asked them to grant him one last request. The bows remained unbent, but the traitors listened.

"In this bag I carry around my neck is the sacred medicine that has kept me alive all this time. If you will let me live, now, I will let you have some of it."

The two sneered at Water Spider's childlike innocence. One said, "First we take it from you, then we will kill you." And they both laughed. Following this, one of them leaned down and cut the drawstring from Water Spider's neck, and as his partner drew near, he opened the small bag. Immediately, four porcupine quills flew out and stuck both in the throat. Reeling, they staggered, fell to their knees, turned purple-faced with poison, and died. Then Water Spider took back the bag and dragged himself through the grass on his belly, until he reached his village. There, amidst much surprise, he was given a hero's welcome. In time, he told all that had happened to him; and this brought him a new name, one which I will share with you when the next big wind blows at the flap of our skin-tent."

So saying, the old chief bade goodnight to the grandchildren gathered around the fire, and left them wondering.

The Story of Snake's Medicine

Sometime after this, Many Names sat himself down by the story-teller's fire and once again took up the tale where he had left off.

"Now, after this, our warrior-hero was known as Snake's Medicine, but by that time, he was so tired of having adventures—and besides, he was all but lame—that he wanted to settle down and have a family, and give up the warrior's way."

"Did he put his lance in the earth?" one of the children asked.

"He did indeed," replied Many Names, "and became a chief known far and wide for his great wisdom and power."

"Did he ever have children, Grandfather?"

And Many Names told them:

He married a pretty young woman named Buffalo Calf, but, it is hard to say why, they did not have any children. They tried, but for them it was not possible. For many years, the two lived in a childless world, a world without stars, a world of winters without spring. And then, one day, while Snake's Medicine was gathering mushrooms in the woods, he saw something that caught his eye: a pine-knot it was, growing out of the trunk of a great pine tree. Now the more he studied it, the more he became convinced that this might be an answer to his and his wife's childless lodge. Here was a burl of twisted wood, a pine-knot, that looked just like the face of a child. He took out his knife and freed the knot, then sat down, and carved the bark off it. *Such a wonderful thing*, he thought, *this little pine-knot looks just like a happy boy.*

When he was through whittling, he brought the pine-knot home to his wife, saying nothing of it except that he had found it on the trail. Buffalo Calf took the pine-knot in her arms, hugged it to her breast, placed it in a fine cradleboard of bead and fur. "Husband," she said, "speak to no one of this, for it is our secret, and no one else's." He agreed, and the two of them fed and clothed the pine-knot, calling it Carving Boy; and they talked to it, and treated it tenderly, just as if it had been their own newborn son. Buffalo Calf fed it stew of boiled corn, and while this, naturally, ran out of the whittled mouth of Carving Boy, the two delighted parents did not really care; for, at last, their wish was granted—they had a child.

Now, eleven moons grew from thin to full, and Snake's Medicine and Buffalo Calf pretended they had a son named Carving Boy; but one morning, as Buffalo Calf was feeding him some crushed berries, he suddenly broke out of his cradleboard, and roared: "Mother, get me some meat!" Well, Buffalo Calf nearly fell over, she was so surprised, but her sense of devotion took over immediately, and she fed Carving Boy a piece of broiled buffalo hump, which he devoured in one bite, without even swallowing. For the rest of that day, he ate whatever she offered him; and he grew quite stout, so that by the time Snake's Medicine came home from hunting, with a deer slung over his shoulder, the starved boy wanted to eat all of it.

Snake's Medicine could not believe his eyes—here was the boy he had carved out of a pine-knot, eating raw deer meat! Nor was that all: Carving Boy could not seem to fill his belly; he ate all of that deer—blood, bones, horns, hooves, even the fur—and there was nothing left for his mother and father, but still they did not complain, for this child was what they had always wanted.

Now, Carving Boy grew very large; in four days he was as big as a skin-tent. And by then, as you can imagine, he was eating horses, popping them into his mouth like strawberries; and when his father's horses were gone, he ate the horses of other people; and when they were gone, he went out on a hunt, and ate a whole buffalo herd. Nor was that all—for Carving Boy now began to eat the hills and the mountains, the plains and the valleys.

At this, the children listening to the old chief, Many Names, became a little uneasy. They began to look over their shoulders, and as the wind moaned around the tipi walls, little shivers went up their spines, and their eyes got big.

"Is he still out there, somewhere?" one of the children wanted to know.

The old chief shook his head.

"He is no longer around," he said, somewhat sadly.

"What happened to him?"

"Well, his father had to kill him with a stone axe. First he chopped off one of his feet, so Carving Boy toppled over; then he chopped off one of his knees; and then he split open his belly . . . and what do you think happened then?"

The children looked at each other with great, wondering eyes; no one could guess.

"Then," the old chief went on, "all the animals Carving Boy had ever eaten came out of his belly and ran away. There were deer, buffalo, elk, antelope, rabbits, mice, rats and squirrels; not to mention the flocks of birds; and the hills and mountains and valleys."

"Was that when he died?" a boy asked.

"Oh," said the old chief, "don't you know that a lie *never* dies, *never* goes away? That Carving Boy is still out there, somewhere, and just like all the lies of this world, he is waiting, once again, to be born."

"Grandfather, what happened to the great warrior, Snake's Medicine?" a girl questioned.

Many Names grinned and, stirring the fire, said: "He is still around."

The children looked all around them.

"You mean he is *still* alive?"

The old chief shrugged. "I suppose so."

"What keeps him alive?" asked the girl.

"Stories." The old chief chuckled. "Stories, and little children, just like yourselves."

The Long Crawl of
Hugh Glass

Roger Zelazny

Amazing people have been accomplishing superhuman
feats throughout history. It is possible, as in the factual case
of Hugh Glass, that the most astounding power is the will
to survive.

*In 1823 an injured hunter named Hugh Glass crawled over 100
miles through the wilderness from the Grand Valley to the Missouri
River.*

Hugh Glass had one chance to kill the bear, and whether his shot
struck it or went completely astray, he never knew. It charged him,
brushing aside the rifle before he could club with it as its paw fell
upon his face, smashing his nose, tearing through the skin of his
brow. Then its great forelimbs came about him, its breath awful, fetid
of ripe flesh and the musky smell of skunk, overlaid with a sweetness
of berries and honey that made him think of a waiting, perfumed
corpse, too long aboveground while distant mourners hurried for the
viewing.

His spirit seemed to turn slowly within his head and breast, a white
and gray eddy of dissolving perceptions, as his blood ran into his eyes
and traced trails down his seamed face into his frosted beard. A large
man, bearlike himself in the eyes of his fellows, he did not cry out,
did not know fear; a great gasp had wrung much of the air from him,
leaving him voiceless, and the attack had come so quickly that there
had been no time to be afraid. Now, what he felt seemed familiar;

177

for he was a hunter, providing game for eighty men, dealing daily death as a business of life. And it was suddenly his turn. It would have been good to say farewell to Jamie, but there are always things undone. The cracking of his ribs was not such a terrible thing through the failing white and the gray; the sound from his thigh might have been a snapping branch in some distant forest. He was no longer there to feel the ground as he crashed against it.

Riding, echoes of his mount's hoofbeats off the hills about him, Jamie saw the shadows flow and merge as he sought downhill for his friend, sky of blood and flame and roses to his left whenever he topped a rise. He could smell the Grand River ahead and to his right. The old man hunted these breaks, was probably camping near here tonight.

"Hugh?" he called. "Hugh?" And a part of his voice rolled back to him.

He continued into the northwest toward the fork, calling periodically.

At the top of another hill the horse stopped short, neighing briefly. For a great distance toward evening the flatlands stretched before him. Below, on either hand, the Grand forked, sparkling, crooked, through haze. He rose in the stirrups, staring, brushed a hand through his sun-gilt hair.

Nothing stirred but the river, and then a rising as of ashes far ahead, with a cawing. A single star was lit above the sunset. A faint breeze came to him from the direction of the water. He called again.

The horse made another sound, took a little prancing step. Jamie touched his mount's sides lightly and headed down the hill, the horse's hoofs clattering in the shale. Level again, on firmer ground, he hurried.

"Camping . . ." he said softly, and after a time he called again.

There came the boom of a rifle from somewhere ahead, and he smiled.

". . . Heard me," he said, and he shook the reins, laughing. His mount hurried and Jamie hummed a tune to the sound of the hoof-beats.

And there, in the grassy area ahead, a figure rose, arms spread.

178

Waving . . . ? The horse snorted and reared, tried to turn. It wasn't a man. Too big, too . . .

His mount wheeled, but not before Jamie had spied the broken heap upon the ground, recognized the shaggy totem shape—beast that walks like a man—that swayed above it. His hand fell to the rifle boot even as the horse bolted. Cursing, he drew back hard upon the reins but there was no response. At his back, he heard a crashing of brush as the great beast fell to pursuit.

Then he drew again upon the bit and sank his spur into the horse's side. This time it swerved, obedient, to the right. The bear rushed by, passing behind him; and Jamie headed for the water, striking sand, then raising a shower of spray as he entered.

The stream was not wide here. Scrambling, scrabbling, the horse protested the rocky bottom, but a growl from the rear seemed to add impetus to its flight. Shortly, they were rising, dripping, from the water, mounting the farther bank.

Looking back, Jamie saw that the bear had halted at the water's edge. His hand went to the buckle on the rifle case, and he turned his mount as he drew the weapon. Still dry.

He swung it through an arc, cross-body, rested it a moment on his forearm, squeezed the trigger.

Through the smoke-spume, he saw the bear lurch forward, fall into the stream, tossing. He watched its death throes, recalling Hugh's instruction on the placing of shots. Immediately, his eyes were clouded for the man who'd raised him like a son.

Shortly, he was back in the water, crossing. He rode to the fallen man and dismounted.

"Hugh," he said, "I'm sorry," and he knelt beside him. He turned his friend's head then to look upon his face, and he gasped at the mass of blood and torn flesh he beheld, nose smashed flat, brows shredded. "Hugh . . ."

How long he watched he was not certain. Then there came a soft moan.

He leaned forward, not sure of what he had heard. There followed a terrible stillness. Then came a catching of breath, another moan, a slow movement.

"Hugh? It's Jamie here," he said. "Can you hear me?"

The man made a small noise deep in his throat, lay still again. Jamie looked about. Hugh had made his camp near a spring, its trickling sounds half-noticed till now. A pile of sticks and branches lay near at hand.

"I'm going to make you a fire, Hugh. Got to keep you warm. You just rest easy now. I'll go do that."

Drawing his knife, he split wood. He built a heap of shavings and twigs near the still form, brought it to a flame, fed it, dragged over the larger branches, added more fuel. The sun had fallen over the world's edge by then, and the stars came on like a city in the sky. Jamie hunkered by his fallen companion, the older man's face even more ghastly and masklike by firelight.

"Oh, my," he said. "Next thing we'd better do is get you cleaned up some."

He made his way to the spring, dipped his kerchief into the water, wrung it out. Returning, he sponged and blotted Hugh's face.

"I remember the day you saved my ass in that fight with the Ree," he muttered. "What was I—fourteen? Folks dead, I rode right out into it. You came after. Killed a few and brought me back. Whaled me later for not knowing enough to be afraid. God—Hugh! Don't die on me!"

Hugh Glass lay very still.

"It's me—Jamie!" he cried, catching up a still hand and clasping it to his breast.

But he felt no life in the hand, and he laid it back down gently. He returned to the spring and rinsed his kerchief. He tried trickling water into Hugh's mouth, but it just ran down his face into his beard.

". . . Jamie," he said, listening for a heartbeat. Was that it? Soft as an underground stream? He washed the face again. He added kindling to the fire.

Later, the moon came up. In the distance, a wolf howled. Hugh gasped and moaned. Jamie touched his hand again, began speaking softly, of their days on the trail, places they'd been, things they'd seen and done. After a time, his eyes closed. Shortly, his words ceased and he moved in dreams.

. . . Riding the keelboats with Major Henry's men, trading for horses in the Ree villages. He saw again the Leavenworth campaign amid flashes of fire. Spring thaws and winter freezes. . . . Dressing game with Hugh. . . . Sleeping on the trail, smell of horses, smell of earth. . . . And storms, and the passing of bison. . . . In the distance, his parents' faces. . . .

The neighing of a horse. His head jerked and he realized that his back and shoulders were sore, his neck. . . . He sprawled, dozing again, dreaming or dreamed of the vast prairie in its moods.

. . . And Hugh's dreams were pain-shot archipelagos of darkness and fire, though it seemed he was not alone in his hurting. He felt he had talked to another, though he was not certain his tongue and lips had really worked. It seemed he had grown roots, extending deep down into the earth, and like a stubborn shrub he held himself to it against a turmoil of weathers, drawing nourishment up into his damaged limbs.

. . . And a horse neighed, and the ground shook. Jamie opened his eyes and the world was full of morning light. His horse stood nearby. In the earth, he felt the vibrations of horses' hoofs. He shook his head, rubbed his eyes with the heels of his hands, sat up. Memories returned as he ran his fingers through his hair. He regarded Hugh, whose head now lolled to one side and whose chest moved very slowly.

The hoofbeats were audible now. Hoping it was not a party of Rickaree, he rose to his feet, turning in the direction of the sound.

No, it wasn't the Ree, but rather Major Henry and his men, come riding into the valley from out of the east. They called and waved when they saw him there, grew still as they approached and looked upon the fallen form of Hugh.

"Jamie, what happened?" Major Henry called out, dismounting and coming near.

"Hugh got mauled by a bear," Jamie replied. "He's in poor shape."

"Damn!" the major said, kneeling and placing his hand on Hugh's chest. "Looks a sight, too."

The others came down from their mounts and moved near.

"We should take him back to the camp, get him more comfortable," one of the scouts said.

". . . And get some medicine into him," said another.

"Bring up that bay packhorse," the major called out.

181

"I'm not sure Hugh should be moved," Jamie said.

"We owe the man every chance we can give him," came the reply.

As the bay was brought up and its pack removed, Frank and Will—the red-haired brothers from St. Louis—stooped at Hugh's head and feet, taking hold of his shoulders and ankles. They commenced raising him, slowly, from the earth.

Hugh moaned then—an awful, bleating, animal-like sound. Frank and Will lowered him again.

"Ain't no way we're going to move that man 'thout killing him," Frank stated.

"I think he's bound to die, anyway," Will said. "No reason to add to his misery."

"Poor Hugh ain't got long," Frank agreed. "Let's let him be."

Major Henry shook his head and put his arm around Jamie's shoulders.

"I think the men are right," he said softly.

Jamie nodded.

"We'll wait a time," the major told him. "In case it happens soon."

And Hugh lay like a corpse, save for a periodic sigh, a groan, as the day warmed. The men made tea and, seated in circles on the ground, conversed more softly than was their custom, of the trails they followed toward the Big Horn, of the recent campaign against the Ree, of Indian activity in the area. Some went off to seek the remains of the bear, to butcher it for its meat.

And Hugh's face darkened and lightened, in token of the struggle in which there can be no ally. His hands twitched as if seeking to grapple; and for a time he breathed deeply, a glassy mask of sweat upon his features. Jamie bathed his face again.

"Soon, lad. Soon, I fear," the major told him; and Jamie nodded, sat, and watched.

And birds sang, and the day continued to warm as the sun rose higher in the heavens. Still Hugh gasped, and saliva trickled from the corner of his mouth; his fingers dug furrows in the earth.

When the sun stood in high heaven, Major Henry moved to study the fallen man. He stared for a long while, then turned to Jamie.

"It could take longer'n we figured," he said. "He's a tough one, Jamie."

"I know," Jamie replied.

"The men are getting a little restless, what with the Ree on a war trail just now."

"I understand," Jamie said.

"So we'd be better off heading to the camp west of here, before moving on. You know the trail we were going to take."

"I do."

"So what I figure is to get a man to stay here with you and help keep the wolves away till it's—over. The rest of us'd move on, and you'd catch up with us farther along."

Jamie nodded.

Major Henry clasped his shoulder.

"I'm sorry about Hugh, Jamie. I know what he meant to you," he said. "I'll call for a volunteer now, and we'll be about it."

"Very good, sir."

. . . The bear approached Hugh again, and he could not run from it. It was as if his feet had grown roots. The bear walked upright, its face flowing like dark water. He saw his father there, and the faces of men he had had to kill. Dark birds flew out of the bear, flapping their wings in his face. He smelled the cloying sweetness and the fetor, the rottenness. . . . Then it clasped him and squeezed him again, and he was coughing. He tasted blood with each aching spasm. It seemed that there were voices—many of them—talking softly in the dark distance. The sounds of hoofbeats came and went. He saw the bear dead, skinned, its hide somehow wrapping about him, its face become his own, bleeding, smiling without humor. Closer was it wrapped, becoming part of him, his arms and aching legs shaggy, his mouth foul. Still was he rooted; still the power came up into him out of the earth. Almost a dark, flowing song. . . .

The hat went round and coins clicked in it, one by one, till Jules Le Bon felt the stirring of compassion and volunteered to sit with Jamie by his friend. A short, wiry man, missing a tooth leftside of his grin, he bade the others good day, stood waiting till they had ridden off. Then he moved to sit by Jamie, clinking as he walked, sighed, and stared at Hugh.

"Amazing strong, that man," he said, after a time.

Jamie nodded.

"Where'd he come from?"

Jamie shrugged.

"So there's nobody you know about—anywhere—to write to?"

Jamie shook his head.

"Shame," said Le Bon. "He was a hell of a hunter. Still, I suppose this is the way he'd want to go—while he was about his business, out on the trail. . . . Buried in one of the places he'd hunted."

Jamie looked away. Le Bon grew still. After a while Le Bon rose and made his way to a fire the men had left where a tin of water was still warm.

"Want a cup of tea?" he called.

"No, thanks."

He made himself a cup and returned with it. Later, he smoked his pipe, drank more tea. The day wore on. Hugh muttered occasionally, grew still again. Le Bon shook his head and looked into the distance.

As shadows slid eastward Le Bon cocked his head.

"Do you hear hoofbeats?" he asked.

"No," Jamie answered.

Le Bon lowered himself to the ground, placed an ear against it. For a long time, he was still.

"Hear anything?" Jamie said.

"No. I was mistaken."

He rose again.

"Little worried about the Ree," he said. "Had me hearing things." He laughed and seized a handful of his hair and tugged it about. "Hate to part company with this stuff, is all."

Later, as they made their dinner of the supplies the major had left them, Le Bon relived his part in the recent campaign. Jamie nodded periodically, watching Hugh. Later still, as the night came on, he covered Hugh with a blanket.

"Amazing strong," Le Bon repeated. "Sad, to have your strength working against you. When there's no hope."

Jamie's dreams were a jumble, of Hugh and the bear and the Indians, of Major Henry and the men, riding, riding, into the distance. He woke unrested in the morning, letting Le Bon sleep as he broke his fast on crackers and tea. Hugh's condition seemed unchanged. Still he struggled—perhaps, as Le Bon had said, against his own strength—moving occasionally, but never speaking, face drawn, gray, fingers at times still ascrabble. How long did it take a man to die?

Later, Le Bon shook his head.

"Looks a lot worse," he said. "Today or tonight will do for him."

"You're probably right," Jamie responded.

"I hope so," Le Bon said. "Not just for our sake—though Lord knows I've seen what those Ree can do to a man—but for him, struggling on that way to no account. It's indecent what dying does to a man, by way of suffering. How old are you, anyhow, Jamie?"

"Sixteen," Jamie said. "Pretty near."

"So you've got your whole life to go yet, lessen it's cut short. Just hope your end doesn't drag out like poor Hugh's."

"Yes," Jamie said, and sipped his tea gone cold.

By afternoon's light, Hugh looked as if he were made of wax, face half-melted. There were times when Jamie thought it was over for him. But always there came a small twitch, a low noise, a bit of bubbling breath. Le Bon raised ladders of smoke, puffing, and watched. Birds passed, to and from the river, uttering shrill notes and bits of softer music. The sky clouded over and there came a rumbling from within it, but no rain fell. A wind rose up and the day grew cooler.

"Wonder how far along the major and the men have gotten?" Le Bon said.

"Hard to say."

"They must feel a lot safer to be on the trail now, heading away from the Ree."

"I suppose."

"We couldn't even hear their hoofbeats for all that thunder, if they were coming up on us now."

Jamie shivered against the cold.

"Guess so."

Le Bon rose and stretched and went off to relieve himself in the bushes. Hugh did not move.

They raised a lean-to of branches for themselves and Hugh, hung a sheet of canvas over it. The rainfall that night was light, drumming. The sound became war drums in Jamie's sleep, and hoofbeats of mounted parties. . . .

The morning came gray and damp, and still Hugh lingered.

"I dreamed a party of them passed us in the night," Le Bon observed. "Maybe they did."

"Then we're lucky."

"So far. My! He looks poorly."

"Same as yesterday, I'd judge."

"Still breathing, though. Who'd've thought any man could hold on so long?"

"Hugh ain't like other folks," Jamie said. "He always knew what to do. He was always strong enough to do it."

Le Bon shook his head.

"I believe you," he told him. "It ain't natural to keep living when you've been tore up the way he has. I've seen a lot of folks a-dying, but none of 'em to hold on like this. You know it's got to be soon, don't you?"

"Seems so."

"Be a shame, the two of us to die for someone who could go any minute."

Jamie went to the spring to rinse the kerchief to wash Hugh's face again.

As they rolled into their blankets that evening, Le Bon said, "This'll be it, boy. I know it. I'm sorry, 'cause I know you're all the family each other's got. Say some prayers, if you know any. I'll do the same, before I sleep."

And the sun shone upon him in the morning. And Jamie's first thoughts were of Hugh. Turning, rising, he stared. Had it happened during the night? No. The pallor remained, but now a small fluttering breath had begun, unlike the man's earlier gasps and long silent spells. His chest moved slightly, with a more rapid, shallow breathing.

"I've seen men like this before," he heard Le Bon say. "Soon it will be over, lad. Likely with God's blessing."

Jamie wept silently. It was wrong to want it to happen, he knew.

"I just want him to stop hurting," he finally said.

"And soon he will, Jamie. Soon he will." Le Bon sounded sad. "There's few as could fight it the way he did. But soon his trials will be over. You can see it."

Jamie nodded, rubbing his cheeks dry against his shoulders.

After breakfast, Le Bon stared for perhaps an hour at the man who lay before him. Finally, he spoke:

"I've been thinking," he said, "about the Ree again. You know I'm scared. I know you are, too. Now, meaning no disrespect, and knowing Hugh'll be gone soon, it takes a time to bury a man— especially when we've only our knives to dig with. All that extra time we'll be running risk they'll find us, when we could be riding away."

"That's true."

"Being practical now—and like I said, with no disrespect—I thought we might dig it now and have it ready. We're just sitting here, anyhow, and whether it gets dug before or after won't mean a thing to him. It's the spirit that counts, that his friends mean to do right by him. It can't hurt him none to make it ready. But it could make a difference for our safety—afterwards."

"Yes," Jamie said. "I guess he'd understand that."

So, drawing his knife, Le Bon rose and moved about to Hugh's far side. He traced long lines in the earth with its point, measuring the man's great length and width with his eye as he did so. Then he plunged the blade into the ground and outlined the first piece of sod to be removed.

" 'Dust to dust,' " he said, "like the Good Book tells us. We'll do fair by him, Jamie. Proper size and deep enough to protect him from weather and the critters. We'll do it right. I know how much you care about him."

After a time, Jamie rose and moved to the plot's farther end. He hesitated a moment, and then began to cut.

They dug all that day, using their hands where it was soft, their blades where the earth resisted intrusion. They removed stones, roots, and a goodly amount of soil. They excavated to a considerable depth, then cleaned their blades in the grass and washed themselves at the spring, before they returned to Hugh's side.

Still that fluttering breath continued.

They ate their meal, and the day's last light touched Hugh's face with color. They watched him till the stars came out, then muttered good-nights and found their blankets.

In all their dreams, Hugh was a part of the earth.

* * *

. . . Hugh dreamt he lay broken beside his grave, his friends riding away into the west. He had heard them speak of going, been powerless to respond. Now he heard only hoofbeats as they went away from him. Felt them within the earth, heard a momentary exchange of their distant voices.

Vaguely, aware of light, he listened to the sounds. The words died away. A tired moon hung above him. He stared at it through a haze. Dawn had leaked a slight light upon strands of mist. There was no wind to stir it. The hoofbeats seemed to grow louder again. He remembered the taste of blood, the breath of the bear. And crawling. . . .

He was awake atop his bluff, and the sounds of hoofbeats were real. He turned and peered downward. Passing through the fog, three Indian horsemen rode on the trail of the buffalo. Almost, Hugh called out to them, for they could well be Sioux, with whom he was on good terms. Yet, they could also be Ree, and he had not come all this way to deliver himself into the hands of his enemies. He lay still and watched them ride by to vanish westward into the mist.

They could well be the outriders for an entire tribe on the trail of the buffalo. He would wait a time and see what followed. With a larger group, slower in passing, he should be able to tell whether they were friend or foe. And then—If they were Sioux, he would be fed, cared for, his wounds tended. He would tell them tales at their fires, paying them in the coin of stories from his wanderings. Then he would walk again, be about his hunt.

He waited as the fog turned to gold, listening, watching. The sun drifted slowly out of the east, over the course of perhaps an hour. Abruptly, a flock of dark birds rose downstream, cawing and flapping, to move westward, settling in a stand of cottonwoods. Then he heard the barking of dogs and the neighing of horses. A little later a band of mounted warriors came into sight out of the brush, to pass the base of his bluff upon that westward trail.

He watched, suddenly aware of his heartbeat. Mounted on a pie-bald stallion, the lead warrior was an older man, face hard and craggy, hair streaked with white; and Hugh recognized him. It was Elk Tongue, the war chief of the Ree, and more and more of his people came into view behind him, rounding the bluff, continuing into the west.

As Hugh watched he saw old men and women, children, the ill as well as the hale, in the procession. This looked to be more than a hunt, for it might be forty lodges that followed behind Elk Tongue, and they bore all their possessions, not just those of the hunt. The Sioux must finally have succeeded in dislodging them from their eastern encampment. They were in retreat now, ponies dragging tra-vois bearing furs, pots, drums, baskets of food, a few metal imple-ments, small children riding atop the heaped household goods; the forms of those too ill to walk or ride were strapped onto other car-riers. Nursing squaws passed by, babies at their backs. All of them looked haggard. Hugh could almost smell their burning cornfields. They would follow the herd, to feed, then continue to the home of their Pawnee relatives on the Platte.

Hugh snorted. "Ree" was short for "Arikara." They had attacked peaceful traders several times, which led to the Leavenworth cam-paign, in which the Sioux had allied themselves with the whites, for they, too, had known unreasoned violence at the hands of these people. The Rees' cousins the Pawnees were more tolerant, less prone to battle and ambush without good reason. Having been a Pawnee, Hugh spoke their language fluently, the Rees' dialect as well, though he was certain that the Rees would not recognize his blood-tie with their kin.

Not that the Pawnees were exactly easygoing. . . .

As the tribe passed he let his thoughts drift back over the years. Where did it all begin? Beyond the Pennsylvania valley of his birth, what had brought him to this point? Chance, he supposed. Chance, and human meanness—the meanness of a white man, a Frenchman, as cussed as any he had met on the plains, white or Indian. No race, nation, or tribe had a monopoly on cussedness; it just seemed a part of being human. He remembered the sea.

After that war in 1812 he'd gone to sea, working on traders in the Caribbean. Never had any real desire to see the mountains or roam the plains. He'd known tropic ports, drunk his share of rum, survived fierce storms and damaged vessels. He had enjoyed the sea and its smells and moods, liked the bright birds and flowers and girls of his ports of call, liked the taste of their rich foods, their wines. He would likely be there still, save for the doings of one afternoon on the Gulf.

When the sleek vessel carrying a lot of sail had first been sighted, no one had been particularly alarmed until she struck her true colors and fired a warning shot.

The captain tried to run, but this was a mistake. The pirate vessel overtook them readily. He tried fighting back then, but this, too, was a mistake. He was outmaneuvered, outgunned, outmanned. Actually, there was nothing he could have done that would have been right, Hugh reflected. Simple surrender at that first warning shot would also have been a mistake. Hugh was to learn all of this later, firsthand, though it was mainly confirmation of rumors he had been hearing for years. The captain could not have saved them from Jean Laffite, who was not of a humor to leave any witnesses to his business that day.

Hugh saw the captain and the other officers cut down. The seamen were treated the same way. This decided him against any attempt to surrender, and he determined to sell his life as dearly as possible. Standing back to back then with seaman Tom Dickens, cutlass in one hand, belaying pin in the other, he killed everyone who came at him, gutting them, clubbing them, hacking at limbs and faces. The deck grew slippery with gore about him, and he bled himself from a collection of wounds. After a time, the attacks slowed; it seemed that the pirate crewmen were holding back, loath to rush in and close with him. Finally, he became aware of a tall individual who stood watching the slaughter. Eventually, the man spoke:

"Let up!" he ordered. "I'll talk to them." Hugh heard the French accent and realized this to be the captain of whom he had heard stories.

"You two," the captain said, as soon as the attacks ceased. "Do you wish to live?"

190

"A foolish question," Hugh replied. "Would we be fighting so, were it otherwise?"

The Frenchman smiled.

"I can have my men wear you down, or I can send for firearms and take you at a distance," he said. "Or you can join my crew and keep your lives. I find myself undermanned again, partly because of yourselves. I can use a pair of good fighters."

"Druther live," Tom said.

"All right," said Hugh. "I'll do it."

"Then put up your weapons—you can keep them—and help transfer the cargo to my ship. If you've any personal effects you care about, better get them, too. We'll be scuttling this scow when we're done here."

"Aye, sir," said Hugh, lowering his blade and slipping the club behind his belt.

Jean Laffite's current headquarters were on Galveston Island. There Hugh and Tom were given quarters. While he made no friends, Hugh became acquainted with all of the pirate crew. There was some resentment of the newcomers at first, and while memory of their display on the decks of the doomed vessel prevented all but two from carrying this beyond words, those two were thick-armed, heavy-shouldered fellows with the battered faces of brawlers. The burly Hugh outwrestled his man and bashed him a few times till he lapsed into unconsciousness. Tom boxed with his opponent, and though his own nose was broken in the encounter he laid the man out. After that, the two shipmates met with no further violence at the hands of the crew and found themselves on speaking terms with all of them. While no real amiability developed, the men were not particularly amiable to begin with, save when drunk, and then it only took the form of songs, gallows humor, bawdy yarns, and practical jokes. Hugh did not trust himself to get drunk with them, for they were inclined to the setting afire of beards and to the removing of a fellow's trousers and painting his bum with tar.

Hugh and Tom sailed with Laffite. There were bloody encounters with merchantmen, for it became apparent that Laffite's policy involved leaving no eyewitnesses ever to testify against him. Hugh fought in the boarding of vessels and he fought to defend himself, but he took what small pride he might in the fact that he never executed prisoners. This changed one spring day when they took a British trader.

Three able-bodied prisoners were taken that day. Laffite faced them—a tall, graceful figure, elegantly clad, one hand upon his hip—and stared into each man's eyes until they fell. Then, as before, he spoke:

"Gentlemen," he said, "I find myself somewhat understaffed at the moment. The exigencies of this work do take their toll in manpower. So I've a proposition for you. Join my crew. You'll have a snug berth, all you want in the way of food and drink, and a share of the booty. There will be occasional shore leave in safe ports to enjoy it. It is a dangerous life, but a high one. Think hard, think quickly, and answer me now."

Two of them agreed immediately. The third, however, asked, "And if my answer is no?"

Laffite stroked his beard.

"Consider it a matter of life or death, sir," he replied, "as you make your decision."

"All my life I've done what I had to and tried to be honest while I was about it," the seaman answered, "though God knows I've had my lapses. Cast me adrift or leave me on some isle if you would. I'd rather that than join your crew."

Laffite raised his eyes and caught Hugh's gaze.

"Deal with him," he said.

Hugh looked away.

Laffite stared a moment longer. Then, "Now," he added.

Hugh looked back, meeting his captain's dark gaze again.

"No, sir," he replied.

"You refuse my order?"

"I won't kill a defenseless man," he said.

Laffite drew a pistol from his sash and fired it. The man toppled, the side of his head gone red.

"Pitch him over the side," Laffite said to another crewman, who moved immediately to comply.

"Hugh, I'm unhappy with you," Laffite stated, stowing his pistol and turning away.

Hugh departed and helped to transfer the cargo.

Later, when they had returned to their base, Tom said to him, "Word's going around you made the captain unhappy."

"I wouldn't doubt it," Hugh replied. "I didn't kill a man he told me to."

"I heard things like that have happened in the past, before our time."

"Oh?"

"Old Jean, he's a real stickler for discipline. They say that nobody as refused a direct order from him has lived too long afterwards."

"How'd he do 'em?"

"Sometimes he holds a sort of court and makes an example of 'em. Other times he just lets it be known to a few he trusts that he wants that man dead. Someone always obliges and puts a knife in him then—when he's sleepin', or some other time he's not on his guard."

"You heard he usually gets rid of them pretty soon after something like this happens?"

"That's what they say."

"Thanks, Tom. Maybe you shouldn't be talking to me much now."

"What're you going to do?"

"I've been thinking for some time about leaving. Now's as good a time to try quitting this business as any."

"You can't steal a boat, Hugh. They watch 'em too careful."

Hugh shook his head.

"Think I'll wait till after dark and swim for shore."

"That's a pretty far piece."

"I'm a pretty good swimmer."

"The water's sometimes sharky."

"Well, that's a maybe, and staying's a for sure."

"What'll you do when you get to shore?"

"Start walking for New Orleans."

"I'm coming with you. I don't much like it here myself. Sooner or later he's going to ask me to do something like that, and the same thing'll happen."

"Make a little bundle of your valuables then. I'll let you know when I'm going."

Hugh waited till the others had started their evening drinking

193

before he nodded to Tom and said, "Gonna take a walk."

They met on the isle's northern shore, lit by a partial moon and floods of stars. Small waves danced in their light as Hugh and Tom stared out over the waters.

"Looks like a long haul," Tom said, "but I'm still game. How long you figure before they guess what we did?"

"Morning, if we're lucky. Sooner, if tonight's the night someone comes by to get me. Even then, they can't do much till tomorrow, and we'll either be drowned, et, or too far gone by then."

Tom nodded.

"I'm ready any time you are."

"Let's be about it then."

So they stripped, bundled their clothes about their possessions, tied their packs to their backs, and entered the water. It felt cooler than the night's air, but their strokes were strong and after a time the exertion seemed to push the chill away. They swam steadily landward, and Hugh thought back over the previous month's piracies. He'd wanted to leave before this, but the danger had held him back. Now he wished he'd left sooner. Stealing, killing, drinking too much every day, and being a prisoner much of the time made him think again of the world's meanness. There was too much of it, everywhere he turned. He wanted to be alone in a big place, away from his fellows, free. He wondered whether the man he'd refused to kill had had a family. He wasn't sure he ever wanted one himself. Another way to be a prisoner, maybe.

Crawling through the water, he lost track of time. There was the monotony of the waves, Tom's steady splashing nearby, and the sameness of the night all around. The two shores were dreams, the crawling was all. One must go on.

At some point, he remembered coming to shore. Now the waters of Galveston Bay seemed the dream, the land they waded toward the reality. He remembered laughing and hearing Tom's laughter. Then they threw themselves flat, breathing heavily, the tingling of ceased motion dancing over their skins. After a while, they slept.

. . . Lying there, still as a stone, he watched the latter end of the procession in its passing, through a haze of fog and trail dust—the

194

lame and the aged walking with sticks, leaning on companions, more squaws with children and packs of supplies. They did take care of their own, he reflected, and he could almost feel a touch of sympathy at their flight from the Sioux, though it was their own cussedness had brought them to this pass. He and Tom had been captured by the Ree on their trek through Texas, but had managed to escape. They were wary after that because of the treatment they had received. But all the wariness in the world didn't amount to much for two men afoot on a plain when they were spotted again by a mounted party.

They tried hiding in the scrub, but the warriors knew they were there and flushed them quickly. Hugh tried the few words of Ree he had learned during their brief captivity, and his new captors showed understanding of them as well as of his raised open hands and his sign gestures. They made it obvious, however, that they were prisoners by taking their knives and conducting them to be confined in their camp.

They were tied and guarded that night, and while they were given water to drink they were not fed, though they were allowed to dine from their own meagre supply of fruit and roots they had obtained on departing from the Rees. The following day they were not molested, though they remained confined, and they spent the second night under guard, also. A considerable babble of discussion emerged from a nearby tent late into both evenings.

The next day they were brought food and treated with some kindness. They were given fresh garments and led about the camp. As the day wore on, Hugh attempted to communicate with their captors, hoping to win their release, but the only responses he received seemed to indicate that they would be permitted to join in a feast that evening.

The day wore on, and at sunset they were conducted to a gathering of the entire tribe in whose company they were seated. Fires burned at every hand, and the smells of roasting buffalo, venison, and fowls came to them. They sampled every dish, as their hosts insisted that they try everything, that they gorge themselves on their favorite fare.

They were infected by the tribe's seeming good humor, and began to relax and try to make jokes themselves. Finally, sated and a little drowsy, they began looking forward to the feast's end, to retiring to a night's rest. Abruptly then, they were seized from behind by several braves and bound hand and foot with strips of rawhide.

"Hey!" Hugh shouted, then added the word he'd learned for "friend."

Nobody answered him. Instead, Tom was taken to a tall, upright stake and tied to it. Squaws cut away his garments, stripping him, and heaped kindling about his feet.

"Let the boy go!" Hugh called. "Friend! Friend!"

They paid him no heed, and the women went to work on Tom with knives, cutting away strips of his skin.

"Stop! Stop it, for God's sake!" Hugh screamed, his cries half-drowned by Tom's own shrieks.

The women continued about their business, taking their time, removing patch after patch of skin, occasionally poking and prodding with the points of their weapons. Hugh became acutely aware of the second stake which had been raised, not too far behind the first. He closed his eyes against the sight, gritted his teeth, and tried to blank out Tom's cries. It did no good. Not seeing was in some ways worse than seeing, leaving even more to his imagination.

The ordeal went on for a long while, till Tom finally pleaded with them to kill him. Even later, they started a fire at his feet and heaped more kindling upon it. Hugh had shouted at them to no avail and had used up his tears early. Now he just watched as his friend writhed within the consuming flames. He tried not to, but his gaze kept returning to the spectacle. Soon it would be over. Then, of course, it would be his turn.

He remembered a small container of vermillion dye which he had borne with him from Galveston Island, as it had some commercial value and he'd hoped to sell it on reaching civilization. He hated to see it burned up, wasted, and it would make fine body paint, a thing his captors seemed to favor. What the hell, he decided. Maybe it could do even more for him here.

He groped with bound hands at the place where he carried it at his belt. Painfully, he unfastened its ties. When it came free and he had a grip on it, he raised himself.

Casting the bundle at the chief, he cried, "Here's a present for you! Hate to see it go to waste!"

The chief stared at the parcel, then extended a hand and picked it up. He removed it from the leather pouch and examined it closely, until he had discovered the manner in which the tin might be opened. When it had been uncovered his eyes widened. Tentatively, he touched the substance with a fingertip, raised it to study it, drew a line with it upon his forearm.

A pair of braves was already headed for Hugh by then, but the chief raised a hand and said something Hugh did not understand. The warriors halted.

The chief advanced then and addressed Hugh, but Hugh shook his head and said, "Present. It's a gift. I do not understand what you are saying."

The chief continued to speak, however, finally calling something back over his shoulder. Presently, a brave approached, drawing a knife as he advanced upon Hugh. Hugh gritted his teeth as the blade's point passed near his abdomen, but the man used it only to cut his bonds.

The brave helped him to his feet, and the chief came forward and assisted him. They guided him back to his quarters, where he sank upon his sleeping skins. The chief said something else then, smiling as he said it, and went away. The man who had freed him remained on guard outside.

He did not think he would sleep easily that night, yet he did. The evening's events returned in his dreams, and in the morning he recalled awakening several times to the sound of his own voice calling Tom's name. After a while a woman brought him breakfast, and he was surprised at his appetite. He finished everything and when she brought him more he ate that, too.

The day wore on and he waited. He was fed again at about noontime. No one approached him other than the woman with the food. He made no attempt to venture beyond his confines. He sat and thought, about Tom, about Laffite, the Caribbean, ships, sailing on a bright day, Pennsylvania summers.

Later they came for him and escorted him back to the site of the previous night's feasting. He surveyed the area hastily, but this time

197

there were no stakes in sight. He moved to settle into the position he had occupied before but was halted by his companion and taken forward, where it was indicated that he should sit beside the chief.

This dinner was different from the previous one in that it was preceded by a speech from the chief and a ritual of sorts where he placed his hands upon Hugh's shoulders and head several times, struck him lightly with bundles of twigs, bound his hair with a beaded cloth, and finally draped a small skin over his shoulders. Then the feasting proceeded in a jovial spirit with others of the tribe passing by to clasp Hugh or lay hands upon him. Gradually, he came to understand that the chief had adopted him, that he had become a member of the tribe, that he was now a Pawnee.

In the months that followed he learned the language, the customs, discovered that he had a knack for tracking, became a deadly marksman with bow and arrow, took him a Pawnee wife, became one of the tribe's better hunters. He learned, too, that the life of the trail appealed to him more than the life of the sea, with its cramped quarters. The plains held all the freedom of the vast and changing sea, without the confining drawbacks. He did not know exactly when he resolved to spend his days on the frontier. The realization grew in him slowly. Before the first winter had passed, however, he knew that he had finished forever with a sailor's life.

Yes, he had enjoyed it. But reflecting upon it now, as the Pawnees' less reputable relatives vanished into the west leaving a cloud of golden dust behind them, he saw that meanness again, on the night the Pawnee women had tortured Tom. True, they'd had grievances against the whites, but a bullet in the brain or a quick knife-thrust would as easily satisfy a need for a death. It was nothing special against the Pawnees, though, who had been good to him during his stay in their midst. Rather, he felt, they had their cussedness because they were members of the same race as all the other tribes of the earth.

He rubbed dust from his eyes then, and licked his lips. Time to crawl down and get himself a drink, see what he could find to eat.

Slowly, he descended and made his way to the river, where he drank and washed his face, hands, and neck. The area about him was too trampled to retain edible roots or berries. He crawled then to the carcass where he had fed the previous evening. It had been picked clean, however, its bones cracked and scattered or carried off.

Back in the direction of the bluff where he had spent the night, beyond the trees, Hugh saw a movement. He lay perfectly still and watched. Some final straggler of the migrant Rees.

He crawled ahead then, among the trees, through the brush, short-cutting a bend in the trail to bring him to a waiting place ahead of the shuffling figure.

An old woman clad in buckskins moved carefully along, bearing her small bundle of possessions. He licked his lips and checked behind and ahead. No one else had come into sight to the rear, and the rest of the tribe was gone from view, far ahead. There was sure to be some food in her pack, and the others would hardly soon miss someone they hadn't even bothered to wait for. Flint, steel, a knife. . . . Even in his condition it would be no problem to take them from her. Her cries would not be heard above the noise of the van.

He watched her move. Ironic, if she'd been one of the ones who'd done for Tom that long-gone day. She shuffled nearer, and he wondered at her life. How many babies had she carried? How many were living now? Just an old woman. . . . He watched as she passed, remained still till she was out of sight beyond a clump of trees.

"Fool!" he muttered, to have let her go by, mother of Rees. It was not the same as when he'd refused to kill a helpless seaman. This was the enemy. He shook his head. "Fool," he said softly. Sometimes he was a fool.

Growling, he turned away, heading back toward the river.

He followed the water's course, down along the trail the Ree had come. It was easy traveling, though the dirt irritated his nose, and he halted to wash his face several times. Berry bushes beside the trail had been stripped, as had the lower branches of fruit trees he passed. He dug a few roots when he was beside the river, washed them, broke his fast with them.

Before long all of the fog had burned away, and the dust had settled. During the next hour he made good progress. The sun spilled some warmth through the yellow and green of the tree limbs, and there was a fresh strength in him today.

Topping a small rise, he halted and sniffed the air.

Smoke. The breeze brought him a hint of smoke. Beginning of a brush fire, or its residuum? Or might someone be camping nearby?

The breeze shifted and the smell vanished. Had it really been there, to begin with?

He crawled forward again, sniffing the air regularly. Nothing now. Still . . .

It was several minutes before it came again. It was still faint, and a breeze's vagary took it away once more. But now he was certain. He had smelled woodsmoke. It was impossible to determine its direction, so he continued along the trail.

Another hundred feet and it came to him clearly. The trail, then, did seem the proper course. He wondered again at what it might represent. Aid? Or an enemy?

He moved off the trail and continued to advance, with more difficulty now, among the trees, brush, and rocks that paralleled its course. It seemed prudent to have a look at any campers without being seen himself.

The campfire smell grew stronger. He slowed when he felt he was nearing its vicinity. Finally, he halted and lay still for a long while, listening for voices. There were none, though he thought he heard the growling of one or more dogs. Finally, he began to move again, deliberately, soundlessly.

After a time, he drew near the periphery of a cleared area. He parted the stems of a shrub and peered through at it. It had obviously been used as a campsite recently. There were no people in sight, but several dogs prowled it now, whining, scavenging.

Studying the grounds, where a great number of people had probably passed the night, he realized that this must have been the Ree's latest encampment. They had proceeded from here past his aerie. He watched a little longer, until he was satisfied that the place had been completely abandoned.

He moved forward then and entered the area. No telling what might have been lost or left behind by a fleeing tribe. Their fires were normally extinguished completely, but with the Sioux at their heels they were moving fast. It would be worth a quick survey. He shouted at the dogs in Pawnee, and they slunk away from him.

He advanced upon the one fire which still smoldered, then halted and lay staring at it. How long had it been since he had seen a fire, sign of humanity? How long since he had been able to kindle one himself? He thought of many he had sat beside—campfires, hearth-fires—and he suddenly felt that he had indeed come a great distance, that he had come back to something. He chuckled in realizing that he lay prostrate before it. His life was wilderness, yet many things set him apart from the beasts. No bear could feel exactly as he did in returning to such a sign of a former existence. He patted the earth beside it, then moved on.

His tracker's eye caught all of the camp signs clearly—the places where the campers had eaten, the places where they had slept, their trails to water and latrine. Even without having seen them go by, he could roughly estimate their number, could separate the tracks of the aged and the children from those in between. The dogs studied him as he explored, but seemed afraid to draw near this man-scented thing of low profile and bestial movement.

With a stick, he stirred the ashes of their fires, where all of their trash seemed to have found its place. All of these others were cold now, and while some of the trash—bits of cloth, leather, wood—had not been completely incinerated, it seemed that nothing of any value lay within. Until the fifth. . . .

Poking within the soft gray heap at the center of a circle of stones, he almost missed the tiny flash. But he did not even pause as it registered. Immediately, he moved the stick again, to knock free its outline and clear its surface. A slim, worn length of whetted steel, its point broken off, haft charred, lay before him in the dust.

He dropped the stick and snatched it up. Steel, serviceable steel. . . .

He wiped it on his pant leg, held it up for closer scrutiny. He tested its edge. A bit dull, but easily honed. And he could wrap the handle with some cloth torn from his shirt. Then, turn up a piece of flint and he could strike a fire whenever he needed it. He smiled.

He could carve a crutch. The hip and leg were feeling somewhat better. It was possible, had he something to lean on, that he might be able to hobble along in an upright position now.

He studied the rocks that ringed the burned-out fires, seeming to recall a small, flat one that just might serve as a whetstone. Yes. Over to the right. . . .

He fetched the stone and began honing the blade. He found himself wanting to whistle as he did it, but refrained.

Later, with a satisfactory edge upon the blade and the jagged point somewhat blunted, he cast about among the trees for a limb suitable for his crutch.

It was the better part of an hour, spent crawling among trees, before he located an appropriate branch, at a height to which he could drag himself by holding first to the trunk, then grasping a lower limb, the knife clasped in his teeth. After notching it and whittling it free, it took him another hour—sitting, back to the tree trunk—to trim it properly, find and adjust to the right length through repeated testing, and to carve a comfortable armrest upon it.

He held it across his lap and regarded it. A knife and a crutch in one morning. . . . If he could use the latter as well as the former, this was a very important day.

Hand against the tree trunk, pulling, left leg straightening, he drew himself up to his full height and then leaned as he fitted the rest to his right armpit. Still holding to the tree with his left hand, he shifted weight onto the crutch. It bore him. He allowed his right foot to touch lightly upon the ground.

He took a step with his left foot, shifted his weight, moved the crutch a small distance, shifted again. He let his left hand fall from the tree. Another step with the left foot. Shift. Move the crutch. Shift.

To be upright again—albeit with aid—not to be crawling—yes, it was an important day. He smiled. He made his way about the campsite. The dogs watched him, but kept their distance, tails sinking when he turned his attention upon them. He thought of killing one for food, but they were wary of him. Yes, he really was human, they must have decided. And a stranger, and odd.

Now. Now, then. Now. Time to search out a piece of flint.

A canvassing of the immediate area did not turn up a chunk of that stone. So he decided to continue on his way, scanning all rocky deposits as he went.

Upright. It did not take long to get into the rhythm of the trail with his new gait. He sprawled periodically to rest his left leg, and his right shoulder. It was difficult to determine whether he was covering ground more rapidly in this fashion or when crawling at his best. Yet he was certain that with increasing familiarity, usage, and strength, this means of progress would soon outstrip the earlier.

He swung along his way into the afternoon till thirst drove him from the trail down among the cottonwoods by the river. And it was there he found his flint. Almost singing, he made his way to the water's edge. When his shadow fell upon it, he saw a darting of forms. Fish had been browsing in the shallows.

After he drank his fill, he used his blade to fashion a spear from a straight stick. Waiting then in such a position that his shadow did not impinge upon his chosen stretch of water, he tried for half an hour before obtaining two catfish.

With some threads from his sleeve and a pile of wood shavings, he was able to start a fire with his new tools. He fed it slowly, and while it strengthened to the consumption of larger sticks, he cleaned his fish on a flat rock and washed them in the river. He grilled them on willow wands, trying the while to calculate how long it had been since he had eaten food that had been cooked. He had to give up, however, as he soon realized he had lost track of the days during his crawl.

After he had eaten he stripped and bathed in the river, remembering that bitter pool near the beginning of his journey. Here, he could tilt his head and drink whenever he wished. And amid his buoyancy and movements he felt that he was coming back together again.

He washed his tattered garments then and donned them wet. He was tempted to loaf the day away, letting them dry on a bush, but he felt uncomfortable this near the Ree. He doubted any would be doubling back to check after pursuit, but it was possible, if the Sioux had indeed pursued them for a time. And though it seemed unlikely there would be any stragglers this far back, some mishap might have slowed someone who was even now hurrying to catch up. So he remained alert as he swung along, ready to depart the trail in an instant at the first sign of humanity.

The afternoon wore on, however, with only the sounds of the birds and a few splashes from the sunken river to keep company to the small thumps of his crutch. A few yellowed leaves came loose and dropped about him. His armpit and shoulder grew sore, but his leg was feeling better, even when he touched it down in occasional testing. His scalp, forehead, and nose were feeling better, also, some of the scabbing having come away as he had bathed. He could not recall when the headaches had ceased.

There were no fruits or berries to be had along his way. The Ree had stripped the bushes and trees as they had gone by. Hugh decided that it would be fish again for his dinner, if they were to be had. He stumped along, realizing, for the first time in a long while, that he was enjoying the day.

He thought back as he hiked, to the time he had spent with the Pawnees, his earlier reverie having breathed fresh life into those memories. He recalled their leader's decision to journey to St. Louis, where a meeting involving large-scale trapping was to be held. It had been decided that it might be a good thing to send a peace mission, to let the fur company know that the Pawnees were a dependable, friendly people, who might be counted upon to provide guides, messengers, labor, in their enterprise. It might benefit the tribe by promoting a preferred status when it came to trading, particularly for metal goods, firearms, ammunition, horses. It certainly seemed worth the effort.

It felt strange, entering the city, being there, back among his own kind—or were they? He had changed, he realized then. It only took a few days, in rooms and on busy streets, before a feeling of confinement came over him. Reading a newspaper was a pleasure he had all but forgotten, though, over a morning cup of coffee. It was there that he saw an ad, in the *Missouri Republican*, which tied in with the Pawnees' journey, and which got him to thinking again of things that had passed through his mind more casually during the past couple of days. The Rocky Mountain Fur Company was looking for men to supplement this year-old trapping company's crew at its Ft. Henry trading post. Major Andrew Henry, after whom the post was named, needed hunters as well as trappers, and especially people with knowledge of Indian languages and ways. He was later to learn that the fort, near the mouth of the Yellowstone River, had lost both horses and men to raiding Assiniboine and Blackfoot warriors.

Yes, it sounded like the sort of enterprise which might meet his fancy, and for which he doubtless was qualified. He had grown tired of the tribal life of the Pawnees. But this—All that movement, and new lands to see. . . . He smiled as he finished his coffee. He would have to go for an interview and learn all of the details.

So he had gone, talked, and been offered employment. His experiences seemed to impress the interviewer strongly, and he had signed him on for the work.

In the days that remained in St. Louis, Hugh met a number of men who had lived in the wilderness—some of them attracted by the fur company's hiring, others just passing through, in both directions. One of these had been that strange man, John Colter, who had actually traveled to the far ocean with Lewis and Clark. There was an odd light in his eye, which Hugh at first took as a touch of lunacy but later decided was . . . something else—something like the look of a medicine man who had been long in the dream-time. Colter did not recite his tales with the braggadocio of the seasoned yarner but with a conviction Hugh found vaguely unsettling. He came away from their talks of travels and adventures with a belief in the man's absolute sincerity, and he was to wonder about him for years afterwards. . . .

. . . Later, as the evening came on, he caught his fish, grilled them, and dined. Then he washed up, massaged his leg, shoulder, and arm for a time, and removed himself a good distance from the trail to make his camp. He fell to sleep with a feeling of satisfaction.

In the morning he dined on berries and water from the river. A few days of steady travel and he'd be accustomed to swinging along with the crutch, he felt. There was a rhythm to it which he was beginning to pick up, and he knew that he was making better time upright, and with less effort.

Each stride took him farther from the Ree and nearer to Sioux country. They called them Dakotas up here. Same thing, though. They'd trust him all right. Henry's boys had always gotten on well with the Sioux. The closer he got to the Cheyenne River and the farther from the Moreau the better he felt. Hard to judge how many days it would take to really be into their country. If it were a few weeks later, with less foliage on the trees, he'd have a better view westward. Could catch a glimpse of the Black Hills then, to know better where he was. At least he knew where he was headed. He'd come a good distance toward Ft. Kiowa, and while it was still a long way off he'd come into a much more congenial piece of countryside. And his strength was beginning to return. Already, long stretches of his inchworm progress had taken on the fragmented quality of dreaming. . . .

He tried to think about meanness—from Laffite and the Pawnee women to Jamie—but his spirits were too high. So he just set his mind to rising and falling with the swells like a ship at anchor, and the day passed through, along with pieces of Pennsylvania, the West Indies, and the mountains, most of them involving days such as this.

He slept deeply that night and did not remember any dreams. In the morning, though, as he headed to the river to bathe and seek after berries and roots, he found a succession of stripped berry bushes, bear tracks and bear scat about the area. This upset him for a long while. That night, after a good day's travel, he dreamed again of the bear, crushing him, breathing into him, with a certain feeling of urgency, as if it were trying to pull him back, to that time, that place, to do it all again, this time not to let him get away. He awoke sweating and shaking. He sought the shadows and sniffed the air, but he was alone in the night. Later, he slept again.

There was no bear sign the next day, and several times it rained causing him to take refuge among the trees. The going was slower because of the mud this produced, and his fear of falling. He was unable to take any fish and dined entirely on roots.

The following day the land began to rise about him, assuming rougher, more hilly features. Eventually, he moved among bluffs and the river was inconveniently low to his left. Still, he crossed the streams and creeks which fed it, and he speared fish, bathed, and drank from these. It seemed to his recollection that this terrain marked the edges of the valley of the Cheyenne. A day or so here and it would be an easy, downhill walk into the safety of that place.

. . . And the pain in his hip was better than it had been since the bear. Even the leg was beginning to feel a little stronger. Every time he inadvertently put weight on it there had been twinges, but none of the terrible pains of a break. Even these had eased during the past few days, so that he began to wonder whether it might have healed to the point where it could bear his weight for a few paces. Gingerly, he began to experiment. A little weight. . . . Not bad. A little more. Still all right. Bit of a twinge there. Try again.

The next morning, as he took his way down a slope, he heard the sound of horses. Immediately he headed for cover.

Two mounted Indians rounded the bend and, from an exclamation one of them uttered, he knew he had been seen. A moment later, two pack horses made the turn, and it sounded as if more were coming behind them. Hugh halted and turned as the foremost reached for his rifle.

He faced them, raising his left hand, open palm facing them. Two more riders rounded the bend, also leading horses loaded with baskets and bags. These riders also reached for their weapons.

As they approached, Hugh grew certain they were Sioux. Thinking again of human cussedness, he waited until they drew near and halted, rifles still upon him.

Then he said, "Hugh Glass," and added "friend" in their language.

God Save the King

■

P. J. Beese and
Todd Cameron Hamilton

Fate is the most common culprit when it comes to making heroes of ordinary people. Some people think fate is over-rated.

The Parliament Tower clock, colloquially and incorrectly known as "Big Ben," arguably the most famous (or at least the most recognizable) clock in the world, was spinning its hands. The real Big Ben, one of the bells hung in the Tower, was striking a resounding 26, 27, 28 . . .

Inside the tower, the clock wardens scrambled about madly, inspecting gears, springs, and cogs in an attempt to diagnose the cause of their baby's infirmity.

29, 30, 31 . . .

On the street outside Parliament Tower, passersby were, for the most part, amused by the false alarms.

32, 33, 34 . . .

At or about stroke 300, people within earshot began to find the constant peal annoying. By ring 500, annoyance had turned to anger. On the 795th ring the clockmaster received a message by courier from the Prime Minister. It was only four words long. "Pull the bloody plug!"

The bell finally stopped at ring 800.

The silence that followed was so loud that the crowd outside was forced to cheer in order to drown it out. One person in that crowd was a beautiful young woman with lush, fully developed breasts that seemed to defy gravity. She stared at her Rolex incredulously.

"800 o'clock? 800! I could have sworn it was no later than two or two-thirty!"

She approached a middle-aged businessman, one of those perfectly turned-out types with a pin-striped suit and a black umbrella.

"Excuse me. Have you got the correct time?"

"Certainly," he answered, reaching into his silk vest pocket to pull out his antique pocket watch. "I've got two twenty-seven."

"No," she replied, shaking her head covered with short blonde curls. "That can't be right. I've got eight hundred." She held out her arm to show her own watch to the stranger. The sun glinting on the diamond bezel made it rather hard to see, but the red LED's did indeed read an unchanging "800:00."

Stiffening his upper lip, the proper stranger asked, "Is this some kind of joke?"

"A joke? A joke, he asks. Oh, sir, I assure you this is no joke. There is nothing funny about this at all!" Her green eyes glittered almost as much as the diamonds had. "Nothing! Nada! Zero! Zilch! Zip!" She grabbed the man by his pin-striped lapels and pulled his face in close to hers. "I think this is the end of the world!" She sighed heavily, and he wrinkled his nose at the mixture of alcohol and tobacco on her breath. "Well, maybe not quite that bad. But it's definitely worse than anything you could possibly imagine." She smiled, kissed him on the end of his still-wrinkled nose, then released his lapels, smoothing them down before she stalked off, muttering, "I didn't realize it was so late. I've got to find him! 'There's so much time and so little to do. Strike that! Reverse it.' I need a drink."

When Mavis St. George returned to her flat in the Mews, she was greeted with derision, as usual, by her puffin, Archimedes. The foul-tempered fowl flapped its wings and hissed excitedly. She cut the display short, however.

"Stow it, Archimedes. I know what time it is. We've got to get to work immediately."

They moved around the disordered room consulting crystals, viewing volumes and perusing parchments half unfurled on overflowing tables. Then Mavis shoved much of the chaos aside, found the phone cord and followed it through the detritus to the actual instrument. Around-the-clock calls followed as she tried to find one man out of all those in Britain.

On the third day of the search, things got interesting. Mavis was accessing the phone records of the greater London area on her Toshiba laptop computer when the puffin quickly flapped its stubby little black wings and ruffled its white chest feathers, its usual way of obtaining its mistress's attention.

"Just a second. Almost done. Just let me finish programming this search and I'll be right with you." She poked a few more symbols into the machine, checked her work on the screen, then pressed Enter. "There, now. What's this all about?"

The little bird flapped its wings again, hopped three times on one orange-webbed foot, then punctuated its request by tilting its head to the right.

"No, I'm not going to take you for walkies right now," Mavis said, looking away, quite peeved at the interruption. "We have work to do."

The bird hopped again, but this time added two head tilts, one right, one left, and a bob for emphasis.

"I said 'no.' Just find someplace discreet. Better yet, use the loo. If a cat can do it, so can you. Then get back to work! The fate of all Britain rests in our hands . . . Well, my hands, anyway. And all you can think of is yourself! You selfish little *Fratercula*! Selfish, selfish, selfish! I swear next time I'll get a cat. I will, just you watch! No more birds! You selfish thing, you!"

At the mention of being replaced by a cat, the small bird indignantly waddled over to a stack of phone books. Hopping up to an open volume, it unceremoniously excreted in the middle of a page. Defiantly it flapped its stubby wings in its best "So there!" fashion, and clacked its brightly colored beak.

Mavis rounded on the little critter. "Not Wales! I need those books! Please tell me it's not the Cardiff book! Anything but the Cardiff book!" Mavis pushed away her terminal and ran to rescue the fouled book. "Oh, damn! It is Cardiff! Have you no decency? It's bad enough that everyone else shits all over Wales! You don't have to!" She wrenched the book out from under the auk, sending it tumbling. "Just look! You've blotted out all the names between Kindrick, Ella, and King, A.! How am I supposed to use this now? One of these obliterated people might have been the one!"

Suddenly the young woman's face went blank and her green eyes glazed over. As if caught in a memory, she focused on something not there. "Hello!" she mused. "King, A.? No. It can't be that simple."

She pressed the page to her forehead, smearing grey-white puffin droppings over her wide brow. "Eenie, weenie, chili beanie! The spirits are about to speak!" she intoned with rising voice. Seconds passed as Mavis St. George stood motionless, entranced, in the middle of her disordered, messy flat with the Cardiff phone book pressed against her smeared face.

"Yes!" she finally exclaimed! "Let me hear you say, 'Hallelujah!' "

The toppled puffin, still a heap of black and white feathers and orange beak, grunted.

"Close enough!" she called, raising her fist in triumph. "Archimedes, we have struck hero!"

Mavis quickly scrawled the address on the palm of her hand with a felt tip marker, grabbed her purse, and dashed out the door. "No time to lose," she chanted. "No time to lose."

Archimedes, with a mighty struggle of wing and webbed foot, righted itself. Flapping its stubby extensions and fluffing out its breast feathers, you could practically hear it calling after her, "You're welcome, you ungrateful, bloody . . ."

The train from London to Cardiff took two hours. The Archwizard Mavis St. George had many other means of transport open to her, some of them all but instantaneous. Mavis had chosen to rail up because she needed the time to decide exactly how to approach this soon-to-be hero—and to make sure she had all of Archimedes's mess removed from her forehead. Nothing like puffin doo-doo to ruin a meeting.

The taxi left Mavis off in front of the fifth row house on Castle Street, Number 17. She approached the canary-yellow front door reminding herself, "Gently, gently. Remember, this is bound to be a shock to him." She stopped, one toe resting on the concrete doorstep. "How do I raise the resonance in him?" she asked herself for the thousandth time. "Hello. I'm Merlin. You're Arthur. Let's go save Britain." She shook her head. "I don't think so. This poor bastard surely doesn't know who he really is, and it's going to be hell trying to convince him. I'll probably have to put a guise on him."

The wizard stepped up, and, still completely undecided as to how to proceed, took a deep breath, closed her eyes, and reached out to ring the bell.

Before she could announce herself, however, the door flew open to reveal a tall, bearded young man.

"Merlin! You really have changed!" He took her arm and pulled her inside, closing the door firmly behind them.

"You know me?" Mavis asked, her face betraying her incredulity.

He leaned up against the wall with one shoulder, and scratched his light brown beard, distorting his face to reach exactly the right spot. "Oh, yeah. I know a lot of things these days."

Mavis took one step forward, putting her face close to his face. "Do you know why I'm here?"

He straightened, plunging his hands into his pockets. "Three days ago I was just Art King. But when Big Ben started to work overtime, so did my memory. By the time Benny stopped ringing, I remembered everything." He closed his eyes.

"Everything?"

"Everything." He opened his grey eyes and peered intently at Mavis. "All of it. Every last bit. It was like someone had superimposed another life directly on top of the life I knew." He closed his eyes again briefly, and drew a deep breath. "I've lived before. I am King Arthur. *The* King Arthur. I know this to be as true as anything around me today."

She smiled broadly, relief washing freely over her features. "Well!" she exclaimed happily, rubbing her hands together. "It looks like this is going to be easier than I had any right to hope. Why don't you just get your hat and we'll be off. We have work to do. A lot of work." She started to turn for the door.

"It's not that simple."

Mavis's hand froze as it reached for the doorknob, hanging in midair like a half-filled balloon. "Come again?"

"I'm not going with you." He responded to her look of disbelief

213

with a broad hand gesture which took in the small hall and the house around it. "I've got a life here! I've got a good job at Inland Revenue, a beautiful wife, friends, a mortgage, and a Volvo that runs reasonably well. I'm not going with you."

"But all of Britain needs you! I wouldn't have bothered to find you if it wasn't necessary! You're a legend! You have a destiny to fulfill!"

Art jammed his hands in his pockets again, and hunched his shoulders. "Don't give me that destiny shit again. The last time I listened to you I wound up screwing my sister, my wife ran off with my best friend, I watched everything I built fall apart before my eyes, and my bastard son by the aforesaid sister ran me through with a pike." He grimaced. "Let me tell you, that pike part was not fun."

Mavis pulled her head up indignantly, shaking her finger under Art's nose. "Don't you go blaming me for Guinevere! I warned you about her. It's not my fault if you think with your gonads!"

"The answer is no, Merlin."

"Mavis, actually," she mumbled, trying to think. "Do you genuinely presume you have a choice in this matter? You're not like ordinary men."

Art met Mavis's eyes. "I was until three days ago," he said softly.

"Exactly my point!" Mavis exclaimed, grabbing Art's upper arm and giving it a shake. "You *were* ordinary. Now you're not! You're Arthur of legend, and the legend states that when England is threatened Arthur will return from the Isle of Avalon. Well, England's in danger, and here you are. Just like old times! See! It's simple! Now, let's go."

Art shook free of Mavis's grasp. "What danger?"

"What danger? What danger! Look about you, man!" Mavis exclaimed, her hands waving wildly above her head. "The place is falling apart! The Irish are bombing the hell out of everything and anything in order to gain independence. The Scots want their autonomy, although they aren't chucking bombs to get it. Yet. The unemployment rate is up over ten percent. The pound is dropping in value. The Labor Party wants to abolish the throne altogether— which might not be a bad idea, considering the bunch of royals they've got running around loose these days. Liz is cool, but her kids!

Forget it! Damned irresponsible, the lot of 'em. That ole Jug Ears! He looks like a poster child for inbreeding! Everyone has forgotten what it means to be a Briton! They need a reminder, a symbol, a guide to direct them back to the narrow path. They need a hero! They need Arthur! They need you!" She ended with her nose only an inch from his, her finger poked deep into his chest.

He stepped back. "I can't help you. I won't."

"Am I not making myself clear?" Mavis was almost shouting, and gesticulating angrily. "I am speaking the Queen's English, am I not? You do know who I am, don't you?"

Art smiled, small and sad. "You're the Great Wizard Mavis."

"I'm Mavis these days," she said, thumping her chest with her fist, "but I'm still Merlin! I'm still the same man!"

This time Art's smile was genuine. "Funny. You don't look it."

Mavis's eyes flashed angrily. "Well, I am. You've seen me in many different guises, many different bodies. Well, I'm still the son of the devil. I'm still the most powerful wizard in all history, and I'm still able to make your life a living hell if you don't do what you should be doing!" Puffed up with her anger, she hovered threateningly over Art.

It didn't work. "Don't threaten me, Merlin. Or is it Mavis?"

"Who gives a shit about my name! Call me what you want!" She puffed up again. "And I'll do more than threaten you if it's necessary!"

"So will I," Art answered quietly.

Mavis threw back her head and laughed heartily, her blonde curls bouncing. "You? What can you possibly do to me?"

A sly, knowing smile slid across Arthur's face, making him resemble a hunting fox. "I work for Inland Revenue. How would you like to be audited this year, next year, the year after that?"

Mavis's hand went to her throat as the color drained away from her face. She was no longer laughing. The very edges of her vision blurred slightly, and she swayed as faintness swept through her. "That's cold."

Art shrugged. "You taught me."

"Too well, it would seem." She turned her head and for the first time looked into the small but impeccable living room. Lace curtains the color of strong tea framed a floral sofa. She moved to it and sat down. "It seems we have an impasse."

"Not really," Art said as he took a chair next to the cleanly swept fireplace. "Not if you're open to suggestions."

Mavis dropped her face into her hands. "Do I have a choice?"

Art shrugged his shoulders in answer before continuing. "It seems to me you need a hero, someone to pull the kingdom together. A symbol of what's good and right."

Mavis raised her head. "Is there an echo in here? I thought I just said that."

"You did. But what you haven't seen is that I don't have to be that man."

Mavis cocked her head. "Come again?"

"Let me finish," Art said. "When we first met—not today. Back then—I was nothing special, just a snot-nosed kid. You took me and taught me. You made me into a king. If you did that for me, you can do it for someone else. Find some poor schmuck. Give him Excalibur and call *him* Arthur. Who's going to know the difference but you and me? I can assure you I WON'T TELL ANYONE!"

The Wizard Supreme opened her mouth to object, but her reply died unborn in her throat. She closed her mouth with an audible snap. "I need a drink. A big one."

"Tea or soda?" Art asked, standing.

"Scotch would be better. A big one."

"Sorry. I've been sober for five years."

"Tea works for me, then." Mavis shook her head, setting her curls atwirl. "You know, this idea of yours could work. Save us both a lot of hassle if you're really not willing to cooperate."

"Of course it'll work," Art said as he extended his hand to Mavis to help her off the sofa. As he led the way to the kitchen he said, "King Arthur isn't a man. He's an ideal for a flawed world. I've already had my turn as an ideal. Fun it wasn't. Get someone else to carry the standard into battle. You're Merlin. You can do this blindfolded."

As Mavis pulled the bentwood kitchen chair out from under the gleaming white table to sit down, she said, "Wart, you always were a pain in the ass."

God Save the King

It took several cups of tea to clear the air between them, but finally they settled down to setting out a campaign strategy for Merlin. Between that and stories old and new passing between friends, the afternoon drifted away. When night finally fell, the Archwizard Mavis St. George left Art in search of three things: a sword, a drink (preferably a large one), and a hero. Not necessarily in that order.

As she stepped out of his tiny, immaculate home, she rubbed her hands together in gleeful anticipation. "It shouldn't be too hard to find someone to be Arthur," she murmured as she gazed at the night sky. "I am, after all, very persuasive. And I've got some jim-dandy spells I haven't used in a while." She started to waltz down the sidewalk. Streetlights flickered in three-four time. "Damn, I'm gonna love being back in action. God help my protege if he messes up." She grinned widely. "I'm not as patient as I used to be."

Contract Hit

Richard A. Knaak

Villains don't have to wear capes and masks. Sometimes they wear three-piece suits.

The night was as dark as a criminal's heart and as wet as the tears of his victims, but the Star-Spangled Adventurer would not let mere elements bar him from his duty. With deft movements and strength born of years of training and use, the scarlet, navy, and ivory-clad scourge of villainy stoically scaled the sides of the once-regal Gotham Building. A mere twelve stories was still nothing to him, even after thirty years of a dedicated battle against the dire evil that ever sought to bring his beloved city to its knees. There was a hint of stiffness in his limbs that he suspected might some day imperil his life, but that was something to worry about another day.

Such a thought did not daunt him; he fully expected to die in the line of duty. It was the way of heroes, the Adventurer knew.

There was a light in one of the windows on the twelfth floor, a lone glimmer in the gloom of the crime-filled night. The Adventurer was not fooled; he was well aware that light sometimes shone like a halo about the greatest of foul fiends.

He climbed to that one window and peered inside. A lone figure, somewhat heavy and with a tiny bald spot forming in the back of his gray-tressed head, sat at an extravagant oak desk perusing a sheath of aged papers.

The Star-Spangled Adventurer rubbed his chin in deep contemplation as he studied his adversary. There was something about him . . .

Professor Khaos had a bald spot like that, he finally thought. *Shaped like an egg . . . just like this one is.*

There was no reason to delay the inevitable. With catlike silence, the Metropolitan Marauder stealthily slid the window open and crept inside. He straightened and turned his blazing stare on the man seated before him.

"Demerest Cline."

The papers in the other's hand went flying with satisfactory velocity. Although he was loathe to admit such things even to himself, the City Centurion enjoyed the effect he had on people like Cline.

Gazing up at six-plus feet of solid muscle clad in the stars and stripes of the American flag, the squat figure barked, "I thought I told them to request that you use the *door!*"

"I have fought too many foes to simply walk through a doorway, Mr. Cline. If I made myself so public, one of them might try to do me harm. Innocents might be hurt before I was able to deal with the miscreants."

Demerest Cline was a man of rock-hard features that had begun to soften like wet clay. His nose was a bird's beak that coincidentally resembled that of the eagle decorating the face mask of the veteran superhero. The mustache below was two almost even slashes of grease. The Adventurer noted that his eyes were beady and close-set. Typical criminal type. "Do you have to talk like that?"

"Like what, Mayor Cline?"

The prime mover of Metra City twinged. In his own rather nasal voice, he responded, "Like a damn special effect! How do you get your voice that deep?"

Striding like a lynx, the Urban Avenger walked around to the front of the mayor's desk. A name plate reading MAYOR D. CLINE was positioned in the middle so that anyone entering would be certain to see it. The Star-Spangled Adventurer raised an eyebrow of impatience at the squat figure before him. *"You wished to speak to me about a matter of import, your honor. Please get to the point; there are misdeeds and dangers threatening the fair city and I must be there to prevent them from occurring."*

"Do you use a script?"

"*What is the urgent matter?*"

"Um, yes . . ." Mayor Cline fumbled with the papers that he had been reading before the Adventurer's typically startling appearance. He shuffled them together, and a look of cool confidence spread across his face. The Adventurer crossed his mighty arms and waited.

"There's a contract with your name on it." The drama of the words was somewhat dampened by the nasal tone.

Every muscle taut, the nemesis of crime in any form and any place nodded solemnly. "*It's not the first, Mayor Cline. You're just two weeks into office, but your predecessor could tell you of seven separate contracts during his four years. The Mafia, the Dartsman, Packwolf . . . they and others through the years have tried and failed in their attempts to have me liquidated.*" He paused for effect. "*Is it that madman, Khaos? The Raven? What about the Family Tree? There are still kin of Doctor Crimson loose. It is truly tragic when such an extended family can turn to—*"

"My speechwriter should talk to you." Cline held up the sheath of papers so that the Superlative Sentinel could peruse them. "And what I mean, Star-Spangled . . . do you prefer just straight 'Star'?"

"*Adventurer.*"

"Well, what I mean . . . *Adventurer* . . . is that this is a contract that *you* signed." The crease that passed for the mayor's mouth arced upward ever so slightly, but the Guardian of Justice and Fair Play for All still noted it with his exceptional vision.

Unfortunately, that same extraordinary vision also revealed to him just what contract the new autarch of Metra City held in his stubby fingers.

"Recognize it?"

"*I do.*"

"Good!" Demerest Cline now looked more like the man who had been running for office on the Tighten Our Belt campaign. The smile was there. The twinkle in those beady eyes was there. Mayor Cline oozed confidence. Oozing seemed to come naturally to him, from what the Adventurer recalled of the election. "This is why I've summoned you here."

"*Is there some question as to its contents, Mr. Cline?*" the People's

Protector asked as politely as his naturally intimidating voice would allow him. *"Mayor Goodman and I thought it the best way to—"*

The new mayor had the audacity to interrupt the Guardian of Freedom. He waved aside the good words of the Adventurer. "No, not in the least. I understand perfectly well what this contract says. In point of fact, by summoning you here, I hope to prove I respect it to the letter."

Somewhere Professor Khaos was no doubt plotting his next plot to seize control of Metra City. Somewhere the insidious Cricket was casing his next theft. Somewhere over the city, the skies were not blue, even barring the fact that it was night . . .

Yet at that moment nothing would have made the Patriot of Justice move from that spot. He arched the eyebrow further and reinvigorated his stonelike stance.

Cline was undaunted by his renewed magnificence. When he saw that the hero would remain silent and steadfast throughout, the mayor simply folded over the top three sheets and held out the contract. After several intense seconds in which there was no move by the Adventurer to read the page, Demerest Cline surrendered the contract to his desk, leaving it so that his guest could study it whenever he chose.

"I'm exercising Section 15, Paragraph (c)." The stubby fingers formed a steeple. "You are being *traded*."

He had faced the hooved doom of the Four Horsemen, the wicked, beguiling advances of Bellamadonna, and the fanaticism of the free press, but those four words spoken by the man who should have been the bulwark of the Star-Spangled Adventurer's backing ripped deeper into the soul of the City Centurion than even the claws of red-capped Sanda.

"Traded? What mockery is this?"

"Section 15, Paragraph (c)." The magistrate purloined a massive magnifying glass from his desk and reached it out to the superhero. "It's in rather . . . small . . . print. You might have missed it the last time you read this. Clearly states that the mayor, whoever he is, has the right as long as it is for the good of the city. It is."

"Traded?" the Adventurer repeated. He was suddenly regretting his decision of neutrality in politics through nonvoting.

Cline put down the unused magnifying glass and reached for another sheath of papers. His beady eyes surveyed the front. "Yes, for a hero named the Dasher and . . . and 'a promising sidekick to be named later.'"

It was fortunate that the American eagle mask obscured much of the hero's stern but resolute visage. "*I'm being traded for a superhero named the* Dasher?"

"And a promising young sidekick to be named later, let's not forget that." The mayor looked up. "You used to have a sidekick; what happened to him?"

Although still mightily disturbed by the wicked turn of events, the Star-Spangled Adventurer yet found the wherewithal to say, "*Which one?*"

"You've had more than one? I thought Flag Boy was your only sidekick."

"*There were seven Flag Boys. Flag Boy One died saving two children from a burning building.*" The Urban Avenger paused in silence in honor of the memory of the daring young lad who had joined him on his crusade against the menaces of crime. "*Numbers Two and Five retired for personal reasons.*" Those personal reasons had had to do with, respectively, getting a young woman in trouble and . . . here the Adventurer got just a bit uneasy . . . getting a young man in trouble. It had taken quite some doing to get those incidents covered up, but the sanctity of the Adventurer name had been at stake. "*Number Three fell prey to the hazards of the city.*" Did they no longer teach children to look both ways while crossing the street? He had thought that a sidekick would at least know *that* rule. Hadn't even been a crime in progress; the idiot had just been jaywalking. At least he had not been in costume.

"And the others?" Mayor Cline was morbidly fascinated.

"*While attempting to hunt down the Yellow Menace, Four plunged to his death.*" Actually, Flag Boy Four had insisted that his powers included the ability to fly, and no coaxing by the City Centurion had been able to convince him otherwise. The Adventurer had never discovered just what it was his sidekick had been high on when he had leapt from the one-hundred-story Rician Building. At least there had not been enough left after he struck the pavement to identify

223

him as Flag Boy. *"Number Six quit and now lives in a remote village somewhere in Europe."* Six had always been a strange one. *"Number Seven . . ."*

"Yes?"

"We never did find out what happened to him."

Cline cleared his thick, short throat. "You don't seem to hold onto sidekicks for very long."

"Number One was my choice. A good, brave lad with a sterling heart and courage unbelievable. The other six were political appointees." As for holding on, Number Five had wanted to do a little too much of that with his superhero. The Metropolitan Marauder often wondered where they had found those six.

"Yes . . . well, I'll keep that in mind."

"Now that I have answered your question, you will answer mine, Demerest Cline." Toned muscles rippled for heroic effect. *"Why have you invoked that all-but-forgotten clause? Why do you seek to trade me for this . . . this Blitzen?"*

"Dasher. That's Dasher as in he's quick. Very much so. He does the mile in two."

"I can do the mile in two minutes. For a hero, that's nothing extraordinary."

The mayor smiled, revealing predatory teeth that reminded the Adventurer of the smile of Mister Mouse. Now *there* had been a novel villain . . . "I mean two seconds."

There was no reply from the Stalwart Sentinel concerning this revelation.

"He can patrol the entire city in less than an hour. He can catch a bullet in his hand. He can run across water."

The Star-Spangled Adventurer waited to be told that the Dasher could also part the sea, but Cline had evidently come to the end of his short but impressive list. Yet . . . *"If he is so great a champion, and I do not doubt his heroic qualities, then why does his fair city desire to trade him for me? Why do you wish him when they do not?"*

"Well, the council of New Biddle has always admired your career, and they—"

"New Biddle?"

"—quite frankly think that your presence will encourage trust in the city fathers. Trust, of course, means growth, with new people moving—"

"*Where in the grand country of the United States of America, a land that I love, is New Biddle?*" The Stalwart Sentinel's voice was low and controlled, but it still cut through the new autarch's rhetoric the way the lasers of Lightbeam had cut through National Guard tanks and, three times, Star Cars.

Even faced by such an onslaught, Demerest Cline persevered where the Shapeshifter had been driven to frightened silence. His smile remained fixed on his plumpish face. "Montana or Idaho, but it's beautiful country, I understand. See, the council feels that a hero of your reputation is needed to prove that New Biddle is a safe place for both family and business. They feel that only you, Adventurer, can turn their home around."

Mightily swelled the Grim Guardian's chest despite the knowledge that he might soon be in Montana or Idaho. "*Despite the Dasher, this New Biddle suffers crime rampant? Hmmmm. It has grown quiet of late. Most of the greatest rogues have either fled the city, are incarcerated, or have quit the business. Professor Khaos has not been seen in months. Baron Black is dead. Skorch is cooling his heels in maximum security. The Mocker has actually reformed and now teaches pet grooming. As for the latest wave of so-called villains and miscreants, there's not a decent arch-fiend in the whole bunch. Perhaps . . . perhaps it is time for new challenges. A new beat.*"

Cline clapped his meaty, ringed hands. "That's the spirit! I have the proper documents right here so if you'll—"

Unfolding his muscular arms, the City Centurion leaned on the edge of the desk, ignoring how the papers beneath his gloved knuckles crumpled like the heads of the robots of Mikros Saaf, would-be dictator. "*First I would know a little more about New Biddle's desperate situation. How dreadful is their crime wave? Who are their supervillains? They must be terrible indeed if this Sprinter is unable to deal with them in some satisfactory manner.*"

"Ummm . . . I don't have that sort of information. You'll have to get it from the town council after the trade is finalized."

Raising one hammerlike hand, the Adventurer pointed at a sheet all but completely hidden by the towers of paper that decorated

Demerest Cline's pretentious desk. "*The very document lies there. I can see just a glimpse of its heading, but my alert and able mind has deciphered the topic with but the two letters visible.*"

"It's really not a good list . . ."

The Adventurer had already seized the tantalizing document in a grip that even the Black Squid would have found enviable. He brought it close and scanned quickly. Scant seconds passed before a darkness spread across his chiseled, masked countenance. "*What madness this? Sheepman? The Potato King? The Bicycle Brothers? Fred— Fred Twizle?*" He looked as askance as the blazing eagle mask would allow. "*Fred Twizle? This is a rogues gallery? This is a crime wave? This collection of minor-league miscreants, who collectively have committed six crimes in five years, has thrown the citizens of New Biddle into despair?*"

"Not exactly despair—"

A human juggernaut, the Watchman of the Weak suddenly leaned across the mayor's desk, almost coming nose to nose with the man behind it. Demerest Cline nearly fell backwards, but he managed to right himself just in time. "*What is the truth here, your honor? This is all piddling shit! It's my age, isn't it? This is the same thing that happened to Captain Collider in Texas! Shipped off to the miners in the Appalachians where there's not a decent supercriminal to be had! He was forced to open a tourist attraction just to earn his keep!*"

Slowly, as if readying himself to pounce, the new mayor tilted his chair forward again. His stubby fingers re-formed a steeple—probably as close as he ever got to the good church, the Adventurer noted. "Many children are fond of Captain Collider's Supercollider Roller Coaster."

"*You want me to be a tourist attraction!*"

"Actually, New Biddle does. The Dasher, homegrown though he is, is never going to be a big attraction. Not enough activity going on to further his reputation. When I sent out feelers for interest in you, they made the best offer . . . the *only* offer."

"*Ridiculous! I have many good years left in me. I am Metra City's son. I am the guardian of young and old, rich or poor. No one who knows of this grand metropolis does not know that I protect it and protect it well from the dire elements of evil! Metra City and I are one!*" He was pleased by the short speech. It was almost as good as the one that he had used on Professor Khaos the last time he had dragged the misguided genius off to the cold, gray walls of prison. Of course, that speech he had practiced for days before the latest epic battle with his archfoe. One had to get them just right; it looked silly to become flustered and tongue-tied during the struggle for decency.

"But you *are* getting older," the mayor needlessly pointed out. Settling into his elegant suede chair, Cline added, "As it is, we still have to cover half of your expenses for the first three years as part of the bargain. Your reputation for . . . new Star Cars every couple months, for instance . . . was a sore negotiation point."

The Crusading Cavalier straightened, openly indignant at the latest words to come oozing out of the new mayor's mouth. "*My rewards have always covered those expenses. They have covered all of my expenses.*"

"Which is robbing Peter to pay Star-Spangled." The mayor reached into the coat pocket of his tailored suit and removed a lengthy, imported cigar. Lighting his elegant cigar with the azure flame of a golden lighter, Cline puffed a bit of smoke, paying no heed to the look of disgust radiating from the Adventurer. "Idiotic provision in your contract, giving you say over those rewards; if I'd been mayor then, it would have been stricken out. You must understand that when the city offers all those rewards leading to the capture of a criminal, the council *doesn't* want all of those rewards to be claimed. We just can't afford it."

"*All my rewards, minus expenses, go to charity.*"

"Yes, and you have a lot of expenses. The Star Car must get destroyed about once every two months. Good thing you collect a lot of rewards for all those supervillains you capture. Never mind that they keep escaping and you capture them all over *again*. Professor Khaos alone has cost the city just over a million in the past four years, even barring how much the publicity of your constant duels brings in the tourists. Some of the money does go to charity, but too much is wasted like that. Don't you think about the strain you put on the coffers of not only Metra but the entire state? The country? Think of all those worthy government programs that are struggling to survive because there isn't enough to go around."

The Adventurer fought the good fight, but could not think of any such programs, except maybe the one that kept road crews happily employed repairing the expressways into eternity. Of course, they had unions.

"That's minor, however, to another provision in your contract. Just what was Goodman thinking?" The mayor looked at his notes. "Aaah. Section 4: Merchandising."

The Adventurer heroically straightened yet more. "*You said merchandising?*"

"Merchandising. Probably one of the sorest points. This contract is a shambles. The city loses out terribly here."

"*Sales of my paraphernalia were at their highest last year. The Adventurer T-shirts alone grossed nearly a third again what they did the year before.*"

Now it was Demerest Cline who cocked an eyebrow. "You do keep track of things, after all."

"*My name and likeness are on those items. I want those T-shirts to be worn with pride and those mugs, earrings, and action figures to ever be utilized with the knowledge that the Star-Spangled Adventurer is always watching over the satisfaction of the purchaser.*"

"Yes, well, while sales are up, the city is currently getting only an eighty-twenty split on all of this merchandising . . . and the quality standards you demand on the items eats into the net profit from which that meager twenty percent derives. Now with a fifty-fifty split, Metra would benefit much more, but even that hardly makes—"

"*I would never accept such a change!*"

"You don't have to. New Biddle is so anxious for your company that they've agreed to the old split. Meanwhile, Metra City will go halves with its new hero, the daring Dasher. We'll also settle this reward thing in a more amicable manner."

"*So it is not merely my age, but also a ruse to take more from the poor souls of Metra in the name of austerity!*" The Star-Spangled Adventurer chuckled in amused triumph. "*I doubt any hero would be so craven as to accept such terms. You'll not be rid of me so soon. Once the Dancer sees these terms, he will never sign, mark my words!*"

Demerest Cline rose to his full . . . five foot eight. He looked the Patriot of Freedom for young and old, rich and poor, in the face and said, "He has and he did."

"*What?*"

"The *Dasher* has signed the agreement. He was quite happy with it. Understand, he will not be as big a draw for the tourists, at least not for a few years. Despite that, the city needs to bring in a certain minimum to keep afloat. When things get better, the Dasher can renegotiate if he wants. By the way, he starts next Monday. Your last day is Friday." From his suit, the mayor magically produced another stack of papers. He held them out toward the disbelieving Defender of Decency. "His contract is available to you if you desire to see it. In the meantime . . ." Cline dropped the new stack atop the old papers. ". . . sign the last page."

The Adventurer folded his arms, albeit not with as much confidence as before. "*I will not.*"

"Then you will be in breach of contract, and I can simply dismiss you."

Professor Khaos had failed to defeat him after two hundred and eighty-six battles. The Packwolf had all but given up after ninety-two. The Star-Spangled Adventurer could list the number of defeats each of his foes had suffered, even down to the lone battle he had won over his very first villain, the Awful Auk, yet none of them mattered now. Now, *he* had tasted the bitter ash of defeat. The sour milk of retreat. The moldy bread of ruination. The leftover treacle of—

"There is one thing that might make this more palatable to you, Spangled."

"Adventurer . . ." he muttered in a voice not heard in years by any outsider. His eyes were still locked on the infernal documents.

"One of the police department's moles overheard a bit of conversation. Seems Fred Twizle and a certain figure well known to you had a conversation. There's rumors of that same figure flying out for a special meeting."

"And so?" He really, really did not care. Maybe this would be a good time to start his memoirs. The notes he had on his life already filled thirteen volumes. He would need two or three years just to shuffle the notes into shape.

"And so that other figure was none other than a certain *Professor Khaos.*"

A familiar trickle of electricity coursed through the tensing body of the masked champion. Renewed purpose peeked its way into his life once more. *"What would the archfiends of two cities, two cities not coincidentally tied together, speak of?"*

Demerest Cline shook his head. Almost there seemed to be some fear in his eyes, fear for both his beloved city and the Star-Spangled Adventurer's new home. "I wouldn't know, but it may be why the town council was so eager to purchase your contract. They may have heard something before this. Our sources did mention he might be moving all of his henchmen there."

The Adventurer pondered the question ferociously. Despite all those defeats, Khaos was still his most deadly foe. *"That has an almost permanent ring to it. The purloining professor might be relocating his operations. Khaos has gone into seclusion before, and the more secluded he becomes, the more diabolical his plans. Now he travels to New Biddle in Montana or Idaho or . . ."* Keen eyes widened in abject horror at the possibilities. *"By Grant's Tomb! This could be catastrophic!"*

"If you sign this right now, I can get you transportation to New Biddle within the hour," Cline offered, looking earnest.

Almost the Adventurer reached for the contract. Yet, he was still not ready to trust. *"If this is a trick, Demerest Cline, I will—"*

Mayor Cline looked aghast. He shook his head. "If you like, I'll even add a rider in the contract, in my own handwriting and initialized, stating that if you find me to have been false in this I will give the Dasher the same merchandising split you had with fair Metra."

"It would almost be worth it if Khaos did not show."

"He will, Star. I'm certain of it. Fred Twizle may be plotting to attack you while you're still becoming accustomed to New Biddle. Khaos would certainly be willing to give whatever aid he could in that respect. Think of it, *Adventurer*. The combined menace of the Professor and the sinister Twizle!"

The hero's mission became clear. Once again, there was a twinkle in his penetrating eyes. He nodded toward the new contract. *"Add the rider. I must be on my way before dawn. I will beat Khaos to New Biddle and thus be able to prepare myself at least a little for what may be the greatest trial of my formidable career!"*

In the end, it took only forty-four minutes before the private jet carried off the Star-Spangled Adventurer to his confrontation with the insidious genius known as Professor Khaos and the madman's latest ally of evil . . . Fred Twizle.

Mayor Demerest Cline did not allow himself a glass of his fine, imported Scotch until the superhero's plane was more than fifteen minutes on its way. The dealing with the Adventurer could have gone very sour, and he knew it. That would have fouled everything up.

Carrying the glass to his desk, he prepared himself for the inevitable.

"*I am here, Demerest Cline.*"

God! Why do they all have to talk like that? Taking a sip, he glanced to his side, where a figure clad in the garb of a Victorian gentleman stood. The man was about sixty, slim but in excellent health. In truth, he looked in better shape than the mayor, who was only in his forties. A Vandyke beard and a monocle enhanced the regal features of the black-haired figure. The gray-steel eyes hinted at a remarkable intelligence. In one hand, he held a cane with a silver wolf's head.

"Professor Khaos."

The master of evil removed his hat, revealing thinning hair, and smiled. "*We must talk, Demerest Cline, of future plots.*"

Settling into his chair, Cline took another sip. "So we should. We should also talk of New Biddle."

The smile faltered. "*New Biddle?*"

"My counterpart there has supplied me with the telephone number of a man you need to talk to before you leave. Fred Twizle is his name. I've attached the number to the top page." As he spoke, the mayor opened a side drawer and brought forth a multipage document. He tossed the document toward the archvillain, looking him in the eye as he did. "You've been good for the tourist business, Khaos, but I'm sorry to say that you've been *traded* . . ."

Origin Story

Dwight R. Decker

Sometimes the "ancient powers" are more than a little out of touch.

I hadn't been living in Phoenix long when I met the superhero who never was. In fact, it was after work the Friday I got my first paycheck from the new job, and I had stopped in an upscale watering hole on my way home to celebrate the milestone with a drink.

I sat at the crowded bar and took my time with the beer, reflecting on what I had lost and gained by coming to Arizona. I was by myself, of course, since I hadn't been in town long enough to meet anyone, and at the moment I preferred to be alone with my thoughts anyway. Next to me sat another quiet, solitary drinker, but I barely noticed him.

The TV set behind the bar was just loud enough that after a while I couldn't go on ignoring it. I finally gave up and watched the news.

I had tuned in just about the time the announcer was going through the results of the day's superhero battles. I can remember when a battle between Jetman and the Skeeter would be the lead story on the national news, and a good rampage by the Gargantuan Glob would keep the pundits on the late-night talk shows busy for hours discussing property damage and insurance coverage. Now there were so many superheroes in so many cities that the network anchors just read off the tally of fight results about the same way they listed NFL scores.

"In Columbus, Ohio, Thunderman single-handedly nabbed five members of the Fat Lady's gang when they tried to hijack a train. The patriotic hero Captain Star smashed a plot by the Hooded Terror gang in Atlanta. Near Chicago, Sun-God Ra used the power of the Solar Staff to foil a break at Joliet State Prison. . . ." And on and on like that. Even kid heroes got into it: "The Teen-Men made a personal appearance at a high school in Los Angeles and came away with two major drug dealers. . . ."

Down the bar, a couple of patrons were arguing about superhero origins and what really made a hero. Back in the Thirties, when the mystery men began appearing, no one knew very much about how heroes got their powers or what made them adopt distinctive or even bizarre costumes and names, but in the years since, enough heroes had retired and written their memoirs that patterns were emerging and Miller Time philosophers could pontificate.

"It's the guy who gets a power by accident and realizes what a responsibility it is," one man said.

"No, there has to be more to it," his buddy replied. "Crooks have to rub out his whole family for him to have a motive to fight crime."

"Oh, come on! That just makes him a psycho vigilante. He has to do it out of ideals!"

I didn't care about that part of it. I was transfixed by the image on the TV screen of Jetman in flight, looking so proud and carefree in his skintight silver uniform as he streaked through the sky. "I'd give almost anything to be a superhero!" I found myself murmuring with an almost embarrassingly sappy sigh.

The man next to me looked up from his drink, the first sign of life I had seen from him since sitting down. "Oh?" he said. "Would you really?"

"Well, yes," I replied, a little irritated that he had overheard me in a weak moment. "The excitement, the glamour, the adventure—that's all worth something, don't you think?"

"Maybe. It depends." He sipped from his glass and swallowed slowly and thoughtfully. "I had a chance to be a superhero once. I turned it down, though."

I'd heard enough barroom commando stories over the years to have a warning sense for oncoming stretchers, but this sounded sincere—or at least like a better lie than usual. I turned to the man with growing interest. "I'd like to hear about this," I said.

He was reluctant to say any more, so I had to work on him a bit. I also took a good look at him and was a little jealous. If I looked like that . . . well, I might still be looking for love in all the wrong places, but I'd have more to show for it by now. He was tall, athletically trim, handsome—just what you would expect a superhero's alter ego to look like. Somebody who looked like he did *should* have been a superhero, so what had been the problem?

My insistence didn't wear down his reluctance until after I had bought him a couple of drinks on top of the one he had been nursing. Finally, he told me his story. . . .

You can call me Jim. I had been working for a computer company here in the Valley and not getting much of anywhere. Then a co-worker named Steve suggested we quit and go into business for ourselves. We started our own little software company and struggled along for a year or so. We were overworked, but happy because we were our own bosses and making enough to get by. We could have spent the rest of our lives like that without any trouble. Well, Steve did have a weakness for weekend trips to Las Vegas, but other than for his showing up at work hungover and broke on Monday mornings, it was never a problem. The trouble started when we suddenly became a success.

I'll spare you the details, but the short version is that a bank had asked us to solve a minor software problem. I looked into it, studied how banking had been done up to now, and worked out a simpler system for routing checks from one bank to another. When you figure how many checks are written each day in this country, the amount of money spent processing them is astronomical, and even a tiny savings in handling each one adds up. We were suddenly rich, and not only that, a big company offered to buy us out. We would never have to work again.

I should have been suspicious when Steve asked me to go camping with him in the Superstition Mountains east of Phoenix the weekend before the sale of our company was to be closed. Steve said he wanted me to help him look for the Lost Dutchman Mine, but I couldn't understand why anyone would want to risk his neck looking for a legendary gold mine when he was already rich. I assumed he looked at it as a hobby to keep him busy in his early retirement now that he no longer had to hope for a lucky strike in Vegas.

After all, any number of better-equipped expeditions than ours had looked for the mine in those mountains over the last hundred years without any luck. Most historians suspect there never was such a mine, and the geologists say the Superstitions are all wrong for gold-bearing ore. One explanation is that the Dutchman had really filled his pockets while working at mines elsewhere, and put out the story of his own secret mine to launder the gold.

If I didn't really believe we might find a lost gold mine, I went along anyway, thinking a relaxing weekend under the stars would be just the thing before coming back to a difficult week of liquidating the company.

We hiked several miles into the mountains, leaving the more tourist-infested areas behind and climbing up the trail into some serious wilderness where it was just us, the rocks, and the occasional cactus. Then I paused on a ledge overlooking a steep-sided valley to admire the landscape stretching out below.

"What a view!" I exclaimed, turning back to Steve. "Now I know why you wanted me to come out here with you!"

That was when he drew a pistol and shot me full in the chest. I toppled over the ledge, dropped ten feet to a steep slope, and rolled another hundred yards into some rocks and brush, finally coming to a stop at the foot of an oddly manlike saguaro cactus.

Steve's mistake was not finishing the job, but he apparently decided I was too hard to reach. If I wasn't dead already, I would be soon, so he could confidently leave me for the buzzards. Whistling a tune that sounded like "We're in the Money," he headed back in the direction of civilization.

I may not have been dead, but the distinction was technical. With the last of my fading consciousness, I tried to think of curses vile enough for Steve. His share alone of the price we were getting for our company was enough to keep him rolling dice and romancing floozies in Las Vegas for the rest of his life, but no, he had to have mine, too.

Perhaps I was hallucinating as the darkness closed in: I had the odd impression that the cactus next to me was changing its shape and turning into a man. I had read casually about near-death experiences, but this didn't seem to fit the pattern. Then the light went out.

When my awareness came up again, I was sitting on a rock and drinking some strange-tasting water from a battered old tin pan.

"Vell, mine friend, how goes it for you now?"

On the other side of the tin pan was an ancient, weather-beaten prospector in a battered old hat, with a long tobacco-stained white beard spilling over his worn and faded denim shirt.

Surprisingly, I felt fine. The front of my shirt was caked with dried blood, but any wound in my chest beneath the round bullet hole had been miraculously healed. The bruises I must have gotten from rolling down the valley slope had vanished as well.

"I never felt better," I said, amazed. "I should be dead. I'm not, I hope—?"

The old prospector laughed. "Nein, you are very much alive. Chust vhat *I* am, now that is another story!"

Suddenly I knew. "You're the Dutchman, aren't you? Jacob Waltz, right?"

He laughed again. "Ja, that is who I am. It is good to be remembered!"

You can't live in Phoenix very long without hearing all about the Lost Dutchman Mine legend. I knew that the Dutchman—actually a German immigrant, but ethnic nomenclature was looser in those days—had died in 1891. At least that was when he was supposed to have died, and there were witnesses. On the other hand, the exact location of his grave was as much a mystery as that of his gold mine. The historical record was vague enough to fit in a fake death, but after a hundred years that didn't seem any more likely than the alternative. I was talking to a ghost. Rather than press that issue, I just asked, "How did you save my life?"

"For that you can thank the Pima medicine man who sold me his Vasser of Life elixir," Jacob said with a grin. "It is a sovereign remedy for vhat ails you, and vorks better than any patent medicine I ever bought from a peddler's vagon."

"Thank you . . . er, do I owe you anything?"

"Chust hear me out. I vant to make you an offer. You are a young man of good character. Your friend, the man you trusted, tried to kill you. You are good, he is evil. I can give you something that vill make you powerful, a force for good in the vorld. You can bring your enemy to chustice, and then go out and fight crime everyvhere."

This was the kind of thing you read about happening to someone else, in a forgotten tomb or even an old abandoned subway tunnel. A wise spirit chooses some worthy candidate to be a superhero and gives him a name, a costume, and superhuman abilities. If I could hardly believe at first that it was actually happening to me, the fact that the wise spirit was the ghost of a dead prospector with a German accent may have kept interfering with my sense of wonder. Perhaps it was true he had abstracted other people's gold instead of mining his own, and he had been put to work recruiting champions of justice as a kind of otherworldly penance, somewhat like Marley coming to warn Scrooge. I was so caught up in the magic of the moment that I could only mutely nod my agreement.

"Good!" the Dutchman exclaimed. "Now put on this ring"—he produced one seemingly out of nowhere and slipped it on my finger—"and rub it vhenever chustice cries out to be done! The ring is an ancient Indian talisman that concentrates the power of the sun and gives you strength and courage!"

I rubbed the ring. There was a flash of lightning, a crack of thunder, and a whiff of ozone, and I was transformed. An instant later, I was three inches taller and bulging with rippling muscles. I wore a skintight red, white, and blue costume and stood legs apart and arms akimbo, with a cape rippling behind me in a breeze that hadn't been there a second ago.

The old Dutchman cackled in glee. "Ja! Now you vill strike terror into the hearts of evildoers everyvhere! You vill fight crime and inchustice as that most noble of heroes—*CAPTAIN SVAS-TIKA!*"

"*What?!*" I choked. I looked down at my chest and flinched in horror. I hadn't noticed the emblem on the blue shirt before, but it was an enormous black hooked cross on a white circle. I glanced behind me, and in the center of the red cape was another white circle with an even bigger black swastika in it.

"My God, Mr. Waltz!" I exclaimed. "I can't wear this!"

The Dutchman looked puzzled. "Vhy not? It is an ancient Indian symbol of the sun, also a good luck sign. Vear it mit pride!"

"Look, I know you probably haven't read the papers much since 1891, but about fifty years ago, some of your countrymen used this symbol for their own purposes. Believe me, *nobody* thinks of the sun or lucky charms when they see a swastika now!"

"Pfui!" Jacob snorted. "You try to be chenerous and give a young man a chance, and vhat happens? In your face he throws it back at you! You don't vant to be a hero? Fine—!"

He raised his hand. There was another flash of lightning, another clap of thunder. . . .

"I woke up again with a ranger from the Forest Service sprinkling water in my face," Jim finished. "In front of me stood the cactus where it had been in the first place. I would have thought it was all a dream, except for the dried blood and the hole in my shirt, and the scar over the healed bullet wound. The ranger told me another hiker had come by along the trail, saw me down in the brush, and reported it to the authorities. The hiker didn't leave his name, but he was described as an old man with a German accent. Even if I insulted him by not taking him up on his offer to make me a super-hero, the Dutchman did me one last favor."

I tried to imagine the effect of a superhero called "Captain Swas-tika" appearing in public—evildoers weren't the only ones into whose hearts terror would be struck—and shook my head. "It's too bad you lost your chance to be a superhero because of a bad choice in costume design," I said sympathetically. "You could have been fighting crime, upholding the cause of justice. . . ."

"Oh, I did plenty of that," Jim said. "I had Steve arrested for attempted murder. I had to come up with some story about the bullet just grazing me, which baffled him because he knew he had shot me point-blank, but it was all pretty much open-and-shut otherwise. He won't be getting out of prison for a long time. I got more satisfaction out of testifying against him in court than I would have had in wearing a mask and costume and beating him up. Now I'm rich, I'm happy, and I don't have any obligation to spend my life fighting crime."

Jim stood up and laid some money on the bar. "I've never told anyone that story before," he added. "No one would have believed me. I'm not even sure you do, but that's all right. I was just glad to be able to tell someone for once. See you around."

With that, Jim was gone.

I stared thoughtfully into what was left of my drink. I had never really thought about it before, but yes, while some superheroes could choose their professional names and design their own costumes, more than a few had their names and costumes chosen for them by some supernatural entity or other. If Major Miracle didn't like his costume's color coordination, he was still stuck with it because it appeared magically whenever he shouted his secret word, and he had no way to change it. But poor Jim. His one chance to be a superhero, and it had to be Captain Swastika. . . .

Someone sat down next to me. I was too deep in thought to pay any attention at first, but then I heard an old man's voice ask for "*Ein Bier, bitte!*"

It was an old man with a long white beard. He was dressed in a modern business suit and not the worn and dusty shirt and overalls of a nineteenth-century prospector, but the coincidence was a little unnerving just the same. *No, it can't be*, I thought.

The old man turned and looked at me, grinning like Santa Claus about to give a good little boy a shiny toy fire truck. "Now, you seem to be a man of good character. I understand you vish more than anything to be a superhero . . . ?"

I stood up, slapped a few bills down, and turned to go. "Not *that* much, Mr. Waltz," I said.

I didn't walk out to my car. I *ran*.

Tu Quoque

■

John DeChancie

Some people are chosen for greatness. Some people are born to it, more or less.

Lunchtime.

Food smells, cafeteria food, the unmistakable effluvium of rancid meat and reheated gravy mixing in the hallways with bathroom disinfectant and the faintest whiff of old vomit dusted up by the janitor long ago. Recess time: from the playground come shouts, taunts, imprecations in singsong rising on the fall air.

Book mold, old wood. School is an insular sensorium, a self-contained universe of smells, sights, sounds: the feel of fresh, slick textbook paper, the smell of its ink; the waxy odor of crayons and the musty one of pencil shavings . . . the slant of afternoon light through rows of classroom windows, birdsong outside—

He walks along the hallway, not very afraid of meeting an adult, because he has a hall pass. Forged, but he is a good forger. He should be out on the playground. Who would suspect him of playing hooky from recess? They might ask to look at the slim book he's carrying, but maybe not. Probably not.

The piano practice room is locked; but he is prepared. A credit card—his credit card, fully functional, with a five-thousand-dollar line of credit—applied to the crack between door and jamb, and he's in. The room is dark.

243

He flips on the light, goes to the piano, a battered console upright with gouges taken out of its faded walnut finish. The keyboard is not locked, and he is glad for that. He sits on the bench and puts the music score up on the rack.

CONCERTO IN A MINOR
FOR PIANO AND ORCHESTRA
Edvard Grieg

Flipping pages, he runs his eyes over the tiers of staves, the various parts: *Fagotti* ... *Violino* ... *Corni* ... Bassoons, strings, horns. He knows Italian and several other languages. The piano solo part is three-quarters of the way down the page. The concerto begins with a tympani crescendo, the piano coming in immediately in a descending series of minor chords.

He puts his fingers to the keys, his long delicate fingers. He can play intervals of a tenth easily. He heard this piece once and fell instantly in love with it.

He plays the first four measures. It sounds like the CD he heard. The arpeggio looks daunting until he plays it. He reads music instantly, easily. He probably could have played this piece by ear—he has perfect pitch—but he wanted to study the score.

There are many parts. He plays the string parts, then the woodwinds, then the brass. Abstracting, he plays them all together, reducing the octave-spanning harmony to accommodate human hands.

He is enjoying himself. He loves music, though most of what he hears coming out of the radio is banal, juvenile, silly, boring. This is different. He likes other sorts of music besides classical, but classical pieces seem to have more going on inside them—structural things: towers of harmony, dancing counterpoint, long, thoughtful meditations on themes—more. "Serious" music is interesting and a lot of it is actually fun.

He is well into the second movement (*Adagio*) when the door opens.

It is the math teacher, Mrs. Schaeffer.

"I thought someone was playing the radio in here."

He looks up at her. He decides to play innocent. He should have brought a portable radio, though. Should have thought of that. Best to hedge his bets—

But she knows. "That was you, wasn't it, Ramon?"

Ramon is silent, regarding her impassively. She is tall with long brown hair. Attractive, for an adult female. Her eyes are steel gray.

She closes the door and leans against it. "Did you ever take lessons, Ramon?"

He nods. "Sure."

"Who gave the lessons to you? When?"

"Oh, when I was . . . younger. A teacher taught me. A piano teacher."

She nods, but she isn't buying it. "You've never had a lesson in your life, have you, Ramon?"

No use denying it. "No. I just picked it up."

She comes to the piano, takes the score, flips through it. "This is hardly the kind of thing you just 'pick up,' Ramon." She smiles a sly, knowing smile. "Grieg. A Romantic. You like Grieg especially?"

Ramon shrugs. "No. I just heard it on the radio."

"You got this score from the public library? Yes. And not only can you play the solo part like an accomplished pianist, you can play the orchestra part, too. You can read music as if you were trained in the best conservatories."

Ramon lifts his shoulders again. "I just picked it up."

"You're a musical genius, a child prodigy, possibly on the order of Mozart or Saint-Saëns—you've heard of them?"

"Sure. I like Mozart."

"But you are possibly greater, at least in theory, because you are self-taught."

Ramon looks away.

She sits on the piano bench next to him, and he feels her thigh against his hip.

"You're in my class, Ramon, and I know you. I've had my eye on you. To all appearances you're a bright student in math, you get good grades . . . but not the best grades. Otherwise, you seem to be an average twelve-year-old boy."

Ramon plunks out a random chord on the piano, then lets his hand drop.

"You hide your abilities," she goes on. "Sometimes the extent of your abilities scares you a little. You know people would think you strange, so you hold back. You learned long ago to hide your light under a bushel basket. Safer that way."

Ramon says nothing. He stares at the concerto score.

"You wonder sometimes," she continues. "You wonder how the human race has managed to accomplish anything at all, because the people around you, the vast majority of them, are so doltish, so inept, so far beneath you that you suspect . . . it's just a sneaking suspicion, something that gnaws at you late at night, when you're about to doze off—just a notion, a stray thought—you suspect that you are not human at all."

Slowly, he turns his head toward her. "How do you know what I think at night?"

"Because I have thought it, too. Do you want to know the answer, Ramon?"

"What answer?"

"The answer to the question. The answer is no, you're not human, not quite. And neither am I."

Ramon bangs out a loud chord. He sneers. "You're crazy."

She smiles again, this time indulgently, condescendingly. "You've read history. Is human history the story of a great and noble race? Or is it the sorry record of a species of pathetic creatures who regularly miss disaster by the skin of their rotting teeth?"

"There are some good things."

"Of course. But most of human accomplishment rests upon the work of a handful of geniuses, men and women at the farthest points along the great bell curve of intelligence, insight, and creativity. You know what a bell curve is, don't you, Ramon?—though we haven't covered it in class."

"Sure."

"Of course you do. Ramon, listen to what I'm saying. We . . . you and me, and others like us around the world, aren't even on that curve. We're off the graph paper."

Ramon laughs. He slams the keyboard cover down. "Listen. Why don't you get to what you're driving at, Mrs. Schaeffer?"

She chuckles. "So you're dropping the kid act? I know only too well that you're an adult—far above a human adult—trapped in a child's body. I know the tragedy of it. The ache, the loneliness. But you don't have to be lonely anymore. *Tu quoque*, Ramon. You know Latin, don't you?"

"A little."

"You're probably capable of reading Juvenal's satires in the original. Juvenal knew the depths of human folly. But you know what the phrase means."

"Yeah. It means 'you, too.'"

"Or 'you're another.' I'm *tu quoque*-ing you, Ramon Sanchez. It's the ancient, customary greeting of our kind, usually spoken in hushed tones. It's the recognition of one superhuman by another."

Ramon gets up from the piano bench and goes to the window. It is a brisk winter day, a bright sun low in the southern sky. He watches his schoolmates mill about the playground like so many ants from a disturbed anthill.

"I say you're crazy."

"Let me tell you a story," she says. "It's about a race of beings, an alien race—noble, powerful, intelligent beyond human imagining—who once ruled a galaxy. Not this one, but another, millions of light-years away. They were called the Kweii. Can you say that?"

"Cut the crap," he says.

She smiles thinly, then spells it for him. "Say it."

"Kway-ee."

"That's right. They ruled with an iron hand, showing no weakness, doing what was necessary to preserve order. They ruled for tens of thousands of years. But a rebellion among the lesser races, one that had brewed for a long time, finally came to a boil. The Kweii were overthrown, dethroned. They were hunted down almost to the last individual, and killed. But a few Kweii managed to escape. And they have been hiding ever since. Hiding here, on this planet."

Ramon interrupts. "Pardon me for sounding like a kid again, but that's dumb. Sounds like comic-book stuff."

"Perhaps, but it's true," Mrs. Schaeffer says. "When the Kweii arrived here, some fifty thousand years ago, they found an almost uninhabited world. Most of the advanced species were doomed to eventual extinction, including the so-called 'dominant' species of bipedal mammals. I don't have to ask you if you know any paleontology."

"Fifty thousand years ago?" Ramon thinks about it. "Neanderthals—but what about the Cro-Magnon?"

"An improved version, our creation. The aboriginal subspecies was simply too primitive. The Cro-Mags and their descendants proved useful. Their improved DNA was complex enough to accommodate and conceal the Kweii genome. Again, I will assume that you know at the least the rudiments of biochemistry and molecular biology."

"You can assume that, yes," Ramon says.

"Then I don't have to spell it out for you. The Kweii genetic material is interwoven with the human double helix. The alien Kweii genome is programmed to produce Kweii individuals now and then, quite at random, regardless of the genetic makeup of the human parents. Not too many racial specimens, not too few. Just enough to maintain a level of racial consciousness across the span of fifty thousand years."

Ramon steps toward her. "Why?"

"Why?"

"Why is the genome hidden?"

"To deceive our enemies, to conceal our presence here. Our life spans are long, but we are not immortal. Many new generations would have to be born in exile. For appearance's sake, we have had to suffer the humiliation of a short life span. There was no other way. Long-lived individuals would surely attract attention. No, the first Kweii generation here had to die knowing only that their progeny would live on, down through the ages. Until the Rebirth."

Ramon nods noncommittally. "I see. How long do we have to stay in this form?"

She answers, "Until the heat is off, to use movie gangster lingo. Until they give up looking. Then we will regroup and return to the home galaxy. And take it back."

Ramon sits on a chair beside the sooty iron radiator. "Won't we be discovered eventually?"

"No. When our enemies observe this planet, as they no doubt have already, they see a race of bumbling bipeds who can't think of anything better to do with nuclear energy than to make big fire-crackers with it, or to heat water. So far they haven't been able to summon the wherewithal to design a simple fusion reactor. Laugh-able. No, our enemies will observe, dismiss Earth entirely, and go on, not even suspecting that we Kweii are here, biding our time, and will one day return to wreak vengeance."

Ramon rises again and begins to pace slowly, the peeling, cracked linoleum gritty under his feet.

"You don't know whether to believe me," she says. "I can under-stand. But if you think about it, if you think back on history, on the human record, it all makes sense."

He turns to regard her, his dark eyes hotly suspicious. "Perhaps."

"It does," she says. "You'll see that in time. And you'll be ready to join us. We have regular meetings, you know."

"You don't say."

"Yes. And the worldwide front organization is one you might even have heard of. Completely innocuous, but one not easily infiltrated. Baseline humans—that's what we call the host race—are a dead giveaway, for obvious reasons."

Ramon returns to his seat. Restless, he crosses his growing young legs. "All very interesting. Extremely interesting."

Mrs. Schaeffer raises her thin eyebrows. "Not convinced? You will be, in time. You'll be contacted when we want you to attend a meet-ing."

"My parents?"

"You'll have a good cover story. Leave that to us. You'll be able to attend the meeting, alone."

"You have everything worked out, don't you?"

She nods. "Of course. Formerly, we could have taken our time with you. But now, time is of the essence."

"Why so?" he asks.

"Recent work in decoding the human-Kweii megagenome is get-ting dangerously close to the truth. Some baselines may already begin to suspect that something anomalous is going on."

"Perhaps the baselines aren't as stupid as we think?"

She dismisses the notion with a derisive laugh. "It's taken them millennia to even begin to glimpse the truth. I suppose there's something to be said for dogged determination, but the notion that they're anything but backward and obtuse is a joke." She shakes her head, and her long hair sways. "I will grant that they've been up to surprising things lately. We've speculated—perhaps the baseline part of the genome has been mutating. But we can't be sure."

"What will happen at the Rebirth?"

"We'll leave," she tells him, her eyes cool and gray and serene.

"And the baselines?"

She shrugs it off. "We might not be able to return to the home galaxy immediately. All evidence of our stay here must be destroyed."

"I see."

"Simple, really. A rapidly mutating and absolutely deadly virus, ninety-nine percent mortality. And the remainder can be dealt with easily. No one will suspect, no one will ever know, including our enemies."

"DNA residue," he suggests.

"No one will think of conducting a racial postmortem. Why?"

He has no answer.

"Come here," she commands.

He remains seated for a moment, then gets up and approaches her. She says, "You will mate with me, when you finish maturing."

"I will?"

"Of course. We will live to see the Rebirth. Our new bodies—our *old* ones. Glorious, transfigured! They are to these flabby lumps as champagne is to ditchwater, as baselines are to their old gods."

He says nothing as she rises and embraces him. He is almost as tall as she. Her warm wet mouth finds his, and her tongue probes deeply. Moments pass.

Suddenly she withdraws. Her gaze is analytical.

"There is . . . something about you."

He meets her gaze levelly.

They stare at each other for a time.

"No," she says finally. "No. It couldn't be . . ."

Her hand goes tentatively to his cheek. "You and I . . . we will be good together. You will see, Ramon Sanchez."

She turns toward the piano. "Finish your playing. You're young, you still enjoy games. Music is just a game, really. A frivolous pastime." She picks up the score and pages through it. "This is mawkish, saccharine. You'll evolve beyond this. And then you'll evolve beyond baseline amusements such as making rhythmic noise."

When she leaves, he reseats himself at the piano, lifts the cover, and plays a bit more. But his thoughts are on the future, and on what he has just learned.

He has had an eye on Mrs. Schaeffer. He suspected her, and she took the bait. Soon he will know more about how the Kweii were organized here. He will infiltrate. That is part of his mission, and the first major step toward his ultimate mission objective.

Yes, she almost intuited it, guessed that he is a plant, a deep-cover agent, a mole. An agent of the Kweii's "enemies"—in reality their victims, races who had suffered under the Kweii yoke, who for countless eons had endured their enormities, their humiliations, their unspeakable oppression.

This is his objective: to destroy the Kweii once and for all, to rid the universe of this curse forever. If all goes according to plan, the plague will come before the Kweii can build their ships and leave the planet, not after. All the Kweii humans will die. And with them all the host humans, every last one of them, but that can't be helped. They all carry the deadly Kweii genome within their genetic structure.

He takes his hands from the keyboard and closes the score.

Music, rhythmic noise. It has much to recommend it. Yes, he has decided. He will recommend that some of these worthy cultural artifacts be preserved. He will also recommend that an attempt be made to resurrect the aboriginal subspecies. Their art might never attain the heights of that of the altered species, but one never knows about these subjective matters. Perhaps the hosts, the baselines, have tapped into something primal, something they had lost.

He cannot absolutely guarantee that he can save anything, or resurrect anyone, but he will try. He will surely try. After all, he and those of his culture are not Kweii. They are not ruthless, cruel, inhumane . . .

251

Theme Music Man

Jody Lynn Nye

Simple logistics would suggest that not every hero gets to move mountains, run at hyper-speeds, or deflect bullets from a chiseled chin. Someone has to provide support services to make heroes look heroic.

The loan officer gazed with open disapproval at the man on the other side of his opulent walnut desk.

"Now, as for your employment?"

"I have two jobs, really," Irwin Katzenbaum said, shifting uncomfortably. "I work for Polyphonic Studios in the audio recording department. I'm a senior technician. I've been there for eight years."

"Good, good," Mr. Gruber said. "And salary?" Katzenbaum told him. "... All right. ... You say you have another job as well?"

"Yeah, but it's not very income-producing most of the time," Katzenbaum said.

"We need it for the application," the loan officer said, sitting back with the smug expression that said he had all the time in the world. Katzenbaum had already pegged him as one of those bureaucrats who enjoyed wielding their petty power against people who couldn't defend themselves.

Katzenbaum muttered, almost under his breath, "I'm Theme Music Man."

The banker leaned forward. "Say again?"

Irwin gave up. "I'm Theme Music Man," he repeated more clearly.

"Really?" Gruber asked, with real interest. "Well! ... Well, we get a lot of people in here claiming to be petty superheroes. Would you mind demonstrating your talent? Um . . . make up a theme for me."

Irwin gulped. He knew what the music would sound like for this odious man: the saccharine violins that they always played in the silent films when the evil banker foreclosed on the house and flung the family out into the snow to freeze. Unwittingly, the music rose about him. It set his teeth on edge, even as it made him want to cry. Other people in the bank turned to stare at them. Katzenbaum fought to contain his talent, and the misery song died away. Gruber looked dismayed and annoyed. Katzenbaum hurried to reassure him. He needed that loan.

"I've been sick with flu the last few days," he said. "Everything sounds like that."

"Oh." The banker nodded, unsatisfied.

"About the loan?"

"Well, we'll need a few days to consider it, check your credit references, you understand." Katzenbaum didn't understand, but he nodded. The banker rose and offered him a hand. "We'll call you."

"Thanks," Irwin said, and hastily left the bank. He could feel the misery song threatening to well up and drown out the Muzak in the beige marble lobby. He didn't want to whine that he needed a lousy three thousand bucks to buy a functional used car or lose the possibility of promotion to traveling sound crew. Superheroes didn't blubber on bankers' desks. Even marginally employed ones who really felt like crying.

Theme Music Man. No one outside the big city knew he existed, but they always suspected something like him did. Whenever a superhero charged into action on television or in the movies, it was to the accompaniment of heroic music that stirred the blood, made viewers catch their breath in awe, fear, and amazement. So where was it coming from?

If the cameras panned a little to the side of the main event, they'd show a modest, medium-sized man in a sort of modified bandleader's uniform. It was coming from him. Music seemed to burst from him spontaneously: the French horns, the kettle drums, the bassoons and trombones. He was Theme Music Man.

Theme Music Man

It all started when he was a kid. He thought he was like one of those people who wrote to the advice columns asking if they were crazy because they always heard music in their heads. The difference was that when it happened to Irwin Katzenbaum, everyone else could hear it, too. He used to get in trouble in school for making noise. The teachers kept sending him to the principal's office until they were convinced he didn't have a concealed radio or tape player. Then they just thought he was a freak.

Not until he fell in with a few of the real superheroes did he manage to find a peer group. It started in his teen years in Boston, when the street he was walking down turned into a shooting gallery. Ten mugs in panty-hose hoods were firing guns at a lone man wearing an immaculate white gi and black hakama trousers. Irwin recognized him at once as Kickfighter, Boston's pride and joy. How he eluded the hail of bullets and whirled in to knock out each man in turn, Irwin could never say later. He just watched with everyone else, dumbfounded.

When it was all over, the news crew summoned to the scene surrounded Kickfighter—and Irwin, who had been generating sweeping, daring musical phrases with an Oriental flair throughout the whole confrontation. Under the red domino mask, the Japanese-American superhero turned out to be a nice guy. He took Irwin under his wing, helped him train his talent, taught him what he was doing and how to control it . . . somewhat. The two of them ran together in Boston for three years, on adventures that came up after school hours, until Irwin graduated. Kickfighter was strict about not interrupting school, even when Irwin complained about missing all the good parts. Then Kickfighter insisted Irwin go on to college and get a decent education. Irwin was reluctant. He'd never have a more appreciative audience, but Kickfighter was adamant. Irwin went. Naturally, he majored in music.

After college, he moved to New York and got a part-time job in Polyphonic's tape library. His essays into crimefighting were a lot more frequent in New York. With an introduction from Kickfighter, Irwin started running with the superheroes he'd heard of all his life. He affected a costume that suited his talent: white tunic trimmed with gold braid, peck-measure cap, white spandex stirrup pants, and boots that used to be a horror to run in until the Wonder Lady tipped him off about a custom shoemaker who worked for the trade.

In spite of the danger, Irwin was thrilled to be involved with people who were admired. Whenever he was with one of the big names, the music he made was grand and heroic, suiting the situation and the hero. Every one of them had a different motif, a different melodic line. When he was with the Superguy, it was all kettle drums and French horns. The Superguy didn't like the fanfare, being a really nice, modest man who lived quietly most of the time. Theme Music Man loved it when he was allowed to hang around. The relationship didn't last because it was hard for the Superguy to sneak up on a crook when the French horns started blaring DAH da da da da DAN DA DA! DAN dadada dah DAN DA DAAA!

The Dark Detective had a moody, film-noir theme on saxophones that TMM really liked to play. It made him feel like he was in the middle of a Bogart picture, but it annoyed the heck out of DD, because an action bridge filling the air was not a conducive atmosphere to interrogate an uncooperative stoolie in private. The Dark Detective was relatively patient for a couple of weeks, then he passed Irwin on to the next big guy who was interested.

TMM thought he would last with Rap Brother, who did his thing as much with tunes as with his fists. RB's cause was getting kids off the streets. Irwin would stand by, generating scratching, samplings, and popcorn beat, and marveling at Rap Brother's sure sense of reality as he told the kids about right and wrong. He was one of the last of the great. Hollywood got him, not an assassin's bullet. It might have been more merciful. Once he hit the boob tube, kids took Rap Brother just about as seriously as the commercials. The producers used TMM's music as the basis for the show's sound track, providing a nice chunk of change for the kitty for as long as the program lasted, which was two seasons.

Since he was not particularly heroic himself, Theme Music Man's personal theme sounded a lot like a mouse sneezing into a kazoo. It inspired no one, not even him.

Where Irwin really shone was at superhero press conferences, because he provided a natural music track for the TV reporters' sound bites. He tried to time it so the big fanfares came right after the superhero made his or her most important statement. The times when he failed to control himself and ran right over the punch line didn't make him popular. Still, he did earn royalties from every time someone played one of his themes on the radio, on TV, or in the movies. ASCAP and BMI sent him a small check once a quarter.

Things had declined for him since all the big guys started disappearing. Bad guys' bullets and fatal traps claimed some of them, but some retired and, like Rap Brother, Hollywood got some of them, too. Without the principal hero, there wasn't much need for a sidekick, however useful. Irwin took on side jobs to help support himself.

When he wasn't scoring press conferences for heroes or cutting together tape at Polyphonic, Theme Music Man hired out to politicians. His reputation for honesty was well known, so his endorsement meant something, ratings-wise. He was approached nearly every week by some candidate or incumbent to generate wonderful music behind the declamation of their latest self-aggrandizing plan. The trouble was that his talent was honest. The pols were counting on *Also Sprach Zarathustra* to rise up majestically behind the sound of their voices. Depending on TMM's faith in their convictions, they might get something like a John Philip Sousa march, or the "WAH wah wah wahhhhh" trombone from missing Bucket Number Six on the Bozo Show. TMM hired himself out to parties, bar mitzvahs, worked with story tellers, but it wasn't much of a life for a superhero.

Crime didn't pay, not for those committing it, and certainly not for the poor slobs who fought it. Irwin got on a bus, feeling sorry for himself.

The personnel department at Polyphonic agreed to hold open the field job one more week, until Irwin heard whether or not he had the car loan. He was on edge until the phone call came three days later. Begging an extended lunch break from his supervisor, Irwin took the bus down to the bank. He was excited; he'd already earmarked a used Chevy station wagon in a lot down the street. With the loan, he'd have enough to pay the title and license fees.

As soon as he got to the loan desk, Irwin knew there was bad news. The guy behind it looked glum.

"I'm sorry to pull you down here for nothing, Mr. Katzenbaum," the banker said, trying to look friendly. "I wanted to see you in person so you would understand there's nothing personal."

"You could have said that over the phone," Irwin said.

"Uh, well, you know, you are a superhero. I wouldn't want any of your friends to misread our refusal to give you a loan."

"Yeah." Irwin could imagine the banker didn't want anyone with superpowers to come up and shove him into the time-lock safe and fuse the door shut with heat-ray vision. Only an immoral jerk like a loan officer would even think of misusing powers like that. "Look, Mr. Gruber, I really need this loan. I'm up for a promotion, but I can't get the promotion without a car, and I can't get the car without money."

"How come, if you're a superhero, you're not rich?" the banker asked.

"Because we don't charge to fight crime," Irwin said. "It's unethical."

The banker's expression clearly said, "Suckers!" He composed his face. "Well, I'm very sorry. Your work record is good, but you just don't have sufficient income to support an unsecured loan."

"But the car—"

The banker shook his head. "First Financial does not want to end up owning a beater, Mr. Katzenbaum. Now, if you were buying a Mercedes . . ."

"Awright!" A harsh shout interrupted them. Irwin glanced up, and realized that the bank was full of guys with shotguns and ski masks. At their head was an unshaven man with a head of greasy blond hair. It was Dirtbag. Irwin recognized him from the blotter police circulated to all registered superheroes. The guy never bathed. He always ended up with a cell to himself in the lockup because the street bums and petty criminals complained about the smell. A whiff of acrid B.O. floated into Irwin's face, and his eyes watered.

"Everyone here on their feet! Up! Okay, you scum!" Dirtbag shouted, thrusting bags over each teller's desk. "Fill 'em up and no one gets hurt!"

Irwin, standing with the other customers and employees, noticed as one teller triggered the silent alarm button (superheroes were trained always to know where that was). In a moment, the cops or one of the big guys would come and rescue them. Dirtbag would end up in the slammer with another sentence.

He waited. The other people in the bank waited. The tellers filled the bags with money as slowly as they dared. No one came.

"All right, you morons, speed it up!" Dirtbag said, leaning over the desk.

"We're working as fast as we can, sir," the first teller said. He made the mistake of glancing toward the front doors. Dirtbag wasn't stupid. He knew that meant someone had called for help. He leveled his S&W pistol at the man behind the counter and backed away toward the middle of the lobby.

"You get that money into those bags, pronto. Nobody comes in or goes out until we're clear." To add weight to his orders, he pulled back the trigger with one grimy thumb. The teller nodded uneasily. Dirtbag signaled with the gun for his fellows to collect the sacks the tellers handed over.

One of Irwin's fellow hostages, a burly man in construction worker's clothes, started forward, fists ready. Dirtbag spun to cover him with the S&W. The man held up his hands, and returned meekly to his place.

"Nobody moves," the villain said. He glanced to one side, where a mother was shielding her young daughter with her own body. Dirtbag reached around her and yanked the girl toward him. He put the gun barrel to the child's temple. "Or she winds up dead."

"You creep!" Irwin shouted. He leaped for the gunman, hands out for the man's throat. Dirtbag, surprised, raised the gun to blast at him, and then dropped it to cover his ears.

Deafening blares of trumpet music filled the room. Rolling thunder from kettle drums echoed off the walls, making the windows shake, and the desks danced on the marble floors. Music burst out of Theme Music Man louder than it had ever done for anyone else, disabling the crooks. He closed with Dirtbag, and chopped him with a quick left to the belly, and a roundhouse right to the jaw. The girl fell on the floor and crawled back, sobbing, to her mother.

As if the music had awakened them from somnambulance, the bank guards dropped their hands and waded into the fray beside Theme Music Man.

Dirtbag threw his arms around Irwin and squeezed. Irwin knew this move from Dirtbag's rap sheet: the perp was trying to use his incredible stink to disable him. Irwin concentrated on the helpless crowd around him. The brass band got louder, and louder, until he could almost sense Dirtbag's fillings rattle in his teeth. The villain let go, and Irwin clasped both hands together. With speed and grace that would have made Kickfighter proud, Theme Music Man spun in a circle, and connected with the side of Dirtbag's head. The robber dropped like a stone.

After one final, glorious crescendo, the music died away to a tweetle when the police arrived. By then, all of the robbers had been rounded up and were being held at gunpoint by the guards in a corner. Dirtbag and his men, heads still ringing, were taken into custody.

The chief of police himself congratulated Irwin personally for the television cameras.

"That was one daring move, Theme Music Man," Chief Hasselrich said, pronouncing the name carefully for the benefit of the viewers who didn't recognize the middle-sized man in blue jeans and zipper jacket.

"I couldn't have done anything else," Irwin said truthfully. In more ways than one. He didn't have a supersuit to protect him, or muscles from another planet, or the pharmacopoeia of a mad scientist to use against villains. It was just him, against a creep who would use threats against a little girl. "In fact, I didn't realize I was making music until it was all over."

"That was some music," one of the guards put in.

"But what were you doing here, Mr. Theme Music Man?" a reporter asked, pushing a microphone under his nose.

"Well, I came in to talk to them about a loan," Irwin said, "but they . . ."

". . . We're always happy to do business with such a virtuous upholder of the law," Gruber said, shoving himself in front of the television cameras and microphones. "Mr. Katzenbaum was about to sign the papers when that gang tried to rob us. We were very lucky he was here." He put a firm arm around Irwin's shoulders, and gave him a big smile. Irwin wasn't about to blurt out the truth. He was going to get his loan, and that was all that mattered. Gruber wouldn't dare to back away on his approval now, not after having announced it on television.

"You realize there's a reward for Dirtbag's capture," the police chief said. "You've earned it, Theme Music Man."

"Thank you, Chief," Irwin said formally. They shook hands, and the crews switched off their lights and rolled up their sound cables. A reporter leaned in quickly with a big still camera and snapped off a flashbulb in their faces.

"Page one tomorrow, Mr. Theme Music Man, Chief!"

"Wow," said Irwin. Still dazed, he went back to Gruber's desk to sign his papers, and wandered out onto the street to catch a bus back to work.

He'd never done that before, foiled a crime all by himself. Since the beginning of his supercareer, Irwin had always been a sidekick. He, skinny Irwin Katzenbaum, whose only talent was being the world's only bipedal jukebox, had helped to capture a dangerous criminal and his gang!

He bounced down the street with a springy step as he remembered just exactly how it felt to kayo Dirtbag, to save the little girl—boy, he was scared! He wondered if all the heroes felt that way when they did their superdeeds.

The symphony rose around him again, filling the street with the bassoons and bass horns. The kettle drums rolled, and he conducted an invisible orchestra with his elbows akimbo. Never had he evoked such incredible music, and it was all for him!

An old woman strode up to him and thwocked him across the shins with her umbrella.

"Young man!" she shrieked, shaking the handle in his face. "Stop making all that noise!"

Irwin gawked at her. In an instant, the fanfare died away. The mouse and its kazoo were back, but it didn't bother Theme Music Man. He was happy.

He walked away humming.

Bicycle Superhero

Dennis O'Neil

Superheroes traditionally have secret identities. They use these to keep the prying eyes of the general public from interfering in their "normal" lives.

He come around the corner off Greenwich like a french fried son-abitch and he smack into this black kid on a skateboard and he don't even slow down, no, he shoots up Charles and hangs a right onto Seventh and he gone, this bastard in a red Corvette.

That's when I seen *him*. Or *noticed* him, really. Skinny dude in the standard uniform, jeans, tee shirt. He's got long black hair that just hangs and he's wearing them rimless John Lennon glasses. Riding a bike. I mean, a bicycle that you pedal, not a motorcycle. Clunker bike. Balloon tires, coaster brake, handlebars rusty where the chrome wore away and stuck in wrong so they ain't lined up with the front fender, and paint scraped away in twenty, thirty places. Bike's a piece of shit, dude ain't even that 'cause you *notice* a piece of shit. Only all of a sudden he *changes*!

Let me remember just how it was: About four in the afternoon, July, raining a little. Dude was over on the sidewalk in front of the pukey green building that's in the middle of the block and for a second a ray of sun got through the clouds and hit him and there was a glare like a somebody hung a hundred flashbulbs on the dude and they all going off at once and then—

He's still there. But different. The glasses are gone. The hair

263

doesn't hang, it lays across his forehead and it's daring you to touch just one tiny strand. The chin, cheeks and brow look like you could bust concrete on them. The jeans and tee shirt have changed into a red spandex racing suit and muscles bulge so his arms and legs look like they was made of strung-together bowling balls. Golden boots, calf-high. The bike's different, too. Slim and sleek and shiny—not shiny like silver, shiny like a *diamond*. Wheels thin as wires and no spokes I could see.

He's facing west. The Vette headed east and after the corner, south. Before the dude changed, he saw the accident—the black kid, remember?—over his shoulder. Then—the handlebars and the front wheel *spin*. A blur there on the sidewalk with blades of pink and blue and orange light slicing the air around it.

I wish I could draw this. It's taken me thirty-seven minutes to relate just this much, and not just because I've been trying to say it as I might have said it then, either; and the whole thing happened in, I'm guessing, less than ten seconds. I'm leaving a lot out, too (the black kid lying on the pavement, the scrawny trees in front of the pukey building, the rain, the clouds, the whir of traffic on the avenue a hundred yards away—a lot.) Anyway, when the blurring stops, the dude and the bike are facing east and for a second they seem to *quiver* and—

Another blur. A horizontal one that starts where the dude was on the sidewalk and moves up Charles, around the corner, onto Seventh with the rain slanting after it filling the vacuum it leaves. The dude and his bike, moving at more than a hundred miles an hour. It's rush hour and thousands of maniac New Yorkers (and maniac Jerseyites, who are worse) are creeping away from their jobs in their usual fury, left hands steering, right fists cramming down their horns, bumper to bumper, a vast, noisy sea of automotives that Moses couldn't have parted with *two* rods and—

Does the dude care? No. He tips up the front of his bike, does a wheelie for a tenth of a second and zooms *onto* the cars. A Nissan Sentra. Leap onto a Ford Taurus. Leap onto a Dodge van. Then— he soars onto the top of an eighteen-wheeler semi, glides over the cab, wafts light as a feather to the pavement inches away from the grill if a feather can waft at a hundred-plus. The Corvette is directly ahead, stopped at Houston Street by a red light and a stream of crosstown traffic. Light changes. Corvette squeals forward. Dude and bike fly over the Corvette, land and stick—not the smallest bounce. Handlebars spin. Dude now faces the driver of the Vette, the murderous hit-and-run bastard. Who freaks. Twists his wheel to the left, which puts him in the path of the semi. Brakes hiss too late. When the noise stops, there's a heap of Plexiglas and aluminum that started the day as an expensive sports car. The driver is a shredded, bloody, moaning mess.

My father was hunched over his drawing board as I entered the apartment. Without raising his gaze, he greeted me. "*Qué es, mi perrito.*" "Little dog" was his pet name for me.

On a taboret by his elbow were his treasures, three Windsor-Newton brushes, and a bottle of india ink, a pen in a jar full of blackish water and the vinegary red wine he'd recently begun to favor: he paid a dollar a quart unless he could get it cheap.

"*Nada, padrecito.*" (I called him *mi padre*, or *padrecito*, because although we both spoke English—you got a sampling of my teenage English a few paragraphs ago—we were more comfortable with Spanish. *Pero mi he olvido el Español.* Even if I did remember it, you might have slept through your high-school language classes. So, *en Ingles:*)

"You got work?"

He looked up, his eyes webbed with tiny red lines, an ink smudge on his chin darkening his whiskers. "Lettering job. From Gruenwald at Marvel."

A nip of disappointment somewhere in the region of my sternum: Lettering paid 18 a page, which was better than the nothing he had been earning for the past two months, but worse than his inking rate of 45 or his penciling rate of 65. And my father wasn't a *letterer*, damn it, he was an *artist*. Back in Puerto Rico, family and friends would come to the little house outside San Juan we'd moved into a year before my mother had died, and pore over his drawings of the great superheroes, his Spider-Man and Captain America and Hawkman and even his Superman, comparing them to the work in the thousands of comics that littered the rooms, and everyone would say my father's renderings were better. Drink beer and praise him as a genius. The editors in America seemed to agree. After receiving a few form rejections, he began to get personal letters encouraging him. One of the smaller companies finally offered him a job, the inking of an eight-page story to run as a second feature in a book about the Korean war. He did it and did it well and a mere week later he took from an envelope a check for 320 dollars, a fine sum for such small effort. The note accompanying the payment said that if he was serious about a career in comic art, he should consider moving to the mainland. A year or two in New York would establish him, and after that he could live anywhere in the world where there were mailboxes. Within a month, he had sold his old Buick and the house and we were on a plane bound for New York.

He took a swallow of wine, swirled his pen in the water and asked, "How was school?"

"Okay."

"Your job?"

"Okay."

"Nobody's kicking my little dog these days?"

"No."

"That's good."

"I saw the notice." Leaving for school that morning. It had been taped to our mailbox downstairs.

"Yes. I called the landlord and told him I would soon have money. He said it did not matter. We have to go."

"We'll find something better, Daddy."

"Of course we will."

I went behind the board to pat him on the shoulder. I looked at the work he was doing. The word balloons were too large, sometimes covering the faces of the characters in the drawings, and the letters themselves were also too large. Because he had not bothered to pencil guidelines onto the board, the lines of copy were uneven and misaligned. There was an inkblot in the middle of one panel where his pen had dripped. I saw three misspellings.

"I'm tired," I said. "You mind if I turn in?"

"A little dog needs his rest. I'll be in myself pretty soon." He wasn't looking at me. His gaze was fixed on the bottle. But he seldom drank when I was present, and I pretended ignorance of his thirst; we couldn't have been falser if we'd been wearing greasepaint and speaking iambic pentameter.

I went behind the curtain that separated our two narrow cots from the rest of the apartment, dropped my jeans and tee shirt on the floor and lay down. I hadn't told him about the Corvette and the dude on the bicycle. I wondered why. Because he wouldn't have believed me? No, my father believed in everything, from saints to lucky charms to succubi to alligators in the sewers. He was the world's finest believer, my father was. Then why? Because, I suddenly realized, he would have felt cheated. *He* had not seen this . . . what? What *was* this bicycled avenger?

I heard loud voices. I raised my head and peered out the window. In the light from the streetlamp I could see two transvestites standing in the street and shrieking at each other. The largest of them, a grotesquely fat man almost seven feet tall, wearing a black cocktail dress and silver pumps, was waving a baseball bat. The smaller, skinny one, in a velvet miniskirt and a sunbonnet, held a clutch purse open and upside down in front of the fat man.

". . . no *money*, silly-billy."

"You gave it to your *wife*."

"Did not."

"*Liar!*"

The fat man swung the bat. It bounced off the sunbonnet and the knees beneath the miniskirt buckled. The bat arced upward, paused, began to descend and—

Stopped. Caught in mid-swing by a sinewy brown hand, which was attached to a muscular arm in red spandex. The dude stepped into the light and whispered, "Enough."

"Hell it is," the fat man screamed and brought the bat around in a flat trajectory aimed at the dude's face. The dude punched. Once. The bat clattered to the sidewalk and was immediately buried beneath a black cocktail dress and a lot of fat.

I must have blinked. The dude was gone. The skinny man was kneeling by the fat man cooing. I lowered my head and silently answered my own question. What was the bicycled avenger? A superhero. No other word for him.

On my way to school the next morning, I fished a *Daily News* out of a wire trash can and scanned it for news of the Corvette. There was a two-paragraph story on page 18 describing the accident, but nothing about the superhero. That was amazing. A couple hundred people had witnessed the incident. Could I have been the only one who had seen what had truly happened? Was that possible?

We left our Greenwich Village apartment the following Saturday and moved into a lower east side tenement. We shared four rooms with a family of nine Cubans, a regiment of rats and an army of roaches. I thought nothing could be worse, that our lives could only get better. I was wrong.

But I survived.

Watched my father deteriorate into a twitching mass of coughing and pain, and survived. In my worst moments, and there were plenty of them every day, when I was tempted to crime, drugs or at least the red wine my father managed to continue scoring, I allowed myself to drift into a reverie. I remembered the superhero. The red-spandexed, golden-booted, silver-bicycled protector of the—I was sure—innocent, the helpless, the kind and the decent. A creature like man, but different, perfected, someone wiser, juster, more compassionate who could compel eyes to raise in willing admiration.

On my eighteenth birthday, I saw him again. I was returning from a housing project in Red Hook, in Brooklyn. I'd gone there to see a girl of wit, intelligence, bilinguality and awesome breasts I'd met at a dance in Bed-Stuy. I'd found her in a playground smoking crack with three guys. She hadn't recognized me. She probably wouldn't have recognized her mother.

I fled onto an elevated platform and waited for a Manhattan-bound train. An old, old woman in a threadbare brown coat with a *Sunday Times* magazine covering her head and three bulging paper bags mended with tape at her feet was huddled on a bench near the stairs. I avoided her. She was muttering and she almost certainly stank. A slim man in a fur coat and grey fedora stood a few feet away staring at his snakeskin cowboy boots. Someone else I didn't want to meet. I gazed up the tracks, trying to will a train into sight. Then I heard a flat, hard *snap*. I turned. Two red flashes in the shadows in the stairwell and, a half-instant later, two more snaps. Someone on the steps was shooting at the guy in the boots, who was tugging an automatic from his coat pocket. He dropped to his knees and fired. *Snapsnapsnap.* It was a gunfight, no rare event in that part of the city, and the old woman was directly between the shooters.

She squeezed her eyes shut and began to scream, "Mother sweet Mary have mercy—"

And there he was. There *it* was. The silver bicycle, riderless, streaking from the darkness at the end of the platform. It slammed into the kneeling gunman and knocked him back, dumping him onto the tracks. A figure in red spandex appeared next to the old woman—from nowhere?—vaulted a railing and dropped onto the second shooter. A pistol spun into the air and a fist struck flesh and a body tumbled to the landing below.

Then silence, except for the old woman's prayer, now whispered: ". . . deliver us sinners . . ."

I put a finger under her chin and tilted her face up. Her eyes opened. "You're all right now, mama," I said. She did stink, but that was okay.

I left the platform and went home. I passed through different kinds of neighborhoods, from shabby to elegant to sordid, across the Brooklyn Bridge, uptown to Fourteenth Street, where I shared an apartment with three other students. I didn't mind the long, chilly journey. I had a lot to consider. To begin with, who *was* my superhero? Did he have a name? Because, if he didn't, maybe I should give him one. I seemed to be the only person who ever saw him—and that was something else to mull: why? In comics, everyone seems to know about superheroes; they're always famous. But suppose the hero didn't *want* fame? Suppose, for whatever reason, he preferred to do his deeds as anonymously as possible. Suppose—this was a weird notion—he felt *unworthy* of his abilities. He'd hide them, wouldn't he? The ability to hide them might be one of his powers. But then, why not hide them from *me*? Obviously, he couldn't. Because I had special training? Since earliest childhood, my father had shared his faith in superheroism with me—I knew that he did believe in superheroes as surely and strongly as he believed in sewer-dwelling alligators—and that early conditioning may have given me a mental warp which enabled me to resist whatever Citizen Mercury used to make himself invisible.

Citizen Mercury?

Where had *that* come from?

It wasn't bad, though. Mercury was the Roman god of speed, and my dude was nothing if not fast. But *Citizen?* Well, a number of heroes had borne military titles, specifically Captain: Captain Atom, Captain America, Captain Marvel, Captains Midnight, Action, Fearless, Flash and Victory, probably more. There had also been a couple of Majors, Liberty and Victory, who was no relation to the captain. Putting a rank in front did lend some cachet to the name. But the military sucked—everyone has known that since Vietnam, and anyone who hadn't learned it from Vietnam surely learned it from the Persian Gulf. So Captain wasn't good; Lieutenant, Colonel or General would have been worse; Private or Corporal would have been silly. "Citizen," though—why not? It implied humanity, humility and identification with the common man, all good qualities for a hero to have. I had to admit it wouldn't have looked good on a cover, and when I said it aloud it just sort of plopped off my tongue, but this was life, not comics, and anyway, nobody would ever have to hear it.

I was wrong about that. Someone did have to hear "Citizen Mercury," someone whose own name was Angeline Gomez. But not for a while.

Specifically, not until I'd seen Citizen Merc in action a dozen more times over the next six years: a purse snatcher; a mugger with a knife in Central Park; a holdup man with a gun in a deli; a baby whose carriage was in the path of a beer truck; a pimp beating on a hooker; a hooker beating on a john; a biker beating on a mailman; a husband pushing his wife out a tenement window; three car thieves; two burglars—all had abrupt and violent dealings with the Citizen.

He had changed. He was bigger, lither. The red spandex suit had been replaced by something darker, looser, somehow more dignified. He'd switched from a Captain Marvel look to a Batman look. I half expected him to appear wearing a cape, but he didn't; I guess he knew capes were passé.

While C. Mercury was dealing with the street realities of the Apple, I was living, as industriously as possible, the slightly ludicrous life of the extremely short. I hadn't grown an inch since eighth grade.

But I had, in approximately this order, developed a sense of humor, stumbled through high school, graduated from New York University, met some women who weren't into the basketball-player physique and had three hot affairs and a cool one, gotten engaged and unengaged, sampled marijuana, cocaine, LSD and various alcohols and discovered, to my relief, that I liked none of them. My father's predilections had been buried with him. He had been dead for six years when I met Angeline and I wish I could say I mourned him, or at least missed him.

"He was a drunk and a dreamer and a loser and I despised him," I told her.

"He was also an artist," she said.

"No excuse."

We were lying on a sofa in her cousin's apartment watching *Saturday Night Live* with the sound off. She was a psych major from St. Louis I'd met the previous summer when she'd come east to spend a month with a cousin who lived in the Village. We'd corresponded, and gotten together when she'd returned three weeks earlier for another visit. Male heads seldom turned when she passed, but she was soft and she listened and seemed to care. Our relationship was dangling between hormones and superego. A condom was a boulder in my hip pocket.

She kissed me, a comforting, sisterly kiss on the cheek, and said, "I'm sure he loved you."

"Not as much as he loved vino and comic books."

"How do you know?"

"He spent time with the wine. He took care of the comics. His little dog he ignored. If it hadn't been for Citizen Mercury—"

"Who?"

I'd uttered it. The name. Without planning to, without wanting to. For a second, I wished I could suck the words back in. But I couldn't, and I couldn't dismiss them with a joke or an excuse either, or change the subject, because, once having said them, I had created a need to speak more—explain, describe, share. The Mercster had been mine alone for years and I realized, suddenly, that I wanted help with the awe and terror of the secret he was.

"You'll think I'm crazy," I said.

"Probably," she said, smiling and snuggling closer.

For an hour, feeling her weight on my chest, her breath on my cheek, staring at silent images on a screen, I told her. Every story, Corvette to latest burglary. I finished and waited in an agony of suspense for her reaction.

She got up, switched off the television and with her back to me said, "He's you. You must know that."

"No way. I don't go around being heroic."

"Maybe not. Maybe you imagined some of it. But you might have *done* some, too. The bag lady and the guns—"

"Sure, I'm gonna go against a couple of nine-millimeters—"

"I'm not saying you did. But you *could* have. In a fugue. A state of temporary blackout. You do things you don't remember later." She turned and leaned forward, almost bowing, hands splayed on thighs as though she were a quarterback addressing the huddle. "How did you get home from Brooklyn that night?"

"On my bike. I was tired and I was gonna take it on the train—"

"So you had your bicycle. You could have thrown it at the guy in the boots and jumped on the other one."

"The Corvette—"

"You were wired. You didn't go a hundred miles an hour or jump over trucks to catch him, you didn't *have* to, not in rush-hour traffic, but you thought you did."

"The witnesses—"

"They might not have noticed a kid on a bike in the excitement. They might not have said anything if they had. They're New Yorkers." She perched on the arm of the sofa. "Listen, I just thought of something. You described the whole scene with the Corvette and the truck pretty completely. Well, you were blocks away, on Charles Street. How could you know what happened, exactly?"

"The story in the *News*—"

"Two paragraphs gave you all *that*? Two paragraphs that didn't even mention a kid on a bike?"

"Okay, I made it up. But the others—"

"The transvestites—you were young and healthy and they were old and drunk and crazy. The same kind of explanation could work for the rest, too."

"Say you're right. Why didn't I take credit, get my picture in the papers, get a reward?"

"You were the little dog. Little dogs don't do great things. Superheroes do."

"All in my head, huh?"

She bumped onto the cushion beside me and squirmed over.

"Yes, but don't sound so sad. Citizen Mercury is *you*, or who you are inside, and it doesn't make any difference if you really did those things or not. *Wanting* to do them is what counts."

If I *was* Citizen Mercury, then the Mercmeister got laid that night.

But he didn't, because I wasn't. No hero would have treated Angeline as I did. I didn't call her the next day and didn't answer the phone when I thought she might be calling me. A week later, she surprised me as I was crossing Washington Square Park and, voice full of hurt, asked why I had been avoiding her. I tried to answer, but all I could find inside me was a mute resentment. I went to a bench and she followed me. We sat.

"Did I make you mad?" she asked.

"You know," I replied, snotty and overbearing, "you'll be a great shrink. You've got the gift. Nice, neat explanations for everything. 'It's daddy's fault, it's mommy's fault, it's your potty training, it's a *fugue*.' Nice, neat boxes. If it won't fit inside a box, it isn't real. Not to you. Not to the hot item from Saint Louie, Moe."

What I was saying I believed. How I said it was loathsome to me.

Angeline stood and hurried away.

I watched her go, hoping someone would appear and undo the damage I hadn't known I would, or *could*, do. Hoping for Citizen Mercury, I guess.

I've seen a lot of New York dawns since then, prowling the neighborhood or staring out my bedroom window. Finally, yesterday, as I was having a second sip of scalding coffee in a Seventh Avenue doughnut shop, I had my flash of enlightenment. The reason I resented Angeline's explanation is this: Citizen Mercury has to be something grander than short, skinny me having a hell of a time. If he isn't, if I merely imagined this demigod whose reality has sustained me, he's no better than my father's faiths, and that's no good at all. That means I'm trapped inside my old man.

Citizen Mercury has to be *real*.

I left the doughnut shop, pillaged my credit card and bought a suit at Barney's. Tie, shirt, Florsheims too—very expensive clothing. Cost almost as much as my father had earned during his entire comics career. I'll wait until midnight and then walk through the grim regions of the city: Harlem, Fort Greene, Red Hook, Bed-Stuy, East New York, the Bowery, in and out of the parks, schoolyards, wino bars, through the crooked alleys in Chinatown and along the vacant stretches between the Hudson piers. Flaunting my finery and my vulnerability. Being an easy victim. Inviting trouble. Sometime soon, I'll be attacked and when I am, I'll look for a savior to burst from the darkness. If he doesn't come, I may die. If he does, I'll call to him, I'll beg him to wait, I'll reach out and touch him and I'll see my hand on his arm, see that he's big and splendid and *not me*, and then I'll thank him and find a place where I might be able to rest.

Captain Asimov

██

Steve Antczak

Is humanity a prerequisite for heroism?

Jeevs cleaned up after dinner, loading all the dishes into the washer, but first washing them by hand as per Mrs. Moynahan's explicit instructions. Then Jeevs vacuumed the upstairs while the rest of the family watched vids downstairs in the holo chamber. Jeevs thought of them as the "rest" of the family, because he was programmed to think of himself as a Moynahan, subservient to the rest of them, but still one of them. Just as he was programmed to think of himself as *himself*.

The upstairs was vacuumed by the time Mr. and Mrs. Moynahan were finished with their family obligations . . . quality time with their children, which Jeevs had figured amounted to an hour and forty-seven minutes and ten seconds for the three of them. The Moynahans sometimes spoiled their children and gave them a full two hours. Then it was off to Social Club with the adults, and Jeevs was responsible for getting the little 'uns to bed. It helped that he was faster, stronger and able to leap taller pieces of furniture than they were. It also helped that he had shock-hands, and if they were bad he could stun them with a quick jolt of electricity and have them tucked into bed before they regained awareness.

It was usually easier to either wear them out with games or read them to sleep. The youngest child was Fermi, and he liked nothing better than to have Jeevs read him the latest superhero comic books. Fermi was too young to actually read, but he looked at the pictures while Jeevs recited the story and dialogue from memory.

"Read *Captain Battle!*" Fermi yelled in his excitement. He had a repetoire of favorites: *Captain Battle*, *Warchick*, *Meathook and Bonesaw*, *Funkiller*, and *The Justice Legion of Avenging Angels*. They were all of the hit-first-and-hit-again-later variety, and Jeevs privately considered them a little too violent for a little boy Fermi's age. But being a robot meant he didn't have the right to express an opinion of such a *human* nature, which was perfectly all right by Jeevs. He was perfectly happy to serve his owners well. It was in his program. To perform poorly resulted in a deep depression which could only be alleviated by going the extra mile, so to speak, with the housework. He had once gotten the carpet so clean he swore he could see his reflection in it. The Moynahans had to take him in to get his optics retooled.

"Captain Battle versus Cardinal Carnage in The Holy Terror Part Three," Jeevs announced in a perfectly pitched, square-jawed news anchor voice.

Fermi clapped his hands and rubbed them together greedily. "*Yeeeeaaaahhh!*"

Next was the only daughter, Jesse, and she didn't like to be read to at all. That didn't mean she could read, because she couldn't, but she had a series of make-believes she liked Jeevs to act in with her. One of them was Jeevs as the White Stallion and Jesse as the Princess, riding through the Enchanted Forest after having escaped from the clutches of the evil Duke. She would climb onto Jeevs's plastiframe shoulders and he would gallop her throughout the entire house. Jesse pretended the door frames were dragons swooping low to grab her off the White Stallion.

"A dragon, a dragon!" she would yell as they approached a door frame, and then cover her eyes with her hands as Jeevs ducked down a mere instant before she would have collided with it.

The oldest was Horace, and he had a jealous streak where Jeevs's time was concerned. He enjoyed having Jeevs read him science-fiction books before bed. He couldn't read either, and was therefore typical as boys his age went. Despite the fact that most of the science-fiction books he liked to hear were hopelessly outdated, he really seemed to like having them read to him by a robot, especially ones with robots in them. Jeevs knew this because Horace wouldn't let either his mother or his father read to him. Of course that might've been because they could only read the primary reader versions of the books . . . like most adults in modern society, the Moynahans were illiterate except on the most rudimentary level. They could tell the difference between the words MEN and WOMEN, for instance, even without the accompanying Greek symbols. They got confused once at a place with GENTS and LADIES. But Horace's favorite authors were Asimov, Bradbury, del Rey, Sladek, anyone with a lot of robot stories.

"Come *on*, Jeeeeevs!" Horace yelled at the robot on the fourth pass through the living room, or, as it was known in this make-believe, the Haunted Wood.

"A ghost!" Jesse screamed when she saw her older brother trying to get Jeevs to stop.

Jeevs was about to duck underneath the chandelier in the main hall—

"A falling star!" Jesse yelled.

—when Horace suddenly rolled a toy truck right at his feet. The robot stepped on the truck, and his leg went flying out behind him. With his inhuman dexterity he managed to maintain his footing long enough to lift Jesse off his shoulders and toss her onto the plush sofa where she landed unharmed. Then Jeevs's footing gave out and he plunged headfirst into the wall.

Blackness. It was not unlike being shut off to conserve his power supply, except this time it had been unexpected. Jeevs knew it probably would have been rather painful too, had he been a human. This was not something he thought while "unconscious." He thought nothing. There were no dreams or anything like that. He just stopped being until somebody turned him back on and he was Jeevs again, ready to work.

Except, when he was turned on, he had other thoughts aside from musing about pain. His head was a-jumble with images from *Captain Battle* and Isaac Asimov's robot stories. The Three Laws of Robotics scrolled through his memory over and over and over . . .

A robot may not injure a human being or, through inaction, allow a human being to come to harm.

A robot must obey the orders given it by a human being, except where such orders would conflict with the First Law.

A robot must protect its own existence, as long as such protection does not conflict with the First or Second Law.

And swimming through these Laws, underlying them, was the cry of Captain Battle: "Fists . . . do the talking!"

Jeevs went back to work, although the children were no longer allowed to play with him before bed like before. The quality time with Mom and Dad stretched another hour into the early news broadcasts on the holo. Jeevs overheard a report about battlebots, designed by the military and sent into any number of small hot-spot countries, where they efficiently murdered hundreds of villagers day and night until self-destructing. The report stated that there was a certain probability that a few of these killing drones had not self-destructed and had continued to mutilate their way through certain South American countries. To top the story with a generous helping of horrific prophecy, the anchor suggested there was always a possibility one could wind up in *your* neighborhood someday, hacking and slashing and shooting to pieces *your* children. Then he ended with his usual, "And may the good news be *your* news."

Jeevs was puzzled. Hadn't these robots ever heard of the Three Laws? Weren't they imprinted with them from day one?

One day Jeevs was outside mowing the lawn, using a push mower because Mr. Moynahan liked to see Jeevs actually working. A remote mower that Jeevs could have controlled from inside while washing the dishes or something would have been much more efficient.

"Hard work's good for you," Moynahan would tell Jeevs, as if speaking to an actual person. "Gives you character."

Jeevs never bothered to wonder just what a robot would do with character.

While he was mowing the front yard, one of the robot street cleaners came down the road. Jeevs stopped and watched it as it approached. It looked very reminiscent of the battlebots he'd seen on the news. Some of the neighborhood children were playing in the street ahead of it, and it sounded several warning beeps as it drew near.

Jeevs turned off the mower, and went inside. Mr. Moynahan was sitting in his massage chair, asleep, and didn't see Jeevs sneak past him and go upstairs. Jeevs went into the Moynahans' closet for winter clothes and found Mr. Moynahan's ski mask, made of a lightweight yet warm material called Nylar. It was red with white circles around the eyeholes, and elastic so it fit snugly over Jeevs's head when he put it on. On the other side of the closet he located Mrs. Moynahan's hot pink cape, the one she wore to the Governor's costume ball and made of the same Nylar yet nonelastic, and fastened that around his neck.

Though he hurried, he didn't fumble or drop anything. He was a robot, with unnatural dexterity. Within moments he was costumed and ready to do battle with the disguised battlebot outside. Sure, it may have the appearance of a street cleaner, but there was something about the way it bore down on those children, slightly faster than a *real* street cleaner so only a robot would really notice. Humans tended to miss subtle clues like that, but not robots and certainly not Jeevs. Dealing with the Moynahan children had trained him to notice any little alteration such as, say, a slight wobble in the mower indicating one of the kids had loosened the wheels so they would come off while Jeevs mowed the grass. Or Jeevs might catch one of the children faking illness to get out of having to go to what passed for school these days. The palms might be clammy, the temperature high on a damp forehead, and then Jeevs would reach underneath the pillow to find a washcloth that had been soaked in hot water.

"They're just the most devilish little rascals, aren't they?" Mrs. Moynahan would ask rhetorically with glee when Jeevs gave her the weekly behavior report.

Jeevs paused to look himself over in the bedroom mirror, to make sure he was sufficiently disguised. He didn't want anyone to identify him, for he knew from having read all those comic books that villains would gladly take out their frustrations at having been beaten by the superhero on the superhero's loved ones. The tight, fire-engine red ski mask and hot pink cape definitely had the effect he was looking for, and the bright colors corresponded to what Jeevs remembered the superheroes in the comic books wore.

His inner brain, the one that handled all the logic and mathematical functions just like any other computer, told him he had just about a minute to get to the battlebot/street cleaner before it "swept" over the innocent playing children.

Jeevs bounded out the open back window onto the gravel-covered back porch roof, ran across it and leaped the chasm between the Moynahan house and the Corman house next door.

"That Corman's a cheese-eater," Mr. Moynahan would say about his next-door neighbor, who was a widower and at least a hundred and fifty pounds overweight. "Cheese-eater" was Mr. Moynahan's favorite way of saying someone was a rat, which usually meant someone in the collection business, which Corman was.

"He won't let the children play in his yard," Mrs. Moynahan would say accusingly while the children nodded their lying heads in agreement. Jeevs knew Corman let the kids play in the yard as long as they didn't hang on the branches of his citrus trees, which they always did.

From Corman's house, Jeevs jumped onto the next one, and then the next one, so that he was then behind where the street cleaner was. He then leaped to the ground and ran as fast as he could, which was close to sixty miles per hour, toward the street cleaner. He saw it as the disguised battlebot, even though he'd seen the street cleaner numerous times before; a hundred and sixty-five times actually, his inner brain told him, once a week for the just over three years he'd been in the Moynahan's employ.

When he neared the street cleaner, Jeevs jumped as high as he could, hoping to land atop the monstrosity and get at its circuits that way to disable it. But a panel on the rear of the machine opened, and a nozzle popped out. A jet stream of water blasted Jeevs in midair, knocking him into the street, sprawled on his back. He scrambled to his feet. The children were shrieking with laughter, although to Jeevs they were screaming in agony as he imagined the battlebot was grinding them into hamburger. Once again he charged, this time deciding the advantage could be gained by yelling out his battle cry.

The problem, of course, was that he didn't have one. In the space of the few seconds between the start of his charge and the moment he was to leap to the attack he reviewed all the slogans and battle cries of Captain Battle, Meathook, Bonesaw and all the other superheroes in the comic books. He couldn't use any of those because of copyright infringement. Besides, he wanted one that would be uniquely his own.

Several occurred to him in the next instant.

"Eat metal!" He didn't like the connotations of that one.

"It's BATTERING time!" Sounded too much like a slogan for a fried fast-food place.

"Kowabunga!" No superhero in his right mind would say *that*.

"Viva Las Vegas!" Hadn't some cartoon already used that?

Finally, as he neared what he perceived as a murderous behemoth, Jeevs came up with one he felt would be both effective and appropriate.

"Yeeeaaaaggggghhhhhhhaaaamama!" he screamed inhumanly in mid-leap. The pitch and tone of his scream pierced the delicate noise sensors of the street cleaner like shards of glass through the diaphanous membrane of a jellyfish. Its balance servos got all out of whack and it stopped. Jeevs landed securely on the thing's wide roof, where he knew the simplistic brain card had to be.

"Warning!" The battlebot (for although Jeevs's sensory apparatus informed him that in every way, shape and form it was definitely a street cleaner robot, his misguided, short-circuited reasoning center still believed it to be a battlebot in disguise) stopped and an alarm started whooping. "Warning! Vandalism of city property is a misdemeanor punishable by fines of up to five thousand dollars, community service, house arrest, and up to one year in the county jail! Warning! This is a series eight-five-three double-ay street cleaner by Hunnington Robotics Incorporated, and is owned by the city of—"

Jeevs had found the brain and pulled the card out, effectively mind-wiping the big 'bot. Still, it wasn't technically dead.

Jeevs broke the thin, fragile brain card, snapping it in two with his hands.

Now it was.

He ran across the roof and jumped down from the front, expecting to find the mangled remains of the poor children beneath the suspiciously missing forward grinders of the so-called battlebot, for he was sure he'd been too late to save them. Instead he was met by the quizzical expressions of small faces.

Suddenly a hovering newsbot approached.

Jeevs was disappointed. He had hoped to spend a touching moment with the children, to make sure they were okay and tell them not to worry because now they had a masked marvel to look out for them. But like any good superhero, the last thing he wanted was publicity. He turned to leap back onto the battlebot and make his escape.

"Wait!" a voice ordered. It sounded too much like a human voice to ignore, but it was coming from the newsbot. "I'm a reporter from Make it Great with Channel Eighty-Eight News! I'd like to interview you, please!"

It *was* a human voice, and the newsbot wasn't a newsbot at all, but a remote. Jeevs couldn't ignore a human just like that, unless an order from his owners overrode that human's requests. Jeevs had no such orders, so he stood and waited to be interviewed.

"Don't I know you?" asked one of the kids, who lived across and down the street a few doors.

"All children know me," Jeevs answered gently, "as their *friend*." Good answer, he thought. He'd never read anything that good in any of little Fermi's comic books, that was for sure.

The news remote hovered up to him, floodlights bathing him even though it was midday and there were no clouds impeding the sun's rays.

"Why did you attack that street cleaner 'bot?" the remote asked.

"That's no street cleaner," Jeevs replied. "It's a battlebot. It was about to rip these innocent children limb from limb."

"No, it wasn't. Don't you know street cleaners are programmed to wait for people to move aside before they can continue?"

If Jeevs could have sighed with exasperation, he would have. "Of course. Street cleaner robots have the Three Laws of Robotics embedded in their behavioral chips."

"The three what laws?"

Jeevs explained the three laws, then said, "I could tell this was a battlebot because it wasn't slowing down quickly enough . . . if that makes any sense. It was my duty to stop it."

"Your duty? Who *are* you?"

Jeevs paused before answering, although Gordon Ferguson would perceive no pause, as it lasted less than a second. Jeevs couldn't give his real name, he knew that, for the same reason he had to disguise himself. He needed a good superhero name, like . . . Several occurred to him: Mightybot, Robohero, Metal Man, Captain Asimov, Tik To—Wait! Captain Asimov . . . It sounded good, and certainly rang true to his mission—to uphold the Three Laws and fight crime. That was *it.*

"I'm . . ."—he paused for effect—"CAPTAIN ASIMOV!" With his modified speaker voice, for calling the children from play, Jeevs was able to add a nifty echo effect. The entire block reverberated with the "*OV! OV! OV!*"

"What kind of a name is that?" the reporter asked through the remote.

Jeevs's inner clock suddenly told him it was getting close to lunch-time the Moynahans.

"I've talked with you long enough," he announced, then turned and leaped onto the dead street cleaner, ran across it, jumped down, and disappeared behind the houses. He decostumed in the Moynahan's backyard and hid the uniform in the tool shed. Nobody ever went in there, so his secret was safe . . . for the time being.

It made the six-fifteen news, exclusive to Channel Eighty-Eight.

"In the suburbs today a city street sweeper was attacked and immobilized by a costumed robot calling himself Captain Asimov. The robot was apparently under the delusion that the street sweeper was a rogue battlebot, such as the type currently deployed by the United States in Iraq, Lebanon, Afghanistan, Los Angeles, Cuba, El Salvador, Bolivia, and North Vietnam. Our research has led us to believe that this robot has named himself after the prolific science writer of the twentieth century, Isaac Asimov, whose Three Laws of Robotics were an idealistic proposition to control the use of robots."

They showed Captain Asimov talking to the kids, included sound when he reverbed his name, flashed a still photo of the writer Asimov, showed some scenes of a real battlebot slaughtering some sheep in a field test, and ended with a picture of the street-sweeper carcass being hauled off by a massive wrecker. Jeevs's inner clock had timed the segment at twenty seconds.

"Hey, Mom! Hey, Dad!" Fermi said as soon as the news bit was over. "Can we get a robot like Captain Asimov instead of just plain ol' Jeevs? *Pleeeeease*? I bet we'd have a *lot* of fun with *him*! He's a *real* superhero!" With that he commenced pretending to be Captain Asimov, beating up on imaginary battlebots (actually his father's footstool).

"Gaaaawwwwd, Fermi, you're stuuuupid," Horace said with an exaggerated roll of his eyes. "Captain Asimov beat up a *street cleaner*! It wasn't any battle*bot*."

"It was *too*," Fermi insisted. "It was in disguise!"

"How would *you* know?" Jesse asked, having decided to take her older brother's side this time. "You've never even *seen* a battlebot."

"I just saw one on *TV*!" Fermi yelled.

"Tell him, Dad, please," Horace appealed. "Mom . . ."

Mr. Moynahan cleared his throat and looked to his wife for guidance, but she only shrugged, as if to say *Tell them, dear, I want to hear too.* "Well," he started, and paused. He came very close to just saying, "Go to your room," but didn't. "If the news says it wasn't really a battlebot, then it wasn't. Whoever this Captain Asmovitz is—"

"*Asimov*," Fermi corrected exasperatedly.

"Well, whoever he is, he must have a chip loose somewhere, to think a robot street cleaner could hurt little children."

"There was that street cleaner that thought it was a dogcatcher for a while," Mrs. Moynahan pointed out. "Until they switched its chip with that dogcatcher that was going around trying to sweep the streets with a net."

Mr. Moynahan nodded as if this somehow proved a point, *his* point, whatever that was.

Jeevs remained unconvinced that the battlebot had really been a hapless street sweeper.

That evening he was relieved from having to read for the kids, since the parents weren't going out. Jeevs cleaned the upstairs while everyone sat watching vids downstairs, and finished early. Since he had nothing left to do, and knew from experience Mrs. Moynahan would handle the putting to bed and tucking in of the children, Jeevs silently climbed atop the roof where he tuned in to the airwaves in search of something for Captain Asimov to do.

Then he heard it, on the police band.

"Unit Twenty-three, Unit Twenty-three, please investigate a possible three fifty-two oh four at Harris Street. Over."

Jeevs wouldn't have been interested had Unit Twenty-three not responded with, "Did you say a three fifty-two oh *four*? Isn't that a *street sweeper* malfunction? Over."

"Affirmative, Unit Twenty-three."

"Where the hell are the city maintenance 'bots?"

There was a pause; then the operator said, "Ah, they're all disabled, Unit Twenty-three. Over."

"*All* of them?"

"Affirmative."

"Jesus. Okay. Unit Twenty-three responding."

Jeevs wasted no time. He was costumed and en route to Harris Street within moments.

He tried to stick to the rooftops as much as possible, with pretty good success since he could leap the gaps between most of the houses and other buildings on the way. His body was constructed mainly of lightweight but extremely strong plastics reinforced by an alloy skeleton. Robots like Jeevs, self-aware and capable of learning, were designed to last a very long time. As Jeevs got farther away from the Moynahans' home, he started to get an unfamiliar and unpleasant feeling . . . as of being lost and alone. He went through the catalog of emotions he could feel, and found the only thing it could possibly be, since he was familiar with the others.

Longing. It started off as a small tug toward home, the urge to think Harris Street was a long way off, he might not make it back in time to have breakfast ready for everyone when they got up in the morning. Jeevs recognized it then. It was something he'd heard of but had never actually experienced until now. In robot lore it was called the Collar. The Collar was supposed to keep a robot home, or within a certain boundary, by making it impossible to even *want* to run away. At first the Collar had been simpler, and crueler, giving the robot the equivalent of a painful jolt if it went past a certain point. This early version of the Collar had been inspired by the late twentieth-century movie *Star Wars*. When self-awareness in robots became a reality, a lobby on their behalf got the current, and much more humane, Collar written into the Artificial Intelligence Act of 2010.

The farther away he got, the stronger the longing got. By the time he was almost to Harris Street he was near panic, but kept it under control as he imagined a *real* superhero would. In fact, it made him feel even *more* heroic!

But there was something wrong. He was at Harris Street, but there was no street cleaner/battlebot. It *had* to be here somewhere! What if it had gotten away? What if it had only *appeared* to break down to *lure* the police there? It could be off hacking up poor, innocent humans *right now*!

Jeevs ran into the street, looking for clues, tracks, something that might tell him where the battlebot went. He was examining the pavement in the street, not finding any recent tracks whatsoever (and he'd know if they were recent; that was one of his most important skills, useful in keeping track of the Moynahan children) when he heard a noise behind him.

He whirled into a battle stance, feet wide apart and fists on hips, to find himself face to face with a robot cop.

"Freeze; you are under arrest," the robot cop ordered.

Jeevs knew from the comics that there existed an uneasy truce between the law and costumed vigilantes. The best reaction to a confrontation with the police was to turn and run . . . as long as the danger was taken care of. But the danger *wasn't* taken care of; there was still a battlebot on the loose somewhere in the city, and *someone* had to do *something* about it.

Captain Asimov was just that someone.

"State your identification," the robot cop ordered. It continued to advance on Jeevs, who stood his ground. Jeevs almost blurted out his formal I.D., which was Jeevs D (for domestic) 35 (for the year of his creation) X-5000 (series letter and model number) Moynahan (for his owner's name).

He caught himself just in time, and though it took a great force of will to overcome the automatic law-abiding response that was as much a part of his self as the Collar, he said, "You can call me . . . *Captain Asimov!*" With reverb and everything. It wasn't *exactly* a lie, which was why he didn't suddenly drop to the ground paralyzed, as would normally happen to a robot who lied to the police.

"Okay, tin-head," a human male voice said from behind the robot cop. "We'll handle it from here . . . give it the *human* touch, eh?"

The robot cop stopped advancing, and replied, "Yes, sir."

Two human police officers, a male and a female, approached Jeevs.

"Okay, Superman," said the woman, "shut yourself down so we can take you in. Don't give us any trouble, and we won't give you any trouble."

Jeevs didn't do anything. He didn't know *what* to do. He hadn't counted on having to deal with the police, and certainly not *human* police. The Collar effect was getting stronger, and that battlebot . . . who knew *where* it was? Killing and maiming and slaughtering. And here the police were harassing an innocent—well, sort of inno-cent—robot.

There was only one thing to do, and it had to be done *now*, be-cause Jeevs knew if he waited any longer he would *have* to obey the police. It was the only behavior control stronger than the one that caused him to obey his owners.

He suddenly broke into a run.

"Hey!" the cops yelled, and started in pursuit. There was no way they could catch him with their organic legs. Jeevs outdistanced them within moments. He ducked into an alley to stop for a bit. Not to rest, but he needed to tune into the police band again to find out if they'd sighted the battlebot anywhere.

But . . . before he could do that, he heard something.

It sounded like wheels, the way a battlebot would sound on pave-ment . . . Jeevs stepped into the shadows, as if that would do any good against the battlebot's heat sensors. But it would! Jeevs gave off barely any heat at all because he wasn't truly alive! He'd have the element of surprise.

"This is the police," came the mechanical voice of the robot cop suddenly. "I know you're in there; please come out with your hands in the air."

The police, again! It was impossible to get away, and Jeevs

couldn't muster the strength to ignore the cop's orders again. In fact, he knew that had the robot cop not come along, he would have wound up back home, for he suddenly realized that was the direction he'd started running in. The constant pull of the Collar, to make him want to be home where he belonged, was becoming too much as well.

He stepped out of the shadows with his hands raised.

"You're going to place me under arrest." It was a statement of fact, and Jeevs didn't know why he said it.

"No," the robot cop replied.

"No? Then what—?"

"You are going to return home."

Home! It was an effort not to immediately start running that way. Right now! Home!

But he stayed, and asked, "What about the battlebot? We have to find it and—"

"There is no battlebot. It was a ruse to trap you. We cannot permit deluded robot vandals running around scaring people. This would be detrimental to human/robot relations."

"I couldn't *hurt* anybody!" Jeevs said. "The Three Laws of Robotics—"

"Science fiction," the robot cop said. "There are three hundred and forty-two laws governing the behavior of robots and the behavior of humans toward robots. You can access the public records concerning all of them, if you wish. Now go, go home, go where you belong."

"Why?" Jeevs asked, even as he started past the robot cop. "Why are you letting me go?"

"It is obvious you present no danger to anyone. I am capable of value judgements without penalty, and have decided it would be best for all concerned for you to go home."

Jeevs went. He took only a few steps homeward before turning back around to thank the generous robot cop, but it was already gone.

"Thank you," he said anyway. He went home.

When he got there he noticed immediately that the downstairs lights were on, even though his inner clock told him it was just past four in the morning. This was quite odd, for no one was ever up at four in the morning at the Moynahan residence, except Jeevs, who used this time to straighten and dust and clean. That way he had the days free to cook, run errands, do yard work, watch the children when they were home, and so forth. He had intended to go in through the rear entrance, but paused near a window to listen. Inside he heard voices, and crying.

He recognized the crying right off. It was Jesse, with her subdued, gulping sob that could go on for days if she felt so inclined, like the time her parents first left the kids alone with Jeevs. That had been a week with breaks only for sleep. He also recognized the sniffling trying-not-to-cry of Fermi.

Then he heard Mr. Moynahan.

"Please . . . please, don't hurt us." His voice quaked with fear. "Take anything, take whatever you want, just—"

"Shut *up*!" This voice was gruff and gravelly, and was followed a moment later by a dull thud, another thud, Mrs. Moynahan's scream, and louder crying. The same gruff voice then said, "All of you, shut up *now*!"

Silence.

Jeevs didn't know what to do. From the tenor of the intruder's voice, Jeevs concluded the man had to be desperate, and obviously capable of anything. If the police were called, would they arrive in time to avert disaster? Probably not. Jeevs was going to have to do something, and do it soon.

There was a problem. Captain Asimov obeyed the Three Laws. One of those laws would not permit him to harm a human, yet another law would not permit him to allow harm to come to a human through inaction. If the thug inside were only a robot, then Captain Asimov could crash in through the window and knock him all the way to next Tuesday . . . but not even actorbots could act *that* human. The man in there was as real as, well, the Moynahans.

There was nothing Captain Asimov could do, unless he found a way to subdue the criminal without hurting him, but the man sounded dangerous, violent, even suicidal—which goes hand in hand with homicidal. Someone had already been hurt, though, while Captain Asimov stood barely twenty feet away, separated by a plate of glass and a nylon drape. Inaction.

It suddenly hit Jeevs. Captain Asimov: superhero failure.

At the same time it also hit Jeevs that *he*, Jeevs, had no such animal as the Three Laws of Robotics constraining *him* from action. If he needed to, he would be perfectly within his rights to punch the villain holding his family hostage so hard it would knock his nose all the way around to the other side of his head.

"You," he heard the ruffian inside say.

"Yes?" he heard Mrs. Moynahan reply.

There was a pause, then a low, throaty, evil, "Come here."

The time for thought was past. Jeevs removed his Captain Asimov garb and dropped it onto the grass.

He stepped back from the window, took half a second to project his trajectory and envision the room inside. Assuming nothing major had been moved, he knew exactly where everything was. Then he jumped.

As he smashed through the glass he heard Jesse and Fermi scream, Mrs. Moynahan faint, and Horace yell out his name.

"Jeeeevs!"

The thug was as surprised as they were, and couldn't react fast enough. He tried, though. He held a black gun in his hand, and brought it around to aim at Jeevs, but by then Jeevs was upon him. He knocked the gun out of the man's hand, sending it harmlessly into a cushion on the sofa. With his other hand, Jeevs plowed his palm right into the man's nose, lifting him off the ground with the force of the blow and sending him airborne to slam against the only unadorned wall in the room. The man sunk to the ground, his nose gushing blood onto his shirt, unconscious. Jeevs quickly ran to the aid of Mr. Moynahan, who was groggily coming to. He seemed okay. Jeevs could detect no damage to the skull, at least.

Fermi had regained his spunk as soon as he saw the bad guy was down for the count—down, in fact, for several counts. "Wow, Jeevs, you were way better than that old Captain Asimov! Wow!"

Jeevs felt something else, a new emotion he wasn't sure he was supposed to be feeling. It seemed linked to the manner in which the Moynahans were looking at him, sparked by the grateful, adoring expressions on their faces. He wasn't absolutely sure, but if he was right, he knew the word for it. Belonging.

Captain Asimov may have been a friend of the children, Jeevs thought, but *I'm* family.

Press Conference

![]

Brad Linaweaver

The President of the United States is sometimes referred to as the most powerful man in the free world. Yeah, sure.

They used to joke that after he was elected President, he'd wish he were back in the Senate where he could wield some real power. He'd taken that sort of thing in good humor. After all, it was only a joke . . . then.

He was a student of history, wasn't he? He was well versed in the imperial presidency—the accumulation of power in the executive accelerating in the 20th century. Every war had helped. The speed of modern communications had done its part. Ever since Truman, the CIA was in there pitching. Sure, there were frustrations. He still had to deal with an unwieldy, vaguely democratic system. He didn't really mind. When it came right down to it, he didn't object to anything that was part of the natural order, as he saw it. In common with many predecessors in the office, he was that peculiar kind of human being who thrived when dealing with political parties, special interests, other nations with their special requirements, and lawyers! He could juggle priorities with the best of them.

He talked about reflecting the will of the people, and he said it with a profound sincerity. Hell, he was good at his job. But the President of the United States had not been prepared for the sudden appearance of The Two. No one in his right mind would have constructed such a scenario. And like all good politicians, the President prided himself on being in his right mind.

Only one month ago the universe had still made sense. It didn't seem all that long ago. Then The Two had come out of nowhere, sharing a nightmare between them as two monsters might suckle a malignant spirit. The world had held its breath, waiting for the last superpower on Earth to *do* something. That meant the President of the United States was expected to perform a miracle. Being a little short on burning bushes, he elected to hold a press conference instead.

And so here he was. The reporters waited for him, eyes wide, mouths wider, under a forest of arms swaying under the lights. What had happened to protocol? Where was his introduction, and "Hail to the Chief" blaring over the speakers? The organizational structure of the White House had gone to hell, along with everything else. On the plus side, every network was carrying him, not just CNN and C-SPAN. Even hundreds of little local stations across the fruited plain were interrupting their game shows and reruns of sitcoms. It had been a long time since a President had received this much audience share.

Gazing up and down the usual row of anxious faces, the President was overwhelmed by his usual emotion toward the fourth estate—contempt. The terror gripping the nation had done nothing to bring out the finer qualities of the White House press corps. Not even the prospect of imminent doom could alleviate their rudeness.

He actively disliked the woman from National Public Radio, so he let her have the first question. Best to get it over with. She didn't disappoint him: "Mr. President, what steps are being taken to deal with the crisis?"

Watching thin lips moving in her pinched face put him in mind of a fish out of water. He thought how this was the same person who had criticized every covert policy and overt military action he had ever taken. Now she wanted action.

Willing himself to be polite, he rattled off the official answer: "Our best experts are working on this problem night and day. Dr. Gerber has taken over from Dr. Shooter, who retired after his theory was exploded . . ."

"Why did Shooter claim it was a hoax?" the NPR reporter interrupted. *That counts as her follow-up*, thought the president.

"He wasn't the only one," explained the chief executive. "The last doubts were not dispelled until the destruction of New York City. Now mankind is united on one thing at least. Next question!"

A pasty-faced man from CBS wasted no time hitting him with: "What about the charges that both of these . . . creatures resulted from a secret government project in genetic research?"

"We categorically deny it," the President shot back.

"So do I!" a voice boomed from behind the President, who slowly turned around to see a man—what appeared to be a man—standing regally with a purple cape wrapped around his muscular frame. A tight, black mask covered his head except for huge goggles over the eyes. Already Secret Service agents were closing in around the President, although a sense of futility pervaded their actions.

The President tried to sound brave but he came off like a ten-year-old making a careful inquiry about the rules: "What is this about, Captain Prism?"

The man in the cape answered: "I'm here to protect you, of course. *He* plans an attack on this very conference. Never fear, he will never prevail while I am guardian of the world." The President had a sinking feeling in the center of his chest. The speaker declaimed some more: "There is no limit to the evil of Mr. Focus. He would enslave the human race with no regard for your free and representative institutions. In fact, the first place he plans to attack is this room! Now, by the cosmic powers at my command, I will move you to the Rose Garden."

"No, wait!" the President started to say, but it was too late. The low, humming noise and glowing lights in the goggles could only mean one thing. In a flash they had been transported to the Rose Garden. It was late in the morning, and a cool breeze made the hot day more bearable. The sky was as clear as an IRS agent's conscience. Everyone was temporarily disoriented, but there was no hysteria. God help them, but they were getting used to this sort of thing.

The President took a quick inventory. The bad news was that, although the television cameras and sound recording equipment had been transferred as well, there was something wrong with the hook-up and the press conference was temporarily off the air. The good news was that Captain Prism was gone . . . for the moment.

A black woman from CNN was first to break the silence. "Mr. President, to your knowledge have they ever deliberately hurt anyone?" While the technicians were busily trying to restore the link, the President relaxed for a moment—put at ease, in part, by the naturalness of the question.

"No, Monique," he said, happy to remember her name. "Even what happened in New York seemed to be an accident, a side effect of their battle. Apparently they'd aimed their beams of force at each other. Neither intended for Wall Street to evaporate. And the way things escalated after that . . ."

"Mr. President," a voice spoke from behind a camera. "We're ready to go back on the air."

Taking a deep breath, the leader of the free world—well, they didn't call it that any longer, since the New World Order—the leader, then, exchanged glances with his press secretary. Time to give it another try. Except they never got that far.

The blue sky suddenly grew dark as the light breeze became a fierce wind tearing papers out of everyone's hands, the fluttering shapes having the appearance of white doves escaping as swiftly as a peace dividend. The other one had just arrived. He was a full head taller than the cowering sound man who had the misfortune of standing next to Mr. Focus.

If anything, Mr. Focus was even more theatrical than his erstwhile foe. He wore an old-fashioned, broad-brimmed hat, as black as the heavy overcoat that was draped over his lanky frame. Although he wore no mask, his dark glasses made one, long strip of unbroken lens bisecting his face. What could be seen of his stern features did not inspire confidence that the rest of the day would be uneventful.

"He's been here," said Mr. Focus, seeming to detect traces of his enemy's presence in the very air. "You've been told the usual pack of lies, I'm sure."

The President was about to respond but he found his already shaky sense of authority further eroded by reporters directing their questions to the interloper. Mr. Focus took over the press conference with the consummate ease of a politician. He answered the red-haired man from ABC, whose question was: "Captain Prism says you're the bad guy. Do you have any response?"

Mr. Focus was clear: "That's typical of my hatred-eaten foe. You know, of course, that he acquired his powers by accident from a stray meteorite, whereas I, through a combination of sheer genius and dogged determination, made myself into what I am today." He paused as if expecting applause, but had to settle for the fear that was palpable in the air.

"That doesn't really address the issue of which one of you is the villain," the red-haired man followed up.

The reply was a bit testy: "The point is that Captain Prism—and in what army does he hold his rank, eh?—is a megalomaniac, out to conquer the world. I'm out to save it."

"Yeah, but what about . . ." someone began but never finished. With a bolt of jagged blue light emanating from his glasses, the cross section of humanity that made up a Washington press conference found itself transported to the oval Blue Room. No one was really disposed to appreciate the French Empire decor, although they were situated very close to a splendid table right next to one of the long windows. That they were standing on the table may have had something to do with the dimunition of their aesthetic sense, along with everything else. They had been reduced in size.

The President of the United States, now exactly six inches tall, was the first to realize the drastic change. "God damn it," he said, oblivious to whether the recording equipment was working. It was a sure bet that no broadcast would be going out in the immediate future. "This has got to stop," he went on.

"No need to thank me," boomed the voice of the now gargantuan man in the slouch hat. "Captain Prism won't expect to find you here. You weren't safe in the Rose Garden."

"That's what you think!" boomed an equally titanic voice. The other one was outside one of the ornate windows. Naturally, he smashed through the window. There was no good reason for this, as The Two could pretty much materialize wherever they pleased. But both of them occasionally liked to smash through things.

If the little figures scurrying around on the table had been asked their opinion, they almost certainly would have voted against the dramatic method of entering the room. As it turned out, they were almost showered with broken glass, the size of which pieces would have proven fatal to a large number of the victims. They were saved by Mr. Focus disintegrating the glass fragments with another of his beams.

"This is exactly what I mean," gloated Mr. Focus. "Captain Prism would have killed you all."

"I didn't see you poor, tormented people," said Captain Prism, picking himself up from the floor and addressing the table.

"It's a wonder you can see anything through those stupid goggles," was Mr. Focus's retort.

Captain Prism wasn't about to miss his turn: "So who shrunk them down in the first place, risking their lives in the bargain?"

The dialogue went on in this fashion for some time. Finally, the enigmatic figure men call Captain Prism decided on a course of action. With a blast of crackling energy, he restored everyone to their natural size; and there is simply no denying that the President was grateful for the restoration of his original dimensions. The only small quibble was that, as no one had been removed from the table, most of them suffered minor injuries as they fell to the floor or through the broken window. The President, in fact, landed squarely on what his political opponents referred to as the most representative portion of his anatomy. His lower back didn't fare too well, either.

"I told you he was the villain," crowed Mr. Focus, addressing the room. "The agonies you suffer today are but a foretaste of a grim future."

"Scoundrel!" replied Captain Prism. "Please, my friends, do not be taken in by his malevolent ruses. This fiend will not rest until . . ."

"*Shut up!*" screamed the President of the United States. "Will both of you just shut up?" The ensuing silence was the first evidence of executive authority anyone had experienced in some time.

Captain Prism and Mr. Focus glared at each other (at least one could assume they were doing this beneath their respective head appliances). Neither would be first to speak in yet another battle of their mighty wills. The lovely silence continued. The press corps was quiet, too. Some of them were preoccupied with their own pain; but there was no one present who didn't appreciate the tenuous nature of their respite. Who would be first to break the silence?

The President basked in his momentary victory. Standing up, straightening his tie, he felt a smile creeping onto his face. *This is the moment*, he thought. *If I can just bring these superpowered lunatics under control, if they will follow my orders just one time . . .* Gathering what remained of his personal resources, putting on the tattered remnants of his father-knows-best charm, he formulated his position. He opened his mouth. That's as far as he got.

An explosion rocked the room. Where before there had been a wall there was now a gaping hole; and stepping through this ragged opening was a tall, athletic, beautiful woman with the single most remarkable figure the President had ever seen (this side of the budget deficit). She looked just like a living Barbie doll, an anatomical implausibility living and breathing, definitely *breathing* only a few short feet away. Her close-fitting red jumpsuit was like a second layer of skin. Her honey-blonde hair swirled around her head as if a halo, accentuating the pleasant fact that she wore no mask.

For one brief moment, the President allowed himself to appreciate her beauty and confident bearing. Then the higher levels of his brain kicked in again, analyzing the new data: explosion, hole in wall, someone in a funny suit. Two words began to hammer in his brain: *Oh, no.*

"I am Lady Lightning," she announced, "of the sisterhood division of the Fabulous Fifty, a loose confederation of teenage mutants whose maturity of thought exceeds the angst of a troubled adolescence."

"Oh, no," said Captain Prism.

She kept right on: "We have chosen this time to make our existence known to the world. We are here to save mankind from this diabolical duo."

"Oh, no," said Mr. Focus.

"The first thing we will do," she said, "is thwart the machinations of these power-crazed villains by coming to your rescue. I will place a protective shield around each of you individually in which your bodily functions will be temporarily suspended. It's the only way."

The President's last thought before he screamed was how much he would miss the military-industrial complex despite its current impotence. At least his emotional display wouldn't cost him with the electorate. They'd never know. And the best part was that the reporters were screaming, too.

Basic Training

Jerry Bingham

Some people live their entire lives as though waiting for one special moment.

His feet bled without pain. Still, he kept his eyes on the dirt, almost unconsciously, searching for the sharper stones or prickly pear or blackberry thorn that might inflict more serious injury. The looser, deeper sand retained more heat, or so he had been told, but he avoided this more for its ability to slow his progress—after all, there were limits to even his endurance, and by the evening of the second day he had realized the importance of conserving stamina.

But his young heart held its even cadence, his lungs were strong, and his legs well prepared for this trial.

He had labored hard as a boy. Had run and won many races. The other boys respected his talent. He remembered that his entire childhood had seemed nothing but a preparation for the trial; this trial that, if he succeeded, would announce to his people—to his world—his *arrival*. He would be a man. He was thirteen.

The mesa, his destination, was yet a narrow lip on the edge of the Earth. The sun god approached, and heat devils rose from the shifting horizon to make the god dance before departing in a fury of orange fire. Far to the south, other demons, tiny, a cloud of them, swirling, darting helter-skelter on wings of hide. Bats. There must have been caves nearby. They would ignore the runner and eventually vanish into the blackening sky.

He looked forward to the night. Though obstacles would hide better by the dull blue light of this half-moon, at least that malevolent sun would be off his shoulders. The cool desert night would prick up his senses and the dark air would insist that he run harder to remain warm. For a short time, crepe clouds threatened to obscure what little moonlight he had, but a determined Santa Ana wind was kind enough to usher them away.

He remembered long talks with The Elder preparing him for this graduation. Tales of other *men*. Tales of gods. Of journeys that changed lives and changed the course of worlds. Of battles that ended in many deaths and changed nothing.

His left hand dropped to the small goatskin pouch at his belt where he kept, among other things, the stone. He loosened the drawstring, drew the stone out, and cradled its smooth, cool surface in his palm. The Elder had presented this gift on his tenth birthday with a warm hand on his shoulder and the words:

"This is a stone. Simple, earthy, yet within itself complex. This stone is reality. It can be hard yet smooth. It can be solid, but it can be crushed to a fine sand and the sand can be fired into fragile glass. A single stone can be pushed by water or eroded by wind and time, yet together with other stones it can be mountainous, a thing of the ages, an intimidation to the gods.

"This is just a stone. It is a reality check. If you feel defeated by life, find a hard place and stand between it and the rock and succumb. But if you wish to fight and survive against crushing odds, grip the stone in a tight fist and feel its solidity, its interior strength, then hurl it in the face of opposition.

"This simple, earthy, complicated stone will be here longer than humankind and surely longer than any troubles you might shovel in your times of despair." The Elder had smiled but his eyes remained stern as if examining the boy's future. The boy was old enough to understand the words as metaphor, but he was young enough to believe that an Elder could know more than average men.

He misstepped once from a loss of concentration and tumbled into an arroyo, scraping skin from his knees and bruising an elbow on a flat rock; but, rolling quickly to his feet, barely breaking momentum, he scrambled up the dead river's far bank and soon matched his earlier pace. He returned the stone to the pouch and pulled the string tightly. He readjusted his headband. His thoughts and his eyes would not stray from the path again.

Breathing, rapid, not his, and the whispering of little feet. A coyote, eyes reflecting moonlight, ran alongside. The twin penlights watched him for a time, curious at the scent of man in this place of no men; the scent nonthreatening but unafraid. Perhaps the coyote thought the runner pursued breakfast. Coyotes knew how to use other animals to find and snare food. He knew of a coyote that kept company with a badger. While the badger would dig into the tunnel of a ground squirrel, the coyote would wander looking for the squirrel's exit hole, where he would lay in wait. The coyote was wise enough to share his catch with the badger, ensuring the badger's continued partnership.

He glanced at the moonlit eyes, the open teeth, the tongue lolling to one side.—Or perhaps the coyote simply stayed with him for the sport.

As night and the half-moon moved on, the coyote watched him less and watched the trail more.

He had spent many hours as a boy spying on coyotes, and he envied their abilities to hunt, to find sustenance in the most meager of places, but tonight especially, he envied the ease with which the coyote ran.

Several times the coyote veered away to become invisible with the darkness, once for as long as a hundred strides. But he always returned, looked at him, wanting to question but settling for the companionship.

As morning's lumbering yellow glow pushed aside the star-beaded shield of night, heralding the return of the sun god, he knew he would lose his companion. The coyote was strong, but strength bows to instinct, and instinct would tell this night hunter to find shelter from the midday heat. The coyote would fail to understand the reasons for the run—but then, the coyote was already an adult.

The coyote stayed on longer than expected. It was nearly noon when the animal, with one last long look at the runner, finally broke the pace and lagged behind.

Some two hundred strides later, the feeling of loss made the youth look back. The coyote stood, small and distant, watching him run on. He turned away and said a silent goodbye and good hunting.

The mesa was larger now. He could see carrion birds riding the thermals along the cliff's steep sides, and he wondered how many runners had fallen and fed the birds. He would not be one of them. The Elder had told him. The Elder had foreseen greater things, a greater way to die, though he refused to be specific. "To know one's destiny would be to alter destiny." The Elder was good at saying simple things in a complicated and often cliched fashion. "Cliches only become cliche because they speak the truth," he would say. "One cannot have a basket of cliches too deep to draw from, just as one cannot know too many truths." *Such wisdom comes with being an Elder,* the boy thought.

The mesa looked large to him, but he knew it was the illusion— "Something standing in the midst of nothing always looks large," The Elder had said. And he knew the foot of the mesa was yet two days away.

The *need* clawed at his belly, and he returned to the goatskin pouch. Before the trial The Elder had given him a root, though he would not say from what tree. He took a small sample of the root in his teeth and held it there for a long while, returning the remainder to the pouch, before swallowing. He untied the small gourd of water, his only other possession, from the opposite hip and, careful not to spill as he ran, touched a drop to his lips and tongue. He had fasted many times as a boy in preparation for this trial. He was grateful for the wisdom it had taught him.

He dizzied momentarily. His knees jellied and nearly dropped him. *Something in the root,* he thought. Then he strengthened and cleared and felt remarkably sated. The sky appeared bluer, the cliffs redder. He smelled . . . the sand, and cactus, and sage, and creosote, and ground squirrels, and coyotes. He heard the wings of a cardinal and the pebbles moving beneath the crawl of a legless lizard. The ground sped more quickly to his bloody feet. Then, wisdom told him to slow his pace. "Do not let the root run the race."

He thought of the others that had tried before him. Many had not returned. Jimmy Crane, Bobby "Little Tail" Hennie. Georgie Sanchez was found after two weeks. He was alive but the sun god had burnt his mind. Now Georgie sits in front of Warren's Sunoco station begging quarters until he can save up enough for a bottle to make him sleep at night.

The runner leaped a dwarf barrel cactus; his eyes blurred at the memory of a younger, nobler Georgie Sanchez.

The next afternoon lightning clouds, heavy with rain, the color of iron, crowded the sky beyond the mesa. A white crack split the iron for an instant, then vanished. Five strides later, the anticipated cannon fire rumbled across the rocks. To the right another crack, this one splitting along several seams. And another, louder fusillade. A warm breeze dragged across his skin and he smelled the bitter, damp dust that always preceded a desert squall. It was better than no breeze.

He examined the lower cloud movement. While he thanked the relief from the day's dead heat, he prayed the storm away from the mesa. The rain would feel good to his parched shoulders, but tomorrow he would begin to climb, and even hard and calloused feet may slip on wet rock.

Night returned, and though lightning continued to fire the sky beyond the rimrock, he felt no more than an occasional sprinkling. The earth remained dusty beneath him. His prayers must have been strong.

The moon hid behind the black cloudwork. The night felt like a tight closet around him, confining. He could see nothing. Only the intermittent lightning flash told him his direction was true. Even the ground was invisible, like running in the emptiness of space. But it did not feel like space.

He fell over something rough-barked. Pushing up and on, another ten strides and he fell again, this time over an invisible knee-high rock. He got up more slowly this time, rubbing his bruised shin. He touched blood there. His chest hurt where he had knocked the air from his lungs. He ran on. He fell many times, but he always dragged his legs up under himself and continued. If he were to stop, if he were to lie down now, he would never get up. He would be feeding the birds by midafternoon. He would join the list: the Jimmy Cranes and the Bobby "Little Tail" Hennies. He would never know the great

305

destiny foreseen by The Elder. His foot caught in a tumble of sage and he went down again. He got up again and ran full-on into a "teddy bear" cholla. A thousand tiny arrows pierced his skin, and he howled in pain for the first time. Lightning cracked the dark as if responding to his cry, mocking him, showing him the demon plant now that it was too late. He failed to repress the tears. And thunder whipcracked as the dark closed around once more.

He forced his legs to move again. Swiping a forearm across his eyes, he resumed the run and began the delicate task of plucking the cholla's quills from his chest. A difficult business in the daylight. Another flash, and the thunder laughed again. Optimism tapped his shoulder reluctantly and whispered, *It could have been worse, boy. It could have been a saguaro.* Little consolation, but a smile snuck across his cheeks nonetheless. Thunder answered him, and he tripped.

Daylight found him still pulling the bristles from his skin. The thunderheads were gone, but the mesa had scarcely moved during the night; he had not run far.

He postponed his plucking to take another bite of The Elder's root and another touch of the water gourd to his lips. The response was immediate and disquieting. The prickling left his chest and arms and legs. He could not feel the stones underfoot and he had to look down to see that his legs were still moving. The scenery accelerated. He ran within striking distance of a sidewinder, who rattled only after he had passed. A company of young javelinas were taken by surprise and ran squealing into the dry tangle of a fallen mesquite. A mule deer raised its head from its grazing, but the danger passed before it could think to run. A large cat growled from afar.

He was aware of all this and more, but he was strangely unaffected. His feet still trod the sand, but his mind flew on ahead. He could see, with an eagle's telescoping sight, details of the terrain ahead. The boulders, the cactus, the dried and ancient riverbeds flew beneath him and the brilliant orange of the mesa wall climbed up, growing out of the earth with the suddenness of Jack's magic beanstalk, the cadmium rock pushing aside the vacant blue sky. A red-tailed hawk ceased its languid spirals and dove away from the intrusion.

His binocular vision scaled the mesa wall as he would scale it, searching quickly for cracks and footholds and loose stones to avoid, thorny obstacles or impenetrably bleak and unpassable stretches of flat rock. Then, suddenly he was off away from the cliff and falling— no, flying, chasing the hawk, then diving away, swooping, letting the thermals carry him, then breaking free of them and soaring to an awesome altitude.

The mesa was below him, a small, ragged-edged table throwing a long shadow on the quilted earth. He paused in flight . . . and the shadow began to move.

Cold talons encircled his kidneys and slowly squeezed. He reined in his flyaway senses. He stopped.

His feet held the earth. The mesa was yet some distance away. His heart kicked like a caged jackrabbit against his ribs and his vision blurred. Nausea. He wanted to fall to his knees, but dared not. He took long, deep breaths. Reaching into the goatskin, he found the smooth stone and held it in his palm. His reality check.

Soon he began to run again.

This night came and moved quickly on. The sky remained open. The moon was closer to being full. He hurt, but he would avoid further injury until morning.

The sun god baked the air he breathed and burned into his back like a hot blanket. He stood at the foot of the cliff looking up. Reaching out, he laid a palm against the first tall rock. The Elder had taught him about the lives of trees and the lives of stones. All things deserved respect. And he nodded a salutation to the mesa. He could feel the pulse of the rock; it seemed to breathe deep. His hand caressed the uneven surface to the top of this first rock. He lifted a foot and found a niche to support it. He began to climb.

This was the test then, he thought. Others had made the distance, though not all. Few had made the climb. None of his generation.

There were other trials of passage. Boys still developed into men, fathered sons and daughters and grew to prominent status within the community. *There were other trials*, he thought, *but none like this*. He shook away any thoughts that might discourage him.

Usually chosen by The Elder, each trial was designed to push the limits of the individual. The Elder never chose *this* trial, because The Elder was a benevolent man. The Elder never wished failure on the boys; the population had thinned enough during his tenure with the tribe. And he loved the boys. He took joy in their passage, their transformation from boys to men.

But occasionally, The Elder had estimated about once every ten years or so, and sometimes not that often, an individual boy would catch his interest. A boy who would play harder than the others; would learn faster than the others; refuse to be defeated in sport; or refuse to come home from a hunting without food to share with the tribe. This boy had a special live cinder glowing hotly behind his eyes, an incentive to best even himself.

The Elder had taken to this boy early on. He had known intuitively that he need not assign this most difficult of trials. He merely needed to mention the trial occasionally in stories of heroic adventure, mention the *"great ones"* that had preceded him, and quietly feed the boy's confidence in himself. He knew that when the time came, the boy would beg to be allowed to give his life for this trial. The Elder would then try to dissuade the boy, offer a simpler path to adulthood, but in the end the boy would win—and in the winning, perhaps lose.

The young one climbed rapidly over the mesa's first hundred feet, barely pausing to secure a grip. The sun drifted quickly toward the edge of the world and the going would be sadistically slow, even by moonlight. Pain crept in, crawling through his bones; nerves dragging and biting at each other; he sucked for air, but the air was woven with motes of glass and his lungs cried with every breath. He worked new muscles now—fingers, shoulders, back—taking some of the burden off his legs, but not much.

His stomach spoke, needing more of the root, but he feared to think of its effect up here where even the saguaro looked dwarfed. He substituted a moderate swallow from the water gourd. This invigorated him slightly and he hastened up the rock, taking advantage of the day's waning light.

Rounding a corner too quickly, he scarcely avoided an active hornets' nest. He nearly left the cliff wall in his frenzied retreat. It took several minutes and many long breaths to steady the muscles in his thighs. The sun winked out. He clung to a fissure in the rocks and waited for his night vision before continuing his vertical crawl; then he went on and up into the black sky.

Two hundred feet above the floor there are no lesser mishaps. A desert cliff face becomes alive, sharp-fanged and deadly. Each crevice can be a lifesaving fingerhold, or it may house a killing pit viper. Reaching fingers may find the sharp needles of a hidden cactus, forcing the climber to pull away, lose footing and fall. Likewise bees, bats, scorpions; a gila monster might fasten spring-loaded jaws around one's hand. Or even minor hazards: a slippery rock from the previous evening's rain could be equally deadly from this height; or step on a succulent plant and not only will the needles inflict a frightening pain, but the pulp would make a flat rock dangerously slick. In the quiet of night, an unanticipated sparrow's flight might give the climber such a start as to send him reeling off a ledge.

Dawn, and he had not traveled far. The previous day's exertions hung to his back and limbs like a buffalo jacket, if there were such things anymore. His wounds stung him in a hundred thousand places. His calves wound in knots whenever he went up on his toes. He had lost one fingernail and pulled another back past the quick during the night climb. And, worst of all, he had lost his water gourd against a sharp rock.

He could not see the top of the mesa. He could only judge distance by looking down, and even at that . . . the ground took on an abstract flatness of pattern after a certain distance. The sun took a position high in the cloudless sky and seemed to stop there where it would be the hottest. Perspiration escaped past his headband, stinging salt into his eyes. Hidden amongst the rocks, cicadas clicked at ultrasonic frequencies threatening his sanity.

He reached and found purchase. He stepped up another notch. He reached again. Still, to him, defeat was not an option. He was not so much afraid of the fall—his dreams had always been of flying, not falling; he had often thought that falling from a great height would be a beautifully silent, graceful way to die—he was more afraid of the failure. Of having come so far, so close to manhood, only to die inches, yards, even miles from achieving same. He reached and pulled his weight farther upward.

The cadmium rocks whispered to him. Taunted. Threatened. Discouraged him. They shifted or broke loose under his step. But such was the boy-man that he laughed at the rocks as he asked them for another toehold. And when he climbed so far, he thanked the rocks that had fallen from the cliffside without him.

He reached on.

Another night, and another day and a night. There was no top, of this he was sure. The mesa would continue to ascend into heaven and beyond.

There was no time. Every moment, every movement had been performed a thousand times before. The repetition of it wanted to make him laugh and throw up his arms to the wind and sing as he fell. Then it made him morose. He became alternately furious with, then accepting of the cruel humor of this life. Then he became merely accepting. This would be the whole of his life—the climb. He lived only for the climb. If he ceased his climb, so too would his life cease. He became a part of the mesa, his movement so slow in the overall grandness of the rock as to be indistinguishable from it. He wondered if the other stones were not moving as well; all the young boys sent on this epic trial. All to become part of the mesa. Sight blurred against the orange rock. There was no differentiation from one rock to the next. The cracks and shadows disappeared. The striations and color variances melded into broad brush strokes. All orange.

Orange, burning into his closed eyelids. The sun god was making his anger known. The whole of his body blazed with orange fire. He fought and shook himself awake, staring mutely into the wide swath of blue. A single wisp of white floated lazily, lonesomely there. He watched it sail for a long time.

The top. He realized, then looked around, then sat up in amazement, then stood, then fell back to his knees, then stood again. The top. He wanted to laugh, to cry out an animal's challenge blaspheming to the gods of the sky and of the mesa . . . but he did not. He simply stood and looked out and a solitary tear hung at the brink of his eye. He was a man.

He sat on the edge of the tabletop. The red-tailed hawk drifted in languorous spirals beneath his feet, miles above the floor. The plain looked less parched from this height; he could actually make out a patch of green to the west, and, blued by distance, hills he had never seen before. Not far off, at least not far from this perspective, he could see a small, dark, mottled patch, two narrow tendrils of smoke twisting into the air . . . his town. The Elder would be there keeping watch over one of the fires, the one burning just for him, a marker from home. They would not know of his achievement yet— well, perhaps The Elder might know. The rest would get word soon.

He sat at the edge of the tabletop and remembered the words of The Elder. All of the tales. Those who made the mesa, and those who did not and survived to tell. They would tell his tale one day. He cried again. He shed twenty tears for every name that came before. More tears for those who did not survive, those less able or those more able whom fate simply denied.

He had made the mesa. And he became so overwhelmed with guilt, that he was somehow more fortunate by accident of birth or of nature, that he nearly threw himself from the clifftop.

To him, this was what it meant to become a legend. He would be a hero to children, and by men less able he would be envied, but to himself he was merely a man like all other men—a little less igno- rant, a little less innocent, a little more cynical.

The dung-colored Ford pickup crunched to a stop on the edge of the gravel drive of Harvey Warren's Sunoco station. The man climbed down from the passenger-side door, the sharp gravel stinging his tender feet, and he choked on the billow of road dust that fol- lowed the truck in. He thanked the driver for the ride.

The driver, who said his name was Dobber Chamas, a face with sad eyes set deeply into skin the texture of beef jerky and hands that gripped the steering wheel like vulture claws, said, "You sure I can't take you all the way home, boy? Your folks is prob'ly pretty worried about where you been."

The man said, "That's okay. I'll walk it from here."

"You think you'd a had enough walkin' out in 'at desert. Hell, you was a hunerd miles from nowhere when I picked you up."

"Thanks anyway, Mr. Chamas. I appreciate the lift." He closed the cab door and started away.

"Hey, wait a minute," Dobber Chamas called through the open window. The man turned to see Dobber's talons fumble the top two dollars off a thin roll of bills. He crunched them into a ball and threw them at the man's scarred chest. "Here. At least get some food in ya. They prob'ly got some Twinkies and soda pop in Harvey's there. Christ, boy, you look like your ribs is gonna break through your hide."

The man stooped to pick up the ball. "Thanks . . ." But the dung-colored pickup spun its tires on the gravel, throwing another cloud of grit into the air, and left the man watching its tailgate. "Thanks."

He walked into the gas station, passing old Georgie Sanchez, who appeared to be asleep sitting up on the doorstep. The man knew Georgie was not asleep. Georgie's ears would have pricked up at the sound of folding money being peeled.

Harvey's name was still on the old Sunoco station, and everyone called it Harvey's, but his daughter owned it now. A few pounds shy of three hundred, Selma Deel ran the register and ate a lot of the profits. She lowered the yellow-paged paperback and said, "After-noon," like she had just discovered the time of day, smiling expansively, grateful to talk to anyone who was not Georgie Sanchez.

"Good afternoon," said the man. He bought a can of Pepsi Cola and on his way out the door, dropped the remaining dollar and forty-seven cents into Georgie's lap.

Georgie looked at the money for several seconds without touching it. Then he looked at the bare back of his young benefactor: the skin there looked blistered and scarred; his elbows mercilessly bruised and patched with dried blood; his naked feet had been tortured.

"Hey!" Georgie called, struggling to stand. The money fell quietly to the dirt. "Hey, did you—?" He took two steps after the man. *"Did you?"* Georgie stopped, his eyes filling with water. The man did not answer or even look back, but Georgie knew.

The man walked down Broadway, the only road through town wide enough to boast two lanes, most of the time. In many places it was even blacktopped. Broadway traffic was meager. Most of the townspeople worked the fields west of here: cotton, alfalfa, onions, any crop the irrigation runoff could support. Of the idlers remaining, many were simply unaware of the young man's graduation. One good mother thought, *Someone should take better care of their children. It's a sin the way some parents treat their young ones.* Two ten-year-olds, chasing each other with crooked sticks, stopped their activity to watch the man pass in silence, then walked off behind one of the houses to discuss the stranger they used to know.

But most either ignored the man or waved hello from their comfortable distance.

The Elder sat at a plain plank table in front of the fireplace in the small adobe walled box he had called home for the past thirty-plus years. The door was open, it was always open, and the man entered.

"Hot afternoon to be burning wood indoors," said the man.

The Elder turned slowly. It was the first time the man had ever seen The Elder smile. The man did not return the smile, but The Elder could not see; brightness from the framing doorway bathed the figure in silhouette.

"Welcome," The Elder said. "You honor my home."

The man's eyes lowered to the dirt floor. "It is no honor." He stepped into the fire- and sun-lighted room where The Elder could better see his features. The Elder's happiness dimmed, and his mouth became a thin straight cut across his features. His eyes narrowed as he examined the dark man.

"Come. Sit," The Elder said. "You must be tired."

"I do not wish to sit."

"Then stand." The Elder turned his face away from the man to stare into the fire. He rubbed at the arthritis in his fingers. "You still honor my home. Can I give you food?"

"You lied," said the man.

"I never lied to you." The Elder was not angry. He understood.

"How many boys have you buried with your fantasies of honor and adventure? You loved them all so much that you would send them out to . . ."

"I never sent you. You chose that path for yourself. I tried to talk you away from it."

"Oh, with so little enthusiasm. But when you told the stories of those that won, of the gods and heroes, your voice danced with the joy of telling."

"It is what you wanted to hear."

"It's what you wanted to tell!" The man slammed the table.

The Elder turned to look at him; his eyes were yet compelling.

Silence traveled back and forth between them until the man dropped onto the empty chair. For a moment he looked as though he would cry—but he was a man now.

"What is it you want to know?" The Elder said.

The man thought, then answered, "What is it I know? I have risked life and gained nothing. I am no older than when I left. I'm tired. I am hungry and I feel as if I've just dug my way out of a grave and walked through fire to get here . . . and I don't even know why I am here. I should've gone home. I don't know why I am here.

". . . I loved you," the man said, unable to look at The Elder's face. He choked. "And now I hate you."

The Elder rose and went to the hearth, where he bent for a moment. When he came back to the table he carried a charred pot in his hands. He set the pot before the man. Steam from the broth made him blink.

"Careful, it's hot," The Elder said and went to the corner of the room he called the kitchen. Cupboards opened and shut. "I'm not much of a cook," he called, "but I know what to eat to get by." The ice chest opened and closed. He returned with a spoon, a plastic cup of milk and a box of saltines, which he placed in front of the man.

The man looked into the pot and wrinkled his brow. The Elder smiled and said, "It's just soup. Campbell's, nothing funny."

The man raised the plastic cup. "Do you steal your glasses from Barry's Truck Stop?"

"The silverware too." The Elder sat back on his chair, interlocked his thick fingers on the table in front of him, and watched the man drink from his cup. After several minutes, the man ate his saltines and tasted his soup. The Elder said gently, "You never hated anything. It is one ability, I am glad to say, you have never possessed. I would not have loved you otherwise."

He examined the knot in the wood-grain tabletop like it was an old friend or a favorite book giving him the knowledge of the tree it was cut from. "Yes, you are tired and hungry and you feel as if you've just walked through white man's hell. But you are here now. You are safe and at my table. And after you have slept, you will have some of the answers you need. And some of your questions will not find answers for a long time. And some will remain unanswered. That's life, as they say.

"As a young man, your questions burn within you; you need to know the meaning in everything. But the point is, you do question. You think on your own, and your questions are no less than a beginning, the birth of independent thought. As a child, we are told what to question. As a man, we question what we are told.

"Your anger toward me comes from disappointment. Your disappointment comes from the realization that I am imperfect, that I do not have the ultimate wisdom, as a child might suppose, or that you have figured out some things that you thought only I, The Great Elder, could know. This lowers me in your eyes.—Guess what, little man." He leaned across the table, his eyes alive with this new secret message he was about to pass on.

The man said the expected, "What?"

The Elder whispered, "I am a man. Just like you. A lot older, a bit wiser because of my age. Your trial? That was only a ritual. Something you had to do for yourself, for tradition's sake. You would have become a man anyway, eventually."

The man finished the meal and talked and listened, and it was late evening when he left The Elder. He needed to see his mother. She would cry and wrap him in her big arms and try to feed him again, and she would talk so much that he would only squeeze in the occasional expletive or nod in response. She would pile all the love on him that she had been storing up since he had been gone, and then some.

The next day, he would visit The Elder again. He would tell the story of his run, and he would experience another kind of pain in the retelling. The Elder would sit, as fascinated as the young boy he once was when he first heard the tales told by his Elder.

The man spent many days in The Elder's company.

In 1969 the man went to war. He claimed Conscientious Objector status, but was refused on the grounds that he followed no organized religion. So he put a red cross on his helmet and went anyway.

He came home alive and sane in time for his mother's funeral. He had been prepared. She had known of the cancer for many years.

He moved to the *big city* where he found a comfortable niche in construction. Naturally, he took to the high rises where his cavalier attitude among the clouds earned him comic-book nicknames like the Human Fly or Daredevil by his coworkers. He didn't mind. He liked the high steel.

In 1987 he ran into his destiny.

It was billed by the media as the greatest high-rise fire in history. Sixty stories of hell and not a sprinkler in sight.

The man watched the tragedy on the television behind the bar where he and the boys spent most lunch hours. He watched as camera crews hustled for the most dramatic shot.

Poisonous black clouds billowed up from the ground floor, where the fire had apparently started, and engulfed all sides of the tower, trapping hundreds of people on the upper floors. The fire company ladders could not extend past the first nine levels. Fire company snorkels poured airborne rivers onto the blaze, but seemed ineffective. Courageous news helicopters braved the blinding ebony air to pluck civilians off the roof. Men and women hung from their windows at the ends of bedsheets, until they could hang no longer. A steady accumulation of dead were being bagged on the street below.

The man went to the tavern door with the rest of the midday bar crowd and looked with deepening horror at the living column of smoke less than a mile away.

Someone said later, "He just went crazy. He got this weird look on his face and he ran out down the street." Then, "I never seen him get drunk before. He musta been drunk."

One of the many he saved said, "I couldn't believe it. One minute I'm coughing my guts over the balcony . . . then I see this guy. He's climbing right up the side of the building, no ladder, nothing. The guy ain't wearing no shirt or shoes, just all these ropes wrapped over his shoulders. And he's hanging onto the side of the wall with his fingers and toes stuck in the mortar cracks. I couldn't believe it."

Another said tearfully, "And then he tied off the ropes and what people weren't strong enough to make the climb, he carried on his back. He must have gone up and down the side of that building twelve times.—I guess it was just one time too many. I'll tell you, there'll be a lot of prayers said at midnight mass for that man."

Basic Training

He was buried in his modest hometown cemetery, and people from many neighboring villages were there. The tale of the man as a boy was legend. The Elder saw to it that the man was laid down with a smooth stone in the palm of his hand. He spoke a good eulogy.

One of the Boys

▮

Lawrence Watt-Evans

Heroes are by their nature different from the rest of human-ity. When it is carried to extremes, this can cause problems.

A fist like a triphammer, the newspapers called it. He tensed the muscles in his arm again in that special way, that way nobody else on Earth could do, and he let the tension go, driving his hand forward.

The metal braces that covered his fingers smashed into the concrete with a sound like a cherry bomb. The blocks shattered, spraying dust and fragments in all directions, and his fist went right through; his arm sank into the wall up to the elbow. Shards of concrete smacked against his armor, rattling and ricocheting, and he didn't so much as blink.

Behind his mirrored visor a grin spread across his face. Punching through a wall—now, *that* was a satisfying sensation. He pulled his arm out and chose another spot, about a foot to the left. He cocked his fist and drew it back for another blow.

"Last chance, Morguson!" someone called from behind. "If we have to come in after you, you aren't gonna like it!"

He paused, fist ready. That was Red, offering the punk a chance to surrender. You always had to give the guy a chance to go quietly. Red was good about stuff like that—he never forgot the rules.

A spray of machine-gun fire came out through the hole he had just punched; bullets rattled off his armor, off his visor.

He didn't flinch; instead, aiming toward the source of the bullets, he punched through the wall again, spattering chips of concrete in Morguson's direction.

"Ow! Okay, okay!" came the shriek from inside. "Okay, I give! I'm opening the door!"

Morguson's voice. The little wimp was giving up.

"Do it, then!" he bellowed. "And drop the gun!"

"Easy, Captain," Red whispered.

He froze, thinking. Had he screwed up, said something wrong?

No, it was okay. Red thought he was losing his temper and wanted to calm him down, that was all. That was fine. That was all in the pattern.

Had he been losing his temper? Maybe he had. Or at any rate, maybe the adrenaline rush from punching through the wall was getting to him.

That assumed it was adrenaline, and of course, nobody really knew. Whatever it was, it certainly seemed to have the same effect on him that adrenaline had on human beings.

Red wasn't mad at him. Red was helping him out.

That was good.

The door, that booby-trapped super-steel door that Morguson had been so proud of, swung open, and Stan Morguson stepped out, hands on his head. He blinked at the bright sunlight, took a moment to locate his opponents.

"Well, at least it took three of you," Morguson said at last.

The Captain took a breath, planning to say something about doing whatever was needed in the name of justice, but he hesitated—was it the right thing to say?

And before he could decide, Swift said, "Hey, it was a slow night, you know?"

Red laughed; the Captain hesitated again, then he, too, chuckled heavily. He supposed that the incongruity of Swift's casual remark, after a life-and-death struggle against a brutal killer, was humorous. Or perhaps it was just a relief of tension.

"All right, Morguson," he said. "Let's go."

"I've got the law waiting down the block, Captain," Swift said.

"And that reporter from Channel Nine, I see," Red remarked. He winked at Swift.

The Captain turned, and spotted three police cars and the Channel 9 news van, all stopped in the street just fifty yards away. He tried to brush the powdered concrete off his armor as he walked toward the clustered vehicles.

Morguson didn't put up any resistance; he kept his hands on his head as he marched along the sidewalk.

The Captain glanced at him. "Glad to see you know when to quit," he said.

"Hey, I'm not stupid," Morguson said. "I don't want to mess with any super-aliens. Everyone knows about you and the Church of Doom, and I heard what you did to the Dickerson monster. I saw on TV what happened to that guy with the laser gun last week, too."

"That was an accident," the Captain protested.

Morguson shrugged. "Well, I don't want any accidents happening to me, thanks. Better I should hope for a friendly jury."

Red smiled; he always liked it when the bad guys were sensible. There wasn't any fun in bringing in a raving loon. And the Captain was always so serious about everything—maybe extraterrestrials didn't have any sense of humor?

But then, it was hard to think of a guy like the Captain as an alien. After all, he'd been raised on Earth from infancy; he was just a regular guy.

The Captain saw Red's smile, but he wasn't exactly sure why it was there. Was Morguson's remark funny? Or did Red find it satisfying, maybe, that their reputation was so formidable?

The Captain wasn't sure just which was the natural human reaction. His own response wouldn't have been a smile at all.

He couldn't let Red know that, of course.

Then he was distracted by the reporter's voice.

"This is Deborah Hatch, on the scene as three of our more famous citizens convince a wanted criminal to surrender to police. The three mystery men who call themselves Captain Cosmos, the Red Rover, and Mr. Swift have apprehended a suspect who may be the so-called Electrothief, the person responsible for the recent rash of high-tech break-ins and killings plaguing the city." She had been facing directly into the camera; now she stepped aside and turned slightly, so that her viewers could see the four people approaching, Stan Morguson with his hands up, Red Rover smiling, Mr. Swift grinning, Captain Cosmos strutting proudly.

"Hey, baby," Mr. Swift called to her.

The Captain threw him a quick frown. That was no way to talk to the press. Swift couldn't seriously be making a pass at a reporter in front of the camera! That was something to be done in private. It didn't fit the heroic image.

"Down, boy," Red muttered.

Swift grinned even more broadly, but he didn't say anything more; instead he waved at the camera.

An officer came up, gun drawn, and took Morguson's arm. "He's all yours, boys," Red said, releasing his hold. "His gun's back in the house there. Pat him down, read him his rights, and take him away!"

Other police arrived, and proceeded to do just that. Deborah Hatch was still talking into her microphone, but nobody was really listening. Mr. Swift was watching her closely, though; the Captain noticed that.

A plainclothes officer was approaching; Captain Cosmos straightened up, trying to look his best. He still had concrete dust on his sleeves, he noticed; he brushed at it.

"You boys want to come on down to the station and give us some statements?" the plainclothesman asked.

The Captain puffed out his chest, but before he could say, "Certainly, sir," Red had replied, "Hell of a way to spend a Friday night, but I guess we could stop by."

"That'd be good of you, I'm sure," the cop said sardonically. "I suppose you'll give us the usual grief about not using your real names?"

Before any of the three could reply, another car pulled up, drawing everyone's attention.

"Oh, Christ," the plainclothesman muttered.

"What is it?" Captain Cosmos asked, instantly alert.

"It's the goddamn mayor."

"Yup," Red agreed, grinning, "It's Hizzoner hisself."

Ms. Hatch was shouting at her cameraman, who swung around

just in time to catch the Honorable Albert Mazilli climbing out of his limo.

His Honor waved to his constituents, as embodied by the un-shaven teenager in the baseball cap and blue jeans with the TV camera on his shoulder. Mazilli took a few seconds to orient himself, then walked—no, *strode*—over to the waiting crimefighters.

The camera followed him every step, and Hatch held out her microphone, calling, "Mr. Mayor, what brings *you* here?"

He waved her away and marched directly up to the colorful three-some. Mr. Swift stood with hands on hips; Red Rover leaned against a lamppost; and Captain Cosmos stood straight, chest out, resisting the temptation to salute.

The mayor thrust out a hand, and the Captain took it, carefully not squeezing as they shook. Red and Swift exchanged glances.

"I just wanted to meet you boys in person," Mayor Mazilli an-nounced, speaking toward the microphone. "To thank you for your amazing triumphs over the menaces to our society, and for the efforts you've made to stop crime in our city."

"Our pleasure, Mr. Mayor," the Captain replied. He threw a quick glance at Red, who smiled and shrugged.

"And I know you're busy men," Mazilli continued, "but I hope you'll be able to find time to attend a reception in your honor, and in honor of all the brave volunteers who have stepped forward to fight crime in the streets and other dangers. I've taken the liberty of arranging one, to be held at City Hall on Tuesday evening." He reached into his jacket and pulled out three square envelopes, hand-ing one to each—obviously formal invitations.

"*Thank* you, your Honor," the Captain said, accepting his. "It really isn't necessary, and I can't say how much we appreciate it."

"Then you'll come?"

The Captain hesitated, glancing at his companions.

"We can't promise anything, Mr. Mayor," Red said, "but we'll try."

Mr. Swift nodded agreement.

Mazilli turned to face the camera, and said, "And of course, the press will be welcome—I hope we'll see *you* there, Ms. Hatch."

She smiled. Swift and Red exchanged glances.

323

"I think I can make it, after all," Swift said.

Mazilli turned back to the crimefighters.

"There's one more thing," he said. "When I heard you men were down here, after this . . . after this alleged criminal, I hurried down here because it was the only way I knew to reach you. Now, of course, you're not the only, um . . . independent crimefighters in town—I believe there are at least two others . . ."

"The Night Man," Captain Cosmos agreed.

"And the Amazon," Swift added.

"Yes, well, I haven't been able to contact them, and I'd like to see that they're invited, as well."

"If we see them, we'll tell them," Red said.

"Well, good, then, that's fine . . ." The mayor smiled, and shook the Captain's hand again, then turned away and, with a wave to the camera, headed back to his car.

"What was all *that* about?" Swift asked, as Mazilli stepped down off the curb.

"Election coming up," Red replied. "I guess Hizzoner has decided we're hot stuff, wants it to look like we're on his side."

"Oh, but we can't take sides in partisan politics!" the Captain said, shocked.

Startled, Swift turned to stare at him; Red snorted.

"Why the hell *not?*" Swift demanded.

"Well, because . . . because we're a symbol, and . . . and . . . it just doesn't seem *appropriate*."

Swift stared at him, and Red said, "I don't recall giving up my constitutional rights just because I like to put on fancy clothes and punch out drug dealers."

The Captain blinked and considered.

It was true enough; there wasn't any real reason that superheroes couldn't take sides in politics. He had had some vague idea that they were supposed to be above all that, and besides, if the truth be known, he didn't really understand politics.

But he wasn't going to argue.

"You boys coming?" the plainclothesman called, rescuing the Captain from having to say anything more.

Giving statements was a familiar routine—not particularly difficult or tiring, but not very interesting, either. Captain Cosmos went through it automatically. Afterward, he waved to the squad room and marched proudly out of the police station.

He was a good deal less proud when he reached the men's room at the Station Square Mini-Mall; he was almost furtive as he slipped inside and took the stall on the end. He stood on the toilet and pushed up the ceiling panel, found his duffel bag, and hauled it down; he pulled out his shirt and jeans, then carefully stripped off his gleaming brass-plated armor and tucked it away.

It was late; for a moment he considered keeping on Captain Cosmos's gleaming black boots, but then he caught himself.

Unforgivable carelessness! He must never let his guard down; enemies could be lurking anywhere. Any clue to his true identity could be dangerous.

Though he wasn't exactly sure how. It was just part of the way this costumed hero stuff was done.

The boots went in the bag, and the sneakers from K-Mart went on his feet.

On the stairs at his building that dark-haired woman from A-21 leaned out and watched as he climbed to his own apartment. She did that a lot; didn't she have anything better to do than watch her neighbors?

Or was she only watching *him*? Did she suspect that he had secrets?

He sighed as he unlocked his door.

He stepped into his living room, into the welcoming warmth and humidity, into the familiar smells from his kitchen, and he relaxed.

It was a slow weekend; he patrolled the city solo most of Saturday and didn't see a thing. The police radio in his helmet didn't mention anything but speeders.

Well, that was no surprise. You couldn't expect to fight monsters or crazed cultists every day. Once or twice a year something like that would come along and make the whole business worthwhile, but usually, he didn't have anything to do that the ordinary police couldn't have handled, if they'd had the time and manpower.

Sunday he and Mr. Swift met up for lunch at Ernie's, and afterward went down to the Projects off 14th and nailed a couple of small-time dealers; the punks ran at the sight of the Captain, and Swift was there to trip them up. Red didn't show.

"I think he's got a date," Swift said.

The Captain nodded. Swift threw him a glance. "You got any hot prospects for the evening?"

"No," the Captain said.

"Spending the evening rereading Dickens, or something?" Swift smiled indulgently. "C'mon, Captain, 'fess up—you're the type who'd rather pick up a book than a girl. Or maybe you've got a wife and kiddies waiting at home?"

"I don't talk about my private life, Mr. Swift," the Captain said. "You know that."

At the police station the booking sergeant remarked, "It took two of you to catch these guys?"

"Slow day," the Captain said with a shrug. He threw a look at Swift, who smiled approvingly.

Monday he heard on the radio that some loon had holed up in his house with a machine gun, holding his own daughter as a hostage; the Captain debated asking his supervisor for the afternoon off, but Red Rover took care of it, getting into the house through a back window, getting the girl out, and then disarming the perpetrator. Nobody was quite sure how he'd managed it.

"Took a long lunch," Red explained, when the Captain phoned him that evening and asked. They'd all exchanged phone numbers.

"No, I mean . . . oh, never mind."

"No, I'm kidding, Cap." Red laughed. "But you know I don't explain how I do my stuff. Any more than you do."

"I don't have anything to explain," the Captain protested. "I was *born* this way."

"Hey, I know, didn't mean to razz you or anything," Red answered, his tone almost apologetic. "But I don't explain, not even to you."

"Okay," the Captain said, accepting Red's decision.

"You going to the Mayor's reception, Cap?"

"I think I will," the Captain said slowly.

Tuesday he changed at Station Square again—it was about the best drop he'd ever found, and it was more comfortable than changing in the car. He knew it would be safer to switch again, but just this once, he thought he could risk it.

The walk to City Hall was longer than he'd thought, though, and he arrived late.

The guard at the door waved him through, and he found himself in a big room crowded with people, men in expensive suits and women in fancy dresses. They stared at him as he entered, and he smiled at them all, his best public smile. Only his mouth was visible below the visor; if his eyes weren't smiling, no one could tell.

He didn't have the faintest idea who any of these people were.

Then he spotted Mr. Swift's helmet; its metallic blue sheen stood out from the innumerable heads of hair in various shades of brown and gold and gray.

And Red's wraparound blade sunglasses were there, too, far across the room. A moment later the Amazon's bronze helmet emerged from behind a pillar near the table of hors d'oeuvres.

Each of them had a small crowd clustered about him or her, and with a start the Captain realized a crowd was forming around him, too. Most of it was people who looked at him and then moved on without getting in his way, but not all of it. A young blond woman in a sleek red gown set herself directly in his path, and smiled up at him across her glass of champagne.

"I've always wanted to meet you," she said.

Disconcerted by the unfamiliar surroundings, he let the natural response slip out: "Why?"

Immediately, he caught himself; he should have said something like, "I'm flattered."

It was too late, though. The woman cocked her head to one side, still smiling, and said, "Because you're a mystery—you're big and strong and brave, so you should have a face like a god, but nobody's ever *seen* your face."

"It's just a face," he said. "Same as anybody else's."

"Oh, I'm sure it isn't like anybody else's," she protested. "I'll bet it's a wonderful face. Can't you raise that visor and let me have a peek?"

"No, I'm afraid not."

"How do we know you're really Captain Cosmos at all, then?"

That stumped him for a moment.

"You don't," he said at last. "And showing you my face wouldn't

327

help any, since nobody's seen it before."

"I bet I could tell."

He didn't bother to answer that.

"You're from outer space, aren't you? That's how you can do all those amazing things?"

"I don't really know myself," the Captain admitted. "Wherever I'm from originally, I came here as a baby, and I grew up right here in the U.S.A."

"An all-American boy, huh? I knew it. Some people say you wear that visor because you're really a robot, or a monster, or something," she persisted. "But I'm sure you're not."

"I'm not," he said shortly. It hadn't occurred to him that anyone might think he was hiding his face because there was something wrong with it. He didn't like the idea. Bad enough to *be* an alien without *looking* alien.

"Now, that's what I said," the woman purred. "I told them I thought you were a real man. I'm sure there's a human face under there, and I'd love to see it. I bet you have the bluest eyes."

"I'm sorry," the Captain told her, "but I couldn't possibly raise my visor in public."

"It doesn't have to be public," she murmured. "I'd be glad to go someplace private with you." Her fingers were stroking the rim of her glass.

Behind his visor, the Captain frowned. This woman's curiosity seemed entirely unreasonable. Why was she interested in seeing his face, and being so persistent about it? Was she a spy for some underworld organization, perhaps, trying to learn his identity so that they could track him down when he was off duty and off his guard?

"I just got here," he said.

"Later, then?"

"I don't think so," he replied. "I should go say hello to the mayor." He gestured vaguely across the room.

She pouted, but let him go.

He made his way through the crowd, making polite noises to various strangers as he went. A murmur drew his attention back toward the door for a moment; he turned to see the Night Man entering, his disreputable hat jammed down even further than usual.

The woman in the red dress was still watching the Captain. She smiled and made a little wave at him. He waved back, unwillingly.

"Who's that in the hat?" someone asked.

" 'It's dusk,' " someone else quoted from the newspaper write-up; the Captain frowned. " 'He's punched in, and he's looking for someone to punch out.' "

"Oh, it's the *Night Man*," the first person exclaimed in recognition.

The Captain was annoyed. That bit was practically the Night Man's slogan now. The darn newspapers had never come up with anything that memorable about *him*, even though everyone knew he was twice the hero the Night Man was.

True, the Night Man probably had more citizen's arrests to his credit, but they were all small fry. He hadn't captured any monsters. He hadn't fought anything like the Church of Doom, or the cave-dwelling mutants with their brain-deadening rays. He didn't have any of the Captain's superhuman talents and abilities. The Captain snorted; he'd like to have seen that punk in the hat even bring in someone like the Electrothief! *He* couldn't punch through a concrete wall!

Then he caught himself. Professional jealousy was unbecoming in a crimefighter; after all, they were all on the same side.

Someone laughed, loudly and brightly; he turned to see Deborah Hatch near the podium, a drink in her hand, talking to Mr. Swift. Her cameraman was nearby, watching disinterestedly. Red Rover and the Amazon were talking over by a pillar.

The Captain supposed that Red and the Amazon were exchanging ideas on crimefighting, and Swift and Ms. Hatch were probably talking about how the media could help in the war against crime. That was all fine.

But what was *he* supposed to do? He started to turn around, looking for someone to talk to, when a man in a black suit strode out to the podium and tapped on the microphone.

The Captain listened intently as the man introduced the mayor, and then as the mayor made a little speech thanking the costumed crimefighters for their efforts.

"We don't know who you are," His Honor said, "but we're glad you're here."

The Captain smiled at that, smiled behind his mirrored visor, smiled his odd, stiff smile that he had taken so long to learn as a child.

He didn't know who he was either, in a way. His adoptive parents had told him what they knew, about how he had been found in a dumpster the night the UFO exploded over the river, about how they'd found out he wasn't really human—but nobody had told him any more than that, because nobody knew.

But no—he *did* know who he was. He was Captain Cosmos, defender of the innocent. Where he came from didn't matter. He had struggled hard all his life to learn to be a human being, and he had managed it, and now he was also something more than that. He was a hero.

"Hi, Captain," a woman said. He felt a touch on his arm and turned to find a young brunette smiling up at him.

"Hello," he said.

"My name's Jenny," she told him.

"Hello, Jenny. Pleased to meet you."

"Do you have any plans for after the reception, Captain?"

"Well, actually, I suppose I'll take a look around for burglars," he said.

She made a disappointed noise, but he didn't really understand why. Wasn't he *supposed* to look for burglars?

The mayor finished his speech, and any further conversation was lost in the applause.

He didn't stay long; he shook hands with a few officials, then said goodbye and left. When he looked back he saw other people leaving, as well. Red and Swift and the Amazon were still inside, as was the Channel 9 news crew, but the Night Man had vanished even before the mayor's speech ended.

On the way back to Station Square he sometimes glimpsed people in fancy clothes strolling along—others who had been at the reception, of course. There was one woman in a black coat who seemed to be going the same direction he was for a surprisingly long way; she had a high collar up, and seemed to turn away every time he looked in her direction, so he never got a look at her face.

He changed in the men's room. When he was out of costume he

felt both better and worse—better because it was a relief to be out of costume, to be offstage, as it were, and worse, because now he was nobody in particular, he wasn't Captain Cosmos anymore, just an ordinary person.

And being an ordinary person was *hard.*

At his apartment he heard someone come in the door behind him; he paused on the stairs to look, and saw a young woman he didn't recognize in the hall below.

She turned to the row of mailboxes and buzzers, and he went on upstairs. As he opened the door to his own apartment he could hear whoever it was down there, talking to the woman in A-21.

That was Tuesday night.

On Wednesday, when he got home from work, he found a woman sitting on the stairs. He hesitated, unsure whether to squeeze past silently, or to say something.

"Hello, Mr. Jenkins," she said. There was something odd about the way she said it.

He blinked. "Hello," he answered mildly. "How do you know my name?"

"Mrs. Almido told me," she said, gesturing toward A-21.

Was that the woman's name? "I didn't know *she* knew it," he remarked.

"She got it off the mailbox," the woman on the stairs explained. "What's the F stand for?"

"Frank," he said, puzzled.

"Frank Jenkins," she said, getting to her feet and dusting off her skirt. "I'm pleased to meet you." She held out a hand. "I'm Rosalie Dutton."

Jenkins took her hand gently, being very careful not to squeeze. He noticed her coat lying on the steps, a black coat that looked familiar.

And there was something about her face, too. He wasn't good with faces, not good at all.

"Have I seen you somewhere?" he asked.

"You might have," she admitted. "Listen, could we go up to your place?"

He hesitated. "Why?" he asked.

"To talk," she said. "Just to talk."

He frowned, trying to figure out what she wanted. "I don't think that's a good idea," he said.

"I think it is, Captain," she said.

He stared at her.

"You want me to talk to the reporters, instead?" she demanded. Her voice was not very steady, he noticed—but as usual, he didn't know what to make of that.

Jenkins glanced quickly around the hallway. Nobody else was in sight, but there was no telling who might be listening through the flimsy doors.

"All right," he said. "Go on up."

She smiled triumphantly—and nervously—and turned and ran up the stairs.

He came up more slowly, trying to think what he should do.

He really couldn't settle on anything until he knew more, he decided as he stepped out onto the landing. He reached past the waiting woman, key in hand, and opened the door of his apartment.

The familiar warmth and smell of home rolled out, and he smiled; that took some of the stiffness and worry out of him, just feeling that hot, damp air.

A new expression flickered across the woman's face, one he didn't quite catch—he was never very quick at these things. Then it was gone, and he waved her in.

Rosalie Dutton was facing her moment of triumph, and somehow, it wasn't quite what she had expected. She had finally tracked down her hero, the man she wanted—but there was something in his face that made her uneasy. His features weren't as regular as she had expected; his hair wasn't the blond she had imagined it would be, but an odd shade of light brown.

And when the door of his apartment opened, the air that rolled out was thick with moisture, hot and heavy, and it carried an odor of ammonia and other things, as if a hundred different cleansers and chemicals had been spilled in there somewhere.

She entered, slowly, looking around. He saw her throat work as she swallowed.

"You . . . you keep it pretty warm in here, don't you?" she asked.

He shrugged. "I guess," he said. "I don't like the cold."

"Oh." She looked around, at the books, the big table, the has-socks, the single chair. She seemed far less certain now than she had on the stairs. He wished he knew what she was thinking.

She had expected to find a modest and tasteful little abode, an all-American setting straight out of fifties television; what else would be appropriate for a big Boy Scout like Captain Cosmos?

Instead, she was in this sweltering, malodorous, vaguely bohemian apartment. There was no sofa, no end tables; the furnishings that *were* there were mismatched and worn.

Her dream was not coming out right.

He closed the door and asked, "Now, what can I do for you, Ms. Dutton?"

She turned to stare at him.

"You're Captain Cosmos," she said.

"What makes you think that?" he asked, trying to sound noncommittal—though he wasn't sure why he bothered; maybe in the comic books people could be fooled out of such discoveries, but he was pretty sure he wasn't going to be able to pull it off. This woman, whoever she was, had found him out.

"I followed you," she said. "I've been following you for weeks, whenever I could, learning your tricks, and finding ways around them. When I followed you from the reception last night I finally managed to see you out of costume, and to stay with you all the way here. I watched you go in that men's room at the Mini-Mall, and I saw you come out, and I was sure it was you despite your tricks, because there wasn't anyone else around you could be, and there aren't many men your size. I mean, I was sure, but I wanted to be *really* sure, so I talked to Mrs. Almido, and she told me about how you go out every night, you're almost never home, you never talk to anybody, never have visitors here—*she* thinks you're cruising gay bars, you're so big and handsome but she never sees you with any women, you don't even talk to women. I don't think so, though; *I* think you're out on patrol."

"And what if Mrs. Almido's right?" he asked mildly. "Or what if I'm a burglar, or a serial killer, and I go out robbing or murdering people?"

"But you're not," she said, without conviction. She glanced involuntarily around at the odd furnishings. "You're Captain Cosmos, the super-crimefighter."

"And what if I am? What would you want with me?" Somehow, her uneasiness seemed to be making him more sure of himself. After all, he was on his own home turf; he could smell that wonderful chloride tang from the kitchen, the air was thick and moist, the temperature was a comfortable 90 degrees or so.

She was perspiring, he noticed; her forehead was damp. She stepped closer to him, very close.

"You saved me from a mugger," she said, her voice low. "Three months ago, on the waterfront, after a late movie."

"Suppose I did," he said. "What of it?"

"I never got to say thank you," she said, a bit desperately. She was almost touching him now.

When he didn't react immediately, she turned and looked at the furniture again, and added, "There's no couch." She knew she sounded like an idiot, and she hoped that she wasn't offending him.

But then, she had come barging in here, invading his privacy—he had a right to be offended, didn't he?

This wasn't at all the way she had envisioned it. She had seen him, after some initial shyness, sweeping her off her feet and carrying her into his bedroom.

Instead, she was standing here talking about couches, and that weird chemical smell was getting stronger and stronger; her nose was beginning to sting. It was like one of those horrible dreams where everything went wrong, where no one would listen to her, no matter what she said.

"No," he said, "I don't like them." After a second's pause, he added, "Have a seat anywhere, if you like."

"What about you?"

"I'll stand."

Desperate for a response, she reached out and stroked his arm. He didn't react.

"I've been trying to find you for months," she said. "When I heard about the reception, I knew I had to be there."

That startled him. "I don't remember seeing you there."

334

"I just watched." She pressed up against him. "I saw those other women talk to you, and you seemed to think they were pushy, or something, so I . . ." Her voice trailed off as she looked up at him. She frowned.

Maybe the whole dream was based on a wrong assumption. Maybe the all-American hero wasn't quite what people thought he was. She was sweating, and the stench was beginning to get to her; she didn't think she could stand any more subtlety—and she wasn't really being subtle at all, in any case.

So she would have to be absolutely direct.

"Damn it, *are* you gay?" she demanded. "Is that it after all?"

"No," he said. He had finally realized what she wanted, though he still had no idea why; he certainly hadn't meant to lead anyone on. He paused for a moment, debating, then decided on the truth. "I don't want men, either," he said.

She stared into his face, his eyes.

His eyes, she thought, were a very strange color, a shade of brown she had never seen in eyes before, and there was something odd about the shape.

Or maybe there was something wrong with her eyes. They were beginning to sting from the fumes, whatever they were.

At least, she thought it was the fumes, and not tears.

"I'm sorry," he said.

"You don't like women?" she asked.

He shrugged. "I like you all fine," he said. "As people. But that's all."

"You don't . . ." She hesitated. This was all wrong. She knew she should just turn and run out, but she had come so far. "You don't, um, want . . ."

He shrugged. He wondered if he ought to blush, but that was something he had never learned to do. "Well, not with anyone I've ever met," he said.

"Are you . . ." She hesitated. "I mean, is there something physically wrong?"

He shook his head. "There's something missing," he said. "But it's not anything simple or obvious. I don't know what it is. I don't know if it's in me, or in all of you, but whatever it is, it isn't there."

She pulled away. "This isn't at all how I pictured it," she said, her voice unsteady, and he could see that her eyes were now as moist as her forehead.

"I'm sorry," he said.

The barrier was broken, and the words poured out in a torrent of confusion and misery. "It's all so weird, I mean, I wanted you so much and you aren't interested, and you keep it so hot in here I can hardly think, and there's no place to sit, and there's that smell, what *is* that?"

"Well, part of it is just the way I like my air," he explained. "I suppose it's like air freshener would be, for you."

"Part of it?" She wiped at her nose, which was beginning to drip. Sweat smeared her makeup.

"Well, there's that," he said, pointing to the tray sitting in the window to the kitchen.

She turned; her vision was beginning to blur, but she could see the tray and its contents.

"Oh, my God." she said. "What *is* that?" She took a step closer.

"My dinner," he said.

She gagged, and turned to stare at him. Her face was pale.

"Ms. Dutton," he said gently, "if I really *am* Captain Cosmos, even given that I came from outer space, have you ever wondered how I could be so strong? How I can see in the dark, and all the rest of it?"

"I thought . . . I thought it was fancy equipment, from your spaceship . . ."

He shook his head. "I was born with it," he said. "I see deep in the infrared, I can bench-press about a ton, and that's just standing here in my regular clothes."

She still stared.

For one thing, if she didn't stare at *him*, she might see that dinner again.

"I'm *not human*, Ms. Dutton." It hurt to state it outright like that, but he knew he had to.

"Then what *are* you?" she demanded desperately.

"I don't know," he replied soberly. "Nobody does. I was a foundling."

"But you *look* human." She could no longer see his face clearly; her head was swimming.

He shrugged.

"You *act* human," she insisted. "I mean, you speak English and everything."

"I grew up here," he said. "I've lived among humans all my life, and I've tried very hard to be one of you." He sighed. "It's been *very* hard, sometimes."

She didn't understand. He was a man, wasn't he? She couldn't think clearly. She tried to fight back to the dream, to the lovely vision of the great handsome hero carrying her off to his bed. "Then can't you . . . I mean, if you grew up here, can't you . . . don't women . . ."

"Something's missing," he repeated. "Maybe it's a smell or something, I don't know. It took me years to figure out what I should eat, you know that? My parents tried, they gave me everything they could think of that might help, but I spent half my childhood throwing up. And as for sex, I haven't even begun to figure it out." His voice cracked slightly as he added, "I don't even know what the females of my species *look* like!"

She stared, and took a step backward, almost stumbling over one of the hassocks. Those flat brown eyes were locked on her own. He flexed his muscles, not like a man might, but like an animal dislodging fleas, unthinkingly; and for the first time, she realized that those muscles moved in ways a man's muscles did not.

Or was that just the distortion of her vision? Everything had become nightmarish; she felt sick and feverish.

He watched her. This was more than he'd told anyone, ever—he hadn't even talked to his parents about sex. He'd told the others, Red and Swift and the Amazon, that he was an alien, but he had never given them any details. When the newspapers had reported he got his powers from outer space, he had never denied it.

But until now, he had never really told anyone what that meant.

"We're different species," he said relentlessly. "We look alike, but that's just a coincidence, or maybe protective coloration, like those butterflies—monarchs and viceroys."

"But then why . . ." she asked. "I mean, why are you a crimefighter? Why do you care about the rest of us, if we aren't the same species?"

"I don't, really," he admitted. "But I *want* to be human. Or at least, I want to fit in. I'm doing what a human would do—aren't I? Isn't that what you're supposed to do, if you've got special powers? Be a hero?"

She didn't dare argue with him. She couldn't keep her words straight, though. "I guess . . . but why do you want to, if . . ."

He did the thing in his throat that corresponded to a sigh. "I may not be human," he said, "but I get lonely. I want a social life."

She blinked, trying to clear the haze. "That's a social life? Chasing crooks?"

"I'm one of the boys," he said. "With Red Rover and Mr. Swift. And the cops, the Amazon, the Night Man, the press people, even the mayor, they all talk to me, and I know what to say back."

She was nearer the door, now, and the air seemed cleaner. She asked, "But couldn't you, you know, get to know your neighbors, go to parties, things like that? You have to go out hunting drug pushers to meet people?"

He shook his head. "It doesn't work, having a regular social life. It's too complicated. I don't get the jokes. I don't pick up the signals. It's all gray and blurry and hard to follow, there's sex in everything, and the food I can't eat, and the body language I never learned to read. I tried. Believe me, I tried. But my brain just isn't wired the same way yours are; all the ways you people just naturally communicate without words, things you take for granted, I don't have."

"So you chase crooks?" she croaked. It still didn't seem to make sense to her.

He shrugged. "You always know who the bad guys are," he said. "You know what the point of the whole thing is."

She didn't say anything. She wasn't sure she could still talk.

"So now you know," he said at last. "Not just who I am, but what I am."

She nodded.

"I don't want you to tell anyone," he said.

Even across the species boundary, she thought the threat in his face was clear. "I didn't think you would," she said, her voice a rasp.

"Or you'd have told them yourself."

"So will you stay quiet?"

She nodded.

He stared at her, hesitating. Then he plunged.

"You know," he said, "I can't read your face very well. I don't understand how you think. I don't know if I can trust you."

"You can trust me," she protested, whispering. "I won't tell anyone."

"I don't know that," he said. "So let me tell you something, Ms. Rosalie Dutton. You aren't my kind. You could ruin everything. If you tell anybody any of this stuff, I will hunt you down, and I will kill you. With my bare hands." He picked a book off the nearest shelf, a thick hardcover, and crushed it between his hands. Shredded paper fluttered to the floor.

She stared in horror at this final ghastly perversion of her dream.

"But you're a hero," she whispered. "One of the good guys."

"Yes," he said. "That's the role I picked. I like it. And I want to *stay* one of the good guys. I don't want to be an alien monster. Don't make me be an alien monster."

"I won't tell," she said. "I swear. I won't say anything. Ever." The room was swimming; she couldn't breathe, her face was soaked with sweat, her hands trembled in fear and confusion.

"Good," he said. He glanced at the serving window. "Would you like to stay to dinner, then?"

She gasped, and fainted.

He watched her fall, frowning.

As he picked up her limp body, he wondered if he would ever really make good on the threat, and he didn't know. He didn't think he would ever need to; he thought Rosalie Dutton would keep her mouth shut, but he didn't really know.

He slung her over his shoulder. Fresh air, Earth air, would revive her, he was fairly sure. He would leave her somewhere safe, and with any luck, when she came to, she would think it had all been a dream, and that would be the end of it.

Of course, if she didn't think that, she might talk. She might go to the newspapers.

If she talked, everyone would say he was an alien monster. Maybe he should just kill her, wring her neck and dump the body some-where.

But if he killed her, maybe that would mean he really *was* an alien monster.

No, he thought, I'm not an alien monster, I am *not*.

He was, he assured himself, one of the boys.

He was just one of the boys.

Truth, Justice and the Politically Correct Socialist Path

John Varley

Ethnocentricity is a basic fact of the human condition. We tend to make judgements of right and wrong based on our cultural upbringing rather than any universal concept of goodness.

Of all the scientists on the planet Xenon, only Mar-Lon was convinced that the world was headed for destruction. They laughed when Mar-Lon made his prediction before the Council of Eminent Scientists, Xenon's governing body.

"It's just a series of Xenonquakes," they said.

Stung, Mar-Lon retired to his mountaintop laboratory with his wife and their infant son, Kla-Lon.

"Our doom is sealed," said Mar-Lon. "But our son shall survive the destruction of Xenon. I have constructed a spaceship with just enough room to carry him away. Quickly, there is no time to lose."

They sealed the tiny payload into the rocket, stood back, and launched Kla-Lon into space. No sooner had the rocket cleared the atmosphere than Xenon was blown to bits, just as Mar-Lon had predicted. So much for eminent scientists.

The rocket sped through the galaxies at pretty close to the speed of light for a time impossible to measure, due to relativistic effects. Finally it sizzled through the atmosphere of a green, watery, fertile planet, third from the sun, known to its inhabitants as *Zemlya*.

❁

341

The rocket plowed into the ground just west of the Urals, about two hundred kilometers south of Sverdlovsk, in the *Rossijskaja Sovetskaja Federativnaja Socialističeskaja Respublika,* or the Russian Federated S.S.R. of the glorious Union of Soviet Socialist Republics. It came to rest, smoking, in a wheat field of the Long Live The Heroes Of The October Revolution Collective Farm #56, not far from where Marina and Pavel Kentarovsky were munching on raw beets as they lugubriously surveyed the flat left rear tire of a twelve-year-old Spirit of Lenin tractor.

The Spirit of Lenin was an exact copy of a 1934 International Harvester except for cast-iron axles and, as Pavel often remarked, "the soul of a pig."

The Kentarovskys hurried over to the space capsule. A hatch popped open. Pavel leaned forward to take a look.

"Phew," said Pavel, straightening quickly. "This looks like a job for you."

Dutifully, Marina reached in and removed the infant. She stripped off his diaper, which had gone a thousand light-years without a change.

"A *malchik,*" she said, which meant it was a boy. "We'll raise him as if he were our own child."

"Well . . ." said Pavel thoughtfully, remembering the three boys and four girls already filling the Kentarovsky household. "What if someone comes looking for him?"

"He fell out of the sky," Marina pointed out.

"Well . . ." said Pavel, meaning he thought it might be all right to keep the child, while at the same time reflecting that someone had gone to a good deal of trouble to get rid of him.

Back at the tractor, young Kla-Lon amused himself eating clods of dirt while Pavel sweated over the balky lugs of the wheel. Hurling an untranslatable Russian oath, Pavel kicked the machine, which promptly fell off the jack and would have crushed him except for Kla-Lon, who reached up and lifted it into the air with one hand.

"Put that down," said Marina, who had firm ideas about raising children, even superhuman ones. Kla-Lon put it down, on its side.

The three of them stood in the Russian sunlight regarding the

Spirit of Lenin, then the two adults regarded the infant in silence. The little *malchik* grinned up at them. Marina lifted him and they began trudging back toward the Long Live The Heroes Of The October Revolution Collective Farm.

"Do you think we should tell the Commissar about this?" Marina asked.

"Well . . ." said Pavel.

"I don't either," said Marina.

They named the boy Kyril. That was the name that went on his newly opened file at the MVD, who also took note of his remarkably short gestation period. This and other odd stories about his childhood were duly noted and passed on to the NKVD, and later to the KGB, with the result that Kyril Pavelevitch Kentarovsky was labeled from an early age as a possible spy, Jew, or reactionary element.

In the same way a cuckoo chick elbows the smaller fledglings from its adoptive nest, young Kyril quickly eliminated his various foster-siblings. One by one they perished in household or farming accidents. Kyril was entirely innocent of any evil intent. He was simply too strong. The elder brothers and sisters fled to distant relatives, while the younger ones kept the village undertaker busy. Kyril quickly became Marina's favorite, as if he had been her own.

Pavel, too, loved the child, in much the same way he loved the State. In the spirit of experimentation, Pavel set out to discover the limits of his son's invulnerability. It was not that he *resented* it when Kyril tossed the communal bathtub through the washhouse wall, Pavel reasoned. Nor was it as if he really *minded* the time the boy turned their home on its side and shook it until all the furniture fell out in a heap. No, Pavel assured himself, it was simply that he needed to find a way to punish the boy, should the need ever arise.

Accordingly, for about a year Pavel possessed no hammer without a broken handle. All Marina's knives had bent points and dulled blades. Day after day, Kyril would return from playing in the fields with tractor tire marks on his face. Kerosene lamps, vats of boiling water, red-hot horseshoes, and anvils had a way of falling from tables onto the toddler. None of it had the slightest effect on Kyril. Pavel withdrew into a moody silence, and tended to sleep poorly and jump at loud noises.

Luckily for him, the Fascist warmonger Adolf Hitler treacherously betrayed the peace-loving peoples of the Soviet Union, and Pavel was called to do his duty in the Great Patriotic War. He endured the Siege of Stalingrad, where he amazed his trenchmates with his ability to sleep through the most harrowing barrage. Captured, interned in a prisoner-of-war camp in Poland, he was apt to turn to the other prisoners and say, "You think this is bad . . . ?"

A rutted dirt path ran from the collective farm to the nearest village, Meilinkigrad. The road had been unnamed until 1918, when the Bolsheviks dubbed it the Praise And Honor To The Glorious Heroes Who Stormed The Winter Palace In Petrograd On November 7, 1917 Expressway.

It was down this path that Marina led young Kyril one fine day in the 1940's. Her intention was to enroll him in school. That she dared do this was testament to her incredible determination as a mother.

He began his schooling without incident. Soon he was steeped in the glories of Marxist-Leninist doctrine. He began a grand dialectic that was to last all his life.

Kyril joined Komsomol, the Communist Youth League. He dreamed of erecting, single-handed, hydroelectric earthworks to harness the mighty rivers of Siberia: the Lena, the Ob, the Jenisej. He would boost Soviet industry, defeat the Fascists, triple the grain harvest, tilt the Earth's axis to warm the frigid north, loft powerful fortresses of Soviet Solidarity into orbit, to the moon itself.

He would fulfill his Five-Year Plan!

He would do all this and more, just as soon as his mother said he was ready.

The Great Patriotic War ended without his help. Benevolent Soviet Hegemony was extended to millions of formerly enslaved peoples in Eastern Europe. The Western powers treacherously betrayed the long-suffering Soviet people at Berlin and threatened genocide to all who would not travel the Decadent Capitalist Road.

Somewhere in these terrible times, Pavel made his way home and sought refuge in the arms of his family.

"Stalin is executing returning prisoners of war," he told them.

"Yes, we know," said Kyril.

"He says we were traitors to be captured in the first place," Pavel went on, draining his first glass of vodka in five years.

"Yes, we heard," said Marina.

"I'll just hide out here for a while," Pavel said. "This should all blow over in three or four years."

"You're safe with us," said Kyril.

"Thank you for bringing this to our attention, Kyril Pavelevitch," said the Commissar, twenty minutes later. "We'll have him rounded up."

"It was my duty, Comrade Commissar," said Kyril.

"Good-bye, Pavelushka," shouted Marina as the boxcar pulled away.

"Good-bye, Father," shouted Kyril. "Enjoy your reeducation!"

"Good-bye, Pavel Ivanovitch," shouted the Commissar. "I hear Siberia isn't really all that bad."

"Dress warm," Marina shouted.

Kyril's teachers reported to the Commissar that they had never found a more apt pupil. The Commissar took an interest, and Kyril received special attention usually reserved for the sons of Party members.

It was rumored around Meilinkigrad that the Commissar was actually Trotsky himself. The wild shock of hair, the glasses, the intense expression, the rigid inflexibility when it came to Marx and Engels—all these contributed to a growing legend that included dark stories of a stooge taking the great Bolshevik's place, dying in his stead in Mexico. The Commissar did nothing to dispel these rumors, knowing that while they increased the people's fear and respect, they were too wild to be believed by those above him. This was fortunate, as he in fact *was* Trotsky.

In the wider world, the heroic People's Army under the leadership of Mao Tse-tung defeated the running dog Capitalist Roaders of the

Kuomintang and forced their degenerate lickspittle tool-of-fascism General, Chaing Kai-shek, into permanent exile in the Chinese province of Taiwan, from where he would soon be forced into the sea. Kyril eagerly devoured the little red book of the Thoughts of Chairman Mao. He liked it so much that an hour later he wanted to read more.

There were two important events in Kyril's life during this time. The first was his beloved Marina's descent into insanity.

"Come here, Kyrilushka," she said one day. Taking him to the basement, she opened a trap door and removed a short-wave radio. "Listen to this," she said, as she tuned to the pirate signal of Radio Free Europe.

"I'm not saying they're right," Marina said, "and I'm not saying Comrade General Secretary Stalin is wrong. But hear for yourself, my darling. I and your father, God rest his soul, used to listen every week."

"Religion is the opiate of the masses," Kyril said.

"Of course, of course, that just popped out," Marina said, glancing around nervously.

"And then I heard the most amazing string of lies," Kyril said to the Commissar, twenty minutes later.

"It does sound serious," said the Commissar judiciously. "Perhaps I should send for a doctor."

"Would you, sir? Thank you so much."

"Good-bye, my darling," Marina called from the open boxcar door as she was taken away for the doctor's prescribed rest cure.

"Good-bye, Mother," Kyril shouted, manfully fighting back tears.

"Good-bye, Leon," Marina shouted. "Take care of my boy."

"Who is Leon?" shouted the Commissar, looking around nervously.

The other thing that happened to Kyril was named Lara Langarova.

She came from Moscow, though she would not talk much about that. Nearly two meters tall, with sixteen-inch biceps and a size eighteen neck, she was the Olympic ideal of the New Soviet Woman. Kyril had never seen anything so lovely. Her thighs were like great tractor springs, her breasts the mighty Urals. Her hands moved with oiled grace, as though mounted on ball bearings. In her voice was the song of a thousand balalaikas, and the Red Army Chorus. She could clean-and-jerk two hundred kilograms. She could bend a large spanner in half. To Kyril, she was the Motherland Incarnate.

And her loins, her loins were the vast, fertile wheat fields of the Ukraine. One day those loins would yield up young Socialists like an inexorable factory.

(There were two young Socialists on the assembly line already, but Kyril did not know that.)

Lara Langarova was equally smitten.

"Hubba hubba," she said to her girlfriend Olga the first day she spied him. "What an incredible example of Socialist Realism."

"I'll say," said Olga. "That's Kyril Kentarovsky. It is said he can piss through armor plate." Lara naturally thought Olga was kidding, but had no trouble imagining equally unlikely and much more obscene feats the dashing peasant boy might perform.

Kyril began bringing her bushels of potatoes and turnips. He sat behind her in classes, and across from her in the library, and their hearts whirred like Diesel turbines, and swooped like MiGs in a dogfight.

Then one day she invited him to the room she shared with her Uncle Vanya and six cousins—all of whom were gone marketing in Sverdlovsk. She was wearing unusual blue trousers.

"Levi jeans," she told him proudly. Then she wound up a victrola and put on a record. She began to gyrate most alarmingly.

"I have not heard this music before," Kyril said.

"It's Louis Armstrong." She showed him a stack of similar records. "I have all the cool be-bop, Jackson. Coleman Hawkins, Thelonious, the Bird, Lawrence Welk. Beat me, daddy-o, eight to the bar!"

"Where did you obtain all this?" Kyril asked, sternly.

"The black market, natch. But it's cool. Don't be cubical, get hep! You can score anything in Moscow. You want some sweet reefer?"

"And then she smoked a funny cigarette," Kyril said to the Commissar, twenty minutes later. Well . . . maybe twenty-five. "And those maddening jungle rhythms . . . I was almost undone."

347

"Degenerate music," the Commissar intoned. "It sounds as if the young lady has fallen under the grip of Western influences. I will handle it."

"Good-bye, Kyril darling," Lara shouted as the boxcar rumbled away. "Be sure to write every day."

"Good-bye, Larushka," shouted Kyril. "Name one of the babies after me."

"Good-bye, Commissar," Lara shouted. "It's all for the good of Mother Russia, and I bear you no ill will."

The Commissar merely muttered, then sought out a comfortable patch of straw beside Kyril as the guard rolled the boxcar door closed, shutting them in. Their long journey had begun. Kyril merely clanked his chains together philosophically, trying his best not to accidentally damage them.

"Cheer up, Commissar," Kyril said brightly. "How bad can Siberia be?"

"How was I to know she was the daughter of the President of the Politburo?" the Commissar whined. "How was I to know she was here to be cured of a slight case of pregnancy?"

"The State has spoken," Kyril said simply. "And we must obey. Twenty years isn't so bad."

In truth, it wasn't so bad for Kyril. He could have done twenty years standing on his head. Siberia agreed with him.

The Commissar was not so lucky, having no superpowers.

They were taken to the Let's All Shout *Khorosho!* To Celebrate The Fifth Party Congress Gulag And Orphanage. Kyril and the Commissar were bunked side by side in a building with Boris Pasternak, Aleksandr Solzhenitsyn, Lavrenti Beria, Raskolnikov, and Cyd Charisse. Also present in the camp were Josef Stalin, V.I. Lenin, three Ivan the Terribles, seven Napoleons, Adlai Stevenson, Jesus Christ, and eight Mae Wests, several dozen Judy Garlands, and uncounted Marilyn Monroes. Kyril suspected that many of them were imposters, and some might be insane.

One certain case of insanity was an ancient, toothless man in the bunk next to Kyril. The old man was convinced that rocks had sexes. Every night he put two stones in a shoebox under his bunk, and each morning he checked it for offspring.

"Today is my birthday!" the old man announced, shortly after Kyril's arrival.

"Yes, Father, I know," said Kyril.

"I'm fifty-five!"

"No, father, only forty-one."

"Fantastic!" exclaimed Pavel. "I feel younger already! And only one more year of my sentence to serve!"

"No, Father. Fourteen."

To cheer him up, Kyril put a handful of gravel in the shoebox that night. All the next day Pavel showed off the newborn rocklings.

"I can't take much more of this, Kyril Pavelevitch," the Commissar whined one day.

"What's wrong, sir?" asked Kyril.

"Well, for one thing, I'm going to have a rectum the size of an SS-20 missile silo," said the Commissar.

At first Kyril thought the Commissar was speaking of an intestinal disorder, a common complaint at the Let's All Shout Etc. Gulag. But no, it was something infinitely worse. Kyril was shocked, flabbergasted to learn such degeneracy could exist in the Soviet Union. For the first time in his life he forgot himself. With the Commissar in tow he marched into the gulag Commandant's office. Two guards promptly riddled him with automatic weapon fire.

Annoyed, Kyril took one of the firearms away and twisted it into the shape of a sickle. Brandishing it at the Commandant, he shouted heroically.

"My friend Comrade Trotsky informs me he is the unwilling sweetheart of half the sexual perverts in the barracks. This is not true Socialism!" His stalwart Soviet upper lip curled in a sneer of disgust. "Each night they have their will with him, whispering endearments such as 'snuggle-bunny' and 'angel-buns.' I have heard these things with my own ears. And I tell you, *this does not further the international class struggle!*"

The Commandant, already white as albino snow, fainted dead away. This took some of the wind out of Kyril's sails. He glanced at the other guard, whose eyes were large saucers.

"Give me that weapon," Kyril said petulantly. The guard was only too happy to surrender it.

"When he wakes up," Kyril muttered, "tell him there will be no more degeneracy in this camp. This will be a decent Soviet gulag, or he'll have to deal with me."

"His balls will become the next two Sputniks," said the Commissar.

Kyril nodded; then, to drive home his point, he ate the guard's Kalashnikov.

"You are quite strong, Kyril Pavelevitch," the Commissar ventured as they waded back through the snow to their barracks.

"I am not of this Earth," Kyril confessed. "My mother says I fell from some great Soviet in the sky."

Kyril then proceeded to demonstrate some of his abilities to the Commissar, running the 100 meters in .00005 seconds, throwing a timber wolf over the horizon, and jumping over the nearest mountain.

"I'd bet on you in the next Olympics," the Commissar conceded.

"That has been my dream for a long time, sir," Kyril confided. "To humiliate the Western powers with my superhuman feats . . ." He sighed dreamily, but the Commissar was shaking his head.

"Resist the temptation, Kyril Pavelevitch," he said. "Comrade Lenin himself warns of the cult of personality. To reveal such superiority to the proletariat would sow the seeds of elitism. It would be counterrevolutionary."

"Lenin also said, from each according to his ability, to each according to his needs," Kyril pointed out.

"Ah . . . no, Marx said that," said the Commissar, smiling, not at all sure who really said it but pleased at the intellectual struggle. "But he was not thinking of such as you. Someday, when the State has withered away, when the New Soviet Man has swept the planet clear of decadent revanchist thought . . . then, Kyril, a man like you, a man who has, if I may say so, leapfrogged over the arduous path of historical inevitability, could take his place without danger to the New Order. Until then, you must do your Socialist duty in other ways."

"And what ways are those, Comrade Trotsky?" Kyril asked, humbled by the vast worldview of this Bolshevik founding father.

"Don't call me that," the Commissar said absently. "The seeds you sow, Comrade Kentarovsky . . ."—and the great Communist paused for dramatic effect—"shall be *the seeds of the Soviet Superman!*"

They both gazed fanatically at the vast Russian sky, eyes gleaming, jaws clenched, biceps bulging, looking just like a poster announcing Chairman Mao's Great Leap Forward, except for the fact that neither was Chinese and the Commissar was so scrawny, stooped, and ratlike.

They held that pose as long as anyone reasonably could; then Kyril spoiled it by furrowing his brow and announcing, "I don't understand."

"Your other powers," the Commissar hinted. "I mean, surely a man who . . . that is, he ought to be a regular *stallion*, if you get my drift, er, um, what I'm saying is, *hoo-boy!* You know what I mean?" The Commissar nudged Kyril relentlessly, dry-humped the air, rolled his eyes, and blushed dark as a bowl of borscht, being a virgin himself.

"I don't know," Kyril said dejectedly. "I might have found out, but I felt it was my duty to denounce Lara first . . . and you know what happened then." Kyril was lying. Perhaps his reticence stemmed from Lara's comment when he was through: "That's *it?*" It doesn't always pay to be faster than a speeding bullet.

"Never mind," said the Commissar. "Why, I'll bet you could cover a hundred Soviet women in a day. No, two hundred! *Three hundred!*"

"I will try," said Kyril, stoically facing his duty.

"I see vast breeding farms," hissed the Commissar. "Crèches, collectives, whole apartment blocks filled with satisfied comrades incubating your brood! I see bright-eyed children by the millions, transforming the Motherland in a single generation into the Socialist paradise on Earth!"

"Yes, yes," Kyril breathed. "And I can begin in only eighteen years!"

"I must see what Comrade Lysenko has to say about this," shouted the Commissar, and whirled and ran toward the camp library.

He got six steps, and stopped in his tracks. He turned slowly.

"What did you say, Kyril Pavelevitch?"

"Just as soon as we've served our sentences, the glorious work can begin!"

Threats were useless. The Commissar tried to reason Kyril out of his adamant position, and soon saw that the youngster's devotion to proper Marxist thought was as invulnerable as his damnable skull.

"We could make an exception just this once," the Commissar wheedled, beginning the argument he was to have every day for the next eighteen years. "Over the wire, and skedaddle to Moscow. Bullets can't hurt you . . ."

"I was sentenced by a properly convened Soviet tribunal, all in accordance with our Constitution," Kyril pointed out virtuously.

"Yes, but it was pure *influence* that got you there. Special privileges for the Politburo. Is this the proper path for the Party?"

"It is true, there seem to be disturbing deviations in Moscow," Kyril admitted, furrowing his brow. "But to escape would be to put my *self* above the will of the State."

This argument consumed ten minutes of each working day. The other nineteen hours and fifty minutes were spent at many other vigorous occupations, interrupted only by the daily meal.

Kyril's favorite job was in the uranium mines. It made him proud to be digging out the raw material from which the purely defensive nuclear weapons guarding his homeland were wrought. His heart sang as he trundled his wheelbarrow full of ore out of the blackness of the stygian pit. He only wished the inmates were provided picks and shovels so they could dig that much faster. At night, they all bathed in a warm glow of accomplishment Kyril swore he could almost *see*.

It was with regret that Kyril had to avoid two other occupations of the gulagites: military testing and medical research. That a projectile bounced off his mighty chest was no measure of the weapon's worth on the battlefield. And as hypodermic needles were blunted by his impenetrable skin, the new experimental viruses and bacteria had to be field-tested in other veins.

Two days before their scheduled release, Comrade Trotsky incautiously stopped to relieve himself against a tree, and froze solid. It was a common mishap in Siberia.

Kyril flew north, to Komsomolec Island, and there established his mighty Fortress of Solidarity. He brought the Commissar's corpse with him and installed it in a glass icebox, where he is still preserved, like Lenin, only standing, with his chin on his chest, looking in some alarm at his cold-shriveled member held in his scrawny fingers. Lenin gets a lot more visitors.

This done, Kyril sped to Meilinkigrad in hopes of finding his true love.

Lara was still there. Shortly after denouncing Kyril and the Commissar, her father had been caught up in a purge. Lara had stayed in the village, married, produced litter after litter of healthy young Socialists.

And she had changed a bit. She didn't recognize Kyril when she answered the door, and he barely recognized her. She had a moustache many a lad would envy. Her nose would have resembled a beet in size and shape and color, but for the road map of burst, purplish veins. Through her laddered stockings, Kyril could see varicosities the size of pythons.

"That'll be three *kopeks* for french, five for around-the-world," she said. One brown tooth and three steel ones flashed in a smile, and she wiggled her four hundred pounds seismically. "How about it, you cossack? Are you man enough?"

"Sorry, wrong number," Kyril stammered.

As he flew away from Lara Langarova's door, a vast weight seemed to lift from Kyril's heart. His last link with the past was cut. His father had died years ago, attempting sexual congress with a large boulder. His mother had vanished into the vast benevolence of the Soviet Asylum network. Comrade Trotsky was safe in the Fortress. It was time to put Meilinkigrad behind him.

It was time to go to Moscow.

He found housing in a nice little two-room flat in the How 'Bout Them Bolsheviks? Revolutionary Modular People's Housing Block

#34923. He shared it with seven other people, only two of whom were KGB informants. It was a 15th-floor walk-up—or it was until the scheduled arrival of elevators in four years—and would be warm and cozy and dry as soon as the roof was installed.

He found an opening for a mild-mannered reporter with *Pravda*, and got the job. He intended to use this as a cover, a secret identity.

Kyril had given this matter much thought, both at the gulag and later in the Fortress of Solidarity. To display superhuman powers as Kyril Kentarovsky would indeed be to court a cult of personality. But what if he assumed another identity, a sort of Spirit of Socialism, a near-mythical character with powers far beyond those of mortal ·men?

He decided to give it a try, and thus Bolshoiman was born.

To aid this deception, he needed a uniform. With the remnants of his indestructible Xenonian diapers and swaddling blankets he fashioned a good, sensible Soviet suit with baggy pants and wide lapels. But he felt a white suit looked too western, so he dyed the ensemble the red of the glorious flag of the U.S.S.R. When he tried it on he found it had shrunk to embarrassing tightness. The legs and sleeves were six sizes too short, and he couldn't button the coat. So he added Red Army combat boots and a T-shirt with a capital "#," for Bolshoiman. Surveying the effect in the mirror, he decided it was just as well, as the shrinkage covered up the sins of his needlecraft.

"It's you, it's you," his roommate Ivan assured him.

"I don't know," said his roommate Yuri. "Maybe a cape . . . ?"

Kyril started out at *Pravda* in the classified ads department, Personals section. It stirred his heart to see how many Muscovites were interested in continuing their education. ("45-yr-old generous Party member seeks stern third-world instructress for lessons in leather and domestic service.") There was also a keen interest in art and history. ("Ukrainian cross-dresser wants to meet husky workers to discuss Greek culture. Include frank photo for quick reply.")

Fascinating as it was, Kyril chafed at being chained to the telephone all day. He longed to be out on the streets, fighting counter-revolutionary elements. He began spending his lunch breaks watching the TASS teletype machines. All night long he haunted the bars, listening to rumors, checking out leads, looking for the story that would break him into the big time.

The city room of *Pravda* was where most of the mild-mannered reporters spent the working day. Most of them were so mild-mannered that they spent the day asleep, waking up only long enough to put their names at the top of stories as they were delivered from the various ministries around Moscow. Some slept atop their desks, some brought in cots, but the majority preferred to lean back in their swivel chairs, mouths open. On a slow news day the snoring could be deafening, and *every* day was a slow news day at *Pravda*.

Only the editor stayed awake all day long. This was because he had not been able to sleep properly for over twenty years.

Comrade Philby took Kyril under his wing. In a few vodka-soaked months he taught his eager young pupil everything he knew about the newspaper business—knowledge gleaned from endless screenings of *His Girl Friday, Deadline USA, Each Dawn I Die*, and *Nancy Drew, Reporter*. Unfortunately, none of it had anything to do with the prudent management of information and propaganda under a benevolent Socialist regime.

Philby also taught him to speak Etonian-accented English. They met daily at The Happy Hungarian, 2 Dzerzhinsky Square—right across the street from KGB headquarters—during happy hour (7 A.M. to midnight), where Hiram the Happy Hungarian poured only three different drinks: 80 proof vodka, 100 proof vodka, and 150 proof vodka.

One day Kyril swam to the surface of an alcoholic haze to hear Comrade Philby's voice coming from beneath the table.

"One day they'll get me, Kyril Pavelevitch," he intoned gloomily. "MI-6 will never forgive me for aiding the struggle of oppressed peoples around the world by giving England's secrets to the Motherland."

Philby was not under the table because he was drunk (though he *was* drunk). It was his habitual seat at The Happy Hungarian. He felt safer there.

"That's why I drink here, even though they water the vodka,"

Philby admitted, gloomily. "I feel safer the closer I am to the KGB. They've kept me alive this long. But MI-6 will have its revenge."

The five KGB agents at the next table had long ago stopped taking notes on Comrade Philby's story; they'd heard it all before. The two KGB agents who were actually MI-6 deep-cover moles wished heartily that they *could* kill the garrulous old traitor so they could steal some *important* secrets, such as the one about the alien superbeing the Russians were alleged to have in hiding somewhere.

Kyril glanced at his watch and noticed it had been five years since his arrival in Moscow. Most of that time had been spent at the Hungarian's. The rest was accounted for by standing in various queues, and dancing the hully-gully with Ludmilla Langarova, Lara's younger sister, who had been his lover for some time now.

It was time to get to work.

He knew where to find Ludmilla. Through the revolving doors of the G.U.M. department store—largest in the world, he thought, proudly—up to the third floor, and there she was near the end of a queue for nylon spandex panty hose from Yugoslavia.

"Ludmilla," he announced, "I must start fighting for Truth, Justice, and the Socialist Way."

"Of course, Kyril dear," she said. "My darling, would you hold my place in line for just a few minutes? I heard a rumor that a shipment of Polish eye shadow has just arrived down at the cosmetics counter."

Three hours later, Kyril arrived home with six pairs of reinforced-crotch panty hose. He trudged up the stairs and kissed his mother on the cheek, pausing only to wipe the drool from her chin.

"Hi, Mom, I'm home," he said. "Hello, Yuri. Hi there, Ivan. Yo, Vladimir, Sonya, Piotr, Sasha, Nikita, Alesandra, Yuri Junior, Alexei Ilyich, Alexei Andreivitch, Alexei Ivanovitch . . ."

Kyril had found his mother while doing a story about the great strides made by Soviet medicine in the field of political rehabilitation. When the doctors realized he was her son, they agreed she was cured, and sent her home with him. And she *was* cured. Twenty years of electroshock and drug therapy had showed Marina the error of her ways.

There had been a few minor side effects, among them partial paralysis, loss of the power of speech, and hair that stood permanently on end.

"It was a small price to pay," she had written in her electroencephalographic hand, shortly after her release. "I repent of the crimes of my youth." At this point her eyes always leaked grateful tears. (These were two of the three sentences she knew how to write.)

"Mother," Kyril announced, "I will now go forth and make the world safe for Marxist-Leninist Socialism."

"Dress warm," Marina wrote.

So Kyril marched down the stairs, his Bolshoiman costume in a shoebox under his arm.

No sooner had he turned the corner onto Kalinin Prospeckt than he spied a crime in progress. There were three parasitic youths lounging around a noisy Western ghetto blaster, chewing on toothpicks, combing their greasy ducktails, sneering at the hearty bustle of workers hurrying along the sidewalk.

"Why are you not at work?" Kyril asked them mildly.

"Work is for suckers," drawled one of the parasites insolently. "Take a walk, you old bolshy."

Kyril hurried around another corner and ducked into a convenient phone booth, evicting the Uzbek family who had made it their home. He went unobserved as he struggled into his costume except for the three KGB cameras concealed in the booth, along with one each from MI-6, Mossad—the terrorist arm of the outlaw Jewish state—and the American CIA. The CIA camera was far superior to the other five, and cost a hundred times as much. It would have delivered high-resolution pictures and stereo sound to its operators in Langley, Virginia, except that it had stopped working three years before.

He left the booth, leaped into the air, and swooped down on the parasites, who looked appropriately surprised.

"Your lives of crime are at an end, social leeches," he announced. "From now on your kind will have to deal with Bolshoiman!" He grabbed one by the scruff of the neck and, warning the other two not to leave the scene, leaped into the sky again.

When Kyril reached a thousand feet and began zooming toward

the local police station, the parasite looked down and threw up all over him.

He reported to work the next day to find the city room of *Pravda* filled with activity. Everyone was working on stories about the exploits of Bolshoiman.

Comrade Philby showed him a sample front page. The headline read: IS IT A MIG-25? IS IT A TUPOLEV-144? NO, IT'S BOL-SHOIMAN!

"What do you think?" Philby asked gloomily.

Before Kyril could answer, a reporter slapped him on the back.

"Nice going, Bolshoiman," said the reporter.

Kyril jumped, then looked around, acting innocent.

"Where?" he asked. "Is Bolshoiman here?"

"Oh . . . that's right," said the reporter, and winked broadly. "He has a secret identity, doesn't he?" Wink, wink. "Well, who*ever* he is, that Bolshoiman is really something, huh?" Wink, wink, wink.

"Comrades!" shouted another reporter, slamming down a telephone. "The Comrade General Secretary himself has requested that Bolshoiman join him at once in the Kremlin!"

Every person in the room fell silent and looked at Kyril.

"I'll see if I can find him," Kyril said grumpily, and stalked from the room.

But it was not Comrade Brezhnev, it was Yuri Andropov, head of the KGB, who greeted Bolshoiman. Andropov stood and held out his hand—then recoiled as Bolshoiman shook it. Kyril felt his ears go red.

"I apologize for the smell, Comrade Andropov," he said. "But I apprehended over a hundred parasites, hooligans, Jews, and black marketeers yesterday, and at least half of them got air sick. On me."

Andropov waved it away, and showed Kyril to a seat a comfortable distance from his desk.

"The General Secretary will be arriving in . . . ah, here he is now."

Leonid Brezhnev was brought in, strapped to a hand truck, followed by a battalion of doctors who immediately began hooking him up to kidney dialysis, an I.V. drip, a heart-lung device, and a cluster of other machines.

"The General Secretary is a bit indisposed," said Andropov.

"Ummm," said Bolshoiman.

A washtub of black beluga caviar was placed convenient to Brezhnev's right hand. He scooped up enough caviar to feed a Park Avenue household for a year, slapped it onto a slab of black Russian bread.

"I've existed for ten years on a diet of caviar and vodka," Brezhnev announced, and ate half the open-faced sandwich.

"That's wonderful, Leonid Ilyich," said Andropov, and turned to Kyril. "All Russia rejoices in your glorious exploits," he said.

Kyril blushed heroically.

"Comrade Brezhnev wanted me to award you this medal," said Andropov. He held up a red ribbon with a gold star hanging beneath it, came around his desk and pinned it to Bolshoiman's chest. "You are now a Hero of the Soviet Union."

"I wipe my ass with sable pelts," Brezhnev announced.

"Marvelous, Leonid Ilyich," Andropov said absently. He frowned. "It's too bad the ribbon is the same color as your uniform. But the solid-gold star stands out nicely." Andropov needn't have worried. In a few days the solid-gold star left a large green stain, setting off the red ribbon.

"Every sable pelt produced in Siberia," Brezhnev announced. "I wipe my ass with it."

"How droll, Leonid Ilyich," said Andropov. "And here, Bolshoiman, is your membership in the Russian Communist Party, voted in at a special session of the Politburo only last night."

Kyril's chest swelled with pride as Andropov handed him the papers.

"No sable is exported," Brezhnev announced, "without me first wiping my ass on it."

"Is that so?" said Andropov. "And one more thing, Bolshoiman. This is my own personal contribution. I thought a cape and a hat might go well with your . . . er . . . rather effective costume. So I procured these, made of . . . erm, ah . . . of the finest Russian sable."

Kyril thought his invulnerable heart would burst as he wrapped the cape around his shoulders, and jammed the hat onto his head.

"What a joke on the decadent capitalist warmongers, eh?" Brezhnev chuckled.

"Indeed, Leonid Ilyich," said Andropov, resuming his seat. He folded his hands and regarded Kyril paternally.

"And now, Bolshoiman," he said. "Tell me what you plan to do to further the aims of worldwide Communism?"

"Well, sir," Kyril said, stammering a bit in the presence of the two great men, "I've been thinking about this a lot." He leaned forward confidentially. "I've begun to suspect there is a great deal of injustice right here in the Motherland. I've heard rumors that certain Party officials have set up special stores where only they can shop, stocked with hard-to-obtain Western goods. I believe that some of these men have established private *dachas* in the woods, or by the shore. It seems certain those with the proper political connections do not have to wait as long to buy a car or other consumer goods. With my own eyes I have seen Party members go to the head of the queue for buying toilet paper." He folded his arms and leaned back resolutely. "Sir, I would like to root out this evil perversion of the classless society and see that the perpetrators get their proper punishment."

Andropov regarded Bolshoiman for a moment in silence. Then he slapped his palm on his desk.

"Wonderful, Bolshoiman!" he crowed. "I applaud your egalitarian spirit." Then he leaned forward. "But I must tell you, we in the KGB are aware of this scandal. I expect to announce arrests within the month. If you blundered into this situation, you might unwittingly undo years of investigation."

"Oh," said Kyril, his heart sinking.

"But I have other work for you," said Andropov. He rounded his desk again, and held out more papers. "Here is your secret membership in the KGB. It entitles you to lie, cheat, steal, sabotage, and murder in the cause of Communism. Here is an American passport and other identity papers establishing you as a U.S. citizen, naturalized ten years ago. And here is your exit visa from the Union of Soviet Socialist Republics."

Andropov took a deep breath, then put his arm around Bolshoiman's shoulders. He whispered intensely.

"You shall go to the United States. You will confound the capitalists with your strengths. *You will work to undermine their decadent system from within!*"

"How diabolical!" Kyril breathed.

"Thank you," said Andropov, and extended his hand. Kyril took it, and they both assumed the pose popularized by the Socialist Realism school of art.

"Good luck, Bolshoiman," said Andropov.

"Thank you, Comrade Andropov," said Kyril.

"I piss in Stolichnaya bottles labeled 'For Export,'" announced Brezhnev.

Kyril and Ludmilla flew to New York aboard *Aeroflot*—the world's largest airline. As soon as their bogus tourist visas were approved, they threw them away and assumed their KGB-established cover identities.

On the way in from the airport, Ludmilla leaped from the moving taxi, vanished into Bloomingdale's, and was never seen again. Once a month her MasterCard statement arrived at 1 Dzerzhinsky Square. Andropov always broke into a cold sweat when he opened it, then paid, significantly reducing the American foreign trade deficit.

Kyril got an apartment in Greenwich Village and took a job in the classified ads department of the *Village Voice*, where he was amazed to discover an American fascination with Greek, English, and French cultures fully as deep as any he had seen in Moscow.

Like many a great revolutionary before him, Kyril decided to begin his campaign for the hearts and minds of the enslaved American people on the streets. He dressed in his Bolshoiman costume and boarded the A Train. No one in the subway gave him a second glance.

He got off at 125th Street, where he quickly spotted a group of young, third-world, unemployed workers. He approached them.

"Crack, man?" one of them asked him.

"Hey, man, who's your tailor, Bozo the Clown?"

"Arise, oppressed workers of America!" Kyril shouted. "I, Bolshoiman, will lead you out of bondage."

"Yo' *mama*," one of the workers commented.

"You have nothing to lose but your chains," Kyril promised him.

Judging the debate had gone far enough, one of the oppressed workers attempted to stab Kyril in the back, but the blade broke off. Another swung his fist at Kyril's chin, breaking every bone in his hand. A third produced a .357 Magnum and emptied it into Kyril's face. This had no effect, except on two bystanders hit by ricocheting bullets. Kyril reached out, took the firearm, ate it, and lifted the surprised worker by his hair.

"I must deliver you to the proper authorities," he said mournfully. "Perhaps you will rethink your politics while languishing in the hell of the American prison system." He took a small white paper bag from his pocket and gave it to the oppressed worker.

"What's this for?" asked the worker.

"You'll find out," Bolshoiman said glumly, and leaped into the air.

"What do you mean, 'lock him up'?" yelled the apoplectic desk sergeant. "I can't even scold him. Did you read him his rights? Do you have probable cause? Was there a lawyer present when the alleged assault allegedly occurred? Do you realize he's eleven years old?"

"What about this?" Bolshoiman said, reaching into the youth's pocket and producing several dozen packets of a controlled substance.

"That? I found that just laying on the street, man. I was gonna turn it in, but along comes bullshitman here and brutalizes me."

"See?" said the desk sergeant. "He found it."

"And this?" said Bolshoiman, reaching into another pocket and finding seven Rolex watches and fifteen diamond rings.

"Them? Them fell off a truck, man."

"See? They fell off a truck. Did you have a warrant for those searches? Do you realize he hasn't seen a psychiatrist yet? You realize just walking down 125th in that outfit is provocation, and entrapment? Here, kid, take this stuff and get outta here. *You*," he said to Bolshoiman, "you I oughta lock up. You're *crazy*. Now get outta here."

Bolshoiman went home and pondered these events long into the night.

At nine A.M. there was a knock on his door. He answered it to find five process servers standing in a line. Each of them handed him a subpoena.

Kyril spent most of the next year in court.

Both of the ricochet victims sued him for negligence in improperly deflecting the bullets. One of them died before the trial, so what with loss of projected lifetime income, pain and suffering to the wife, three children, mother and father, four grandparents, and punitive damages, Kyril had to pay seventeen million dollars. He got off easier with the survivor, whose lawyer could only manage to find nine hundred thousand dollars in damages and was so ashamed he gave up the practice of law.

The youth who cut himself on the broken knife blade sued for doctor and hospital bills of $4398.03 and fifteen thousand dollars in pain and suffering. The fellow with the broken fist contended that he had lost his means of livelihood—mugging, purse-snatching, and leg-breaking—and won a judgement of a million five.

"Sorry about that," said Kyril's court-appointed public defender after the fourth verdict against him. "But this next case is frivolous. No jury in the world is going to convict you for stealing that kid's gun and destroying it."

"But it's a criminal charge," Kyril worried.

"Trust me," said the public defender.

"But just what does a sentence of six months to life *mean?*" Kyril asked, through the wire mesh screen of the visitors' room at the Tombs, two weeks later.

"Three, four weeks, tops," said the public defender. "I gotta run. Keep your nose clean, and don't drop the soap."

Back in his cell that night, one of his three cellmates crept close in the darkness and whispered in Kyril's ear.

"I represent ABC television," said the man. "I bribed the guard to get in here. ABC will pay ten thousand dollars for exclusive rights to your story. We plan a two-hour movie of the week."

"Twenty thousand, and a four-hour two-parter," whispered the cellmate from CBS. "Plus a guarantee to air during a sweeps week, Thursday or Friday."

"They're robbing you," whispered the cellmate from NBC. "I'm prepared to offer thirty-five thousand, and *The Cosby Show* as a lead-in for the first episode of what we envision as a six-part miniseries."

"We're gonna call it *Bolshoiman: The Risks of Involvement*" whispered the man from ABC.

"We're gonna call it *Bolshoiman: The Peril of Getting Involved*," whispered the man from CBS.

"We're gonna call it *Bolshoiman: Is Involvement Worth It?*" whispered the man from NBC.

"Why don't you just *all* do it?" Kyril sighed, and rolled over and went to sleep to the sound of whispered bidding.

Kyril was paroled after serving two months. He walked home to find a little man in a tweed suit sitting in his living room.

"Good morning," said the little man briskly. "I'll get right to the point." He opened his briefcase and produced a sheaf of papers, which he fanned out on Kyril's coffee table.

"I have here your 1040 forms for the last ten years. In none of these years do you list an income exceeding seventeen thousand dollars. Yet it has come to my attention that you recently paid out judgements in the amount of $19,419,398.03, and you paid in cash. May I ask where you got this money?"

Kyril had charged it all to his KGB-backed American Express Gold Card, but began to wonder if perhaps he should have squeezed lumps of coal into diamonds instead.

"By the way," said the little man, with a brisk smile. "Did I mention I'm from the Internal Revenue Service?"

Kyril was sentenced to fifteen years for tax evasion, and remanded to the new Jails 'R' Us privately operated minimum-security rehabilitation facility outside Orlando, Florida. He was issued a loud Hawaiian shirt, a pair of Bermuda shorts, sandals and sunglasses and a ball and chain, and the bellhop showed him to his two-room efficiency cell/suite. It was furnished by the same people who do Holiday Inns. There was a small color television, a K-Mart bottom-of-the-line "stack" stereo with miserable speakers with practically no bass response, and no telephone. He had to share the Jacuzzi with nine other inmates. When Kyril arrived the inmates were on strike, demanding compact disc players and a better grade of suntan oil.

He settled easily into prison life once more. He spent his time reading the *Daily Worker*, plotting the overthrow of the U.S. government by force and violence, and wondering if he should escape.

Sometimes he had the weird feeling that prison was his destiny.

While he thought about these things he freebased a lot of coke and gained over fifty pounds on the prison diet. He tried to sweat it off in the daily aerobics class, but then Sunday would roll around again.

"That damn brunch is my downfall," he often lamented to the ex-cabinet officers, federal judges, and Congressmen. "I swear I'm just gonna have a bite, and the next thing I know all the cheesecake is gone."

When he tipped the scales at an alarming three hundred and fifty pounds, he decided he had to make a break for it. He punched a hole in the floor of his cell and began tunneling like a tubby, supersonic mole.

After a few miles he lifted a manhole cover and poked his head into the Florida sunshine again. He was in the Fantasyland section of Walt Disney World. He took a slow look around, then zoomed back through the tunnel to the safety of his cell.

No matter how he tried to avoid it, Kyril's first parole hearing came up after only two years. He was told not to do it again, and set free.

He carried out of the prison gates only his Bolshoiman costume, two hundred pounds of blubber he hadn't come in with, and a monkey on his back bigger than Mighty Joe Young. He was met at the gate by seventeen gorgeous women offering to marry him. The networks had taken his advice and all aired his story. The part of Bolshoiman had been played by Tom Selleck on ABC, while CBS opted for Arnold Schwarzenegger, and NBC, in a lighter vein, went with Chevy Chase.

He rented a small apartment in Miami. It was okay, except for the vampire bats poking their heads through the walls, the giant slugs in the bathtub, and the billions of invisible ants that crawled over his body day and night. While going cold turkey, Bolshoiman wasted down to a hollow-eyed ninety-eight pounds. His costume hung on him like a deflated zeppelin.

He decided America would kill him if he stayed any longer, so he swam to Cuba, where he was imprisoned for eight years. He never was clear about the charge, but it seemed to have something to do with his costume.

China had about as much use for him as Russia. He only did three years there.

Bolshoiman now lives in the People's Stalinist Republic of Albania, where he is reasonably happy. He resides in Cell #5, The Enver Hoxha *Glasnost*-Free Repentance Academy, 45 Revolution Square, Tirana, where he is serving 850 years to life.

He is currently at work on his manifesto.

About the Authors

Steve Antczak

Steve Antczak, a comics fan since third grade, developed his own universe with a full line of titles by age ten.
Steve sold his comics collection to pay for a car, then sold his car to pay for college. He dropped out. He now realizes he should have kept the comics.

P. J. Beese and Todd Cameron Hamilton

P. J. Beese has a passion for history, fine jewelry, and carnivorous dust bunnies. She writes novels and short stories with her literary partner, Todd Cameron Hamilton. Todd delights in art nouveau architecture, sculpture, and long walks. They are both residents of the greater Chicago area.

Jerry Bingham

Jerry Bingham, the winner of the comic industry's Kirby award and the Golden Apple award for best graphic novel, is an illustrator of books, magazines, and comic books. He has also written comics, magazine articles, and a stage play performed so off-Broadway that it was in San Diego.

Richard Lee Byers

Richard Lee Byers worked in an inpatient psychiatric facility for ten years before becoming a writer and teacher. He lives in the Tampa

Bay area, where most of his published adult and young adult horror novels take place.

B. W. Clough

B. W. Clough worked as a mild-mannered reporter for a metropolitan newspaper after growing up overseas. She has written several fantasy novels and a children's book set in Virginia in her cottage at the edge of the forest.

John DeChancie

John DeChancie was born and still lives in Pittsburgh, Pa. He began his career writing for TV and film, directing and producing many of his own projects. John is a classical music aficionado and an amateur musician, and plans to write symphonic music in retirement. His latest fantasy novel is *Magicnet*.

Dwight R. Decker

Dwight R. Decker became hooked on superheroes by the old Superman TV show. Dwight is a technical writer by trade. He has translated German science fiction and European comics and now publishes his own small-press comic, *Rhudiprrt—The Prince of Fur*.

Alan Dean Foster

Alan Dean Foster is a prolific author of numerous novels and short stories. In addition to his very popular Spellsinger and Flinx series, he has written many movie novelizations including *Alien*, *Star Wars* and *Dark Star*. He resides in the sunny state of Arizona.

Roland J. Green and Frieda A. Murray

Roland J. Green is the father of Violette Green and the pet human of a large black cat named Thursday. He writes heroic, high, and historical fantasy, military science fiction, pastiches, and reviews of sf and fantasy for the American Library Association and the Chicago Sun-Times.
Frieda A. Murray is the wife of Roland Green, the charming mother of Violette Green, and a Federal civil servant. Her writing includes *The Book of Kantela*, the first book in a high fantasy trilogy. She was Program Chairman of Chicago Women in Publishing.

Laurell K. Hamilton

Laurell K. Hamilton, in addition to being a snake charmer, is the lovely author of fantasy and science fiction novels and short stories. *The Laughing Corpse*, Laurell's most recent book, is the second in a contemporary fantasy series featuring a detective who is a vampire executioner.

Gerald Hausman

Gerald Hausman is a teacher, translator, and author of more than a dozen books on Native American subjects. He recently collaborated with Roger Zelazny on a historical fantasy novel of two "superhuman" mountain men.

Richard A. Knaak

Richard A. Knaak writes several ongoing fantasy series and is a long-time contributor to the Dragonlance series. He is currently working

About the Authors

on a new modern fantasy, *King of the Grey*, and a new series featuring a disreputable character, Andros Macab.

Paul Kupperberg

Paul Kupperberg is a veteran writer in the international comic book field with over five hundred stories to his credit including work on *Superman* and *Batman*. He has written *Superman* and *Tom & Jerry* syndicated newspaper strips and two novels. He is currently an editor in DC Comics' Development Group.

Brad Linaweaver

Brad Linaweaver has appeared in periodicals as diverse as *National Review* and *Monsterama*. An active libertarian, he has written for many publications of pristine obscurity. Brad was a Nebula finalist and Prometheus Award winner for *Moon of Ice*. Currently he is scripting for radio and movies.

William Marden

William Marden was a newspaper reporter and editor for twenty years before writing fiction. As a freelance writer his work includes sales to the *National Enquirer*, true detective magazines, and comic strips, and he has edited a medical textbook. William currently teaches and writes reviews.

Jody Lynn Nye

Jody Lynn Nye was turned onto comics at age four by her maternal grandfather. Her favorite hobbies are reading and playing with cats, though not at the same time. Jody is the author of the *Mythology* fantasy series and has collaborated with Anne McCaffrey and Piers Anthony.

Dennis O'Neil

Dennis O'Neil began his career as a journalist, then worked as Stan Lee's editorial assistant at Marvel Comics. He has written a nonfiction book, a novel, hundreds of comics, reviews and stories. Dennis is now the editor at DC Comics in charge of *Batman*, teaches, lectures, and writes occasionally for television.

Mickey Zucker Reichert

Mickey Zucker Reichert is a pediatrician whose novels include the *Renshai* trilogy and the *Bifrost Guardians* series. Mickey lives in backwoods Iowa with a wolf, a dog, three cats, three horses, one son, three stepsons, a partridge in a pear tree and a handsome, exciting, intelligent husband who writes her bios.

Mike Resnick and Lawrence Schimel

Mike Resnick is the multiple Hugo-winning author of *Santiago*, *Ivory*, *Purgatory*, *Prophet*, *Lucifer Jones*, and the Kirinyaga stories.

Lawrence Schimel has just graduated from Yale, but has already amassed more than a dozen science-fiction sales.

Josepha Sherman

Josepha is the author of numerous fantasy novels including *A Strange and Ancient Name*, *Castle of Deception*, *Child of Faerie*, *Child of Earth* and

Windleaf. Her writing also includes several children's books, over ninety short stories, *A Sampler of Jewish-American Folklore* and a sf television script.

Michael A. Stackpole

Michael A. Stackpole grew up in the woods of Vermont but now lives in the desert of Arizona. His novels include over a dozen game-related books and unrelated fantasies. Aside from writing and designing computer games, Mike plays indoor soccer, collects comics, and engages in a bizarre form of self-torture involving a NordicTrack machine.

Brian M. Thomsen

Brian M. Thomsen is the executive editor and head of TSR's book department. As an editor, he was a Hugo nominee and as a writer has sold numerous short stories to various theme anthologies. A lifelong fan of the DC Comics universe, he fails to be "marvelled" by their less-than-super competitors.

John Varley

John Varley, a multiple Hugo, Nebula and Prix Apollo award winner, is the towering author of numerous novels, film scripts and short stories. *Steel Beach*, his most recent novel, returns his readers to the popular, infamous "Eight Worlds" universe.

Lawrence Watt-Evans

Lawrence Watt-Evans taught himself to read at age five so he could read his big sister's comic books. He went on to write a score of novels and won the Hugo for short story in 1984. Lawrence is probably best known for the Ethshar novels, most recently *The Spell of the Black Dagger*.

Roger Zelazny

Roger Zelazny is a multiple Hugo and Nebula Award-winning author of more than fifty books. He is probably best known for his "Amber" series. Roger's most recent collaboration, with Gerald Hausman, is a historical novel of the Wild West, *Colterglass*.